Love, betrayal, and con

At midnight, when V and Jerry could transfer ... desk lines to his portable phone, he filled the fireplace with fresh logs and dimmed the Great Hall lights except a few over the desk.

Drawing Carol to the sofa, he poured two steamy cups of hot chocolate. For a few moments, they sipped them wordlessly, while fire from the new wood hissed in the background.

As Carol tipped her mug to drink, a blob of marshmallow stuck to her face. Jerry reached up to wipe away the white dollop with his thumb. They both giggled as removing it took several attempts.

On the final try, however, Jerry's hand lingered on her cheek, and he turned her face in his direction. Laughter ebbed into sighs, as Jerry saw that the event that the entire day had been moving toward was finally within his grasp.

As Jerry at last pulled Carol into his arms, he felt her hands simultaneously move to the back of his neck and lace themselves together there. Their lips met in a tender kiss, warm with surrender, while the flames crackled and Jerry's heart threatened to literally explode from the joy of it all.

In that ecstatic moment, Jerry knew he had found in Carol the prescription for the past six months of pain. The last lips that his had touched were those of Natalie, a week before the plane crash.

Until just yesterday, Jerry believed that he'd spend the rest of his life without someone to fill that void.

Yet even amid the triumphant feeling that washed over Jerry then, a warning light flashed deep within him. *If she knew the real me, she'd run,* an inner voice trumpeted.

As desperately as he hoped that this sweet analgesic would never wear off, something inside him knew better.

1

I run in the path of your commands, for you have set my heart free.

Psalm 119:32

WHEN THE HEART SOARS FREE

Kay Moore

To Grace—
may you
be "Amazing
Grace" &
Grace in
many in
your
ministry.

Kay
Moore

2/05

Hannibal Books
A Division of KLMK Communications, Inc.
Richmond, Virginia

Copyright 1999
by Hannibal Books
A division of KLMK Communications Inc.
(Lyrics and music to "Remembering You" on pages 6-8
Copyright 1999 by Kay Moore)
All rights reserved
Printed in the United States of America
by Lithocolor Press, Inc.

ISBN 0-929292-87-1

Library of Congress Card Catalog Number: 99-90645

(Use coupons in back to order extra copies of this and
other books from HANNIBAL BOOKS)

Unless otherwise noted, all Scripture quotations are taken from
the New International Version of the Bible.

This is a work of fiction. The characters, dialogues and
incidents are not real and are the products of the
author's imagination. Any resemblance to actual events
or persons, living or dead, is purely coincidental.

Hannibal Books
P.O. Box 29621
Richmond, VA 23242

The Hannibal Books World Wide Web site address is
www.hannibalbooks.com

to
Katie

who reminded me
I had one more mountain
to climb

Remembering You

(Jerry's Song at Sky Ranch)

Words and Music by
KAY MOORE

Slowly

1. Re - mem - ber - ing you and all our times to - geth - er; Think - ing of days we've laughed and loved and grown. Though we may part, our ties no one can sev - er; With you in my heart I'll nev - er be a - lone.

2. Re - mem - ber,

Music and Lyrics © Copyright 1999 by Kay Moore.

please,   in   all   of life's to - mor - rows,

God's in con - trol;   He   sees the big - ger

plan.   Al - though— the   past   might

have   its share of   sor - rows,   we can— look

back and see His   faith - ful   hand.

3. Re - mem - ber - ing   you,   how God brought us to -

geth - er; E - ven through trials He's

kept us safe and strong. Our hearts— soar free de -

spite the storm - y wea - ther. It's been His way to teach us

all a - long. My heart's been true; Al- ways I'll

be re - mem - ber - ing you. To all of

you, al - ways I'll be re - mem - ber - ing you.

Remembering You — 3

Contents

Acknowledgements

Soli Deo Gloria. No other proper words exist to begin this list of acknowledgements. From my teenage years, the Heavenly Father began stirring in my heart a desire to write a novel with the picturesque setting of a Colorado ski lodge at its core, and the characters of Jerry and Carol came to life for me as I mentally mapped out their pilgrimage. Through the refiner's fire of life experiences, He was faithful to shape and mold and develop the story line. He illumined for me two promises, 1 Samuel 12:16 and Matthew 17:20, to claim for assurance of its publication. On days when I sat down to a hopelessly empty computer screen, He graciously gave me actual words to compose, to the end that I felt as one with the ancients who penned Scripture, so acquainted was I with the "God-breathed" process of writing in my own journey. *When the Heart Soars Free* is His story. I pray He will use it to accomplish His purposes among His people.

I owe a huge debt to my prayer warriors, chief among them my husband, Louis; my children, Matthew and Katie; my mother, Mable, and my aunt, Frances. Their and others' prayer cards of encouragement framed the window surrounding my computer screen. Always faithful to affirm, inquire, and uplift, these two dozen "called-out ones" regularly stormed the Throne Room of Heaven with their entreaties for this book and its future. In intercession, they tirelessly offered themselves as partners with God for what He desires to enact with *When the Heart Soars Free.*

I am thankful to my early mentors, Drs. Donald Williamson, Doug Fitzgerald, and Dan Cox; the late Rev. Gary Haaland, and Barbara Sanders, MSW, who applied psychological concepts to biblical principles. They helped me fully understand the meaning of the verse, "As a man thinketh in his heart, so he is" (Proverbs 23:7, KJV).

To Dr. Tim Sledge, whose sharing of self in *Making Peace with Your Past* broke new ground in helping churches reach hurting people, I say thank-you with a gratitude that is huge. Countless thousands benefit daily from *Making Peace* concepts, many of which underscore *When the Heart Soars Free.*

To LifeWay Christian Resources, I applaud its courageous act in the early 1990s to launch the LIFE Support Group Series, which has led scores of participants to break down the barriers of painful pasts that separate them from fully comprehending God's love. For my LifeWay years as editor of these life-changing materials, I'll forever be grateful.

For Marti Hefley, a passionate and discerning wordsmith, a giant thank-you for caring enough to provide the gift of editing—in just the right places, at just the right time. To Marti and Jim, founders of Hannibal Books, we look forward to continuing your vision for quality, Christ-centered materials that point people to the Father.

Thanks to the Crested Butte/Mt. Crested Butte, Colorado Chamber of Commerce and Visitors Center for helpful background on your exquisite, incomparable town and to the people of Crested Butte for sterling hospitality—Valley Lodge style—on my visits there.

Also, herein, I recognize the endeavors of a colorful ancestor, William F. Kimmell, who arrived with his young family in Gunnison County, CO, in 1881, full of high expectations that were reflective of that mining era, and sadly left a widower, his fortunes carrying him to other climes. It is a privilege to honor his memory with a novel set on the same glorious Rocky Mountain soil on which he pinned many hopes and dreams.

Kay Moore
Richmond, VA
August 1, 1999

ONE

Hearts and Skies of Lead

❀

The friendly bouquet of daisies—Natalie's favorite—did little to brighten the dreary waiting area, where a rotating beacon could barely be seen penetrating the bisque-thick snow.

This morning, Jerry Rutgers had eagerly toted the perky flowers to the airport to greet his fiancee's plane. By mid-afternoon, both he and the blooms, still tight in his clutches, were withering fast.

"Natalie, where are you?" Jerry murmured into the window, his breath forming an "O" of mist on the glass as he trained dull eyes upward again and again.

The only reply came from ice crystals spitting sideways against the thick pane, more clamorous now than they had been even thirty minutes earlier.

An arm on his powerfully built shoulder, drooped with worry, attempted to console.

"Here, Jerry. Drink this coffee. It'll help you. I promise." Dave, his sidekick at the ski apparel store where Jerry worked, had rushed over after Jerry phoned to see if anyone there had heard from Natalie or her dad, pilot of the missing Cessna 310.

Jerry brushed Dave's arm away irritably, sloshing some of the proffered French vanilla brew out onto the waiting room carpet. "Why did they try it today? Why?" he pled. "Why didn't they wait until the storm passed?"

"Probably thought it was too late in the year for this to happen," Dave ventured, meting his words out cautiously as he studied his beleaguered friend. "Boulder doesn't get many howling blizzards like this in late April. The weather report last night mentioned only a chance of flurries."

"You trust those weather guys? They're nothing but charlatans on that newscast, with their spray-plastered hairdos like they expect a hurricane to sweep through the set." Jerry, his blue eyes blazing, was bellowing now, so loudly that it bolted a catnapping traveler from his slumber in a nearby chair.

"Look, Jerry," the friend suggested, "Mr. Fulmer's an experienced pilot. Maybe he thought a few Colorado snowflakes wouldn't amount to much. I'm sure he's flown in worse."

"Mr. Fulmer's an idiot!" Jerry retorted angrily, dashing the pathetic-looking daisy cluster to the ground. "And Natalie knows it. She can't wait to get out from under her daddy's thumb. She can't wait . . ."

Dave's aghast look halted Jerry's railing briefly.

"I'm sorry, buddy. Let's not argue," Jerry recanted, patting Dave's elbow penitently as his eyes raked the ominous sky yet another time. "Why, I bet in just a few minutes, we'll hear over the intercom that they've landed. Natalie's going to be OK. Don't you see? The plane's just fine. Just fine."

Jerry resumed his sentinel by the window, straining to locate some hopeful dot on the horizon that would herald an end to this anguish.

Another time, Jerry's blood would have spiked with adrenaline if an unexpected, late-spring snowstorm had dumped on the Rockies. A last-minute serendipity like this would have summoned him back to the slopes and to his obsession. He could have proved himself one final time this season at the skill he did best.

Now, today's stupefying snow only brought heartbreak. It threatened to take the love that sustained his life, as Natalie's fate hung in the balance.

After another forty-five minutes of his vigil, Jerry inched a few steps backward and sank into a chair. His stooped torso signaled that the earlier burst of optimism had run its course.

"It'll be OK; it'll be OK!" Jerry sputtered as Dave slumped down beside him and touched his arm lightly.

"Jerry, it's no use. You know they didn't have enough fuel to circle forever," Dave said woefully, barely above a whisper.

"Sure they did! Maybe they found another airport. Maybe they could get in at Denver."

"Jerry, I just talked to the airport personnel. This whole region has blizzard conditions. Hazardous weather advisories are out everywhere. They checked the Denver airport for the plane. Other places too. No sign at all. I don't see how they can make it, buddy. I'm so sorry. So very sorry."

Jerry began frantically working Dave's arm like it was a tire pump and dragged him over to the window. "Look—don't you see it? There's something in the distance there, don't you think? See that little speck? Doesn't it look like it's . . . ?" His voice broke as his heart filled with dread, and Dave again slung an arm around the weary shoulders of his friend.

"Jerry, the people at the desk want to help. Maybe if they called a chaplain . . ."

"No!" Jerry snapped, his clenched fist punctuating with a thwap on the window rail. That was the last thing he needed—some wimpy cleric spewing out empty religious talk that wouldn't help a bit. It wouldn't make Natalie appear. Nothing would.

Suddenly limp and weeping, Jerry plopped into his seat, dragging his fingers through long, blond forelocks until his hair stood wildly on end. Dave was probably right. He might as well face it. He likely would never again gaze on the countenance of his fiancee.

15

The image of a pixie face, cropped brown hair, her trademark loop earrings, and laughing eyes sprang unbidden into his mind. All their plans, their wedding in two weeks . . . Natalie and her dad had been flying in to Boulder to talk to the caterer and florist one last time, to nail down final details.

She can't leave me now, Jerry thought desperately. *I need her so. Without Natalie, I have nothing. Nothing!*

"Natalie! Natalie!" The strong, cover-boy handsome features of his lean face were quaking under the strain, and he buried them into locked fingers.

"Oh, Natalie, what will I do? " Jerry begged, his voice trailing into a moan. "What will I ever do without you?"

T W O

An Almost Perfect Union

Jerry absently restacked a pile of down jackets as customers milled about, occasionally bumping up against him as they crowded in for Alpine Gear's legendary July sale.

"Got a fitting room somewhere?" one muttered, toting a trio of ski bibs he wanted to try on. As Jerry stared blankly and stood frozen, one of his co-workers quickly cut in with directions.

"Through that door in the back, sir," the other salesman motioned, squiring the man toward the wall. Jerry shrugged lamely. *Guess Phil will get the commission on that one, but what difference does it make?*

Months past, Jerry would have attached himself in bulldog-aggressive style the minute any customer set foot in the ski apparel store. But that was before Natalie's fatal crash three months earlier. Now Jerry moved through Alpine Gear like a zombie, himself more dead than alive.

One elderly shopper who scrutinized the clerk with the chiseled, all-America good looks and athletic build wouldn't let him off the hook so easily.

"Weatherproof jackets, son," the customer barked forthrightly, striding toward Jerry until he could tug on his elbow. "Heard the Alpine Gear ad on the radio and drove all the way over from Crested Butte. Show me what's on sale."

Although few smiles crossed his lips these days, something about this particular shopper suddenly struck Jerry as amusing. His face couldn't help twitching into a slight grin. As he watched the man paw through the stacks of outerwear, Jerry realized this customer was almost an Albert Einstein look-alike, with a leonine thatch of unruly, gray hair frooming from under his navy beret.

That, plus the man's reference to Crested Butte, site of last year's U.S. Extreme Skiing Championships in which he had competed, brought back an energizing memory and lit a fire under Jerry for a change.

Suddenly a vestige of the old, personable salesmanship returned, and Jerry couldn't do enough to show this extroverted customer around.

"You *have* come a long way to shop," Jerry commented, feeling strangely animated. "Took me three hours to get over Monarch Pass in traffic last year when I drove over to ski in the Extremes."

"Ski a lot, then, do you?" the Einstein clone queried, continuing to study the blond salesman with the dip of hair that he frequently waved from his brow.

"Yep, my dad razzed me that I came all the way from Boston to the university here to get a business degree and turned into a ski bum in the process," Jerry shared, a tinge of sadness passing over his face.

"Bum, indeed!" his co-worker, Dave, hooted. He feigned a miffed look at Jerry as he overheard the conversation. "I wish I had one-fourth of his energy. Jerry was tops in sales last year, in addition to all this."

Dave had become Jerry's self-appointed cheerleader in these days since the crash. As Dave gestured to the wall behind the cash register, the man's eyes followed a line of photos showing the muscular clerk proudly receiving medals in various ski events.

"Hmm," the customer murmured. He scanned the photo display perfunctorily and then turned his attention back to some snowshoes on the discount table. Jerry sensed the subject was forgotten and went on back to stacking his merchandise.

But the older man clearly was continuing to cogitate on the co-worker's remark while he rifled through the sale items.

A few minutes later, when he could pull Jerry out of earshot of the others, the man thrust out an eager hand. "Eldon Hartley," he volunteered cheerily. "I run a little lodge on the mountain there at Crested Butte. Valley Lodge. You know the place?"

A bittersweet memory jabbed at Jerry.

"Yes, I've been there," Jerry admitted, his gaze lowering as he fought off shadows that towered over him. "Earlier this year." Natalie's father had liked the steaks at the lodge's Rippling Rock grill. Despite Natalie's protests, he had dragged the young couple halfway across the state in his airplane to dine there with him just after they announced their engagement.

"Good," the customer continued, breaking Jerry's reverie. "Since you're familiar with my hotel, I've got a sort of unusual question for you. Working here at the ski shop, and skiing like you do, you probably get around . . . know lots of folks. Truth is, I need to hire an assistant, someone who could be a sort of second-in-command. Thought I had someone trained, but the deal fell through. You just seemed . . . well, like you might have contacts."

Jerry's eyes widened at the man's inquiry. *I don't know anyone who would be that nuts,* he thought to himself. Valley Lodge might serve legendary steaks in its restaurant, but it also sparked snickers with some people in the trade. It was the rare ski-area hotel that banned alcoholic beverages in its food service and held chapel services every Sunday in its lobby. *So this is the man behind all this eccentricity,* Jerry mulled as he surveyed Mr. Hartley quietly. *Why would anyone want to limit his clientele just because of some personal scruples?*

19

"You see," Mr. Hartley continued with his monologue, taking Jerry to be rapt with interest, "I need someone who could be trusted implicitly, who learns fast, who has a lot of business sense. Someone appealing in looks. Someone who might even be groomed to take over Valley Lodge. I'm not getting any younger, you know."

Jerry had noticed that Mr. Hartley had seemed to totter with a pained gait as he padded around the store. He punctuated his sentences with short bursts of breath, and occasionally Jerry saw him rub his eyes under the thatch of gray, as though he were straining to focus.

"Crested Butte's a great place to work," his sales pitch continued. "Gets more snowfall than almost any Colorado ski area. An unpretentious little town, straight out of a Currier-and-Ives print. We're like a family at Valley Lodge. It'd be a real plum job for someone. Besides," Pop continued, glancing down at Jerry's left hand and seeing it missing a wedding band, "many a young love has blossomed under the glow of our streetlamps. *Heh heh.*" He looked pleased with himself as he tossed out what he thought would be an appealing hook.

Jerry bit his lower lip at the painful mention of romance.

"I see, Mr. Hartley," Jerry interjected, a little snappily, hoping to end the PR spiel, but the customer interrupted, "It's Pop. *Ple-e-ease.* That's what everyone else calls me. Now, since you've been there, you know our trails. You know what a world-class ski area we are."

Jerry did know the trails. Frankly, for regular-season skiing, his preferences leaned more toward the playgrounds of Vail or Aspen. But as he thought about Crested Butte's uncrowded mountains and the expert terrain in its extreme limits, a surprising rush pumped him.

"It's the world's most perfect location," Pop rattled on doggedly. "Why, I bet anyone . . . well, even someone like yourself," he said, clearing his throat loudly, "would give his eye teeth to live there."

Truth was, Jerry couldn't picture himself living anywhere but Boulder, his home since university days. The place had been a safe cocoon for him after officials confirmed that Mr. Fulmer's plane indeed had crashed into a mountain during that April blizzard. Friends in the college town had hovered around Jerry protectively, inviting him out to dinner and including him in their plans. Customers inquired about his health. The solace of work kept him immersed in busy, predictable activity.

Occasionally, Jerry thought about finding another kind of job—especially one that would make his father happy. Dad had reminded him, "Surely you can do something better with a business degree than sell these toys." The meddlesome words still rankled him a little. What right did his father have to chastise him, since he'd helped very little on Jerry's college expenses and left Jerry to work his own way through?

Actually, the job at the ski shop did use very little of his college training. His dad was right. He really should apply for something that taxed his intelligence more than vegging out in Boulder, pricing ski gear.

However, work there kept him connected to the slopes, the love of his life, next to Natalie Fulmer. With predictable 8-to-5 hours, Jerry had time to stay in condition during the non-ski months by a regimen of in-line skating, weights, and mountain biking. The ski shop pay wasn't the best, but the job held minimal prospect of failure, which Jerry knew he must avoid at all costs.

Curiously, though, as Pop blathered on to Jerry about how he needed to train someone who was slope-smart as well as business-wise, Jerry found himself starting to hang on Pop's every word—for reasons he couldn't explain. Pop had become so absorbed with his story, he seemed to have forgotten all about the Alpine Gear sale, but Jerry kept pulling more and more jackets from the racks for Pop to see. Maybe if he looked busy, his boss wouldn't call him away to another customer.

"Maybe you know someone who'd like that kind of job. Have dinner with me tonight, and we'll talk some more," Pop persuaded him.

"Sure, Mr. . . . I mean, Pop," Jerry managed warily, his lips stumbling over the name. *What could a dinner hurt?* he theorized. *I'll probably get a free meal out of this geezer, and besides, I have nothing better to do with my time—any more.*

❀

As they sat down to Thai food that evening in one of Boulder's eateries, Pop grabbed Jerry's sleeve confidently.

"Son, I checked you out thoroughly this afternoon," he announced, his clinched jaw jutting from under the gray locks. "The Chamber of Commerce gives you highest marks. I know you'll do just great."

"Me?" Jerry sputtered, struggling to find his voice. "But I thought you . . . but I was just here to . . ."

"Nonsense, son. I don't need to look any further. You're the perfect candidate for the job I have." It was stated as fact, as though the septuagenarian sensed some urgency and knew he must cut the deal quickly. "I just knew the Lord was going to direct me to the right person, and you're it," he added confidently.

Jerry startled even further at this last remark. No one had ever identified him as God's solution to anything. God was no friend of Jerry's, especially after what He'd done to Natalie.

"God has directed me like this every step of the way, ever since I opened up with the goal of running a ski lodge on Christian principles," Pop elaborated. "It's paid off. God's been good to me these twenty years."

Jerry sliced a little too loudly into his ginger chicken, trying to hide his disdain. *Why give God credit?* Jerry thought acidly. *It's simply good business breaks that have pushed this guy forward.*

But the more Pop insisted that Jerry pull up roots from the familiar and move with him to Western Colorado, the more Jerry felt a peculiar compulsion to investigate. Jerry wasn't at all sure if he should trust someone with the parental nickname of "Pop." People in that role always had it in for him. His own father was a critic of the highest order. With reluctance, Mr. Fulmer agreed he could marry Natalie, but Jerry knew he had never been good enough in Mr. Fulmer's estimation—never quite worthy of his precious daughter, who didn't hold her dad in the same high esteem.

Odd that this fatherly older gentleman seemed to express confidence in him. *That's a switch . . . affirmation for a change,* Jerry mulled thoughtfully.

Maybe he really was desperate for a new trapeze to swing on. Right now he had no goals or dreams—all of them died three months ago with Natalie. Valley Lodge, with its weird rules that ran somewhat counter to Jerry's lifestyle, didn't seem a very likely place for dreams to surface, but the more Pop talked, the more Jerry seemed to lose his objections to the idea.

I really do need to get out of Boulder and try something different, Jerry thought to himself. Feeling more relaxed than he had in weeks, Jerry poured out to Pop about the twists his life had taken during the past three months and why a new setting might benefit him. Pop nodded sympathetically and patted the younger man's arm in a way that continued to woo Jerry.

"I'm so sorry, son. Sounds like it's been tough for you." His eyes, with unkempt gray brows hooding them, were comforting.

Then Pop threw in another zinger.

"Why, I bet you've been praying for something like this, too, haven't you?" Pop queried him persuasively, his head bobbing all the while. "I bet you've been asking the Lord to give you some new direction."

"Well, I . . ." Jerry stammered. Jerry knew he needed a change of focus, but taking his request to a Being who bore the brunt of his anger right now was absolutely the last thing on his mind.

"Sometimes God's plan for us is right under our noses, it's so obvious, but we can't always see it. Don't you think so?" Pop continued to wheedle him. He almost swiped his shirt sleeve in the rice bowl as he leaned over the table exuberantly.

"Sounds like you do, for sure," Jerry responded, dodging again. *This guy's so enthusiastic, he's letting me duck his questions,* Jerry observed cautiously. *I need to set him straight. I've got to set him straight—tell him I'm not some kind of holy weirdo. But if I do, I'll botch the whole set-up, just when the idea is starting to grow on me.*

"Of course I do. I . . . ." Pop's gasp, stronger than his customary ones, cut his sentence in two. His hands involuntarily pressed his chest as a pain appeared to blindside him.

Jerry caught the gesture and shot him a frightened look. "Are you OK, Mr. . . . Pop, that is?"

Pop straightened quickly, patting the air with outstretched fingers as if to dismiss Jerry. He reached into his pocket and slipped a small, white pill under his tongue. "Fine. Just fine. Indigestion, I guess, from this peppered pork. Now," he resumed, focusing intently on Jerry again, "It's a deal then." He sealed their talk with a spirited handshake. I'll call up some more references that the Chamber suggested, and I'll be back in touch."

Three days later, Pop was on the phone, summoning Jerry again.

"Completely solid," Pop appraised into the telephone. "You're just like one of the rocks in my fireplace here. Everyone tells me what an asset you'd be. Come on over here to Crested Butte, and we'll talk again."

Meanwhile, Jerry had done some checking of his own. From phone calls to a ski shop in Crested Butte, he learned that Pop was a widower whose whole life was his work.

"Go for it," his contact advised. "The place is an odd bird, but it's quality, and the tourists keep coming. Go on and stay a few days at Valley Lodge and see for yourself."

With this visit, the cozy, 250-room hotel nestled up against the powerful peaks took on new dimensions for Jerry as he now viewed it through the eyes of a prospective employee.

As he stepped from the airport shuttle and into the lodge's Great Hall, he heard a cheerful, recorded voice announcing, "Welcome to Valley Lodge, the happiest little hotel in the Rockies." Jerry remembered this chirpy, curbside greeting from his previous visit. Originally he thought it was annoying—trumpeting the same message

24

again and again in a cadence that could churn your nerves into mincemeat. Now it seemed almost charming—Pop's way of trying to display warmth in every amenity he could offer.

In addition, Pop outfitted his bellmen in mountaineer costumes. He insisted on family-style dining in the Rippling Rock. He offered guests nighttime sleigh rides in the historic town below. For two decades, Pop had used this folksy brand of hospitality to lure ski buffs to Valley Lodge over some of the larger, pricier places in this booming Colorado ski area.

Something about this is stimulating, Jerry thought, a little surprised at his spurt of interest. *Maybe a fresh start in a new location is what I really need.*

That night, as the two of them talked into the wee hours with the dramatic Great Hall fireplace as a backdrop, Pop prayed aloud that Jerry would seek God's will as he made his decision.

What in the world does that mean? Jerry had wondered, his teeth set on edge again by Pop's mention of spiritual matters. *Decisions are decisions, based on what I feel in my gut. After all, God was the one who tore Natalie away from me. He's dealt me a bum rap all my life. Why should His "will"—whatever that is—be something that I'd want or desire?*

Still squirming a bit from Pop's overt religiosity, Jerry wasn't at all sure what God had to do with any of this. He knew he really ought to warn Pop that the two of them might not see eye to eye on spiritual matters.

Pop had been kind, however, and Jerry didn't want to cut off his prospects by discouraging his new mentor. Jerry had to admit that despite his personal beliefs, Eldon Hartley had been successful at Valley Lodge in its prime location at the Mt. Crested Butte ski base. Under that disheveled gray mop was a head full of business sense that had served Pop well. Hitching his own wagon to that type of success couldn't be all bad.

Within two weeks, Jerry's bags were packed as he left the ski shop behind to see what life held for him in his new adventure with Pop.

"This union is providential," Pop gushed to Jerry as he welcomed him at the Great Hall door and into the Valley Lodge family. "Just as close to perfect as I could ask for."

Pop scooted a luggage rack in Jerry's direction so he could begin moving into his picturesque new home. As his boss shuffled away with an even more decided lurch to his step than Jerry had noticed back in Boulder, an empty feeling broadsided Jerry.

Close to perfect, Jerry reflected, squirming a little. *How can I tell him otherwise? How can I possibly tell him things are different from what they seem?*

THREE

Struggle in Paradise

❊

When Jerry arrived in August, he appeared to have three months to shadow Pop and learn about the business before the new season's guests began pouring into the valley and onto the slopes.

And shadow he did, as he and Pop explored seemingly every inch of the hotel operation.

"I'm going to keep you busy, son," Pop adjured him on his second day on the job. "Today we'll go over the housekeeping services. I want you to spend tomorrow with the clerical staff and Friday with the servers in the Rippling Rock."

Jerry didn't object to Pop's frenetic itinerary and found it invigorating. *Anything to numb me and keep me from dwelling on what I've lost,* he thought gratefully, as he pondered the intense schedule.

"It'll be super to have a real pro involved with the ski instructors for a change," Pop mused. Another of Valley Lodge's perks was to provide its own staff of employees to offer personalized ski instruction for every level of ability. Pop wanted Valley Lodge's hand-picked coaches to be a cut above those employed by the resort for guests in general. He wanted them to demonstrate strong character and exceptional skill.

"Why don't you get out with them yourself and show them a thing or two?" Jerry queried Pop, as Pop outlined his standards.

"That'll be a balmy day in January!" Pop chortled. "I haven't had my feet in a pair of skis in more than 20 years. I'm a perfect klutz on the slopes." He elaborated, "I look for strong assistants in areas where I'm weak. Why do you think you're here?"

As weeks went on, Pop observed that Jerry's youth and charisma—and knockout physique—were a big hit with the staff, especially the young, female contingent. His recruit was dovetailing well with the Valley Lodge operations. Several times he praised Jerry for catching on so quickly and demonstrating that he was a natural in the business.

"You're the best decision I ever made, son," Pop had beamed warmly over dinner one night. Jerry was actually starting to feel like a son to Pop, who exuded an unfettered, fatherly warmth around all he supervised.

Jerry had noted that not all employees responded as positively as he had to Pop, however.

One day Pop good-naturedly gave an employee an encouraging slap on the back in the presence of other workers. After Pop walked away, Jerry heard one member of the staff grouse to another, "Too bad that glad-handing doesn't translate to my paycheck." It wasn't the first trace of discontent about salary he detected as he circulated among lodge personnel.

"What's going on here?" Jerry asked the disgruntled bellman. "What's wrong between you and Pop?"

"Nothing that a few extra dollars wouldn't cure," the man replied sourly. "He's just a penny-pinching old curmudgeon, that's all."

Jerry halted and took a decisive step backward.

"He really seems to care about the staff," he protested, waving off the remark. "He praises everyone for the smallest gesture. My boss in the ski shop certainly didn't do that." Some things in life—like the affirmation Pop dispensed toward him—were worth more than a pay raise. Jerry tried to dismiss the bellman's disparaging outburst and decided not to ask more later.

❀

While on one hand Pop's adulation was welcome, it also caused fear to grip Jerry's throat like an invisible hand. What Pop didn't see behind Jerry's confident exterior and quick mind were the nights that Jerry slipped from his lodge apartment after most guests were asleep—poring over books, struggling to master the computer system, puzzling over the mounds of paperwork that had stacked up of late.

I've never done anything like this before, Jerry thought, panic starting to grip him. *Pop expects so much of me—more than I can handle. He's had years in the business, and he expects me to absorb in three months what he's learned in a lifetime.* With only weeks before the season began, Jerry quietly wondered if he hadn't leaped too quickly at Pop's offer.

Then there was the matter of his slope-time. With so much bureaucracy to manage, Jerry wondered when his schedule would allow him to ever make periodic checks on the instructors—much less have the type of ski immersion he envisioned when he took the job. He really did need to sit down with Pop and try to discuss this. He needed to tell Pop about the apprehensions that were descending on him like the season's first snowflakes that were beginning to arrive.

This and all else were quickly pushed to the back burner one morning when Jerry made his customary early brush through the staff dining room.

Pop was alone, slumped over his coffee, the gray mane drooping over his cup. Jerry thought he was dozing. Maybe Jerry had kept him up too late last night going over the bookkeeping. He leaned over his boss solicitous-ly, then recoiled in horror. Pop wasn't snoozing; he had collapsed.

"Call an ambulance quick!" Jerry's shrill order pealed through the dining hall, sending a waiter scurrying.

By the time paramedics who arrived at Valley Lodge to give Pop medical attention loaded him up for the hospital journey, he had sustained two cardiac arrests.

"What can I do for you, Pop?" Jerry frantically queried the ashen Pop, as paramedics revived him and then urgently strapped his limp form onto a gurney. Through the oxygen mask clamped onto his face, Pop murmured almost inaudibly, "Pray, son. Just pray."

So Jerry prayed—though the silent words came uncertainly and stiffly. Prayer hadn't passed through his lips since his childhood "Now-I-lay-me-down-to-sleep's" that he had recited by rote, with little meaning.

God, please help, he attempted.

Though he tried to beg God for Pop's recovery, anger seemed to always seep through his desperate petitions. *God took away Natalie, and now He'll take away Pop, too,* Jerry found himself muttering bitterly. *I have Him to thank for all the awful things that have happened to me. Why can't Pop see things the way I do? Maybe now that he's sick, he'll see how God abandons you. Maybe he'll back off from some of this God stuff.*

Pop's religious ardor did anything but cool as he struggled daily for life and breath. The days before Pop's quadruple bypass operation were mini-evangelistic crusades in Pop's tiny hospital room. Rev. Dawson, the chaplain who led the weekly worship services at Valley Lodge, visited regularly to read Scripture passages of comfort and assurance.

One day Jerry arrived to find the ailing patient and two nurses warbling "The Old Rugged Cross" at his bed-side, at Pop's request.

The night before his surgery, Pop and Jerry talked lengthily, covering many last-minute bases about the business. Then Pop launched another of his unsettling missiles.

"Who is God in your life? How have you seen him active lately?" Pop inquired of Jerry, leaving him scrambling for words, as always. With time on his hands during his bed confinement, it dawned on Pop that in his haste to get Jerry in place, he and his new assistant had had only surface conversations about personal beliefs. Now might be a good time to find out more about the details of Jerry's spiritual life.

Jerry thought quickly to avoid a trap. "He's the one who needs to bring you through this tomorrow," he fired back in a feeble attempt at humor.

"No, son, I'm serious," Pop pressed, his eyes darkening without their characteristic twinkle. "Tell me about what being a believer means to you."

"What kind of believer am I? One who believes you'll come through this OK, Pop," Jerry again bantered awkwardly. "We need you back at Valley Lodge. After the doctors get through with you tomorrow, you're going to be just fine."

Pop smiled weakly and dozed off. Thankfully for Jerry, Pop's pre-op sedative kicked in before Jerry had to fake it further.

Jerry had to concede that God—or someone—did deliver, as Pop survived the surgery. He rebounded so well, in fact, that doctors decided to release him early from the hospital.

Oddly, however, Jerry detected that some staff members seemed less than overjoyed at Pop's return. An undertow of sarcasm—and lax work attitudes—had permeated the ranks while Pop was away.

One afternoon he had returned from the hospital to report Pop was improving. "They say I can spring him tomorrow," Jerry announced happily to Sadie, the staffer who helped him run the registration desk.

To Jerry's surprise, Sadie grimaced.

"Oh, really?" she commented with a caustic tone, rolling her eyes dramatically toward the ceiling.

Jerry's face became a mask of confusion. "Sadie, what's the deal? Aren't you happy that Pop's getting well?" Jerry had pictured Sadie as true-blue loyal—the last person who would ever pan Valley Lodge.

Sadie looked as if she were about to burst with something. After a studied silence, she pulled Jerry over. "You know what they're saying," she told him, feeling pressed to confide in someone, even if it were the boss' assistant. "They're afraid Pop WILL recover from this heart attack. Then things for sure won't change around here."

No longer able to ignore this pervasive undercurrent, Jerry saw that Sadie seemed eager to spill.

"Look, Sadie, you can level with me," Jerry finally ventured, struggling to keep his voice even. "What's going on here? You've got a great place to work. You've got a boss who really cares about people and a lodge that guests flock to. What's everyone's beef?"

"So you've been duped, too," Sadie shot back, looking sullen. "It may seem like paradise to you, but some evil things are happening—that's what they say. Most of us haven't had a raise in five years. I guess any chance of one is now eaten up in Pop's high-priced medical bills. The ski instructors get any of the rest of the leftovers," she said, raising an eyebrow at Jerry, "and I guess you will too, now, since Pop's got a real uptown assistant. But the peons like us—the folks who make this place run smoothly—we get peanuts. 'Peanuts for the peons'—I've heard them say this, and now I believe them." Sadie nodded as she spewed out the last statement, her nod coming like a proud exclamation point over the fact that she had gotten something off her chest at last.

Jerry didn't know who the "they" and "them" were that spangled Sadie's monologue, but he tried to act unruffled. Privately, he sensed that dissent must run deep if perceived loyalists like Sadie were feeling the heat.

Once back at Valley Lodge, Pop began barking orders from his bedside command post like a general in a war flick.

He returned not one minute too quickly for Jerry, who had felt the pressure of Pop's absence as no one else, since it occurred just as Jerry began to get his feet wet. So many unanswered questions about the ski lodge awaited Pop, yet Jerry didn't want to stress out his recuperating boss and send him into another coronary.

"Get your rest, and we'll talk later," Jerry retorted any time Pop mentioned that the two of them had some catching up to do.

When Pop felt chipper enough to return to his desk for a few hours one morning, Jerry decided he could wait no longer to see what, if anything, he knew about these murmuring employees.

Pop looked blase as Jerry related Sadie's troubling conversation.

"It's nothing for you to worry about," Pop assured. "I've talked to several of them before and explained to them all of their benefits. I think it'll blow over. It's just that Hilliard in the kitchen who tries to stir up trouble." He referred to Henry Hilliard, the Rippling Rock's assistant chef, who Jerry had sized up merely as being an inveterate clown and cut-up but never suspected that he harbored actual ill against the boss. "We've been through little upsets before. Believe me, they die down. People can't beat the working conditions at Valley Lodge. They know that."

The day Pop had sauntered into Jerry's shop and enticed him to leave Boulder, he could have sold the proverbial icebox to an Eskimo. Today, he was less than convincing. Despite Pop's casual air, Jerry noticed that by the end of the conversation, the older man's chalk-colored lips were so tightly drawn that the imprint of his teeth showed through.

Now, in hindsight, the picture for Jerry of Pop's almost frantic efforts to hire him began to sharpen. Pop had sensed trouble brewing—in both the staff and his health—and rushed to snare Jerry away from the ski apparel shop as a panacea for his desperation.

For Pop he tried to put on a brave, bold front. In his less-guarded moments Jerry continued to stew.

So someone else has let me down. I thought the big rush Pop gave me was because he genuinely liked me and saw potential. Now I see I was nothing more than a vehicle hired in desperation to preserve his dream.

Henry Hilliard's brief note was the first to appear on Pop's desk the next day.

"I'm resigning effective immediately to take a job at the Ski Chalet," read the brusque announcement, with not even a hint of a thank-you for Pop's past goodwill.

Two bellmen left similar notes taped to Pop's door, stating that Ski Chalet had hired them, too. Sadie was the fourth to resign—following "them" to work for the same competitor just up the mountain.

By day's end, Jerry had never seen the even-tempered Pop so angry. "They'll see how wrong they are," he squawked. "I've been good to them and they know it. But I think the boil is pricked, now. The mad ones that Hilliard managed to stir up are gone. Everyone else is loyal."

The next day's house mail contained three more resignations, however—all from housekeeping. Valley Lodge was now on the verge of crisis.

"Burt Umphrey at Ski Chalet thinks he'll raid my staff for his pricey new lodge. I'll raid him right back," Pop charged.

Jerry saw quickly it was all bluff. Unless someone acted fast, the acclaimed Valley Lodge would be seriously crippled as it faced the season opening only a few days away.

Ads for help quickly sprang up in local newspapers. Jerry called the state college in Gunnison for the names of students seeking work. S.O.S. calls went out to Pop's business contacts in Crested Butte, where he was a man-about-town and a long-time member of the Chamber of Commerce.

Fortunately, a faithful, threadbare crew refused to join the walkout. Among them were Doug and Henny, the portly husband-wife team who oversaw the restaurant end of the business. Jerry had found this couple personable from the start. He thought they resembled a pair of affable dough people like the ones on refrigerator biscuit advertisements. He regarded them even more highly when they stayed.

"We're just crushed, Pop Hartley," Henny said with conviction, as tears pushed to the corners of her eyelids. "We've never had anything like this happen before." Pop had hired the loyal Doug and Henny away from running their own mom-and-pop diner in Crested Butte 15 years ago. Even with several restaurant staffers missing, Pop knew the Rippling Rock could maintain its reputation amidst the walkout if Doug and Henny were in tow.

The brunt of the strain to keep the lodge afloat continued to fall on Jerry, who had been perilously close to buckling even before Pop took ill.

Now, in one hour's time, he might clean a dozen toilets, run several washers full of sheets in the lodge laundromat, and unload the luggage of guests who continued to pour in, oblivious to the difficulty.

Undaunted by his recent surgery, Pop felt duty-bound to pitch in, clattering about the lodge despite his weakened state.

His foolhardiness caught up with him quickly. On the third day of the walkout, while changing a lightbulb, Pop swayed from exhaustion. He barely managed to crawl down from the stepladder to avoid a serious fall.

"Pop, this is absurd!" Jerry practically shrieked when he came upon this frightening development. "You're going to bed and stay there before you get killed."

Gratefully, the doctor who arrived at Valley Lodge to treat Pop echoed Jerry's manifesto, only more sternly.

"What do you have, a death wish?" he queried Pop none too kindly. "I'm telling you, Hartley, you almost died a few weeks ago, and you're trying to put yourself back in the grave. If you want to see this lodge survive, you'll stay in this bed until you're thoroughly recovered. What your employees need right now is your history and your common sense. You can distribute that just fine in a prone position." He ordered him confined to his lodge apartment, where Pop had relocated several years back after his wife Hannah died and he sold their home in town.

One night, as Pop was distributing those orders with Jerry at his bedside for the umpteenth time that day, Jerry nodded off with Pop in mid-sentence. Pop was instantly compassionate.

"Poor Jerry, I've dumped so much on you," Pop said soothingly. "You're not resting or eating right—I just know it."

Then he inserted, "Why, what you need is a wife!" He obviously was thinking of Hannah, who had been a partner to him in running Valley Lodge before her passing. "A wife would keep you going."

Jerry roused to Pop's words. He sighed bitterly, *A wife. I would have had one by now if things hadn't happened the way they did.* Suddenly, he realized that days had gone by since memories of his fiancee had even entered his mind. *Natalie! Oh, Natalie! Look what's happened to me—I'm so stressed out, I haven't even had time to think about you. I'm letting everyone down—even your memory.*

All at once, an avalanche of guilt and hopelessness engulfed him. At that moment, if he could have, Jerry would have burst from Pop's room screaming from anxiety and bounded from Valley Lodge, never to return.

One look at the ailing man's face reminded him, *I must be strong for Pop at all costs. I can't let on. I CAN'T. He leans on me now, more than ever. If this lodge crumbles, it's all my fault.*

All too soon, it was opening day for the new ski season. A frown furrowed Jerry's brow as the bright, recorded voice booming, "Welcome to Valley Lodge, the happiest little hotel in the Rockies," wafted from the outdoors and over the registration desk.

The normally upbeat greeting was a grim reminder to Jerry that on this day that should be one of the year's crown jewels, Valley Lodge was anything but happy. Neither the spirited announcement nor any of the other promised perks at Valley Lodge would keep tensions at bay for much longer. Guests were growing noticeably irked at the uncharacteristic wait they experienced in the check-in line that snaked through the Great Hall.

"I thought this place had good service," one guest muttered, causing Jerry's temple to pound like a mallet striking an anvil. Despair was etched on each line of his face as he pondered what to do next with these crowds.

"Here, young lady, let me take those bags from you," Pop's voice emerged unexpectedly from somewhere behind Jerry.

Before Jerry could protest, Pop had swept in from his Valley Lodge apartment where the doctor supposedly had him under house arrest. He pushed to the front of the registration desk where Jerry stood and began hefting two bulging suitcases, one under each arm.

The female guest shot the older gentleman a grateful look. She had languished in this slow-moving serpent for forty-five minutes now. The prospect of finally getting settled into her room was much welcomed.

"Pop, you mustn't," Jerry whispered frantically, laying a restraining hand on the older man's arm.

"Nonsense, Jerry; I want to impress this young lady with my muscles," returned Pop, grinning back at the guest beside him. Ignoring Jerry's caution, he bounded up the stairs, stooped by the luggage he hoisted.

Jerry heaved an exasperated sigh. It was one more proof that nothing—not even a doctor's strict orders—would stop Pop when he made up his mind to do something. Hadn't Pop proved that the day he struck up the conversation with him at the ski apparel shop in Boulder—the conversation that changed his life?

Why'd I ever do it? Jerry brooded. *If I had stayed there, nothing like this would be facing me. The lodge is sinking, and it's up to me to save it. I'll never pull out of this hole.*

In better times, Jerry might have just now been off on the mountain giving last-minute coaching to the ski instructors whose classes were about to kick off for the season. Sadie and several other former workers would be amply covering the desk that he staffed alone.

The way things were going, Jerry wondered when, if ever, he would ever see his beloved slopes again.

It was a curious thing. The lobby of the Great Hall by now was packed with people—people pressing him on all sides for rooms, baggage handling, and a host of other needs.

He even was vaguely aware that many called his name—"Jerry," not because they knew him, but because they saw it on his badge and thought a familiar address might net them quicker attention.

Yet, in the midst of more people than he probably waited on in several months' time in his comfortable old ski shop in Boulder, Jerry had never felt so sadly, desperately, alone.

FOUR

A Lift and a Lifeline

❀

"You look as if you need some help," called a soft voice that broke into Jerry's reverie. Two luminous, sympathetic brown eyes met Jerry's tired blue ones as he glanced up from the computer to the other side of the registration desk.

For a few minutes, he had been vaguely aware that a trim, chestnut-haired form had been leaning over the desk rail trying to get him to notice. But the fog of thoughts and exhaustion that swirled around him seemed to freeze him at inattention, temporarily unable to respond.

"Sorry," Jerry muttered when the words finally came. "Have you been standing there long? I was involved in something on the screen here." It was a lame excuse for his lack of alertness—one he suspected the female guest saw through anyway, since she clearly had been observing him for some time.

"It doesn't matter," she replied insistently, shaking her chin-length locks free of the parka hood that framed her face. "But seriously, you're about to collapse. I saw you nod off for a second while you were looking at the computer. Look, I worked in a motel office some during college. If you'll let me behind the counter, I can at least help you get some of these names processed."

"Me, too," joined in a second voice. A petite blonde suddenly sidled up alongside the brunette guest. A knit headband held back a mop of curls that bobbed as she spoke.

Waves of embarrassment swept over Jerry. How incompetent he—and the esteemed Valley Lodge—must look, for two total strangers to act out of pity and volunteer to aid him after he dozed on the job! Jerry straightened himself and tried to muster as professional an air as possible after the gaffe.

"You're very kind—both of you," he said to the women. His eyes drifted past them to the lobby that continued to teem with noisy guests. "We're a little shorthanded today, and I do appreciate your patience. But if you'll tell me your names, I'll get your accommodations right away."

"Carol McKechnie," replied the first. "Shannon Wilder. We're from Ohio," injected her blonde friend.

McKechnie . . . Wilder . . . As Jerry entered the names, things clicked in his head. These weren't just guests at Valley Lodge. These were the two ski instructors he'd been waiting for—with special permission to arrive late after other instructors had been in place for several weeks. He remembered that their university, the College of Wooster, had granted sabbaticals from their jobs as P.E. instructors to work at Valley Lodge this season but had required them to complete the first nine-week term of classes before they could leave.

As Jerry typed their names, FACULTY quickly flashed on the screen, confirming his assessment.

"Am I sorry *you two* had to wait!" he murmured apologetically. "If you had only pushed to the front of the line and told me you were instructors, I would have gotten your rooms immediately. You could have registered ahead of the other guests. You need to be checking out the slopes."

"We don't need special favors," Carol replied, her voice still soft yet now laced with a determined tone strangely reminiscent of Pop's. "I've already seen my teaching schedule here. My ski classes don't start for two more days. I'll have plenty of time to investigate things."

She grabbed the key and the lodge map that Jerry placed on the counter and began to wheel her luggage away. "Just as soon as I unload my things, I'll be back down to help." She and Shannon, who would be roommates at Valley Lodge, bounded out of the lobby before Jerry had a chance to protest.

Although a bit bemused at their offer, Jerry figured that was the last he'd see of the two ski instructors from Ohio that afternoon once they got a glimpse of the lift station that their rooms overlooked.

In a relatively short time, however, Carol appeared again. She had managed a quick change from the denim overalls she wore for travel. She now had on a white cable-knit sweater and white pants that made her look as if she belonged in one of Valley Lodge's promotional brochures.

More alert than at their first meeting minutes earlier, Jerry suddenly noted the attractiveness of his new acquaintance. "I'm back, just as I told you," she announced, striding behind Jerry and determinedly planting herself beside him at a spare computer at the registration desk. "Now please give me a job to do."

Carol's boldness stunned Jerry. Other than Pop's initial conversation with Jerry that day at the ski shop in Boulder, he had never met a total stranger who instantly exuded such confidence and such a take-charge attitude. Despite his exhaustion, Jerry found this situation at the same time refreshing and exasperating.

"Look," he said sternly. A slight, condescending smile played at his lips. "This is really nice of you to want to help, but I can't let you on the computers. I'm sure you're trustworthy, but you're not bonded. We deal with financial matters at check-in. Now, please go on back to your room. Things will be just fine."

"Look yourself," Carol replied, matching the sternness of Jerry's tone and refusing to be patronized. "Things *won't* be just fine, either, unless you get some help. I read Mr. Hartley's letter. Unless the situation's changed much, you're dreadfully short-staffed right here at peak season. Shannon and I overheard people from all over the building coming up to you and making demands you couldn't meet. The phone was ringing off the hook, and we saw what happened when you gave those two guests back the wrong credit cards a moment ago."

Before Jerry had time to respond, Carol went on. "Now, I've come a long way to Valley Lodge," she continued, speaking carefully. "When I got the letter, it was too late for me to change my plans. I've worked long and hard to get this sabbatical, so I'd like for it not to flop. From the looks of my schedule, I don't have much spare time, but I can put the few extra minutes I have to good use. If I can't help you at the desk, surely you can find some place for me to pinch-hit. Shannon will, too. She had to make a phone call, but she'll be down in a minute."

Jerry's eyes shifted downward. Now he understood. Unlike other guests in line, for whom Pop had insisted that the lodge maintain a business-as-usual front, Carol and Shannon had known the truth about Valley Lodge's employment situation.

Jerry remembered that as soon as the crisis hit, Pop had dispatched a quick letter to all ski instructors, putting the most positive spin possible on the walkout but giving the faculty an option of teaching elsewhere. In the letter, Pop had told about Jerry's ski pro credentials as an enticement to the group. He wrote that he and Jerry, his assistant, "will do our best to make your stay enjoyable despite possible minor inconveniences."

A few minutes ago, when Jerry had described the lodge as a "bit short-handed," his comments must have appeared to the two women like a cover-up. Now he was doubly embarrassed. What a dolt he must seem.

When he lifted his grim face and looked at Carol again, Jerry saw no condemnation—only those same soft, insistent eyes.

"I forgot for a minute that you were notified," he finally shrugged. "Most guests don't know."

When Carol made no reply but continued to stand in front of him determinedly, Jerry heaved a sigh of resignation.

"OK, do you think you can fold some laundry?" he asked, weakly. "We'll have someone from the temporary service down there tomorrow, but today we're way behind. The supervisor called me a minute ago. They can't get the linens out fast enough to get the beds made for new guests."

"Just tell me where, and I'll go," Carol nodded, unflinching.

Carol's attire again caught Jerry's attention. As he suddenly thought how her front-desk-perfect outfit was hardly suitable for the laundry room, he couldn't help notice the contrast of her dark hair as it curled under against the winter white.

"You might want to change into something else," Jerry cautioned, gesturing a bit awkwardly in the direction of her sweater. "Things get pretty steamy in the basement with all those dryers going."

Carol, noting his concern, flashed him an appreciative grin. Her smile called attention to a pair of full, expressive lips that were freshly outlined in a flattering shade of plum. "I'll be just fine," she assured, turning to go. "Now the basement is where?"

"The stairs are just past this hallway," Jerry waved. "Ask for Jessie. She's in charge. I'll call and tell her you're on the way."

"Send Shannon down, too," Carol called, her voice trailing as she headed out.

As he turned back to his computer, Jerry realized he had forgotten to say thank you—and that he had failed to introduce himself, although it was clear that Carol had readily deduced his role. *Just add that to my list of blunders for the day,* he thought to himself.

Then Jerry realized something else. As he and Carol had their brief exchange, a curious sensation began seeping in around the edges of his thoughts—a sensation he thought himself incapable of experiencing again, a sensation he thought died with Natalie.

Jerry realized he had actually noticed the beauty of another woman.

Shannon, with her perkiness, was button-cute and friendly as a cocker spaniel, but her dark-haired roommate, though outgoing and confident, had something of an ethereal quality about her that drew Jerry instantly.

Certainly, he had been around numerous females in the months since Natalie died. Customers often tried to flirt with him, and coeds from the college had routinely swooned over his good looks and impressive build. Friends had even lined him up with dates in an effort to jump-start Jerry's social life again. None of them had piqued his interest the slightest bit. Jerry had worked hard to keep his emotions shut down because of his overwhelming sense of loss and his loyalty to Natalie.

Something about just gazing at Carol for those few moments had felt satisfying and good, like drinking a big mug of marshmallow-topped hot chocolate following an afternoon on the slopes. He was sure his boorish behavior in the past few minutes had been anything but winsome to these two new females.

Despite that realization, Jerry suddenly felt a bit more alive than dead—a contrast to the past few months. It was just a tiny lift, but a lift that he needed—a lift that carried him through the rest of the afternoon as he faced the endless line that still awaited him in the Great Hall.

The sound of mirthful female voices mixed with the drone of clothes dryers greeted Jerry when he finally descended the basement stairs and peered into the laundry room late that afternoon. A temp sent by the personnel service in town had come out to staff the registration desk for the evening shift. Jerry was grateful for the break. He imagined that Carol—and her roommate, who had joined her just as Carol anticipated—probably had long since wearied of their brief burst of altruism and returned to their rooms.

To his surprise, four eyes peering over piles of freshly folded towels and sheets told him he was wrong.

"Hi, Jerry," called Shannon cheerily as she spotted the lodge's good-looking assistant. "Are we doing a good job, or what?"

"Spectacular," Jerry responded. He surveyed the orderly laundry room that had been hopelessly backed up last time he checked only hours ago. "But what keeps you here? You're wiling away your first afternoon here in this furnace. Don't you have more interesting things to do?"

"They seemed to need us," Carol interjected amicably as she arranged a stack of towels bearing the lodge's "VL" insignia. "Jessie said our extra hands really made a difference. Plus, we got to meet Pop. He came by to introduce himself."

"He's awesome!" Shannon chimed in. "I can't believe he just got over surgery. And already back at work—what a constitution he must have."

"He's so much like my father, who died last year," Carol added. Her eyes misted a bit at this remembrance. "Really indomitable, and such a caring person. Pop made me feel instantly at home."

Jerry winced a little at Carol's description. *Like her father—indomitable, caring.* What adjectives would come to mind to describe his own dad? *Negligent? Remote? Undependable?* Certainly none that Carol cited. The contrast to his personal history pushed Jerry's insecurity button afresh and made him feel badly inadequate.

Shannon's familiar chirp broke through his thoughts. "I guess we *had* better knock it off and get something to eat, though," she said, tapping her watch as she glanced at her friend. "That turkey bagel on the airplane is a distant memory."

Suddenly Jerry remembered one of the reasons for his basement visit. On the chance that the duo might still be on the scene, Jerry had come down to offer his brainstorm.

"If you don't already have plans for dinner, I have an idea," he suggested. "I can reserve one of the horse-drawn sleighs down in town. It's something special we provide guests for evening outings. I could take you to The Wild Goose. It's a Victorian-themed restaurant down the mountain in the historic area. Maybe I could give you two a better opinion of Valley Lodge than the one you got this afternoon."

Deep in Jerry's imagination sparked the thought of seeing Carol's imploring brown eyes over the candlelit tables that gave The Wild Goose its special, romantic aura. This afternoon, he had probably been a little snippy at her offer, which continued to perplex him a little but which he saw was no doubt sincere.

Although he knew the evening would involve making pleasant conversation with both Carol and her chattery roommate, Jerry could, if he maneuvered carefully, seize the opportunity to learn a bit more about this intriguing, dark-eyed beauty.

The women's delighted response, "Oh, wow! Could we?" to his proposal sent Jerry scurrying to the lobby phone to make the arrangements.

As he hastily ordered the sleigh, Jerry recognized a lilt in his step that had lain dormant in the press of recent weeks.

"Oh, and Joe, get some flowers for the horse's hat," Jerry instructed the driver as an whimsical afterthought. He wanted to make it an evening that wouldn't be forgotten soon.

FIVE

Snow in the Forecast

❀

Flakes from the fresh winter snow blanket that had just begun to settle on the town clung to Carol's lashes as she and Shannon loaded into the horse-drawn sleigh. A three-mile drive down from Mt. Crested Butte in the lodge's Land Rover put them out at the train station, where Joe and the equine team awaited.

"How picturesque!" Carol exclaimed, as Jerry spread a shawl over the two women's laps. "Brand new snow—in honor of our arrival."

"You'll see much more of it soon," Jerry assured her. He waved to Joe to give the horses the reins. "Snow's in the forecast for the next three days. Maybe it'll keep folks on the slopes and out of the lodge for a while."

Jerry instantly regretted the remark. *Why doesn't someone just zip up my mouth?* he fumed. *Why don't I just rent a billboard saying that Valley Lodge is a loser—and that I am, too?*

Carol responded immediately. "Well, my offer still stands," she told Jerry as the snow-muffled sleighbells jingled behind them. "I'll need to spend a couple of hours tomorrow morning learning about my duties and check out the 'bunny slopes' for my classes. After that, I can be back to help out around the place."

Jerry decided not to comment. Instead, he began pointing out to the women the Old City Hall and the other quaint buildings that had just come into view as the horses clopped their way down the streets at a slow, rhythmic pace.

He hoped the atmosphere of the laid-back mining town, which looked like an old-fashioned Christmas card in its fresh winter whitewash, would work its magic and wipe all thoughts of the crippled ski lodge from their minds.

The conversation at The Wild Goose was convivial. Over grilled Ruby Trout, Jerry and his two dinner guests delved into each other's worlds a little with some tentative, get-acquainted conversation.

The women laughed as Jerry recalled how the colorful Pop boldly squired him away from the ski shop. Then it was Jerry's turn to listen, as Shannon and Carol shared tales about some of their P.E. students at the College of Wooster. They talked about the women's volleyball and softball teams they coached, respectively.

The light-hearted banter, plus the restaurant's ambience, made Jerry feel relaxed and successful for a change. *This is really working well,* Jerry thought to himself. *Maybe I've raised myself a notch or two in their estimations. Maybe they'll forget how dismal things looked at the lodge when they arrived.*

His companions definitely seemed entertained. Carol's eyes danced with merriment when she talked about her dream of teaching children to ski. "I've wanted to do this since I was a kid, when my dad started taking me to the slopes in Vermont," she disclosed sunnily.

Although Jerry conversed politely with both women, he found his eyes glued on Carol, whose soft features looked all the more alluring in the dusky light from the candle on their table. Sometimes he found himself tuning out Shannon's chatter to drink in Carol's face, which had turned increasingly in his direction.

How nice it was to be the object of a woman's attentions again—especially a woman that other restaurant patrons were admiring, too.

Later, after they finished off their desserts of marble cheesecake—another Wild Goose specialty—Carol again brought up her insistent offer to help. This time Jerry couldn't resist probing.

"You need to explain something to me," he ventured, leaning in over the empty plates as he spoke with intensity. "Why would you do this? You came here to be a ski instructor. You just told me how this fulfills a dream for you. You didn't come to Valley Lodge to be a chambermaid. Much as I'd like to, I can't pay you even an extra penny for your volunteer work."

"Oh, that's just the way she is—always doing good," bubbled Shannon. She cast an appreciative side look at her brunette friend.

"But you helped me this afternoon—and you didn't even know me," Jerry persisted. "How can someone be so generous? You enlisted your roommate as well. You didn't know you were going to get a dinner in return," he continued, laughing slightly.

Carol lowered her eyes, a little embarrassed at the attention Jerry continued to focus on her offer.

"I suppose if it were up to my basic nature, I wouldn't be generous," she explained, after some thought. "I'm sure I'd be rather selfish with my time."

"But," she went on, her face erupting into a contented smile, "since I have a personal relationship with Christ, I try to do what Jesus would do." She disclosed this just as casually as she had chatted about her college and her students and her sports team. She pulled back her sweater sleeve to reveal a bracelet with the letters "WWJD" woven into it.

Jerry had seen some of these woven bracelets in the lodge gift shop, which sold Christian books and accessories. The gift shop operator had given him one with a bunch of samples. He was vaguely aware that the bracelet had to do with something religious, but he hadn't known until now what the letters meant.

"So, how about you?" Carol continued, with that same confident lilt in her voice that seemed to be her trademark. "I guess I really don't feel like I know someone unless I know about his relationship with Christ."

Jerry grimaced. *That subject again,* he thought miserably. *She's like Pop in more ways than her confidence.* He pondered how he could bluff his way out of Carol's probing, just as he had with his mentor. After all, hadn't he been the top salesman at the Boulder store? Carol probably assumed that anyone hired to help manage this high-principled ski lodge would share Pop's religious fervor as well.

"Oh, you have one, too," Jerry finally answered, gesturing to her bracelet in an attempt to hedge. "I guess I forgot to wear mine tonight. They're pretty neat, huh?"

Carol telegraphed a slightly quizzical look to Jerry. He saw his reply hadn't completely satisfied her, but the evening's ebullience made her willing to drop the subject for now.

Jerry tried to thwart any follow-up questions by turning to pay the bill. He felt his buoyant spirits nosedive at this turn in the discussion.

Part of him found Carol's—and Pop's—outlook about their faith intriguing. It seemed so personal to them—such a motivating, present force in their day-to-day activity and decisions. But bitter, resentful feelings continued to bubble up whenever he thought about God's role in his life. With Natalie, he never had to deal with such topics, since his fiancee had been a backslidden church attender, if at all.

I simply must find a way to avoid this subject in the future, Jerry vowed uncomfortably.

The crisp night air and snowfall helped snap Jerry out of his dour mood as Joe brought the horses to The Wild Goose door. As he assisted Carol into the sleigh, his hand touched her elbow to boost her over the high step. A surprising shiver of delight coursed through him, as his hands tingled with the awareness of her.

Shannon seemed to detect the chemistry that had begun between her roommate and their blond, engaging

50

host. Unlike the sleigh ride to the restaurant, where Carol and Shannon occupied the same seat, Shannon quickly planted herself down across from Carol, leaving Carol's side free for Jerry to occupy.

Jerry happily seized the opportunity and nestled close to Carol. They all huddled under extra blankets Jerry produced from under the seat. The sleigh threaded its way through the frosty night and back to the lodge's Land Rover, which returned them up the mountain and to the lodge door.

Removing their coats in the lobby, they all teased Carol about her pink nose which the cold had colored to the exact rose hue of her cashmere sweater. For a few minutes the three clustered in front of the Great Hall's fireplace and warmed themselves from the biting weather. Their voices were gleeful in the afterglow of a pleasant evening.

A heated discussion that drifted over from the registration desk snapped Jerry back into a business mode.

"I called you last week," he heard a stern voice storm angrily. "What do you mean you don't have me in your computer?"

"Jerry, can you help?" the temp who had taken Jerry's place for the evening pled urgently.

"Sorry, ladies," Jerry apologized to Carol and Shannon, his voice mottled with more regret than he intended to show. "Sounds like I'm being summoned."

Shannon immediately thanked Jerry for hosting them and headed for the stairs. Jerry sent the temp home for the evening and seated himself behind the desk. He saw that Carol was lingering behind, and he felt his pulse quicken. After he settled things with the irritated guest and sent him away with a bellman, she approached the desk curiously.

"So, who comes to handle the night shift?" she asked, a caring look crossing her face. Surely Jerry wasn't expecting to go back on duty after such an exhausting day.

"You're looking at him," Jerry confirmed, managing a grim smile. "The temp's not ready to take this on yet. After midnight, the phones get quiet. Things get easier."

51

"But how much will you sleep—and when?" she persisted.

"Not much right now, of course," Jerry replied. "This is prime time. Lots of night activities, and everyone needs something before bedtime. During the wee hours, things settle down. I sometimes even manage a nap on the sofa when I turn on the night bell and take my phone with me."

Carol frowned, and Jerry wondered if a lecture were coming. He could hear her lambaste him: with no more sleep than this, he could always expect to nod off while registering guests.

But when Carol spoke after processing this information for a moment, her voice held no hint of recrimination, only concern.

"Well, wish I could stay up and keep you company, but it's been a long day," she said, with an understanding smile. "Maybe some other time."

Some other time, indeed, Jerry thought, his insides growing tingly as he pictured Carol's companionship through some of the quiet, lonely hours that had been his lot since the walkout. He would eagerly wait for that moment. The prospect of it would keep him going for the next stretch of evening.

Carol's and Jerry's eyes locked one more time across the registration desk—the spot that had been the scene of their first meeting hours earlier. As Jerry realized this coincidence, he marveled at the wild ride his emotions had been on since he first cast Carol that sleepy, embarrassing, yet momentous glance.

Then the two of them blurted out in unison, "Thanks for everything."

A flurry of self-conscious giggles followed. Through ripples of laughter, Carol exclaimed, "I've been a lodge-hand for less than a day, and already I'm talking like you."

"Well, at least you have good taste," Jerry followed. On that cheerful note, Carol gave him one last smile and disappeared up the stairs.

For what seemed like an eternity, Jerry's eyes stayed fixed to the spot where he last saw Carol. Only the annoying ringing of the phone brought him back to reality—wake-up calls to record, room-service orders to transfer. Jerry had little time to wander in his thoughts—to reflect on this mortifying day that somehow had taken a magical turn.

But any time the noise died down and Jerry's mind trailed off to the few minutes of enjoyment the past few hours had brought, it was tinged with a trace of dread.

How am I going to continue to fake it? Jerry wondered, shifting uncomfortably.

When Pop had brought up the issue of his faith earlier, he was distracted and sick—easier to bluff. Jerry had danced around the answers enough to say what he thought Pop wanted to hear.

Carol was another matter. Sharp and intuitive, she was likely to see through every word he uttered. Jerry suddenly felt ganged up on by Pop and Carol, so effervescent in their beliefs. They were pressuring him to be something he wasn't—as if he didn't feel enough pressure already with his work load.

Then Jerry was struck by another thought. Carol might already have a boyfriend back in Ohio—someone with whom she was more in step, someone more attuned to her spiritual leanings.

Jerry gritted his teeth determinedly. He would simply have to be more on his toes and watch out for these land mines. If not, he might see this woman, who was already having an overwhelming effect on him, disappear as well.

SIX

Prescription for the Pain

❄

Jerry stirred on the sofa as he roused from the few hours of sleep he'd managed to grab. A sense of eagerness enveloped him, and he struggled to orient himself. His eyes opened, and he attempted to focus.

The first beams of daylight pushed their way into the Great Hall where he had fallen asleep, as was his custom lately, in front of the fireplace. They reminded him that it was time to make a sprint to his apartment, shower, and shave his stubble-covered face. He would have to be back before 6 a.m., when snow-obsessed, early-rising guests would begin pouring into the lobby.

Something was different, Jerry knew, as he struggled to hoist his tired body from the sofa.

For the first time in more mornings than he could count, Jerry actually felt a starburst of excitement about facing the day. He could hardly wait to bound downstairs to the staff cafeteria for breakfast after the new temp arrived for the registration desk.

Carol would likely be there, he knew. As her face flashed across the screen of his mind, yesterday's events fast-forwarded before him.

This time one day ago, the name of Carol McKechnie had meant nothing to him. Yesterday, he had set out on his duties as a broken, weary, overwhelmed man—with little light, little hope.

Today he was, undoubtedly, still weary and overwhelmed. But part of him felt less broken, more healed, more whole.

Just as quickly, insecurity gripped him. What if Carol didn't match his eagerness? His own eyes longed for another glimpse of her—another day to look for little snatches of opportunity to be by her side.

But would the feeling be mutual? Despite his snow-job last night at the restaurant, what if the image of him that stuck in her mind was that of the fumbling desk clerk that she first saw yesterday afternoon?

There was still much he didn't know about this pretty, personable ski instructor with whom he had spent last evening. Before today would be over, every other guy on Mt. Crested Butte would have their eyes on her, too. Once she hit the slopes, she'd be thoroughly inspected by those who were there for girl-watching instead of skiing.

Granted, he and Carol had passed some pleasant moments in a romantic restaurant, where her eyes hardly left his face during much of their meal. That didn't mean that he would still matter to her in the fresh light of day.

Jerry's step halted a bit sometime later when he moved to the entrance of the staff dining room and spotted Carol among the tables, acquainting herself and Shannon with the workers already gathered there. He was glad he had taken a few extra minutes to dig out his new teal fleece pullover instead of the usual frumpy sweatshirt he often wore to breakfast.

But the moment Carol caught a glimpse of him striding through the doorway, her face lit up like a million sunrises. *Down boy,* Jerry cautioned himself. *She's just being courteous. She'd react this way to anyone who took her to dinner last night.*

Still, his heart raced at her immediate, delighted response.

"Jerry! We've got a spot for you," she commanded. As though she were the veteran at Valley Lodge instead of the newcomer, Carol instantly began rearranging people seated at her table. She made a place for Jerry and motioned for him to join her.

"You were about to leave," Jerry observed to Carol, spotting her empty plate. He hoped the disappointment in his voice wasn't as obvious as it sounded to him.

"I've got a few minutes," Carol replied. She made no effort to rise. "But I've been talking to some of these old hands here, and I'm just dying to get out and try out the ski area."

A fashionable, lemon-yellow jacket and matching yellow goggles were draped on the back of her chair. It told him that Carol was headed straightway for the slopes. Jerry imagined how this bright flash of yellow light would look, poles poised, on a downhill coast, a spray of white powder preceding her.

Daggers of envy knifed through Jerry. Today's skiing conditions would be absolutely perfect in this outdoor paradise after last night's new snow. How many weeks had it been, now, since he had known the thrill of the wind at his back as he pushed off on skis? Routine pleasures like these that he had anticipated when Pop recruited him for Valley Lodge had been traded for a desk job of endless days and abbreviated nights.

"I'll be back at one o'clock sharp to help you," he heard her continue, through his reverie. "Be thinking of what I can do."

Jerry again demurred, as he had yesterday. "Please. It's really not necessary," he told her, this time trying to mean it. "Go on and enjoy yourself. You need to be outdoors, not shut up inside on a great winter day."

"You'll see me at one," Carol stonewalled, closing the case. *That Pop-like determination again,* Jerry thought, as Carol whisked from the table and out the door.

None other than Pop himself greeted Jerry when he returned to the lobby minutes later. His shaggy hair looked even more riotous than usual as the Great Hall's morning beams filtered onto it.

"So how was your social engagement?" Pop asked brightly. His eyes danced with an interest that Jerry could not readily interpret. "Joe tells me he took you and a couple of young ladies for a night on the town. Glad to see you getting out, son."

"It was fine, Pop, just fine," Jerry mumbled. He brushed off Pop's query as nothing more than small talk.

Pop pressed further. "That Carol, she's something else, don't you think?" So Pop obviously knew who went with Jerry to town. "When I met her yesterday, I thought, 'She's as godly as she is gorgeous—just what Jerry needs.' I would have figured out a way to play Cupid myself, but looks like you did just fine on your own." Pop turned away, chuckling a little as he sauntered off.

Jerry should have been amused—even honored—at Pop's would-be matchmaking. Instead, he smarted with resentment. It was just like his own father's meddling—trying to dictate what profession he entered, where he went to school, even his recreational pursuits. How disgustingly like Dad was Pop in some ways, to be so refreshingly different in others.

What if I wasn't successful with Carol? Jerry wondered. *What would Pop think of me then?* He already suspected that Pop was eyeing him critically about the vast amounts of work he wasn't managing well with Valley Lodge in chaos. He feared that Pop would eventually sum him up as a flop as his manager-in-training. Then, if he were unlucky in a courtship that Pop arranged, he'd be a two-time loser in Pop's eyes.

He also bristled at Pop's hint that Carol was some kind of cure-all for his spiritual condition. Did that mean that Pop saw through his shallow answers, after all?

Jerry felt ill-tempered and cross throughout the morning. His face was still creased in a scowl when Carol swept in at 1 o'clock, fresh from the slopes. She was ready, as she predicted, for her afternoon tasks.

Her face was happily flushed from a combination of windburn and excitement at finally experiencing Crested Butte's world-class ski runs. One look at her, and Jerry shifted into present tense, his sourness losing its edge.

"Absolutely stupendous," she gushed breathlessly. "There are some awesome skiers out there." Jerry inwardly hoped that some of the powderhounds she mentioned weren't of the oggling male variety.

Carol switched gears quickly. Soon she was a streak of activity—making beds, restocking linen carts, stepping in so the gift-shop clerk could go on break.

Jerry was incredulous at how quickly order reigned when Carol's cheerful efficiency took hold. He popped in and out of her work area whenever he could, trying to feel less embarrassed about conditions and more encouraged as he saw her willingly take over.

Over the roar of vacuums and washing machines, she yelled questions to him about the ski area and her upcoming classes. When she described her first pratfall of the season—on the beginner slopes as she tried to dodge some clumsy five-year-old "bunny busters" that morning, Jerry found himself laughing harder than he had in months. This soft-spoken, glamorous instructor had her witty side too, Jerry observed.

Shannon stuck her head in briefly, only long enough to call out in passing, "Sorry I can't help today. Maybe tomorrow."

Jerry saw that Carol's sidekick continued stepping out of the way a little to make sure her roommate had plenty of time with the dreamy, blond desk clerk. Despite her slight ditziness, Carol's roommate had more savvy than Jerry would have reckoned.

Suddenly it dawned on Jerry—Carol had never eaten lunch that day. To keep her word, she had rushed in from her morning on skis and had never stopped for a meal, working solidly until five o'clock.

"You must be faint with hunger!" he chided her. How like Carol, to sacrifice her own needs to keep her promise. He had never known anyone to be so giving, so consistent.

Jerry offered to buy her dinner at the Rippling Rock, and Carol fairly jumped in assent. He dashed off to make sure the evening temp was in place for a few hours and promised to meet Carol shortly.

The Rippling Rock itself was quite picturesque, with its floor-to-ceiling, glassed-in fire pit where steaks were grilled as a focal point in the center of the room. Tables overlooked an illuminated, outdoor ice rink. Dinner guests in the darkened restaurant were entertained by ice skaters gliding gracefully in the night.

Once they had placed their orders for two of the Rippling Rock's biggest steaks, Carol leaned in and faced Jerry squarely.

"I've been waiting to tell you something," she said quietly, with her usual, to-the-point directness. "Pop filled me in on one of the main reasons you came to Valley Lodge. He told me about your fiancee and the horrible accident. Jerry, I'm so sorry. It must have been a terrible thing for you."

Jerry almost choked on the cracker he'd just loaded with cheese spread.

So Pop had taken this step for him, too—revealing something to Carol that Jerry would have preferred to disclose in his own good time. Anger, mixed with a rush of painful memories, combined to form a giant lump in his throat. Jerry gulped hard to force it down.

"Yes, it was tough," he finally managed to sputter. He studied the lines in his palms as he tried to gain equilibrium. "But I coped, and it's behind me, now."

Jerry had already planned to tell Carol about Natalie soon—maybe even tonight, if the right moment came. Pop's well-meaning meddling had left Jerry unprepared, and he wasn't at all sure how he was coming across at that moment. He hoped the shock mixed with disdain at Pop's revelation wasn't as obvious as it felt.

If Carol detected any of this inner turmoil, she indicated nothing. She touched his arm softly, wordlessly, and all his fury at Pop melted. Actually, he was a bit relieved that some of his painful history was out in the open.

Then it was Carol's turn to disclose. "I guess I came to Valley Lodge to make a break with the past as well," she confided.

Jerry's eyes widened as she described just ending a long-term relationship with a fellow college instructor. The two of them ultimately had little in common—especially the love for the outdoors. He was bookish and quiet; she was bold and adventuresome. With him, skiing—Carol's passion in life—was out of the question. Finally, they decided that things were too dead-end to continue.

"It seemed like a good chance to pursue a goal of mine," she concluded. "When the school approved my sabbatical, I took it to be a fresh start."

Part of Jerry wanted to shout in glad relief. So Carol wasn't attached somewhere—that is, if she truly wasn't still carrying a torch for the other guy. That left things wide open, just where Jerry wanted them.

Then, Jerry remembered he needed to react to Carol's news with sensitivity, too, just as Carol had to his. The hand that she had sweetly placed on his arm moments before was still just inches away. Jerry gently reached for her fingers and enclosed them in his, empathetically.

"That's not easy to go through either," he said consolingly.

For a moment, the freeing feeling of having unloaded their individual losses enveloped them, as their eyes held each other's gaze in silence. As each had leaned in toward one corner of the table to hear the other's low whispers, their faces had moved closer together. *Close, tantalizingly close,* Jerry reflected.

With little effort, he'd only need to incline his head just slightly over the sleeve of her emerald silk blouse to brush his lips against her cheek. He was close to doing this, his courage building, his heart pounding.

Carol's words cut through the quiet, tender moment., startling him. "Yes, it hurt a lot, but God helped me get through it. Is that how you felt too?"

Confound it, Jerry thought. The color rose in his cheeks, and he squelched the urge to slam his hands on the table. *Why couldn't she leave that topic out of things?*

Before Jerry could concoct a reply, Carol added to his angst.

"My friends at church were a big support. Did your church friends rally around you, as well?" she queried. She looked at him searchingly, while a tempest in Jerry quietly raged.

It was asked in all innocence. Certainly, after his misleading answer to Carol's question last night, she would naturally assume that Pop's top assistant was an active church-attender. It was time for one more ambiguous statement, to add to the others he'd handed Pop and Carol up to now.

However, in the face of Carol's guileless, transparent honesty, Jerry knew it was time to at least stem the tide of this charade, even if it undid everything that had occurred between them within the past 24 hours. *Just when I was at the brink,* he thought miserably.

"Actually, no. I haven't really gone to church in a . . . in a while," Jerry confessed, pushing away from the table in frustration.

Even that admission wasn't the whole truth, Jerry realized. He didn't dare add that "in a while" actually meant since early childhood—a childhood where concern about his dad's erratic whereabouts, his alcoholic binges, and his demanding, critical rages left little time for anything but survival. In the few times his mother had taken him and his younger brother to church, it was done to convince the neighbors that things were OK in their family and weren't the disaster they seemed. Carol would never understand this. Her own home life was obviously so markedly different from his.

Where would this conversation lead now? Jerry wondered, anxiety squeezing him like a vise.

After an interminable time, Carol finally replied with a single, "Oh." Jerry wondered how one word could be so heavy in the air that it seemed to thud to the ground like a croquet ball dropped to the floor. Her lovely, pink-tinged lips seemed to freeze in a perfect "O" as she formed the word. Jerry held his breath and braced for the worst.

Then, just as quickly, Carol collected herself—her chin lifted, her shoulders erect. "Well," she said, matter-of-factly. "I'm sure that can be remedied. Pop says Valley Lodge has chapel every Sunday in the Great Hall." She darted him a glance he had seen numerous times in the brief period he'd known her. That familiar, take-charge look promised that she'd have him at services from now on, even if she had to drag him.

Jerry sighed with relief that she had dropped the subject.

He noticed that the room suddenly had grown warm—*no, uncomfortably hot.* He rubbed his neck where the collar of the shirt under his V-neck sweater had begun to chafe. He needed to get out—outside—away, and fast.

Glimpsing the skaters as they moved skillfully across the pond, he pushed back his steak that suddenly tasted like a shoe sole and tossed out a suggestion.

"I have an idea," he said, frantic to get in his comfort zone after the distressing conversation. "How would you like to go skiing—tonight?"

Jerry realized that Carol only knew him as a harried lodge hand. He needed to do something quickly where he had half a chance of seeming successful—that is, if he didn't tumble down from lack of practice. If they hurried, they could rip down the slopes a couple of times before he had to relieve the night temp at the desk.

"I'd love to, but how?" she inquired excitedly, her eyes thankfully reflecting no strain at all from the discussion just ended. "I thought Crested Butte didn't have night skiing, like some places do. People in town don't want the bright lights bothering them, is what I've read."

"Where there's a will, there's a way," Jerry replied, managing a laugh and trying to take charge of the conversation after its sudden, desperate turn. "On nights like this, when the moon is full and bright, I've done some great skiing on the hill behind the lodge. It's perfect, if you don't mind a little climb. You up for it?" The trek up the hill would be tough for the uninitiated, but he took Carol to be in top physical shape. The climb would probably, at worst, only leave her breathless.

Carol grinned eagerly. "Just show me the way!"

"Great. Go get changed. We'll go do a little field research for your classes."

❁

The vacant, moonlit hill had a haunting yet enchanting aura as Jerry and Carol hauled themselves and their gear to the top, with Jerry leading the way. Jerry's hoisted poles fairly danced in his hands at the prospect of planting them on the trails once more—and in Carol's enthralling company, to boot.

The part of the Butte that jutted up behind Valley Lodge was rapidly ceasing to become the area's best-kept secret for those who had a hankering for skiing at night. Usually when Jerry slipped away to try it, he ran into several other adventurers.

Luckily, tonight Jerry and Carol seemed to have the untracked snow all to themselves.

He picked out a simple run to explore first. Taking this less-challenging trail would make it easier for them to stay together. Jerry didn't want to take any chances of getting separated from Carol since they were utterly alone on this massive mountain without even the ski patrol on duty.

He encouraged Carol to push off first, so he could stay behind at a protective distance.

Jerry was totally unprepared for what he observed when Carol took off on the hills bathed in the celestial light. Even on the simple slope, he could see that her form was perfect, controlled, artistic. As she effortlessly swerved back and forth on the powder, he thought he had never watched such a natural skier.

Although it was her first time on this unfamiliar trail, she worked her way down effortlessly, confidently, her skis perfectly parallel—her lithe body becoming liquid poetry in motion. The moonlight danced on the ice crystals and turned the entire area into a gleaming, alabaster palace.

Watching Carol, Jerry wondered if he was actually in the company of a real-life Ice Princess instead of the ski coach of the bunny slopes.

"What are you doing teaching the Kiddie School?" Jerry demanded, racing to catch up with her after she reached the bottom first. "Carol—you're fabulous! I've never seen anyone have such smooth form."

Her grin at his praise lit up the dark night.

"It's perfect out here—so deserted," she enthused, beaming with exhilaration. "Not having to dodge other skiers does wonders for your confidence. Thanks, Jerry, for suggesting that we do this."

"Can you make it up again? We've got time for one more," he exulted.

As they hoisted their way up and Jerry pointed them to a bit more challenging side of the hill, the bitter night chill bit to the bone. With no protest from his partner, Jerry wrapped his arms around a shivering Carol to help her warm up a bit after the twenty-minute hike to the top. Wearing caps, goggles, and all the layers they could muster against the cold, their dancing eyes peering through the slits of their masks stayed locked on each other in the sheer ecstacy of the moment.

This time, as they chose the steeper trail down, it was Carol's turn to be wowed. With Carol skiing alongside him most of the way, Jerry coasted through the turns and heard her shouts of encouragement as he zipped along. Jerry had never felt more buoyant—with Carol matching him bump for bump. Carol was obviously in her element, too, her grin so broad that her eyes almost vanished into slits behind her ski mask. Jerry could have skied all night without tiring in such an arrangement. He took in a deep, satisfying breath and tried to memorize the moment.

When they reached the base, an exuberant Jerry howled giddily. He held out both arms wide in celebration of their experience. Carol slid into them unhesitatingly.

"I might ask the same thing of you, Mr. Rutgers," she said, moving her face closer to his mask-covered ear. "What's a championship skier like you doing at a desk job? I've never seen anything like you, in any competition."

The bright eyes behind Jerry's goggles suddenly saddened. "I've wondered the same thing myself many times," he replied.

He bent down to click out of his skis to hide his frustration. "I hope to have more times like this, and often," he commented wistfully.

Carol caught the note of distress and moved to pull him out of it.

Kneeling beside him, her voice suddenly heavy with intimacy, she murmured, "Jerry, can I tell you something? Keith—the guy I told you about while we were having dinner—he would have never done anything like this. Do you understand? You'll never know how much this means—the fact that you arranged for us to ski like this tonight."

All the prizes, all the cheers, all the photographs snapped as he had crossed the finish line in times past—none of these rewards could have done for Jerry what Carol's affirming, penetrating words did at that very moment.

After feeling like a loser for more days recently than he could count, Jerry believed he finally was going home with the gold medal.

The substitute night clerk was pacing anxiously, ready to go off duty, when Jerry and Carol rushed through the lobby and dropped off their ski gear. Shaking the snow from his jacket, Jerry quickly kicked into his sneakers, slid in behind the counter, and prepared for the late-night shift.

He steeled himself for Carol to disappear as she had last night, bringing an abrupt end to another roller-coastery, yet storybook day.

However, this time Carol grabbed a magazine and flopped down in a chair near the front desk. Jerry dared to hope that she, too, was reluctant to say good night.

"I'm still good for a few more minutes," she grinned at him mischievously. "I think I'll stick around and see what it is you REALLY do in the wee hours."

"Well, hang on for some wild excitement!" he clowned back, his heart somersaulting with delight. "Valley Lodge is a swingin' place at two in the morning, believe me."

The late-night hours did turn out to be more eventful than usual. Crested Butte police appeared at the door, escorting home a couple of teen-age guests who had loitered suspiciously in the town.

A guest's steam iron temporarily set off a smoke alarm. A honeymooning bridegroom had ten dozen roses delivered to the Valley Lodge bridal suite, with delivery specified at 11 o'clock at night.

Carol snickered afresh with each development. "These things never happen when you're not here," Jerry kidded her.

"Well, I'll just have to keep you company more often," she retorted blithely. Their easy, comfortable repartee was a pleasant contrast to the emotion-laden atmosphere over dinner and the ethereal invigoration of the ski slopes.

At midnight, when the lobby at last grew hushed and Jerry could transfer the desk lines to his portable phone, he filled the fireplace with fresh logs and dimmed the Great Hall lights except a few over the desk.

Drawing Carol to the sofa, he poured two steamy cups of hot chocolate. For a few moments, they sipped them wordlessly, as fire from the new wood hissed in the background.

As Carol tipped her mug to drink, a blob of marshmallow stuck to her face. Jerry reached up to wipe away the white dollop with his thumb. They both giggled as removing it took several attempts.

On the final try, however, Jerry's hand lingered on her cheek, and he turned her face in his direction. Laughter ebbed into sighs, as Jerry saw that the event that the entire day had been moving toward was finally within his grasp.

As Jerry at last pulled Carol into his arms, he felt her hands simultaneously move to the back of his neck and lace themselves together there. Their lips met in a tender kiss, warm with surrender, while the flames crackled in the background and Jerry's heart threatened to literally explode from the joy of it all.

In that ecstatic moment, Jerry knew he had found in Carol the prescription for the past six months of pain. The last lips that his had touched were those of Natalie, a week before the plane crash.

Until just yesterday, Jerry believed that he'd spend the rest of his life without someone to fill that void.

Yet even amid the triumphant feeling that washed over Jerry then, a warning light flashed deep within him. *If she knew the real me, she'd run,* an inner voice trumpeted.

As desperately as he hoped that this sweet analgesic would never wear off, something inside him knew better.

SEVEN

The Principles of Love

❂

If Carol were the prescription for Jerry's pain, she became the miracle cure for Valley Lodge's difficulties. As she continued to make good on her vow to be a substitute lodge-hand, Jerry had never experienced anyone with so much enthusiasm, so much boundless energy—and such a sweet, delightful desire to personally help lighten his load.

Daily, after her ski classes for children ended, Carol changed from her ski attire into jeans and a Valley Lodge sweatshirt. She showed up as a trouble-shooter in spots around the lodge where Jerry had identified a personnel shortage for the day.

If nothing were tremendously pressing in any of the other lodge's service areas, Jerry deployed Carol, who was now bonded, to the front desk. This freed him to interview prospective employees as he pressed on to fill the lodge's vacancies. Jerry was amazed at how much her drive, sprinkled in the appropriate places where momentary needs arose, went such a long way to break the back of the employee crisis. No longer humiliated as he was at first to have her help, Jerry relied on Carol more and more. He always breathed a sigh of relief when he saw her arriving for her afternoon assignments.

Carol, in turn, continued to draft the perky, helpful Shannon, as well,. The two of them became known among the staff as the "Ohio Avalanche" because of the way they swept down from the mountain each afternoon and came shooting in to straighten up some precarious situation in the lodge's inner-workings.

One afternoon when Carol looked especially tired from her day, Jerry insisted that she take time off and rest. She would hear nothing of it.

"*You* don't get the afternoon off to catnap," she answered, attempting to end the matter. "Why should I?"

"But your 'bunnies' need you," Jerry protested. Carol's face regularly wore a glow now when she breezed in from her morning ski classes with the younger set. She and her clutch of kids had a rapport that was obvious every time Carol encountered some of her charges in the lobby. They climbed on her and hugged her and hung on her every word.

"Well, I hope you do, too," she responded, donning a hurt look that melted Jerry's heart afresh.

After that, Jerry never protested again and let her volunteer no matter how weary she looked when she showed up for service.

Their increasing time together had done nothing but drive Carol and Jerry closer in a partnership that went beyond their joint interest in seeing Valley Lodge pull out of its doldrums.

Since the evening of the moonlight ski adventure and their late-night kiss, Jerry and Carol had seized any moment possible to be in each other's company. The striking brunette and the muscular blond were becoming a regular and talked-about item. More and more, the staff saw them with heads inclined together over meals or holding hands at the pizza parties which Pop staged to boost morale.

Then, when Jerry found any rare second to pursue his art, he joined Carol on the ski slopes. They continued to stagger each other with their respective skills and relish in the joy of their mutual passion.

Other staff members commented appreciatively to Jerry about the courtship they saw developing under their noses.

"What a match made in heaven!" Henny cooed to Jerry one afternoon after Carol had filled in for a few hours in the kitchen. "I can't imagine anyone so perfect for you."

"You're absolutely precious together," Jessie, the housekeeping supervisor, added at another time when Carol had served a stint in the laundry room. The first afternoon I saw her come down here, I said, 'Now that Jerry better latch on to this one.' I'm glad to see I was right!"

Chief among those interested was Pop, who appeared to privately beam whenever he saw Carol and Jerry paired off somewhere. Pop's original dream for Jerry as heir apparent was still alive and well—the employee walkout had only set the timetable off a bit.

When Carol entered the picture, Pop clearly began looking on her as a daughter. With a little luck from Cupid, she could easily grow into the role of the lodge's First Lady—like Hannah had been in the years before she died. What a team Carol and Jerry would be, he had told several people delightedly.

Pop mentioned this vision to Jerry.

"Son, she's exactly what you need—the wife that I've been praying for," he said in his most paternal of tones. "With you at the helm of Valley Lodge, I can't think of a more fitting partner. Why, with your smarts and her drive, the two of you could really put this place on the map. I could enlarge my apartment some to make a nice first home for the two of you."

Pop's mental meanderings about Carol continued to irritate Jerry in a way he was still at a loss to understand.

"Pop, just let me write my own script for things," Jerry snapped, his cheeks flaring red as he spoke.

The older gentleman literally jumped backward in surprise at the volley.

70

"Jerry, my gracious!" Pop gasped. His face turned so blanched and his breathing so raspy that Jerry wondered if he'd set off the old heart problems again. Pop had only just now resumed office hours since his relapse. His health was still very fragile. "Whatever was wrong with what I said?" Pop begged.

Jerry was instantly awash in guilt for his sharpness. He sucked in a breath and struggled for an explanation.

"Look," Jerry finally got out, as he flailed his arms in the air. "You have to understand. I know that's what you think—that's what everyone seems to think. But what if it doesn't happen that way? What if this isn't the kind of future that Carol wants? We've never even talked about things like that. But if, and when, we do, she may have other ideas. Then I'd feel like a total failure—I'd let everyone down."

Pop smiled in what he thought was understanding and felt compelled to encourage Jerry a bit more.

"Oh, I see," he ventured. "You wonder if the feeling's mutual. You wonder if Carol has the same tingles that you do. Well, from the looks of things, son, you don't have to worry. You're such an opposite from that loser of a guy she tells me she was involved with in Ohio—who didn't know one end of a ski pole from another. Take it from an old-timer. She's thoroughly smitten with you, I can tell. "

What should have set Jerry's heart leaping fell flat instead. Jerry's mood turned even more downcast. Pop's words continued to jab at him for the remainder of the day.

Carol offered to rent a video for them to watch during the late-night shift, but that didn't set well with Jerry, and he sullied like a wounded animal. The sad, strained look on his face warned her not to push him on her invitation that day, and she retired early for the evening.

When it came to chapel services, however, Carol didn't give up so easily. True to her earlier gritty commitment, Carol gently but firmly pressed Jerry to sit by the Great Hall fireplace with her on Sunday mornings when Rev. Dawson visited Valley Lodge to conduct services. Many people knew Valley Lodge was clearly identified as a Christian guest house and stayed there because of it, so the chapel services actually had a rather respectable attendance most Sundays.

Before Carol arrived at Valley Lodge, Jerry had managed to busy himself elsewhere during the services. Like Carol, Pop had urged, but Jerry's excuses that some lodge matter needed his attention during that time always seemed to satisfy him, or at least persuaded Pop to drop the subject. Pop's weakened physical condition often kept him bedfast on Sunday mornings anyway. He didn't always know about Jerry's absences, and he was in no situation to dig in his heels with his second-in-command.

Carol's earnest brown eyes stared directly through any alibi Jerry offered about skipping out. She remained firm.

"Just bring the portable phone with you, and we can take turns staffing the desk," she insisted the first Sunday after their conversation in the Rippling Rock. "We'll sit near the back. If somebody needs attention, one of us can slip out."

When the minister offered prayers, Carol habitually reached over and squeezed Jerry's hand lovingly as she bowed her head.

Who wants to fight this? Jerry found himself wondering, as her manicured fingers sweetly laced with his.

The words from the devotional messages seemed to Jerry like a pointless monologue. He felt detached from the worship experience that Carol—and others—were wrapped up in.

"What does God say to you from this passage?" Rev. Dawson would query. He sometimes invited dialogue with the audience about a Scripture portion he had just read.

Jerry wondered why others could hear the same verses that he heard and suddenly spout volumes about how they applied the passage to their lives.

God hasn't said a mumbling word to me, Jerry found himself thinking. *Where do they get off with these ideas about God, like He was in everyone's hip pocket?*

Once, the minister even called on Jerry to pray as the service ended. Jerry had been listening intently—even leaning forward with his chin cupped in his hands and his elbows propped on his knees. As usual, he was straining to make some sense of the discourse he had just heard.

The pastor mistook Jerry's serious gaze and called on him for the closing prayer. Jerry, ever the salesman that he was in Boulder, by now was able to mimic some of the prayers he'd heard Pop, Carol, and others voice.

"Dear God, we thank you for this day . . ." he attempted.

Jerry did a fairly commendable job of parroting back some of the same words they had uttered to God many times. From listening to his prayer, few people would have known he hadn't spent his life in church.

Afterwards, Carol and Pop radiated their pleasure. *They think they're making progress,* Jerry observed to himself dryly.

Throughout the afternoon, the experience haunted him—the hypocrisy of what he had done, the unwitting, pressurizing gang-up by Carol and Pop.

Jerry wasn't actually opposed to having a spiritual life. He had come to truly envy the personal relationship that Carol and Pop seemed to have with God. In the time he had known her, Carol had spoken of her daily quiet times of meditation and prayer. She made frequent and comfortable reference to God's guidance in her life. She talked openly about Scriptures that offered her promise and hope.

"What Scriptures have meant a lot to you?" she once queried him. *She thinks if she probes long enough with me, she'll hit paydirt eventually, even when there's nothing there,* Jerry fumed.

"Well, Carrie," he answered, calling her by a nickname he had affectionately tried on her lately and that she seemed to warm to. "I've always been partial to 'Jesus wept' myself."

Carol frowned and decided she'd try again when he wasn't in a clowning mood and could take her question more seriously.

It wasn't that Jerry objected to her way of life. It was just that to him, God simply wasn't available. He couldn't be trusted, He was waiting to zap him, and He didn't care for him a whit.

In a strange way, Jerry found himself wishing that Carol wouldn't be so tolerant of his glib, shallow answers. Sometimes he wished she'd actually shake him by the shoulders and demand to know what caused him to trivialize these matters.

Maybe that way he would find out himself why the subject always seemed so pointless, so blastedly painful.

Shaking Jerry by the shoulders was completely opposite of anything that Carol seemed to be about, however. The closer they grew, the more lavish Carol became with her affection, which sent the blood coursing through his veins in a way that Jerry had thought was lost to him forever.

Most evenings, Carol continued to join him for the late shift just as she had since the second night of her arrival at Valley Lodge. As the lobby emptied and the two of them moved to the sofa, the evenings continued to end in a tide of increasingly exhilarating kisses and embraces. Carol was like velvet in his arms. When he held her, he perceived that they were two souls joined as one, in an ecstacy he thought he'd never again experience.

One night, when he sensed he could easily move things to an even more intense level of passion than previously, Jerry breathed in her ear, "Let's go to my room. I'll transfer the phones over. Things will be OK for a few minutes or so."

To Jerry's amazement, Carol balked. Brushing the brown wisps of hair from her eyes and looking at him directly, she replied, laughing a little, "We'd better not. In fact, we probably better go raid the snack machines for ice cream, before things get out of control."

Jerry looked dumbstruck. "Out of control?" he blasted. "What gives with you, Carol? You acted like you wanted this. You seemed like you enjoyed all this . . . this closeness. Enjoyed it a lot, in fact. So how come you now want to sound the whistle?"

"I do love for you to kiss me, Jerry," Carol replied, her smile fading and her voice tinged with shock that such explanations were even necessary. "But if you want to go to your room, you're talking about more than kisses. If we went, we might be tempted to go further. That's why it's best to stay here."

Jerry was perplexed. "I don't understand," he finally muttered, raking his hand through his hair. "You went with Keith for three years, you said. Don't tell me that during that time you didn't . . . you didn't have . . . those moments. You can't go with someone that long and keep things nice and sweet and Sunday-school perfect."

"You can do anything you feel principled about," Carol replied, her eyes smarting with hurt tears. "Sleeping with someone before you're married is not God's way. And no, nothing like that happened with me and Keith. I'm surprised you'd even suggest it."

The protracted, agonizing silence that followed deafened both of them. Carol lowered her eyes, and the tears that had already darted to the corners of her lids flooded out unrestrained, drenching her cheeks and plopping into her lap.

Jerry sat helpless, wanting to reach out to her, yet knowing better.

Then Jerry looked down as well. On the heels of her disclosure, Jerry knew what obviously came next, and fear clutched his throat. If Carol had remained sexually pure during her three-year courtship with her fellow professor, she would clearly presume Jerry had done likewise during his recent relationship. After all, he and Natalie had only known each other for a year, the last half of which they were engaged.

Carol would think he had followed the same standards, saving himself for marriage, just like she had presumed the best of him from the very beginning. She had thought he'd be a religious clone of Pop, she expected him to have a deep spiritual life, she had envisioned him to be a lot of things . . . And like the other times, on the issue of chastity, he knew he was about to disappoint her—cut her to the very quick, again. Jerry wanted to run, hide, jump . . . do anything to avoid Carol's next words when the dark, tear-ladened eyelashes finally lifted.

Too soon, however, before he could even give another thought to splitting the scene, Jerry felt two brown, sorrowful eyes penetrating him again. He suddenly realized that there weren't even going to be any words in this inquisition—there didn't need to be. Carol's expressive eyes did all the interrogation—eyes that held out a smidgen of hope that what she wanted to suspect about Jerry was true—that he, too, had acted on principle and used restraint during his last courtship, yet eyes that seemed braced for what she now knew was the inevitable confession.

So Jerry looked into her face, and Carol met his gaze steadily. Looking at those deep, inquiring eyes, he said nothing but merely nodded.

Her small, dry sob broke the silence, and a desperate Jerry rushed to embrace Carol. His arms ached to hold her, to make things right.

"Look, Carol, it didn't mean anything, I promise you," he cried, kneeling on the floor in front of her and attempting to wind his arms around her waist. "I promise, when Natalie and I were . . . when we did, it was nothing. It doesn't have anything to do with you and me. Whatever you say, I'll do. We don't have to go to my room. We'll go by your rules. It's not that important, believe me."

Carol looked at him like she had been struck across the face.

"What do you mean it didn't mean *anything*?" she spouted back. "It should mean *everything*. Making love with someone should be life's ultimate experience, because it's supposed to occur inside a marriage commitment. They're not my rules; they're God's rules. And you're wrong! It has plenty to do with you and me—PLENTY!"

"I'm really sorry, Carrie," Jerry muttered, swallowing back his own tears and feeling more helpless than he'd ever felt in his life. He buried his face in his hands, his penitence real.

By that time, Carol was halfway across the lobby, leaving a trail of sobs in her wake as she disappeared. He started to run after her, but she warned him back with an arm extended behind her as she fled in the distance.

Jerry threw himself down prone on the sofa and felt every ounce of blood being drained from his veins.

So, is this the way things are to end between me and Carol? he wondered *After all these days together, is she going to throw me over—over this? She can't—I won't let her. A quarrel like this can't split us up! It wasn't anything.*

Then, just as surely as he thought this, Jerry realized with sinking heart that he was minimizing again, cavalierly, just as Carol had accused him. He felt flooded with remorse that he could not come to her with a clean slate, an unblemished history.

Maybe if he had known people like Carol and Pop earlier in his life and seen another way of looking at things before he began making mistakes, things would have been different. He might have had a different measuring stick, a different set of principles about love. He'd have had a different set of role models—people whom you could respect, people who lived their faith in front of him.

Before, he'd always thought those who lectured about abstinence were narrow-minded and prudish—people who had no fun. But Carol and Pop didn't seem prudish at all. Life-loving and ebullient, they had values and beliefs that were dear to them, and they stuck to them.

All he had in terms of a role-model was his own father. Dad never made any attempt to hide his numerous affairs and flagrant betrayals of his mother while he was out on his drunken escapades.

Is it any wonder that Carol's rules seem strange to me? Jerry asked himself.

Suddenly, it seemed to Jerry that he was no longer himself but that he actually took on the shameful identity of his father, all their indiscretions melding into one. He was hopeless; he couldn't change; he was done for.

A sleepless, miserable, gut-wrenching night followed. Unlike other evenings when he had lain on the Great Hall sofa, eager for the daylight to bring him further opportunities to see Carol, Jerry delayed rising as long as usual, hoping to avoid the inevitable.

His heart broke already when he thought about the icy glare that Carol undoubtedly had waiting for him when she came down to breakfast. Would Pop and the others detect that the twosome that had become the darlings of the lodge had had a critical rift?

When Carol at last appeared, however, there was little to distinguish her demeanor from that of any other day. The fuschia nylon ski bib that she wore under her instructor's jacket made her look stylish and delectable as always. She bounded down the stairs with hand-clasps and hugs for her pupils, fellow ski instructors—everyone she saw in her path.

All that appeared different was that she seemed to have made a valiant effort to cover her swollen eyelids with an extra layer of eyeliner. The shoulders seemed to be forcibly held high—the same suck-it-in, I-can-fix-this mode she had rotely flipped into at other times in the past when he had let her down by word or deed.

Instead of the snub he dreaded, Carol seemed to strategically seek out Jerry in the midst of the lobby crowd that milled about, eager to head for the slopes. She kissed him lightly on the temple.

"Good morning, Jerry," she said, not avoiding his eyes at all but looking at him directly. "Will that make up for the good-bye I forgot to say last night?"

She pulled him into the staff dining hall, her business-as-usual carriage obviously the way she was choosing to deal with last night's conflict. It was her way of letting Jerry know she was dismissing the subject.

Part of Jerry wanted to cry in relief. So this was *not* the way it was to end, he thought gratefully. Maybe they could pick back up where they left off. He would be on his best behavior, Jerry thought. He would let her set the direction of their physical relationship. He could live with that. He'd be willing to sacrifice a lot of his druthers, just to have Carol. He *needed* her. Last night's events made Jerry realize just how desperate he was for her love—yes, he was beginning to be sure that's what it was he felt. *The "L" word.* Jerry was convinced now. He loved Carol. He hadn't told her yet, but he was sure it would occur soon. He couldn't imagine life without her and the way she completed him—a completion he thought he'd never know again.

Yet, as thankful as he was that Carol might be willing to put their painful conversation and his stained past behind her, part of Jerry felt angry—a dull, amorphous anger that he couldn't pinpoint but that nevertheless made his stomach churn.

He was relieved that Carol seemed determined to forge straight ahead with their relationship in spite of their quarrel. Yet something in Jerry wished that after last night's incident, she would finally call him on the carpet royally—to give him the tongue-lashing that he merited.

I don't deserve her, really, an inner voice told Jerry. His thoughts drifted into another sphere even as he vaguely heard Carol make small talk at the breakfast table and attempt courteously to draw him into conversations with others around them. *I don't deserve anything good to happen to me. Carol's so pure, and I'm so scarred. I'm not worthy—that's what I've heard all my life. Why can't she see it and do something about it?*

What was it that made Carol merely blink at his inadequacies that seemed projected in front of her like images on a big-screen TV? Was it a merely sweet, forgiving nature that caused her to blot out all wrong?

Or was it deeper than that? Was she truly so fed up with Keith and his incompatibility that she would gloss over Jerry's faults just to find someone who was a skier? What kept her from seeing that as a couple, on the outside, they were dynamite, but on the inside they were a disaster?

At breakfast they conversed casually, with the cares of last night seemingly swept under the table. Part of Jerry's heart rejoiced that Carol remained his for yet another day, that he hadn't lost her, after all.

A deeper part of him, at some level far below consciousness, begged for Carol to cry out and force him to address the problems that threatened to sweep them under.

EIGHT

The Couple on the Wedding Cake

❁

The days rolled on into December, and Valley Lodge seemed destined for a special Christmas gift. Because of Pop's tenacity, a number of key staff vacancies had been filled lately, and things were looking up. Once Pop felt well enough to return to regular office hours, he re-connected with all his contacts who might give him good leads on workers. His digging paid off.

The first break occurred when two former Valley Lodge staffers who left to join Ski Chalet sent word that they wanted to come back to work for Pop. Pop considered that these two were innocently duped and were not part of any insurrection at Valley Lodge. He looked on their situations more kindly than he would have some. They had balked at the militaristic style of Burt Umphreys and missed the family feel of their former workplace. When Pop got wind of this, he personally solicited them. They asked for forgiveness and he granted it, gladly restoring them to the fold.

Then, a couple of workers that the temp service sent out asked to become permanent. They had proved themselves to be good help, and Pop was happy to have them. Pop also pursued several fruitful contacts at other resort areas, and these brought results.

Soon, more than half the vacancies were filled, while several more candidates looked promising. Valley Lodge wasn't out of the woods yet, but it seemed to have taken a turn for the better. Pop was especially glad to staff the late-night shift. This enabled Jerry to get more rest and averted a physical collapse by Pop's top assistant.

"I want you to get out on the slopes more. Go spend more time supervising the instructors," Pop told Jerry, as things improved. "I'm feeling much stronger these days, and I can fill in some of these gaps for you."

Jerry nodded agreeably but still proceeded with caution. Pop had a bad track record for over-extending himself. A few too many hours at the grindstone, and they'd be back in their original crisis, with Pop relapsed—or worse.

Besides, Jerry knew exactly what motivated Pop to thrust him outdoors to check on the instructors. Jerry knew his job was to help these employees. But he also knew that Pop particularly wanted him to monitor one kiddie class—and not because it needed it.

Over the weeks, Jerry saw that Pop and Carol had fused in a special bond. Sometimes Jerry actually felt a tinge of jealousy as he observed the two of them hanging out together. It made him wish he could regain some of the closeness he had felt with Pop in the beginning before life around Valley Lodge became so difficult.

As Jerry breezed by Pop's office door, he sometimes spotted Pop and Carol with their heads bowed in prayer. Jerry suspected that they often prayed and talked about him. Pop had tiptoed around the subject since the day it brought Jerry's ire, but Jerry knew that Pop was still maneuvering behind the scenes to fuel his and Carol's liaison.

As satisfying as it was to have the ship running more smoothly, Jerry felt mildly agitated at the turn of events. Pop publicly gave Jerry all the credit. Deep down, Jerry knew Pop was window-dressing.

"Son, this wouldn't have happened if it hadn't been for you," Pop assured him. "You kept things running and made Valley Lodge a good place to work. You took good care of the temps and caused these to want to stay on."

Jerry knew better. He knew Pop's praise was specious, at best. It was simply a skillful management tactic designed to keep Jerry motivated and in position, where Pop needed him. Jerry acknowledged ruefully that he had been totally in survival mode during most of the time of the walkout. He had merely struggled from day to day. He had little time left to strategize how to bring in new people. He had interviewed many and had actually hired a couple—one of whom didn't stay—but he knew he hadn't demonstrated any particular ingenuity. The two who returned from Ski Chalet had flocked back on the strength of Pop's contacts.

Pop expected more of me, and I've missed the mark with him, again, Jerry thought. *I'm no administrator, and he knows it now.*

The improved conditions at Valley Lodge, particularly the new staffer on the evening shift, did allow Jerry to spend time with Carol in some settings that were a welcome change of pace. It brought a new level to their courtship, free of laundry-room dryers and incessant desk phones.

One afternoon, he went with Carol to take some of her students on a winter horseback ride at a dude ranch. She had organized the trip as a special bonus for bunny slope "graduates." Jerry went with her to help keep the group together. He watched as she patiently organized them and herded them into a shuttle for the trip down the mountain and to the ranch. Later she sweetly comforted a few youngsters who cried because they were afraid of the horses.

"You were like the Pied Piper. They would have followed you anywhere!" Jerry admired as the field trip ended and they safely handed the last child off to parents, back at Valley Lodge.

"It's amazing, Jerry," Carol confided, excitement filling her eyes as she and Jerry drank some cinnamon tea in the snack bar. "Before this, I would have sworn that my special gift was working with college students. But since I've been here, I've realized just how much I love children. I get along just great with them. Now I feel like I have a whole new vision of what God wants me to do down the road."

Jerry didn't pursue her statement that moment, but he continued to try to grasp some outline of whether, and how, that future was supposed to include him.

Some of their best times continued to be on the ski slopes. The late afternoons, now suddenly unencumbered, gave Jerry and Carol new opportunities to explore the endless maze of ski trails. At high-adrenaline moments like this, the stress of managing the lodge was momentarily forgotten, and the skill of his sport was at the forefront. Jerry felt less gripped by his fears.

Maybe there is hope here, he found himself theorizing. *Maybe I can feel more strong about this relationship I want so desperately.*

For weeks, the subject of their quarrel that night on the sofa in the Great Hall was like an immense chasm between them. It was never mentioned, never hinted at, but it was clearly on both of their minds. Jerry was at all times on his best behavior. He honored Carol's wishes about physical limits. But every time they embraced, the memory of their talk and of his tacit confession still hung there.

Then one night they took in a holiday play at the community theater and arrived at the lodge after a quiet, late-night dinner for two. As they passed through the lobby entry, Jerry brought Carol under the mistletoe that Pop installed there. All evening Jerry had been especially captivated by Carol in her midnight blue velour pants and matching shirt with its jeweled collar. A pair of iridescent, dangling earrings added to the sparkles she set off as the outdoor lights played on them inside the darkened entry.

As they stood under the mistletoe, his arms tightening around her in this spellbinding moment, Jerry sprinkled her face and neck with lingering kisses and nuzzled his face in her hair that was heavy with her perfume.

84

Carol tossed her head back and teased, lightheartedly, "Is this mistletoe getting to you, Jerry? I think Pop put this up for the guests, not the staff."

"Yep, it's the mistletoe, alright," Jerry mocked, good-naturedly. "It has nothing to do with my date who stands here, glittering like diamonds." He kissed her again, lingeringly, and murmured, "Guess we'd better go get some ice cream." He laughed softly. Both of them knew he referred to the comment she'd made to him just before their last discussion on this subject grew volatile, several weeks back.

Carol lowered her eyes at the remembrance and sighed deeply. Then, determinedly, she pulled Jerry through the lobby and to the sofa. The moment had arrived for them to clear the air.

Twining her fingers through his and facing him squarely, Carol said, "Jerry, you've been so precious about this. I really appreciate how respectful you acted after we talked that time. Thank you for taking it seriously. I feel very comfortable and very cherished. It means more to me than you'll ever know."

She leaned across the sofa and planted a small kiss on the corner of his mouth, her lips warm, her voice indolent.

At this, words that welled up inside Jerry came tumbling out unheeded, and he couldn't have restrained them if he'd tried.

"When you love someone, it's not tough to do," he murmured as he inclined his head toward her.

Carol's eyes grew big as plates. The half-laugh, half-sob she choked out seemed to reverberate throughout every corner of the Great Hall.

"Jerry Rutgers, did I hear correctly? Did you just tell me you loved me?" she begged. Her face radiated the joy she seemed to have held back for this very moment.

"Surely I didn't have to tell you," he answered. A playful smile sauntered across his lips. "Surely you're not surprised."

An endless pummeling of questions followed. "When did you know?" Carol demanded breathlessly. "When did you figure it out?" Each question was punctuated with an excited hug. She brought her eyes back to his each time. The magnitude of what just transpired etched every line of her face.

Jerry pretended to study the matter. He replied with a grin, "It stemmed back to the day I looked up from my computer and saw some murderous brown eyes about to saw me in two because of a long wait in line."

"My eyes weren't murderous," Carol insisted, warming at the memory. "But that's exactly when I can trace it to, as well. I love you, too, Jerry." The sweet, unbridled honesty and devotion in her declaration twisted his stomach with that same puzzling mix of longing, loss, and terror to which he had grown accustomed where Carol was concerned.

The fresh glow of excitement that seemed to engulf Jerry and Carol after this tender moment fit with the lilting holiday spirit that emerged around Valley Lodge as Christmas neared. Staff members made holiday plans. Some would stagger their schedules in such a way that permitted them a few days at home; some would save their trips until the season slacked; and a few would celebrate at Valley Lodge with family visits right there around the Great Hall's giant tree.

One of the latter was Carol, who announced one day that her mother planned a trip to Valley Lodge from Ohio for Christmas Eve and Christmas Day. Since her dad's passing a year ago, Carol knew her mother would be lonely in her first solo Christmas after almost 30 years of marriage. Carol wanted her to have a change of pace this holiday, and the sparkle of Crested Butte in December would charm even the Grinch.

Besides, Carol was eager for her mother and Jerry to meet.

"My family is close; it's tough for me to be away at this time," she confided. "This will tide things over until I can get back home for a visit. What about you?"

Jerry knew what Carol envisioned: that he'd also parade in a line-up of folks to meet her—the new special someone in his life, after his earlier heartbreak. Truth was, he felt light years removed from any of his relatives right now. He thought about his father, whom he hadn't seen since his sophomore year of college, living in some town in western Kansas. Dad had found a small business to buy after his most recent layoff. It hadn't even upset Jerry when he realized he'd misplaced his dad's new address. He figured he wouldn't need it anyway.

His mother, now on the East Coast with her third husband after divorcing his dad and later another man, was preoccupied with a new raft of stepkids from her latest marriage. She probably hardly gave Jerry a thought.

His brother Bo was the only family member with whom Jerry kept in semi-regular contact. Bo had called Jerry a year ago and asked him to visit at a ranch for recalcitrant youth that Bo ran in Kansas. Jerry knew he should have better relations with Bo, who genuinely seemed eager to make connections, but he and his wife Sally seemed sufficient unto themselves with their huge population of boys. He declined Bo's invitation, thinking he'd feel like an outsider.

Again, his contrast with Carol chilled him to the bone. "Guess it won't work to see my folks this year," Jerry muttered. He half hoped his answer would spark an outcry from Carol—some kind of shocked response that would prompt her to ask, "What's wrong here?" But as usual, it produced none.

The contrast with his troubled family couldn't have been more apparent when Carol's mom did arrive. She was obviously clued in to Carol and Jerry's connection. The diminutive woman, whose youthful features belied her prematurely white coiffure, greeted Jerry warmly the moment they were first introduced.

"Jerry, I feel like I know you," she enthused, her face awash in smiles. Sincerity seemed to ooze through every pore. "You and Valley Lodge have shown Carol such a good time since she's been here."

Instantly affirming, Carol's mother, Fayma McKechnie, greeted all the other lodge players boldly as well, with a charisma that could charm the fillings out of someone's teeth.

I should have known she'd be a Carol clone, Jerry thought. *Carol can't help being confident and self-assured with this lady in her family.*

Fayma insisted on taking Jerry along with Carol out to dinner one evening. They went to The Wild Goose, which Carol had identified as the scene of their first outing weeks back. Although she was a nonskier, Fayma prodded Jerry to tell her everything about all the competitions he had won and show her his photos and trophies.

When she and Carol opened family Christmas gifts around the giant tree in the Great Hall on Christmas Eve, Fayma had wrapped Jerry a present as well. It was a navy and tan snowflake stripe-patterned sweater that she had knit herself. It was the first handmade item Jerry had ever owned in his life. He was awe-struck as he tried it on to model it for the women.

Everyone delicately tiptoed around any reference to Jerry as a prospective family member. Not one scintilla of a mention was made by anyone about any kind of future plans. However, Jerry knew that Carol must be confiding plenty about their burgeoning relationship to her intuitive, animated mother. Jerry also saw Fayma and Pop huddling one afternoon. He could only guess the subject of their talks.

"Now you be sure to come to Ohio to visit us," Fayma invited as she told Jerry good-bye at the end of her trip. "Maybe by that time I'll have knit a cap to match your sweater."

Fayma's personal interest in Jerry was flattering. He couldn't help thinking he'd love to spend more time around this nurturing, maternal figure.

However pleased he was for Fayma's tacit seal of approval, the comparison with his own situation continued to make him edgy and ill at ease. The day that he might eventually have to take Carol home to meet his own family members was a day he'd prefer not to think about at the moment. Carol's concept of relatives and kin was based on the loving yardstick Jerry just experienced. He feared she would find his distant ones very disinterested, at best.

It had been different with Natalie, whose own family history was not unlike his—marked with parental divorce and relationship breaches aplenty. He and Natalie had spoken the same language when it came to childhood hurts. Jerry knew that language would seem like Greek to Carol with her background of stability.

The Valley Lodge staff observed none of these misgivings as they saw Carol's mom warmly treating Jerry as family over the holidays. Several began ribbing him, calling it a "future in-law" visit.

"When you gonna pop the question, Jer?" Doug, the chef, cajoled. "I'm just dying to cater an engagement party for you."

Jerry thought he detected a small bit of disappointment in Carol when he presented her a tiny, gift-wrapped box on Christmas morning. Her eyes clouded initially after she saw the box contained a pair of pearl and diamond earrings. He was sure she hoped it would be a sparkler that would seal their future together.

Jerry knew it was time to do some serious thinking about where their courtship was headed, but he also knew that some things still needed to come into focus. Too many questions gnawed at him to get a clear picture yet.

One afternoon, Pop ran, breathless, through the lobby in search of him. When he found Jerry, he seized him by the arm, portending an emergency.

"Jerry, have you seen Carol's letter?" he panted. Jerry didn't know what letter he meant. Was there bad news in her family—something wrong with Fayma, perhaps?

"What about?" Jerry inquired. Actually, Jerry *did* recall seeing Carol walking through the dining hall at noon, a buff-colored envelope under her arm, but she didn't mention it, and he didn't ask.

"It's from the College of Wooster," Pop replied, his brows still knit with worry. "They're asking her to firm up her contract for next term. They're even giving her some added responsibilities. She's gotta answer them right away."

Jerry swallowed hard. Carol would be expecting him to state his intentions about their future. She needed to know whether to accept this important offer. The decision he'd been processing couldn't simmer on the back burner any longer. The make-or-break time he'd been dreading was here.

Pop draped his arm around Jerry's shoulders. He walked Jerry to his office, gesturing toward a chair.

"Son, you know how I feel about this," Pop shared. "I've told you before. I'd do anything to help you and Carol. I believe the Lord led her here just for you. I'll do whatever I need to make it so she doesn't have to return. The offer's still good about my apartment. We can create a job for Carol. We'll give her an added role to make it worth her while to stay. You know your own future is certainly bright here. I'm getting too old for this place, anyway. Just don't lose her, son. She's God's gift to you, remember?"

Jerry shut his eyes and tried, as always, to feel grateful. "We'll talk about it soon," he promised. He sensed Pop's relief clear across the desk from him.

Carol's eyes at dinner that night looked strained from an afternoon of anxious deliberating. Despite Pop's proposal, which Pop had stated to Carol as well, Jerry knew Valley Lodge would have little to offer her compared to her teaching post at Wooster unless she had a permanent, more compelling reason for staying on.

"What do you want to do, Carrie?" Jerry asked. He was eager to hear her spin on things without Pop's biased slant. "I know how much your job at the college meant to you—coaching your teams and all. Would you really be happy giving that up? It's a big chunk of your life to say good-bye to."

"Like I told you, God already seemed to be moving me to work with children," Carol answered. She deliberately steered clear of the real issue that underscored this discussion. "It's like He was preparing my heart to make the break, if I needed to." She said little more. It was obvious that she was placing the answer to her dilemma squarely back on Jerry's shoulders.

Jerry's night was tortured and sleepless. *Pop has things fixed up in such a tidy package,* Jerry fumed, feeling utterly torn inside. *I feel like his marionette—he's pulling the strings and I'm jumping. Even Carol is totally bought in to his arrangement. I'll be the bad guy for sure if I don't totally walk in step.*

The alternative, though, was losing Carol—something too unthinkable to bear. Thousands of guys would trade everything to be in his shoes. A perfectly exquisite woman was in love with him. A mentor adored him. His entire workplace, oddly, looked to him as their future hope. He'd be the biggest fool in the world if he got squeamish and failed to seize this opportunity.

So Jerry pondered about when he'd broach the subject to Carol, and how.

In the end, few words were necessary. An emergency in the Ripping Rock kitchen provided the uncanny setting. The next night, Roger, the pastry chef, begged for help in getting a giant tray of cakes ready for an anniversary reception. Jerry and Carol cut short their time night skiing and volunteered.

After the work ended and they were alone in the kitchen, Jerry grabbed an icing tube and a leftover sheet cake that Roger gave them as "payment" for their service. In blue icing over the chocolate frosting, he scrawled, "Will you marry me?" He iced a huge heart around the lettering.

Giving Carol two forks and a plate, he shoved the cake in front of her. "Let's celebrate getting this job done," he said resolutely. He knew if he acted quickly, he'd be less likely to have a mind change.

Carol started to cut the cake, then gawked at Jerry's handwriting. Her screams of joy could be heard all the way to the lift station.

"You're proposing to me?" she exulted, blinking in disbelief. She sank a big kiss on Jerry's lips and kept looking back at the cake and the writing on it.

Then, taking a knife, she cut the word "will" from the cake and aimed it on a fork for Jerry's mouth. It was her reply to his question.

"I'll never forget this night as long as I live," she fairly yelled. Her voice reverberated off the kitchen walls.

"Guess it would have been more romantic in front of the fireplace, but I couldn't pass up the moment," Jerry replied mischievously. "I figured if I put it in writing, there couldn't be any confusion."

"And you got my answer in writing as well," she teased. She seized his shoulders and kissed him again.

When Carol's joyful shouts died to a murmur, Jerry hoisted himself onto the ledge beside the metal sink and pulled Carol up beside him.

"Can you possibly bear to live apart from Shannon when she goes back to your college?" he inquired.

"It'll be sad, but I'll be getting an even better room-mate," Carol replied, her face resplendent at the prospect.

"Are you sure you won't be lonesome for Ohio?" Jerry suggested. "It's really different here—out West."

Her dancing eyes suddenly grew puzzled. "Are you trying to talk me out of it, Jerry?" she said, half-kidding, half-serious. "You're tossing out so many protests, I can't tell."

Jerry gulped. Had his misgivings been that obvious? Was he really trying to dissuade her so she would never say yes?

"Of course not," he said, trying to sound reassuring. "I just wanted to make sure that you're sure. It's just a lot to commit to, that's all."

Then she dropped in the dynamite.

"Jerry, this is such a memorable moment—the night we've decided to marry. I always thought it would mean a lot to pray right now. It would be a kind of good way to get things started. Would you do it? The husband is supposed to be the spiritual head of the home, right? So this could kick things off, kind of like your first act in spiritual leadership. Would you mind just saying a prayer that God will bless our marriage?"

Jerry knew that somewhere within him must be some reserve of strength to help him rebound from Carol's question, but at that moment, he couldn't find it.

Pray, here? In a kitchen? Just the two of us? he thought, panic-stricken, his cheeks suddenly turning the color of oatmeal.

Praying aloud in church the Sunday the pastor called on him was one thing. He could merely regurgitate someone else's pietistic phrases. But winging it, alone, with Carol? This was the ultimate bad idea. He was trapped, with nowhere to go and nothing to say. He knew his face must be an absolute road map of his horror.

One look at Carol, with her head already bowed and her eyes squeezed closed, told him he had no option. Earnestly, she pressed his hand and awaited his words.

"Thank you, God, for Carol and for me and for this blue icing that brought us together," he mumbled, words tumbling out so he could get through this quickly. "Help us to be good at being married. Amen."

For what seemed like an eternity, Carol kept her eyes closed, as though she were hoping for a longer, more serious, prayer, after he quipped through this one. Finally, when nothing more was forthcoming, she opened first one eye, then another, and met Jerry's gaze expectantly.

Then she did the shoulder-raising thing again—her signature gesture. It had come to communicate that she was settling for less but was determined to forge forward in spite of it.

"You're really growing, Jerry; I know you are," she said, as though pronouncing it would make it so. "Maybe we can take a couple's Bible study together after our wedding."

She always has the solution, Jerry thought, frustrated.

Growing was the exact opposite of how Jerry felt at that moment. *Shrinking's more like it,* he thought sadly. *At the moment in my life when I should feel taller than Mt. Crested Butte, I don't think I've ever felt so small.*

Heaving a sigh that, for the life of him, he couldn't read and dragging her fork through the chocolate frosting, Carol turned her attention back to her cake slice in front of her.

"This is all so perfect, Jerry, this special way you proposed to me. And—I just thought of it! It's almost prophetic with what my mother said," Carol said triumphantly, a coy smile lighting up her face.

"What in the world did she say?" Jerry replied. His concentration was just barely returning after the prayer incident blindsided him.

"When she was here, she thought you were so debonair and so charming," Carol reported, beaming. "And she said that . . . well, if things ever did happen for us . . . if we ever did happen to get married, we were so ideal for each other that we'd be just like the little plastic couple on the wedding cake."

So Jerry had his mother-in-law's imprimatur. He should be thrilled.

Yet, at that moment, Jerry could feel nothing but that dreaded, old triumvirate of love, longing, and terror. This time, it originated at the tip of his toes and wormed its way, wrenchingly, through his gut.

He was glad that Fayma wasn't around just now to perceive what he did: that the fairy-tale model that she idealized already had a crack in the plastic.

NINE

Indelible Scars

❁

Word trickled out quickly about what transpired that evening between Carol and Jerry in the unlikely setting of the Rippling Rock kitchen. Although Carol had cut out the crucial word "will" to answer the question Jerry posed, three other, highly important words remained written in on the chocolate cake that bore Jerry's marriage proposal.

A beaming Carol stepped from the kitchen, toting the leftover cake back to her room to show Shannon. As she did, one or two curious lodge workers spotted the tell-tale phrase "you marry me?" They reacted with glee.

Corinne, the new night clerk, stopped a hurried Carol while she breezed through the lobby and begged to see what was in the mysterious cake box that Carol held so tenderly.

"Ooooooh, we're going to have a wedding!" Corinne bellowed, as others hovered around.

Before Carol could reach the stairway, a small crowd had formed to prod her for the news. Jerry, arriving on the scene, suddenly felt his back pounded and thumped with congratulatory greetings.

"Thought you'd never ask her, ole buddy!" one of the bell-staff members chided him, good-naturedly. "If you hadn't moved in quickly, I was gonna claim her myself."

The whole lodge staff was in much more celebratory spirits these days now that the vacancies were almost abated. Soon everyone was caught up in the excitement of the idyllic union that had occurred right under their very noses.

True to his word, Chef Doug immediately began planning an elaborate announcement party. It would feature, among other things, an ice sculpture of two skiers as the focal point of the room.

"We'll spare nothing. In fact, you might as well go on and marry her now. The wedding will be anticlimactic after this reception," Doug boasted.

Pop strutted peacock-like around the lodge after Carol and Jerry brought him the news. "We simply *must* ask Pop to be best man at the wedding, don't you think?" Carol insisted happily to Jerry. "It only seems right that he be the one."

In truth, wedding plans were about as far from Jerry's mind as the North Pole at this point. He was still seeking his equilibrium after the proposal and the subsequent realization of what was coming to pass. He knew Carol would soon press him to set a date, but that would require more foresight than he possessed at this confusing moment. The adoring lodge community was pressing him, too. They had become, in Jerry's eyes, almost annoyingly possessive of the upcoming event.

For now, the next order of business, at least on Carol's timetable, was finding an engagement ring. Pop had arranged a deal with a local jeweler whereby Jerry could enjoy a massive discount on whatever bridal set he and Carol picked.

After a long siege of looking one afternoon and poring over display cases in the jeweler's showroom, Carol lit on an eye-catching custom design that would require several weeks to special order. The large, round center stone was surrounded by several smaller diamonds on a heart-shaped gold mounting. The heart was flanked by numerous tiny baguette stones set along the width of the gold band.

By any other standards, the dazzling ring would have been totally out of Jerry's financial reach, but Pop had finagled with the shop owner. His dealings, plus Jerry's proceeds from the recent sale of his car since Valley Lodge provided him one, made it possible for Carol to have her wish.

"This heart's symbolic, since you had one on the cake," Carol cooed. "The rest of my life, it'll remind me of how you proposed to me. Isn't it great how Pop arranged this?"

Jerry knew he should be jubilant, but he found it somewhat disconcerting that Pop would have his stamp on this matter, too, as he seemed to on all others.

Carol's mother was delirious with joy. She booked a flight back to Valley Lodge so she could be with Carol during the engagement party. Fayma's childless sister, Carol's Aunt Claire, who had doted like a parent on Carol from childhood, would come along, too. The three of them could refine Carol's wedding plans, which Carol assumed by that time would be fully under way.

When Carol announced this to Jerry, it set off a whole new wave of moroseness about how he would deal with his own family about this milestone.

She'll wonder soon why her *future in-laws are not on the scene,* Jerry pondered. *It's beginning to look odd now that my family is still so far in the background.*

Finally he mustered enough courage to at least write his mother, in Pennsylvania. He braced himself for another wave of rejection if he failed to receive even so much as a reply to his note.

Bo and Sally were a different matter. If he notified them, his brother and sister-in-law might even drive all the way over to Colorado to help him celebrate. They had offered to do this for his and Natalie's wedding plans, if they could manage to break free from the hoard of troubled boys that surrounded them.

There was also another factor about Bo and Sally to consider. Until he met the devout Pop and Carol, Jerry had regarded this duo as a pair of religious fanatics—the most fervent believers he had ever run across. Bo had "gotten religion," as Jerry had always categorized it, after he married Sally several years ago and started the ranch that they identified as distinctively Christian—a lot like Valley Lodge, now that he thought of it.

Pop and Carol are enough of this variety right now, Jerry decided. If his brother and Sally were here, he'd feel such a gang-up with his two current tormentors that he'd never escape.

Let's skip them until I have to, Jerry concluded. *There's no point in digging a deeper hole for myself than the one I'm already in.*

Then he realized what word he'd used for Carol—*tormentor!* Was this any way to think about his fiancee that he loved—that he worshiped? Yet even times with Carol, since the proposal, had seemed to lose some of their sizzle, in a way he couldn't identify. Lately, when Carol wanted to snuggle up to him on the Great Hall sofa or shower him with kisses in her joy, Jerry seemed less than enthusiastic—sometimes even curt, to Carol.

One night when Carol impulsively threw her arm around him, he found himself pushing her away irritably. He hadn't meant to, but a sort of growing malaise with her welled up in him. He responded with an involuntary reaction to an emotion he couldn't place.

Carol reacted instantly to the rebuff. "Jerry, what's wrong?" she queried, hurt clouding her face. "You've never done anything like that before."

Jerry was himself clueless. "Carrie, I'm sorry," he mumbled, almost inaudibly. "All of a sudden I didn't feel like hugging; that's all."

Carol sized things up quickly. "Engagement jitters—that's it," she diagnosed. A glimmer of relief replaced the hurt look earlier. "Buying your sweetie a rock like you just did is enough to make anyone a little cranky." She gave him an understanding pat on the arm and excused herself for the evening so he could get an early bedtime.

Sleep didn't come to Jerry for several hours. Oddly, for some reason, thoughts of Natalie began flashing through his mind for the first time in months. Once again, Jerry was mystified why these strange mental patterns should occur.

I love Carol more than life, Jerry thought, bafflingly. *I put aside all emotional ties to Natalie the moment Carol came into my life—before that, actually, when I got so stressed at the lodge I hardly had time to think about her any more.*

He felt sure Natalie wouldn't have wanted him to spend the rest of his young life wasting away in mourning. It's the same thing he would have wanted for Natalie if the situation had been reversed.

Yet now, finding himself in the state of being engaged again, he wrestled with feeling strangely disloyal to his first fiancee.

I could never discuss this with Carol—it would devastate her, and she'd never understand, Jerry mourned. *I could never discuss this with* anyone—*Pop would be mortified, too.*

Jerry knew that Carol was relieved to have him in her life to replace the miserable relationship she had with deadbeat Keith. She'd never be able to relate to what he was struggling with right now.

What was with this inexplicable reluctance to get married? Jerry continued to interrogate himself. After all, he hadn't had this kind of queasiness during his first engagement.

On balance, Carol was perhaps more perfectly suited for him than Natalie had been. Although Natalie had a beauty all her own, in looks she was no match for the thoroughly ravishing Carol. He and Carol by far had more common interests, and a much brighter future lay ahead. When Jerry was engaged to Natalie, he had only a dead-end job as a shop clerk. Now, he was heir apparent to Pop's empire.

Then, Jerry realized he may have hit upon the answer. It was because the future *did* appear brighter, at least from other people's perspectives. The ski shop was predictable, routine. Jerry had worked at the job for several years and was a master at it. It was no threat. Despite all these months at Valley Lodge, his work still left him panic-stricken most of the time. Even with all of Pop's exaggerated affirmations, Jerry still felt incapable, unsure—still paralyzed with fear of failure. And if that happened after marrying Carol, after another person's happiness became linked with his, it would be catastrophic. He'd end up destroying Carol along with himself, and it would be a total disaster.

Besides, what role models did he have for marriage? His own parents' marriage was definitely not one to model. With Natalie, it didn't matter so much—her own family so torn asunder by divorce and a multiplicity of estrangements. He had figured that he and Natalie would lean on each other—two refugees from war-torn childhoods, with domineering fathers who came up lacking, hoping to make something better together than they had experienced.

But Carol was the product of a 30-year, rock-stable union with a loving father whose loss she still mourned. She would want Jerry to be like her Dad—one more expectation he couldn't meet. And she was far different from Natalie, who like him, hadn't darkened the door of a church in years. Carol posed a challenge to his moral fiber and his spiritual condition.

In every way in this engagement, unlike his previous one, he felt handicapped—trapped and helpless, by the indelible scars that no one else seemed to recognize.

The closer the party date grew, the more it shaped up as the social event of the season. Since it had been recently decided that their wedding would be in June in Carol's hometown in Ohio, Pop theorized that the engagement party would be the only time most people in the area could formally extend their good wishes to the couple. He wanted to make sure it was the celebration that the event deserved.

Although the party was originally designed for lodge staffers, Pop had quickly expanded it. He first included some of his colleagues from nearby hotels and businesses but then enlarged it to invite prominent townspeople and officials.

Pop strategized that this would be a good time not only to share Jerry and Carol's good news but to also "introduce" Jerry as the future leader of Valley Lodge. In the end, everyone from the mayor to his chief competitor, Burt Humphreys, received one of Pop's custom-designed invitations featuring two skiers with a heart surrounding them engraved on the cover.

The day before the party, however, the weather threatened to overshadow all the well-ordered plans of Pop and the staff. One of the most massive fronts of the season was forecast to drop a barrage of new snow on the area.

"You ladies got here just in time," a relieved Pop announced when a motorcoach bearing Fayma and Carol's Aunt Claire finally pulled up to the Valley Lodge entrance. "That snowstorm on its way will close the airport, for sure."

"Why, we wouldn't have let a little weather get in our way, Mr. Hartley!" countered a radiant Fayma. "Nothing would have kept us from being here for Jerry and Carol."

Aunt Claire exuded the same brand of effusive warmth that was the family's trademark. "Oh, you're just so precious—just like they said," she told Jerry, as the two of them met. She dug deep into her tote bag and handed her nephew-to-be a colorful tin package. "Here's a container of fudge I made for you just before I left. I know how guys sometimes get left out in big events like this."

Jerry reacted with stunned silence. He couldn't believe these people! First Fayma had arrived at Christmas bearing a sweater she had made for him, sight-unseen. Now a second gift came from a prospective relative who had never laid eyes on him, either. It was totally removed from his frame of reference of how relatives behave. As he expected, his own mother had written him a terse letter to decline, with not even so much as a "good luck" or "best wishes." Jerry only hoped he had responded to Fayma courteously instead of like the blunderbuss he felt at the moment.

True to Pop's predictions, the morning of the party dawned with blizzard-like conditions outdoors. While Pop stayed glued to the phone to assure invited VIP's that the party was still on, Jerry drove the lodge's Land Rover to town to pick up the ring for Carol so he could present it to her that evening after Pop made the official announcement.

The specially crafted ring shone even more brilliantly than he remembered as Jerry removed it from its red moire box and held it up to the window. The light poured in brightly because of the almost blinding sheets of snow outdoors.

At least Carol will get one thing tonight that is worthy of her, he murmured sadly.

Back at his room, he stuffed the ring into a small plastic jewelry bag and slipped it into the pocket of his tuxedo trousers so he could produce it when Pop gave him the nod. He dressed and clipped his bow tie in place. He looked in the mirror at the face of a man who was about to receive the Olympic Gold but who had the lifeless appearance of one who was marching away to a death sentence.

In contrast to his, Carol's face shone like galaxies a few minutes later when Jerry showed up downstairs. The lodge's Aspen Room had been transformed into a glittering ice palace for the engagement party. Jerry gasped as he surveyed the incredible amount of work that Doug and his helpers had expended. They wanted to make this night unforgettable for the engaged duo and for Pop's special mission that evening.

"Darling, can you believe this?" Carol cried ecstatically. She slipped her arm through Jerry's when she spotted him and led him to the ice sculpture of the skiers that Doug had promised.

Doug's crew had not missed a detail. Simulated ice crystals spangled the ceiling. Swags of silk magnolia leaves sprayed silver and wired to white silk blossoms were draped from doorframes and arranged on damask-clothed banquet tables. Food stations featured eye-popping spreads of fruit, cheese, shrimp, and other hors d'oeuvres. The kitchen crew had pulled out every silver serving piece in the lodge's collection. The glint of the silver as the room's spotlights hit it added to the elegant atmosphere that the caterers had tried to create.

The true centerpiece of the party was Carol, every inch a vision as she hung on Jerry's arm and moved around the room to the background music of a string quartet. The champagne crepe sheath dress with its back that dipped almost to her waistline clung to every contour of her small, well-proportioned frame. The sparkle from her sequined, trumpet sleeves was a perfect complement to the Aspen Room's glittery setting. Her dark hair was pulled into a French braid with small sprigs of baby's breath tucked into it. It set off the handsome gold and pearl earrings Jerry had given her for Christmas. A double-strand, pearl choker necklace accented the high neckline of her bodice.

"You're marrying well above you, I see," the town's mayor complimented Jerry. He surveyed the glistening Carol on his arm as they made their way through the crowd.

I know that all too well, Jerry thought to himself bitterly. His smile felt more plastic by the minute as he attempted to make small-talk with Pop's connections.

The evening moved on toward Pop's first staged, important moment. He ushered Jerry to the podium set up at one corner of the room and introduced him to the guests as part of Jerry's first business sendoff.

"With Jerry Rutgers at the helm in the near future, you'll see more innovations than ever out of Valley Lodge," Pop announced, to the guests' polite applause. "This is only a sign of great things to come at the happiest little hotel in the Rockies. In a moment, I'll tell you about an even happier development here."

For the next few minutes, Pop's business contacts milled solicitously about Jerry. Even Burt Humphreys had at least a perfunctory handshake for him.

"I wish you the very best as you attempt to fill Pop's shoes," Pop's competitor said dryly.

The man's comment stopped Jerry in his tracks. *Fill Pop's shoes—I can't do that!* Jerry thought desperately, as sweat drops beaded up across his brow. *Can't they see? This whole thing is a charade! Pop knows I'll fall on my face; why is he putting me and himself and the whole town through this pretense? It's simply, absolutely not going to work.*

Those last four words grew from a whisper of self-talk in Jerry's mind to a deafening chant. It drowned out the strings players, drowned out the chatter, drowned out the tinkle of crystal as white-gloved servers poured party punch.

It's not going to work, his thoughts demanded. *It's not going to work. The business, the marriage, none of it!*

Suddenly, the collar and bow-tie on Jerry's tuxedo shirt grew so suffocating Jerry thought he would choke on the spot. He slipped out of Carol's view as she turned her attention to yet another well-wisher.

Jerry stepped to the corner of the room and slid behind one of Doug's flower-bedecked trellises. He unlatched the neck of his shirt and tried to draw some deep breaths. Momentarily, the pressure eased.

Jerry gathered his wits about him and straightened his shirt. He took a few steps forward to try to rejoin the gathering before anyone noticed his absence.

But when Jerry moved only slightly, the room began swimming around him in a dizzying whorl. His chest again constricted with air that couldn't find its way out. Jerry caught onto one of the room pillars to keep from toppling to the floor. His heart clamored so violently he thought he perceived the whole room shaking because of it.

I've gotta split, Jerry determined, in a panic. *I can't stay a minute longer.*

With one last, backward glance at the magnificent Carol, too deeply immersed in her own crowning moment to notice him gone, Jerry managed to slip through the doors of the Aspen Room without attracting attention and fled up the stairs to the lobby.

TEN

Into the Darkness

As Jerry scrambled past the registration area, making a nosedive for the stairway to take him to his room, the loud, provoked voice of a female guest penetrated the edges of his haze.

Leaning on the desk, with her considerable baggage surrounding her, was a woman clearly in need of something. She was gesturing angrily and complaining vociferously but to no one.

"Don't they have people to help you in this place?" she muttered, crossly. "First, I go through the plane flight from hell, and now this!"

As her words jerked Jerry into reality, he noticed that the lobby was, indeed, like a ghost town. Everyone had disappeared downstairs to join the party. In his current state of confusion, he couldn't at that moment remember who was supposed to be on duty this evening, but not a soul was in sight at present. Pop had ordered everyone who could step aside from their duties even for a minute to attend the reception.

"They're at a . . . at a party," Jerry stumbled over his words, apologetically. His eyes skimmed over the lobby for someone—anyone—in the lodge crew who might help this customer. All he wanted was to escape to his room and rest his throbbing head.

"Well, *you're* not at a party," the guest snapped. Jerry realized he still had on his lodge badge that Pop insisted that everyone—even the guest of honor—wear to the reception. The angry woman obviously pegged him as someone who might be official. "You're *here*," she seethed. "Can't you help?"

"Of course," Jerry replied dully. He realized he was stuck and struggled to pull himself back to attention.

He stepped mechanically behind the desk and got his first real glimpse of the woman. The words she used to describe her current predicament began to soak in gradually. His eyes widened, then blinked in disbelief. Short brown hair . . . closely cropped against a diminutive face . . . large, loop earrings . . . halter top and black leather pants . . . harrowing plane flight.

This woman could be Natalie! he thought with a gasp. After an interminable time, he found himself literally having to rip his eyes from her face to break his obsessive gaze. He knew she recognized he was staring.

"You're looking at me oddly," the guest stated puffily, her voice still irked from having to wait.

"Sorry . . . I'm s-s-sorry," Jerry replied, still stumbling over his words and trying to shake free of the fog that curled around him. "You just . . . just reminded me of someone, that's all."

Forcing himself to be businesslike, he turned to the computer and typed in the woman's name—Cindy Cortland. She was just in from Oklahoma and was meeting up here with two other single girlfriends.

"I got in on the only flight they'd let in all day because of the snowstorm," she complained.

Jerry tried to concentrate on his computer while she ranted on.

"It was dreadful," she continued. "The pilot circled for an hour until they let him land in the blizzard. We got so pushed around by the wind, people were up-chucking everywhere. I thought the jerk next to me was gonna yank my arm off, he was so scared. I was glad to get free of him. Then, when I finally arrived here, I'm totally ignored. It's too much."

Jerry groped for something that would shut down the daggers darting from her eyes.

"We'll give you a free room night—will that help make things more comfortable for you?" Jerry offered in desperation.

At that, the guest's face relaxed a degree or two. "That's very kind of you," she replied, struggling at civility and forcing a slight smile.

Again Jerry studied this strange figure that appeared before him. Now that he had his bearings more about him, he could see that the guest was a little shorter, a little younger, the face a little more angular, the brows a little thicker than the way she looked originally, when it seemed for a moment that Natalie's ghost had come back for him when he was still reeling from the panic attack he'd experienced at the party. And, as she had just informed him, her plane *had* landed safely.

What in the world came over me? Jerry asked himself, confounded.

Although he was more in touch with reality now, his eyes were still riveted to Cindy. Strangely, he found himself not wanting to let her out of his sight.

She bent to pick up the handles of her luggage. Max, a bellman, who had been nowhere around only seconds ago, suddenly breezed up to the desk.

"Take your things, ma'am?" he offered. He grabbed a luggage cart and studied the number on the room key Jerry had placed on the counter.

"No, Max," Jerry interrupted, gruffly. He drew in a sharp breath and literally jerked the key from the porter's hand. "You go on and join the party, like Pop said. I'll take care of this."

Max flashed him a baffled look. "You sure, boss?" he questioned. "You shouldn't be here at all, you know." Max was right. In a few minutes, Pop would be stepping to the podium downstairs to announce Jerry and Carol's engagement. A frantic Carol would be looking for him, searching, awaiting the ring that right now rested in the pocket of his trousers.

"It's OK, Max," Jerry barked. He gestured the employee away irritably. "I've got it."

Obligingly, Max left for the stairs, but his puzzled eyes remained latched on Jerry. He watched Pop's assistant over his shoulder, as he disappeared in the distance.

Jerry directed Cindy toward the elevator, and Cindy struck out ahead of him. The heels of her boots tapped out a still-perturbed beat as she walked across the lobby floor. From behind the brass luggage cart on which he loaded her suitcases, Jerry continued to stare, transfixed, at Cindy until they reached her room door.

He slid the key in, opened the door, and moved inside to set down the items. Her roommates weren't here yet, so the room was dark and the curtains drawn.

He stepped over to her bureau and clicked on a lamp so Cindy could survey her accommodations. He watched as her eyes skimmed over the furnishings, peered into the bathroom, and looked around the window curtain to check out the view of the high-tech lifts outside. He had the swift sensation that she was deliberately looking for something wrong with her room so she'd have further cause to grouse about Valley Lodge. Finding everything to her liking, however, she turned her attention to getting settled in.

Waiting for her verdict and hearing none, Jerry continued to stand by the baggage cart. Suddenly he was in no particular hurry to leave.

As she tried to transfer her hanging items from the cart, the hook on her bulky bag snagged on the cuff of the dark crepe jacket that covered her halter top.

"Drat!" she exclaimed, and struggled to keep it from tearing the fabric.

"Let me help," Jerry offered, and zoomed in quickly to lift the bag out of her hands and position it in her closet. He made the same gesture with her suitcase, moving it to a luggage rack near the dressing area. He located her

TV remote and showed her how to call up the ski information channel.

By this point Jerry realized that he, oddly, had begun deliberately looking around for other courtesies to perform for this guest. Light from the nearby outdoor skating area crept around the edges of the window curtains. It cast an interesting pattern of shadows onto the burgundy-hued walls.

Once she was finally ensconced in her room, Cindy appeared more peaceful. She looked up at her new, helpful acquaintance with large eyes that actually appeared grateful.

"You really went out of your way for me. I appreciate it," she told Jerry. He noted that her voice actually had a pleasant quality about it, now that the irritation was dissipating. "I hope I didn't sound too rude down at the desk," she added, somewhat meekly.

Then it was Jerry's turn to be meek. "And I hope I didn't offend you by staring," Jerry responded. He himself felt freed up a little, now that he was away from the pressure chamber that had surrounded him downstairs for the past hour at the party. He could sense his disorientation abating, the more the minutes wore on.

"Well, I'll have to admit—you looked at me like you'd seen a ghost," Cindy ventured. She tossed her head back in a half-laugh, having absolutely no idea the significance of her casual statement.

"I thought for a minute I had," Jerry's muted voice breathed. He was embarrassed now at how his eyes had played those inexplicable tricks on him a few minutes before. "Actually, you could almost be a twin to my fiancee. Your clothes, your hairdo, everything I saw about you—for a second, it was just uncanny how like her you were."

"Your fiancee?" Cindy interrupted. "Where is she?"

Jerry cleared his throat, self-consciously. "She . . . she's not here. I mean, she died. In a plane crash. During a snowstorm." His words emerged awkwardly. "When you said your plane had trouble . . well, my mind did some funny things, I guess."

"How horrible!" Cindy answered him. She sounded genuinely sympathetic. "No wonder you looked white as a sheet." Her eyes surveyed his blanched, perspiration-beaded face that surrounded two blazing blue eyes. "In fact," she pronounced, "you still do. Maybe you'd better sit down for a minute and rest." She gestured to the small sofa close by in the living room area of her suite.

Suddenly Jerry was determined to do anything to avoid leaving this quiet sanctuary away from the noisy, pressurizing party. He was even more hesitant to leave this mysterious, magnetic guest. At her offer, he found himself sinking down onto the plump cushions, with only the dim light from the dresser outlining them. As he sank, he removed his tuxedo coat, which still had pinned to it the white rose boutonniere he wore as the guest of honor. He shoved it onto a nearby chair out of his line of vision.

Idly, he wondered if she might think it odd that a desk clerk might be wearing a tux and a flower, but it was a random curiosity that he pushed away quickly. He suddenly wanted to dismiss any thought that reminded him of the party he just left.

In contrast to the heat of the Aspen Room that had threatened to suffocate him, Cindy's room—and her voice, now that she was no longer hostile—were cool . . . so cool . . . like the sudden rush of deep powder on his face when he skied into a turn. Something about him wanted to curl up into this untroubled haven and never find his way back.

Cindy's voice soothed even further as she turned the conversation to Valley Lodge. Since this lodge staffer was on her sofa, she would simply take advantage of his presence and query Jerry about ski conditions in Crested Butte. She wanted to be knowledgeable tomorrow when her slope-crazy friends from Texas arrived to join her. What were the most challenging trails? When were the lift lines shortest during the day?

"And, most importantly, can we find some hunky ski instructors?" she threw in, laughing provocatively. "We're looking for single, available guys on this trip."

Her teasing laugh was contagious, and Jerry found himself reveling in it.

"Why, certainly. We aim to please, ma'am," he replied, catching her playful mood.

Talking about skiing—his heart's passion—was like a balm to Jerry's feverish spirit. Downstairs he'd had to dodge troubling questions that he had no answers for and that had only made him feel incapable. Guests had queried him about his five-year organizational plan for Valley Lodge and whether he'd throw his hat in the ring to run for town council, now that Pop was retiring. Talking with Cindy about the nonthreatening subject of the area's ski runs was the most gratifying break he could imagine. He realized that his headache was gone and his muscles were unknotting.

Before either of them knew it, a full hour had passed as they made slow, unhurried conversation in Cindy's suite where Jerry had initially intended to only unload her baggage. He still made no effort to leave, and Cindy, who was by now increasingly taken with the attention of this cover-boy-handsome acquaintance, made no effort to ask him to.

As the night advanced, the shadows in the room grew darker, and it seemed that Cindy's voice became more velvety, more drugging the longer he listened to it as she sat on the small love seat beside him. Although she wasn't Natalie, the conversation carried him back to a less-complicated time—a time he would give his whole life to be able to re-create right now. If he could have delved into the depths of Cindy's sea-green eyes and remained there, he would have, never having to come up for air. The longer they talked, the closer to Cindy Jerry discovered himself moving on the sofa. He found himself emotionally plunging deeper . . . deeper . . . away from everything that bore down on him, everything that entangled.

As he plunged, something inside of him buckled. Cindy's arm, covered by the slim sleeves of her crepe jacket, had lain draped over the back of the sofa with her hand so close to him it almost touched his temple as he tilted his head back onto the upholstery. He reached up for it and dragged her hand down, pulling her to him in a sudden, determined embrace.

Cindy surrendered without protest. At his purposeful touch, she wrapped herself around him like Velcro around a boot cuff. She was supple and compliant and caught the back of his neck to maneuver his head closer to her. They kissed with abandon, his mouth crushing hers, on the sofa for a few minutes, until Jerry realized that by moving only slightly, they could step over to one of the hotel room beds.

At that, Jerry rose and pulled Cindy to the edge of the mattress, again without any hint of resistance. The two of them sank down on top of the quilted comforter. Jerry felt his senses slipping totally away, and Cindy obliged Jerry's every move and desire. The minutes wore on, the sighs grew more intense, the touches less tender and more desperate.

His formal attire and her halter top and pants soon lay in a knotted heap on one corner of the bed. The duo that had worn them moments earlier now rolled and entertwined on the other end, as Jerry gave in to the overwhelming magnitude of irrationality that engulfed him. He took Cindy, as well as his hopes for happiness with Carol and his bright future at Valley Lodge, down with him.

An incessant, unanswered knock sharply pierced the silence. From a deep swirl, Jerry caught the tap-tap-tapping which tried to break in on his trance. *How long had it gone on?* Before he could tear his thoughts away from his partner, he heard a key turn in the lock. Then he heard Max's deep baritone saying, "No one seems to be here, Miss Carol, but this is the room where he was headed."

The door swung open, and Jerry looked up from the frantic coupling into which he was lost at the moment and into the face of his fiancee.

For a tortuous eternity, Carol was silent. Her disbelieving eyes absorbed the picture in front of her. She saw the tangle of clothes on the bed that included the shirt and bow tie Jerry had worn moments earlier at their engagement party, the tangle of bodies that defied all logic, all reason.

Her eyes, struggling frantically to focus in the dim light, locked on Jerry's upturned ones. Carol's were searching, questioning, momentarily denying the horror of the unthinkable that stretched out before her.

In front of her lay the grim truth that affirmed exactly where Jerry went when he fled from the party, sending Carol off in search of him after he hadn't returned an hour later.

Then, her single, silvery scream filled the room. It was followed by racking, furious sobs that trailed off in the distance as Carol ran down the hallway yelling, "Pop . . . Pop . . ." at the top of her lungs.

Max lunged after her, but missed. "Miss Carol, come back," the bellman cried helplessly, as he watched her wild, red-rimmed eyes disappear down the stairway.

Jerry, instantly jarred into action, jumped from the bed. He jerked up covers and threw on clothes.

"Carrie, wait!" he pleaded, his face reddening, his shouts occurring too late and too insipidly to impact anything.

Max's mortified face peering through the doorway was all that Jerry saw—his face and that of Cindy, now herself quivering in the darkened room. She looked dumbstruck because of the baffling roller-coaster ride of emotions and experiences in the previous minutes.

And, although they weren't present, he also visualized the faces of Pop, of Fayma . . . and of Carol. His mind froze on the last, horrifying glimpse of his fiancee as the scream of reality at his betrayal left her lips.

Suddenly, the lives that he had just crushed by his rash, imprudent actions of the past hour flashed in front of him—the plans, the dreams, the love now in ashes. Jerry knew he had only one alternative.

He must bolt—not just to his room or into town until things cooled down at the lodge and he could come back and muddle through some explanation.

This time, Jerry knew he had to bolt for good. He had to leave Valley Lodge, go somewhere—anywhere—where he could permanently escape the pressure and the expectations and the worthlessness and the loss.

114

He raced from the hotel room past the stunned Max, without so much as a word of explanation to Cindy, or to anyone, for that matter. Jerry knew he didn't have a second to spare. Pop, and others in the lodge when word got out, would pursue him like bloodhounds as soon as Carol's story reached the lobby. There was no time to even stop by his apartment to grab some belongings. Jerry dashed the length of the upstairs hall and reached a little-used stairway that emptied out onto the back of Valley Lodge.

Finding the exit door, Jerry started to bound out into the cold night air. Then glancing up at the snow blowing sideways from the relentless storm under way outside, he hesitated. He would freeze to death in minutes if he ventured out with only the starched white shirt and thin, tuxedo pants that he wore.

He looked around for a quick solution and spotted a small storage closet a few feet down the hallway. Sometimes people from the maintenance crew left work jackets hanging on pegs near the door. Jerry reached into the dark closet. As luck would have it, he dragged out a coat. Although stained with oil and mud, the jacket at least would give him some protection.

Then, as Jerry dug into its pockets, he miraculously found a frayed knit cap stuffed in one. The cap would shield him from the wind as well as give him some anonymity as he raced into the darkness. Jerking it tightly down over his ears, he took one last, backward look at Valley Lodge.

When he arrived there so triumphantly six months before, he had believed it to be a little slice of heaven.

Now it represented nothing to him but a living hell.

Resolutely, he disappeared into the night. Jerry knew nothing of where he was going—only that he was thankfully, finally, unalterably, going away.

ELEVEN

Adrift and Alone

❀

Jerry clambered his way through a back route from the lodge, down the mountain, and into the silent, snow-encrusted town. It was a toss-up as to what blinded him more—the flakes that flew mercilessly into his face, or the sharp, stinging tears that blurred his vision.

He knew that no one in his right mind would venture out on a bitter night like this one with temperatures in the single digits—especially no one clad only in formal wear and party shoes. Already he could hardly remember what his toes felt like, protected from frostbite only by thin, nylon socks. Bits of the snowdrifts he trudged through clung to his ankles and slid down onto the insteps of his feet.

Beyond that, Jerry realized he was practically penniless. At the last minute before he left his room for the reception, he had removed his wallet and keys and tossed them on his dresser. Other than barely a dollar's worth of change, and Carol's ring, which he might have to hock for his own survival, Jerry had no resources on him—no money, no credit cards, no identification of any sort.

Just exactly how far do I think I'll get in this predicament? he lamented, his despair building. *I have a job, a home, money, yet here I am on the lam like some kind of common fugitive.*

As the white-mantled town came into view, Jerry saw the lights of the bus station and momentarily considered leaping onto the next shuttle that was outbound to Gunnison. Once he got to Gunnison, Traveler's Aid might help him with some cash and some money for food until he determined where he should go and what he should do.

Then Jerry laughed at his foolishness. *How stupid to think that stopping for the shuttle is an option for me!* The drivers all knew Pop—and consequently, him. These were some of the guys that Pop guzzled coffee with at the Columbine Cafe, or at least used to until sickness confined him. Someone would surely recognize Jerry and wonder why Pop's assistant would be trying to skip town at 10 o'clock at night with no funds and no suitcase. He couldn't even begin to invent a story that wouldn't prompt a call to Pop immediately.

He also knew better than to try to duck into The Wild Goose or any of the other eateries that were open at this hour. Immediately he would be known, and the predictable array of questions would follow. Most of the restaurant proprietors would realize that the party in Jerry's honor was still going on at Valley Lodge. They would be horrified to recognize that Jerry, who they thought was currently being regaled as the toast of the town, was a runaway.

Yet despite these dreary circumstances, returning to Valley Lodge was absolutely not an option for Jerry, he knew most assuredly. By now a mortified Pop would be scrambling to make excuses for Jerry's absence to the guests who were there for the big announcement. By now some folks would have helped Pop comb the place thoroughly and be aware that Jerry appeared to have fled—putting Pop on the spot even further.

By now a grieving Carol would have poured out her story of horror at Jerry's unfaithfulness.

By now Fayma and Aunt Claire and Shannon would be hovering around her—trying to help her make some sense out of the baffling events.

By now the staff would be wagging their heads as the story leaked out about the scene that Max had stumbled onto in the hotel room.

By now Doug would be sadly putting away the ice sculpture and the swags and wondering how a party so lovingly planned could have ended on such a disappointing note.

By now Cindy would start to bear the brunt of the staff's anger that was no doubt already being siphoned her way.

No, no, I can't go back there—ever! Jerry railed to himself. *I'd be lucky to escape with my life.*

With that decision fixed, Jerry knew that he also would soon be a wanted, hunted man, if he were not already. Even now, Jerry knew that the Crested Butte police probably were on the lookout for a 26-year-old blond, broad-shouldered male last seen wearing gentlemen's party attire and thought to be fleeing on foot from Valley Lodge. A sharp eye would have noted fresh tracks in the deep snow outside the lodge's back entrance and pointed toward the mountain road. It would seem only logical that he had headed toward town.

In only seconds, if he lingered on the snow-covered sidewalks outside the Victorian storefronts, someone might spot him and return him to the scene of his disgrace. Jerry's only alternative was to make his shivering legs work fast and get to the highway—his only hope for making a getaway.

He pulled his cap down even further over his brows and ducked against the blowing snow. Jerry stepped up his pace and moved with his back to the traffic. He knew he'd be safer facing the cars headon, in these low visibility conditions. But the glare of headlamps in his face might come from just the very driver who would recognize him.

Some of Carol's and Pop's prayers would sure come in handy right now, Jerry thought in his desperation.

But even that prospect was futile, Jerry believed. *I've made such a miserable mess of my life, even God himself would turn His back on me.* His breath turned into a vapory puff that circled around him as he muttered aloud.

Once Jerry reached the highway, fresh anxiety gripped him. He had only hitchhiked once before in his life—as a college student, when his car went dead. He knew the risks involved—especially if some unsavory character who gave him a lift reacted in anger because he had no wallet, credit cards, or money to steal. As car after car sped by him, ignoring his upturned thumb, Jerry envisioned his gagged body dumped in a ditch somewhere, at the mercy of the elements on this night that was colder than any he ever remembered.

Yet the alternative to finding transportation—*any* ride at the hands of *any* driver at this point—was equally formidable. Jerry knew he'd be a candidate for hypothermia if he didn't soon find himself inside some car or truck.

He lifted both hands in the air and began waving them more frenziedly. *I'm acting like a wild man—maybe that's what I am,* Jerry thought. *Maybe someone will pick me up and take me to a mental hospital.*

A psychiatric ward actually sounded appealing as his teeth chattered so violently that his whole body shook. *At least there I'd have a bed and food and a warm blanket over me.*

Finally a car in the distance appeared to slow a little. Jerry watched it as it approached, continuing to decelerate. The early model navy sedan was close enough now that Jerry could hear a pronounced rattle as it moved.

I don't care what kind of clunker it is—it will be like a chariot of gold to me if this driver would take me in, Jerry thought. Still it slowed, the car braking further. *Thank you, thank you,* Jerry almost cried out in relief.

Then, as Jerry continued to watch, he saw the driver swerve impulsively—first pulling off the road toward him and then careening for a minute back into the flow of traffic before veering a second time to the shoulder. A white car in the outside lane barely missed striking it as it turned back into traffic. A van behind it almost rear-ended the white car in the confusing melee. Jerry gaped in disbelief at the near-collision he just witnessed.

As the navy car pulled fully onto the shoulder and came to a stop just in front of him, Jerry heard loud, raucous music pouring from the open windows. Then laughter, then profanity.

These people are drunk, Jerry realized. *They could have caused a bad accident just then.*

"Hey, buddy," one of the passengers yelled. "What'cha waving for? That won't keep you warm on a night like this." As he peered into the window, he saw booze flowing freely among these occupants. He counted five of them, including the driver. The stench of alcohol wafted out of the car and enveloped his senses as he stood there, contemplating how to answer.

"I need a way to Boulder," Jerry finally managed, his vocal chords so frozen that he had to force the words out.

"Well, what d'ya know? That's where we're headed—back to school," the driver yelled at him. "Hurry up and get in. We don't want any cops comin' around." More obscenities peppered his speech as the driver revved up his engine and prepared to swerve back onto the road within seconds if Jerry didn't act quickly.

Jerry sucked in a fright-riven breath and pondered his dilemma. *Should I really ride with this bunch of drunk students? Who knows what else might be in this car besides liquor?*

Yet, what else might happen to him if he continued to stand by the side of the road in the knifing cold? Jerry wondered. *Choose your poison,* he told himself. His eyes roamed frantically over the surface of the navy car as he studied his fate.

More curses, this time at Jerry's impatience. "OK, buddy, time's up," the driver yelled. He turned his wheels sharply and began pulling onto the highway without him.

Jerry made a sudden, frenetic choice. "Wait! Wait!" he yelled, lunging after the car's door handle and grabbing it like the disappearing lifeline it was as the vehicle moved away. The back door swung open on the passenger side. Jerry hoisted himself in while the driver floored the accelerator and wove back into the traffic, narrowly missing a pickup in his lane.

The driver squealed on his brakes to avoid his third near-collision within a matter of minutes. He vomited anger at Jerry.

"You jerk! That's what I get for trying to help someone who won't make up his mind. Where you trying to go in Boulder, anyway?"

Jerry adjusted his body to the shelter as he sardined himself against the other three back-seat passengers. He thought about the driver's question.

Where am *I going in Boulder, anyway?* he repeated the query to himself. Up until this point, his only thought had been minute-to-minute survival—getting warmth returned to his fingers, ankles, and quaking chest. Boulder, his old home, was the place that automatically came to his mind when he had to cough up a destination to the driver.

If he actually survived this car ride and made it to Boulder, he could always call on his friends there—Dave, his buddy at the ski shop, or some of his college chums who still lived in town.

But the last time Jerry had seen these old colleagues, he had been off in the glow of glory—to work at what he thought was his dream job, in the ski lodge with Pop. For all his well-wishers knew, things had gone swimmingly for Jerry, and he had been a success.

Facing them the way he was now would only add to his deep humiliation. Besides, Boulder would be the first place Pop would imagine Jerry would head. Pop might have already alerted Jerry's old contacts there, and they'd be in cahoots with Pop to rally around and send Jerry back home.

He would have to think beyond Boulder—some other destination, provided he made it to this first one safely.

Clank-rattle-clank. The noise of the dilapidated car and the occasional jerk of the wheels as the driver fought against inebriation rocked Jerry in and out of drowsiness. In front, the students were boasting about how they spent the weekend partying in a mountain cabin up near Schofield Pass, above Crested Butte, and showshoeing in after parking their car several miles away.

Jerry caught only snatches of their boisterous conversation. As the odor of their guzzled beer infiltrated his nostrils, it provoked a far-distant memory as Jerry and sleep did a dance together in the back seat of the car.

Pictures in his subconscious began to take shape. *You little twerps come out from wherever you're hiding.* He and his brother were back home again, cowered in a corner of the living room, ducking behind a chair. Dad had come in drunk and raging one more time.

Don't worry, Jer. He won't hurt us here. Bo was the younger of the two by eighteen months. Yet in these scary times, he had always hovered over Jerry—protecting him, calming him until Dad's anger had passed.

Jerry realized he had found his answer. *That's it. I'll call Bo.* Perhaps his only sibling could protect him once again, in this latest, most urgent siege of his life. Bo and Sally's ranch for troubled boys was about four hours away from Denver, off Interstate 70 in the western part of Kansas. If Jerry could make it to Denver, he could throw himself on Bo's mercy. *Maybe he'll come for me.* Jerry hadn't seen Bo and Sally in several years and hadn't talked to his brother since Natalie died. Bo probably wasn't even aware that Jerry had left the ski shop and moved to a new location.

It wasn't that Jerry had anything particularly against Bo. In their growing-up days, the two of them had been as friendly as two siblings could be who had to survive in their broken environment. Bo had a hairtrigger temper that didn't take much to set off. They had gotten into typical scuffles, many of them physical. Fortunately, none of them had left any major scars that Jerry could recall.

In his sober days, when Dad was home for a while and an uneasy calm descended on the household, Bo seemed to be able to ingratiate himself to Dad more easily than Jerry had. When Dad took the two of them hunting, it was Bo who held the rifle correctly, Bo who had sure aim, Bo who got the kudos when the rabbit fell.

In Dad's eyes, his firstborn was the klutz, the one who never quite measured up, the one who entered the wrong profession in later life. All that in spite of the fact that Jerry was his namesake—Edward Jeremiah Rutgers Jr. The senior Mr. Rutgers—Eddie—always seemed paired up with his second son.

Then Bo married Sally and had the religious experience which prompted him to leave stockbrokering and begin a new life at Sky Ranch. It was Bo who sought out Dad in his hermit-like existence in the far southwest corner of his state. It was Bo who now had frequent contact with their father, bringing him to the ranch on occasion and visiting him in his home. Meanwhile, Jerry remained out of touch, with the breach very much still alive between father and son—and, to an extent, between brother and brother.

Bo had urged Jerry to join him on these visits. He assured Jerry that Dad had mellowed in his older years—that he had given up drinking, that he wasn't the meddler and scalawag of days gone by. But Jerry wasn't interested. *How could Bo possibly be objective? He's the only son that Dad would be happy to see.*

Because Jerry was now a recalcitrant—just like some of the troubled youth that Bo and Sally sheltered—he could appeal to Bo's good graces—even if he had to endure Bo's sermonizing. *Bo is the only person I can think of that might keep me without Pop's knowledge, so I can get a grip on things.* He would get the driver to drop him off at somewhere near the Boulder turn-off; then he would use his calling-card number, which he had in his head, to contact Sky Ranch.

So, as the highway veered to the north to carry the rowdy students back to their home, Jerry's car door swung open on the access road near a gas station that doubled as a diner, and he was at the mercy of the elements again.

Thankfully, as the car moved closer to Denver, the polar blast had abated. Although temperatures in this new spot were still sub-freezing, the absence of the blizzard gave Jerry more hope, in case he had to hitchhike again.

"Hullo?"

Sally's voice was heavy with sleep when Jerry finally managed to obtain their number from directory assistance and rang Bo's ranch house on the grounds of the boys' home. Jerry knew that in their line of work, he wasn't the first person to awake his brother and sister-in-law at three in the morning with a distress call. Still, having to slink like some worm back into his brother's life in the middle of the night made Jerry's throat contract in his embarrassment.

"Sally . . ." his voice rasped hoarsely, as he barely mouthed the words, "this is . . . this is Jerry—you know, Bo's brother?" *Can't believe I blurted out that last part,* Jerry fretted, instantly regretful. *Just points out how strained things are between us.*

"Jerry . . . where are you?" Sally asked, jarred instantly awake. "You sound bad. Real bad. Honey," Jerry could hear her voice muffle as she turned aside to awaken Bo, "it's Jerry. Something's wrong."

Good ole intuitive Sally. Jerry knew why Bo was so successful in his current work. Sally was his antenna—reading intonations, hearing past words—even with an in-law she had seen only a fistful of times in her life.

Bo quickly grabbed up the line. "Jerry. It's been months. What's happening? I'd lost all track of you." Bo's voice was grave. Emergencies in the wee hours were his stock and trade, and he flipped on his professional tone automatically despite sleep.

"Bo, you've got to help me," Jerry begged, tears ripping through his voice as the anxiety of his last few hours on the run broke over him. "I can't go into detail, but I had to leave abruptly from the last place I worked—a ski lodge out West. I'm sure they have a tracer on me by now. I can't go back, Bo. I think I'm losing my mind. I know I haven't been the brother to you I should, but Bo, you're my only hope. Can I count on you, Bo? Can I?" Violent, exhausted sobs shook him as he pled. Jerry knew he probably wasn't the first person who ever stood at a pay phone at some stopover for transient losers, blubbering like a baby, but he ducked his face into the cubicle so no one would see.

"Have you broken the law, Jerry?" Bo interrogated. Jerry might be his brother, but there was business to attend to, and Bo needed the facts.

"No, not the law," Jerry sniffed, the words spurring fresh tears. "Just some hearts. Just some people I let down, including myself. Don't call the police, Bo—I beg you. Just take me in—let me get somewhere so I can think."

Bo thankfully didn't press.

"Where are you, Jer? Where can I find you?" he asked.

"I'm at a gas station—west of Denver, I'm not sure where," Jerry whispered. "I hitchhiked here. I don't have money—just a little change, and the calling card number in my head. I can't stay here forever. They'll get suspicious. It's not a place that I can loiter."

"Do you think you can get to Denver—somewhere like the bus station downtown, where you'd be safe, somewhere they won't suspect you and that you can rest?" Bo inquired. His voice was laced with concern.

"I've made it this far; I'll try to get another lift," Jerry sighed, eyeing the tough-looking characters who continued to file into the roadside stopover.

"Good," Bo affirmed. "If I leave now, I can be there by 7, 8 at the latest. I'll have my cell phone with me. Call Sally when you land somewhere, and she'll let me know where to find you."

Jerry sighed in thankful relief, his trembling hands clutching the phone as if to anchor him to the one lifeline he had. "Thanks, buddy. You won't regret this, I promise," he told Bo.

Then, a desperate thought panicked him.

"Promise you won't call anybody, Bo. I can't take it right now," Jerry pressured.

Bo was accustomed to the same kind of pleading from teen runaways. He shot back immediately. "For now, no, I won't, although I can't promise what I might need to do in the future," he replied firmly.

Then, sensing Jerry's fragile mental state, Bo issued his parting shot, even though he knew Jerry would be rankled by it.

"Jerry, be careful," Bo warned. "I care about you—Sally and I do. And God cares. That's most important. He knows about this, and He's there for you. Don't push your luck. Get somewhere you can be safe, and call so I can find you. But don't give up."

Bo's remarks might normally have made Jerry cringe, but in his current condition, he found himself almost wishing it were true—that a kind, all-knowing God took pity on his helplessness.

I can see why they say there are no atheists in foxholes, he thought grimly.

Clinking down the phone, Jerry looked around to plot his next steps. Pungent coffee fumes drifted over his way from the diner counter of the truck stop. Jerry thought how good the coffee and a heaping plate of scrambled eggs looked as the short-order cook served them up to some customer. *I'm so hungry, I could eat the silverware right now. It's been hours since I've consumed food.* The buffet spread at the reception had looked tasteless at the time, and he had skipped dinner earlier as well. Probably lunch too—he couldn't recall. Hunger had begun to weaken him. He dug into his pocket and examined his change.

A dollar eighty-two cents. That'll buy coffee or my bus fare. Not both, Jerry reckoned.

Jerry knew he'd better save the money for a time when he needed it more. Hunger would just have to be his companion for a while.

At first he headed for the doorway, prepared to brave the weather to flag down a ride again like he had in Crested Butte. Spotting the row of customers who sat on stools at the counter, Jerry paused for a moment. Maybe if he polled each one, he could hit paydirt.

"I need to go to downtown Denver," he blurted out, nervously, for each to hear. "Are you headed that way?"

126

Most of them remained expressionless, saying nothing, or ducking their heads in a way that answered his question tacitly. Still another curled his lip up at him in disgust. He turned his stool away to break Jerry's gaze.

Only one man, a portly individual so heavy-set it seemed the stool that supported him might break under the weight, replied. Angling his head so he could peer at Jerry through the bottom part of his bifocals, he eyeballed the insignia on the pocket of Jerry's work jacket. "What's a Valley Lodge?" he asked, dryly.

At the very mention of the painful name, Jerry jumped like he was shot. "I work there," Jerry finally stammered, caught off-guard by the inquiry.

The man skimmed his eyes over Jerry's party attire. "Then why ain't you there now?" he prodded, suddenly erupting into laughter so forceful, it caused the entire counter to quake.

Jerry could feel all the blood draining to his toes. He realized now that the jacket insignia listed Valley Lodge as being in Crested Butte, Colorado.

Can this man tell I'm a runaway? he thought quickly, guilt and terror rising in him afresh. *If I dash out of here, he could suspect me and turn me in. How in the world will I answer this lunatic?*

It turned out no answer was required. "Let's go, kid," said the big guy, who Jerry saw, despite his apprehensions, had only been making conversation. "I'll take you in to Denver. But I'll have to drop you off at a shopping center outside of town. Maybe you can hop a bus to take you the rest of the way." Nudging the driver on the seat next to him, the man added, "Guess I can take my chances with this kid. Doesn't look too much like a mugger, with these fancy duds on."

With that, he shifted his bulk off the stool and lumbered out into the early, cold darkness, with Jerry following. They climbed in his pickup, no more questions asked. Before Jerry knew it, they were well down the road and pulling into the shopping center parking lot.

As the truck driver sped away, Jerry pulled out his change again and was grateful he had bypassed the coffee. Walking to the parking lot's covered bus stop and reading the route list posted there, Jerry saw it would take almost every penny he had to pay for the fare and the transfer he needed to get him downtown.

More than two hours later, after huddling against the cold in two different bus-stop enclosures and asking endless directions from drivers and riders, Jerry was finally deposited in the downtown area, within about six blocks of Greyhound.

Jerry had never seen a more welcome sight than when the large red, white, and blue sign over the station appeared in his view as he rounded the last downtown intersection, on foot. His journey into the night, adrift and alone, had begun eight hours ago. He was drained to his last ounce of energy.

As he dragged himself into the bus-station lobby, Jerry had just enough reserve left to pull himself to a phone booth and give Sally his whereabouts. That accomplished, he flopped down on a seat so loudly that he drew raised eyebrows from those nearby.

By that point, Jerry was oblivious to everything. He had finally reached a secure waystation. Here he would rest until Bo hopefully found him, some two hours hence. He threw his head back on the seat and drifted off as soundly as the straight-backed chair would permit. He didn't stop to ponder his future or dwell on his past.

At that point, all that mattered to Jerry was escaping into sleep—tentative, troubled sleep, but sleep, nonetheless.

T W E L V E

A Ranch for Recovery

❀

A hand gripping his shoulder jarred Jerry from his upright slumber. He awoke to peer into blue eyes that matched his in hue and intensity.

"Jerry, I'm here now. Time to go." A voice pushed through Jerry's drowsiness, and a hand continued to rock his shoulder gently.

Crawling from out of his fog, Jerry tried to make sense of where he was and to identify this opaque form that bent over him. He gazed on a blond crew-cut, partly covered by a cap that said "Sky Ranch."

Then he remembered. *Bo. Shelter. Security. Help.*

Bo was Jerry's same height, but where Jerry had the tapered bulk of a body-builder, Bo was lean as a lamp post. As his brother's appearance took on meaning, Jerry leaped from his chair and embraced Bo so forcefully that both of them almost fell backward from the lunge.

"I can't believe you came for me, Bo! Thank you, buddy. From the bottom of my heart, thank you!" Jerry's voice broke a little as he continued to cover his brother with frantic, grateful hugs, oblivious to the crowd in the busy bus terminal that morning.

Finally Bo stepped back. Using a professionally trained eye that he had engaged in the past on other emergency missions, he surveyed Jerry carefully.

"When did you eat last?" he queried. His eyes scanned Jerry's pale, ravaged face and the legs that wobbled like a newborn colt's as Jerry struggled to stand.

Jerry managed a nervous laugh, now that relief was in sight. "I think it was light years ago," he answered, dragging his hands through unkempt hair. "Maybe I had a little lunch yesterday—I don't know."

"Let's get you some breakfast, then," Bo answered. "My truck's out here." Flinging a protective arm around his brother's shoulder, Bo directed Jerry out of the bus station and onto the downtown street that hummed with early-morning traffic.

Bo motored to the edge of town, where he pulled into a drive-through. He loaded up on breakfast muffins and hot coffee, with a large to-go container of scrambled eggs and sausage for Jerry.

The two brothers said little until Jerry wolfed down his take-out food and felt strength begin to seep back into his limbs. Bo patiently sipped from his coffee mug and waited for the story that Jerry needed to spill.

Finally, as he revived, Jerry remembered something he had to do.

Digging into his pocket, he pulled out the heart-shaped ring, encased in its plastic jewelry bag, just where he inserted it yesterday as he left his room for the engagement party. The iron clamp around his heart tightened as he took the ring out to show Bo.

"Here," he said, removing the piece of jewelry from its container and thrusting it in front of Bo's eyes. "This is the only thing I have in the world right now. But it's all yours, brother. You can get a good bit of money for it, I promise you. This is to pay you for what you're doing for me—for letting me stay with you."

The ring caught the early-morning sunbeams as they filtered through the window of the truck and threw hundreds of tiny, iridescent sparkles onto the ceiling. Bo's eyes widened at its size and beauty.

He reached out and took the item, depositing it in his own shirt pocket.

"I don't need your money, although I'll be glad to keep this for you for a while," Bo replied. The huge sparkler would be safer with him than subject to Jerry's whims in his current, confused state.

"But I do need to know what's going on here, when you feel like telling me," Bo continued, his voice quietly insistent. "You didn't get this ring out of a gum-ball machine. And I doubt that you bought it just to carry around in your pants."

Jerry's Herculean sigh almost drowned out the hum of the truck engine. He knew Bo certainly deserved more than the vague details Jerry had sputtered out during the middle-of-the-night telephone call that had brought his brother west.

So, as Bo's truck wove its way across the Colorado border into the western plains of Kansas that would lead to Bo's home, Jerry poured out the details of his past four months of love and anguish at Valley Lodge.

With the lines of his face etched deeply in regret, he told of Pop's persistent recruitment at the ski shop, Pop's illness and the worker walkout, and Carol's arrival and their subsequent romance.

He explained about Pop's meddling into their courtship, his deceit of Pop and Carol on matters of faith, his cries for help that everyone ignored, his panic attack at the engagement party, and his fatal involvement with Cindy that sealed his doom and thrust him into the cold.

Jerry half-expected that Bo would react in horror when he related his tale. He was sure his brother would judge him for his moral failings and for pretending he was a believer.

Instead, Bo merely nodded affirmatively throughout most of Jerry's story. Occasionally he quietly clarified some detail. Once or twice he replied with surprising compassion, "I'm sure that really hurt," or "That must have been terribly embarrassing for you."

131

When Jerry told about his bitter feelings toward their father and how Pop unwittingly took on some of their dad's traits, Jerry was sure he saw Bo brush away moisture that brimmed in the corners of his eyes.

As Jerry finally collapsed back into his seat, Bo reached over and patted his brother's arm. "I'm so sorry," he murmured quietly, turning sympathetic eyes toward Jerry briefly as he looked away from the road.

Jerry was incredulous that no tongue-lashing occurred. "Sorry?" he bit out sharply. "You mean you're not going to preach to me, to tell me how disappointed you are in me? Haven't you heard me? Your big brother is a loser. A LOSER—big time!" Jerry was practically yowling now, amazed that his brother could resist the urge to rub his nose in his sins.

Bo's countenance never altered during Jerry's outburst. "There's no need for *me* to berate you," he replied stoically. "You're doing a pretty good job of that yourself. It's not me that convicts of sin. That's God's job. Some people call that process their 'conscience.' I like to think of it as the Holy Spirit. Sounds like He's already working overtime, without my even saying a word."

As Jerry chewed on that statement for a minute and stared dead ahead, Bo continued to speak: "No, Jer, nothing you've told me surprises me. To tell you the truth, I knew that something like this might happen to you some day. Please understand—I don't mean this harshly. I wouldn't want to see you hurt for anything in the world.

"But I had my own day of reckoning a few years ago," Bo went on, "when I hit bottom and hit hard. It took something drastic like an emotional collapse to get my attention and cause me to turn around. If I had it to do over again, I wouldn't take one tortured second away from that day that I began to see the light."

He cut a sideways glance at Jerry, who had leaned his head back in the seat and squeezed his eyes shut. Seeing that his remarks hadn't raised Jerry's hackles so far, Bo went on.

"Jer, we're cut from the same cloth," he said, his voice growing more gentle. "We're products of the same painful upbringing. This life we grew up in—it leaves no one unscathed. We all have to come to terms with it sooner or later, or it'll rip us limb from limb. Mine just happened sooner and yours later. The end result is a good one, if you'll let it be. This could absolutely be your lucky day."

Jerry bolted upright. "What lucky day? Look at this," Jerry laughed almost hysterically. He turned his pants pockets inside out to display only a few coins and a wadded-up tissue that he had grabbed in the men's room of the truck stop. "I have nothing. I have no job, no home, no good name. You expect me to believe that things are going to smell like roses?"

A small, confident smile rippled across Bo's lips. "In my life, I found that when I came to God with empty pockets and an empty heart, that's when He did His best work," he told Jerry. "When I'm totally dependent on Him is when He loves to step in and show me just how powerful He is."

Part of Jerry wanted to shake Bo. *You just couldn't resist, could you?* Jerry wanted to scream, his defenses rising. *You just had to get your religious two-cents in, with me here as a captive audience.*

Yet another part of him was struck with Bo's testimony. So Bo had been at the bottom of the heap, too. His kid brother had also suffered residual pain from their childhood—despite the fact that he'd been the favored one. Jerry hadn't known. He just knew that Bo married Sally a few years back and suddenly began sending him religious tracts and telling him of spiritual changes in his life. Jerry merely presumed it was part of Sally's agreement to marry him—that Bo would embrace her faith. He wasn't exactly sure what kind of collapse Bo had, although Jerry had to admit that he had done little to communicate with Bo over the years.

Jerry tried to swallow back his temper and resist the itch to pick a fight. After all, Bo was carrying him to safety—after a terrifying night of believing he might die out in the weather. Bo had left his home at an ungodly hour with only a smidgen of explanation. Jerry supposed he could put up with a few of Bo's ridiculous attitudes in exchange for the rescue.

He steadied his voice. "So, what do I have to do to be your boarder?" he asked Bo, as he cupped his face in his hands. "I'm sure you have some floors that I could scrub."

"Nope. Sorry," Bo replied, his lips twisting in a small, crooked smile. "The floors are squeaky clean. The boys take care of that part of the ranch."

"OK, then, shear some sheep? Slop some hogs?" Jerry continued, his voice becoming tinged with acidity.

"Wrong again," Bo replied, refusing to rise to the bait. "We're a ranch, not a farm."

Silence hung for another minute, until Bo detected Jerry was ready for some serious conversation. Then he outlined the plan he had mapped out that morning during his long drive to Denver.

"Truth is, Jer, I seriously need an athletic coach. These guys need to learn sports. Many of them couldn't afford to do Little League when they were younger. A few have been in high-school athletics, but most really need some very basic training. The last person I interviewed for the job didn't work out. Now I see why. My jock of a brother was waiting in the wings."

A different kind of thought gripped Jerry. These clearly weren't prep-school kids—different from the privileged ones that skied at Crested Butte.

"Am I gonna get mugged or something?" he asked Bo, guardedly, as anxiety coiled in the pit of his stomach. "Are any of these kids ax murderers? You haven't said exactly who lives at Sky Ranch."

"You'll find some lawbreakers, sure. The state correctional system is one of our contracts," Bo explained. "Some minor offenses only—marijuana possession, petty thievery, property damage. That sort of thing."

Most of the boys at Sky Ranch have struck out in other school settings, Bo elaborated. "They might be truants, runaways, or poor achievers academically. A few have mentioned suicide. Some might simply need behavior-modification, or a more structured learning environment than they had at home.

134

"Sky Ranch goes by strict rules and swift consequences," Bo continued. "The boys attain various levels of compliance. At level 2, they get to fold up their sleeping bags and move to a bed. At level 3, they can phone home. After level 6, they may leave. The average stay is about six months, although some remain as much as two years. The length of stay is basically how long it takes them to learn to act appropriately again."

"Slow learners, then?" Jerry asked, his curiosity building.

"Actually, many of them are quite bright," Bo elaborated. "Sally teaches the younger ones. It's amazing what she's been able to get them to do. In some of the older teens, we've gotten their test scores up to the point that their parents can't believe it—at least, those parents who give a flip. That's been the whole solution in many cases—just getting these kids around people who care."

Bo's eyes took on a paternal glow as he talked about the teens he supervised. *Maybe I can still contribute to society, even with the mess I've made of my life,* Jerry pondered. He visualized himself dusting off some skills he'd scarcely used since high school, when he lettered on every athletic team. Jerry began to relax a little and actually started to relish the prospects.

"So those are my conditions? Room and board, in exchange for playing all day? Such a tough life, Bo," Jerry quipped, breathing a shaky sigh of relief. "That all there is to it?"

Bo cleared his throat and smiled back at Jerry's banter, but his eyes maintained their serious gaze.

"Well, actually, that's not *quite* all," Bo said. "I *do* have a few more things that would be part of the bargain."

Bo would arrange for Jerry to consult with Dr. Naylor, the counselor who drove out from nearby Colby to do individual therapy with the boys weekly.

"I owe everything to Dr. Naylor," Bo explained when Jerry's face begin to writhe in protest. "He's the one who helped me get to the root of what was eating at me, and the one who then persuaded me to take over Sky Ranch later on. When I started my therapy, it was tough work. I must have called him every nasty name in the books at first. He patiently waited things out with me, and it was worth every minute I spent in his office. Every dollar as well. But, Jer, you won't have to pay a cent. Dr. Naylor's on a retainer with us, so you can have regular consultations with him, just like the boys do."

Am I supposed to be grateful, or something? Jerry mulled. "This isn't necessary, Bo," he spat back. "I'm sure that after I'm away from that pressure chamber of Valley Lodge for a few weeks, I'll be back to my old self. I can get a job somewhere. I can start over. That's all I need— just to be free of all those demands. I don't need some shrink prying into my life."

Bo kept his cool. "You probably do feel that way Jerry," he answered softly, his voice remaining steady. "But I found that my troubles always followed me. Oh, the setting and the players might change. But the same patterns of hurt and anger and guilt kept reappearing. Until I got at the core of what caused them, I never made any permanent fixes."

Jerry sat silent and sullen, taking in Bo's words. *Why did I ever call this twerp of a brother, anyway?* he fumed. *What does he think he knows? Here he is sounding like he's some Ph.D. I should just tell Bo no dice and for him to put me out at the next town.*

In the middle of his angry reverie and the thick silence between them, Bo began talking again.

"It's also going to be necessary to make some contact with Valley Lodge," Bo went on. "There'll have to be some closure there. They need to know your whereabouts before I get in trouble for hampering a police search."

"NO!" Jerry shouted, his face reddening to back up the words. "Stop the truck right now," he demanded, clutching the door handle. "I can't take any more of this. It clearly was a mistake for me to call you up. Now, this is good-bye."

To Jerry's surprise, Bo acquiesced. He eased off the gas, braked to pull off the road, and halted the truck, with the engine running.

"Sure, Jerry. Whatever you want," responded Bo, looking dispassionate. "We're just out here in the middle of the plains of western Kansas, with no town and no gas station for miles, where you know no one. You're already exhausted and half-frostbitten. As you pointed out, you have no money. But go ahead. Resist help." He sat quietly, arms crossed, his foot intermittently revving the motor, while he waited for Jerry's decision.

"Can't you call Pop for me?" Jerry finally begged weakly, as pain stabbed at his heart. "I can't face him yet. I don't want him to know where I am. He's just determined enough to send a posse for me. And I can't talk to anyone else—especially Carol. I'm just not ready."

Bo waited patiently until Jerry's fury ebbed. "I never said you had to, did I?" he finally explained. "Someday you *will* need to make the contact. For now, I could do the deed without telling Pop exactly who I am or WHERE I am. I'm just a relative who has you in safe-keeping and who thinks it best at the moment for you to avoid contact with other folks. We can arrange for a post-office box in Colby, where Pop can send your things, if he's willing. You *would* like to get your wallet and your identification back, I presume?"

Jerry raised his eyebrows as he sat frozen. It was the first time he'd thought about retrieving his belongings or starting over the tedious process of getting a new driver's license.

Bo continued, "Oh yes, and just in case Pop decided to sue you for damages the lodge incurred because of your departure, we'd need to offer to settle up financially."

Jerry slammed his hands down on his knees angrily. "Good grief, Bo. Pop would never do that!" he yelled.

"Oh, no?" Bo replied. "People do things that seem out of character for them when they're hurt or when their plans are foiled. Some money-hungry attorney in town might try to influence Pop. My point is, it's best for us to go on the offensive. We need to settle any monetary matters in a gentlemanly way before we have to defend ourselves."

137

Jerry forced his eyes to focus straight ahead, on some unidentified point on the horizon. Then he realized that Bo's truck had continued to sit on the side of the road with the engine still running while they conducted their debate.

With a sweeping gesture toward the highway, he waved Bo to get back on the pavement, to proceed on. In tacit acquiescence, Jerry crossed his arms submissively and turned his body toward the passenger door.

Bo ignored the body language of avoidance. "Glad that's settled," he said, still cheery despite Jerry's frustrating maneuvers. "Now, there's just one more thing I need to tell you about what's expected of people at Sky Ranch."

Jerry grunted but stayed turned away. What more could Bo possibly hit him with? Why did he feel like he was some captive being led off in chains?

"Sky Ranch is a Christian establishment, so everyone goes to church on Sundays, plus we set aside 10 minutes every night for the boys to pray and read the Bible," Bo continued.

Dead, barren silence followed. *I should have known,* Jerry thought grimly, his lips tight with rancor. *Everywhere I go, religion gets crammed down my throat.*

As he started to bleat out his usual objection, however, something struck Jerry. Curiously, Jerry did have to admit that something *had* taken hold of Bo in the past three years and made a difference in his younger brother. The firecracker temper of Bo's youth—the temper that prompted Bo to pop off at Jerry at the slightest provocation—had been replaced by a spirit of gentle restraint and quietude. For several hours now, Bo had endured Jerry's pelleting—his protests, his sarcasm, and back a few miles ago, his efforts to bolt from the truck.

Yet, the entire time, Bo had not yelled but had been composure personified. His steel-willed forcefulness had shone through many times. Bo hadn't let Jerry run over him, but he had held his ground in a calm, sympathetic way. Truly, there was some character change at a deep level in Bo that Jerry couldn't identify, and he wished he could experience it as well. Unlike in bygone days, in Bo he now saw a mien of peace, acceptance, confidence, serenity. At that moment Jerry would have given the whole world to have those qualities.

Maybe if he really tried to fight God a little less this time instead of conjuring up another rebellious act as he had at Valley Lodge, he could find happiness.

So to Bo's last condition, Jerry merely shrugged and replied in a wooden voice, "Whatever."

"Good," Bo nodded, closing the subject. "Now, get some sleep. We're about an hour away from Sky Ranch. We'll have to hit the ground running once we arrive. The boys will be involved in their morning chores. Everyone—faculty included—has a job to do."

Sleep was one suggestion to which Jerry offered no resistance. Folding his arms wearily, Jerry inclined his head onto his seat back and nodded off as the truck continued to vein its way over the Kansas turnpike to Sky Ranch and to Jerry's uncertain future.

THIRTEEN

Answerless Days

❁

Jerry's first glimpse of Sky Ranch was a red bandanna head scarf darting rapidly across his field of vision. The woman wearing it energetically shook out a throw rug. A big gust of wind flapped the rug loose from her hands, and two dark-haired male youths raced after it as it tumbled into the yard nearby.

"Looks like Sally has some help today with cleaning," Bo chuckled. He nodded in his wife's direction, as the two residents retrieved the fly-away object. They helped Sally restore it to the porch across the front of the lemon-colored house.

Jerry realized he had still been asleep when Bo turned the truck off the highway and onto the road that led to the ranch house. He looked back and saw that the road wound past a gleaming white fence and under a wooden archway.

The scene would have looked like any other ranch entrance except that two attendants had begun bolting the gate shut as soon as Bo drove through, and the fence was about two feet higher than would be typical. The mountains that had been Jerry's home for the past six years were now flattened out—replaced by a huge expanse of horizon that gave Sky Ranch its name.

Catching sight of Bo's truck, Sally began running toward it, and the two brothers hauled themselves down from the cab.

If Sally was put off by the fact that Jerry's hair hadn't been combed in more hours than he could count and that his clothing looked—and probably smelled—dowdy, she showed no sign of it. After giving her husband a brief, welcoming kiss, she raced to Jerry's side, beaming.

"Jerry, it's great to see you again!" she gushed, tightening the scarf over her blonde curls. "May I give you a hug?" He noted that Sally waited for his permission before reaching around him in a friendly embrace.

"Sure, if you think you can stand to be near the fella who waked you at three o'clock this morning," Jerry replied. He received his sister-in-law's greeting appreciatively and thought how easily and naturally she reached out to him.

In the few, brief times he'd been around Sally, Jerry had considered her to be a fitting match for his robust brother. She was bright as a Tide box, with a perennially bronzed complexion that gave her a healthy, wholesome appearance. As he gazed down into her sincere brown eyes, he knew he probably looked on the real dynamo behind Sky Ranch and behind his brother as well.

"We'd do anything to get you to visit us," Sally replied cheerily, dismissing his comment. "Now, what do you need? I bet a shower and some lunch might help after all this time on the road."

By this point, Jerry had begun to attract a crowd. Several youthful residents had wandered up to survey the newcomer. Although he wanted to make a good first impression with the teens he would be coaching, Jerry felt awkward in his attire, and probably looked it, too. He knew it wasn't every day that someone showed up wearing party clothes.

"Bo told me this was chore time," Jerry answered Sally. "I don't want to interfere. Give me a job to do now, and I can clean up later."

Bo shook his head, a bemused grin on his face. "Jerry, I've reconsidered your role in chores this morning. I don't think you're quite dressed for the occasion. Let Sally walk you to your quarters, while I help out down at the barn. After lunch, the boys will be back in their classes, and I can show you around this little outfit."

Bo's grin of pride in the ranch he supervised was jarred by a giant tug at his shoulders. A slightly-built, dark-skinned youth began pulling at Bo insistently.

"Bo, you've gotta come quickly," the wiry boy demanded. "Where have you been? I've been waiting for hours to tell you. Choya is about to foal. You've gotta come see, Bo. You've gotta come see."

Bo quickly glanced at Sally, checking his facts. A slight shake of her head wordlessly advised Bo that no birth was imminent just yet and that Rico only needed his attention.

"OK, Rico, thanks for letting me know," Bo told the boy. "Sounds like you're excited about Choya's new baby coming. By the way, Rico, I want you to meet my brother. Jerry, this is Rico."

Jerry extended a hand, but the boy merely scowled, continuing to yank at Bo. "Bo, come quick. Come to the barn, Bo, and let me show you."

Bo lowered himself so that his eyes were level with Rico's. Never changing his tone, he replied directly, "Run on to the barn, Rico, and check on Choya. I'll be along soon." The boy stomped away haughtily but disappeared as Bo instructed.

"Rico feels abandoned when I go away, even briefly," Bo explained when Rico was out of earshot. "He sticks to me like a gum wad. He lived in several foster homes before coming here. Later on, I'll spend some special time with him. He's at a point in his life when he really needs a father-figure."

As Bo followed Rico to a barn that was painted the color of a green highway sign, Jerry absorbed the interchange he had just witnessed. Bo obviously had become very skilled at dealing with the challenges of his work. Part of Jerry felt pride welling up for his sibling. Bo had done the Rutgers family proud, with his ranch operation out here in Kansas.

But another part of Jerry felt jealousy broadside him. *Bo is successful, while my life is a mess,* Jerry thought. *I just botched the best job I'll ever have, and now here I am at my younger brother's mercy.*

Sensing that Jerry's mood had taken a nosedive, Sally motioned for him to follow her on a path that wound past the ranch house and around to the first in a trio of barracks.

"I hope you'll be comfortable here," Sally told him. "Your room's an old storage closet that we converted, but the intern who used it this summer seemed to get along OK. The showers are all public, of course; you'll have to share with the boys. At least you can sleep in privacy. The 'A' barracks you're in is the smallest and quietest of the three."

The room that Sally led him to was indeed spartan. Lacking window or closet, it was furnished with only a single bunk bed covered with a faded, chenille spread. A goose-neck lamp pulled out from the wall, and a small, three-drawer bureau clearly had seen better days. The only decor was a picture of praying hands and a Bible that lay on the dresser. The scent of pine cleaner threaded its way throughout the empty barracks. Jerry deduced that the boys had just finished their morning scrub-down of the bathroom before they moved on to work elsewhere.

On the bed, Sally had laid out some piles of clothes— several pairs of jeans, a few shirts, and even some socks and underwear. "I guessed at your size," Sally confided. "People donate things to us. Some of these have never been worn. If nothing works, let me know. I'll raid Bo's closet if I have to." Jerry tried to smile his thanks.

As Sally left, he thought of the irony of what he was doing—removing a tuxedo that he had worn yesterday at a party that was the social event of Crested Butte to don discarded jeans that do-gooders had given to charity. The weight of his circumstances pressed down on him again. Jerry hurled himself face-down on the small bunk bed mattress that smelled of sawdust and sobbed afresh.

Alone in the windowless room that was all the home he had in the world right now, Jerry reflected for a minute on what this day would have been like if he were back at Valley Lodge. Yesterday's gala would be a sea of pleasant memories, staffers would be glad-handing him, and Carol would be showing off her ring. Pop would be preparing for his move into management, and the future ahead would be bright.

As it was, the lodge was probably still reeling in stunned disarray, Carol's engagement ring was stuffed away in Bo's shirt pocket because Jerry couldn't be trusted with it, and the only job he had on the horizon was to work with a bunch of socially unskilled troublemakers.

Angry tears soaked the flat, mildew-smelling pillow into which Jerry pressed his face at that moment, as desolation held him in its grip again.

When his grief was spent, Jerry caught a whiff of his musty shirt and thought about how good a shower—even one in a public stall that he would soon share with twenty teen-agers—would feel right now. He grabbed the toiletry kit that Sally had thrown together for him and headed for what might be his last chance to bathe in private for many, many days.

With a freshly scrubbed body and clean clothes at last, Jerry decided the world felt brighter, so he made his way down for lunch. He walked in the direction that an arrow pointed to the dining hall and prepared to meet up with Bo.

About a hundred boys were trying to push through the entry door all at once as they scrambled for their meal. Unlike shy, unsociable Rico had been that morning, one of them spotted Jerry, obviously a guest, and sauntered right up to him.

"Hiya. You're new here, aren't you?" he asked, shaking Jerry's hand in a surprisingly bold manner.

"Yup, sure am," Jerry replied. "My name's Jerry. I'm the brother of Bo, your director."

"I'm Greg. Greg Jefferson. I'm from Virginia," answered the copper-haired youth with a sprinkling of freckles dotting his nose.

"Virginia?" Jerry gasped in astonishment. "You're a long way from home." Jerry found himself wondering what could have possibly brought this boy to Sky Ranch. Bright and gregarious, he didn't seem to fit the picture Bo had painted of the rebellious misfits.

"Uh-huh," nodded the clean-cut boy, his dancing eyes suddenly cast down at his toes. "I'm sure homesick. I hope I get to go back soon."

Jerry wasn't sure whether Bo would consider it appropriate for him to ask Greg what brought him to Sky Ranch, so he resisted the urge. Instead, he tried to change the subject quickly.

"Well, Greg Jefferson, you have the same last name as another famous red-haired Virginian," Jerry said, making conversation as the two of them placed their trays on one of the long dining tables. "You wouldn't be related to that well-known American, Thomas Jefferson, would you?"

"Sure," Greg replied, dead serious. "He's my great-great grandfather, with a few more greats added."

Surprise skittered across Jerry's face, and he gaped at Greg. "Really?" he asked. Bo had told him that a few kids from prosperous families were at Sky Ranch, but he hadn't expected to meet one this well-heeled.

As Greg started to nod, an older youth who had overheard the conversation yelled over the din of the eating area, "Aw, Greg. Are you telling that story again? Mister, don't believe him. He always feeds new people that baloney, until they realize what a liar he is. His name is Jep-per-son, with a 'p.' He's not who you think he is."

Greg shrugged the whole thing off and buried his face in his hamburger. For a moment Jerry felt perfectly foolish. He looked gullible in front of a couple of boys he would likely coach. He studied the fizz in his soda as he pondered what to say next.

Then, a thought hit him like a stick of dynamite exploding. *Greg's no different than me,* Jerry said to himself sadly. *A charmer and a con-artist, just like I was at Valley Lodge. I'm just like these kids. Shows I truly belong here—to get remediated like the rest of them.* Although he tried not to let his crestfallen spirits show while he finished his meal, Jerry found himself feeling empty and weak once again. *How seriously I need help!* he thought. *I hope Bo is right about this being a place to heal.*

Bo appeared from behind Jerry. "Ready for your tour?" he asked. Jerry, ripe for a change of pace after the embarrassing incident, jumped up eagerly. "Let me show you what God has created out of a fistful of dreams," Bo directed.

The unseasonable warmth of the January sun was a balm to Jerry's frayed nerves as he strode beside Bo along the walkway that linked the numerous structures comprising the Sky Ranch complex. Jerry had already seen the barracks, the dining hall, and the ranch house, where Bo and Sally lived. Beyond that, Bo showed him classrooms and a picturesque chapel where the boys filed in for Sunday services. In the barn and stable area, residents learned to care for the horses and a few head of cattle as part of their rehab program.

As they passed an open field that Bo envisioned using for football practices, Jerry offered the beginning traces of a smile. An adjacent baseball diamond, already outfitted with a backstop and some small bleachers, sat idle and overgrown. "Just waiting for you," Bo beamed in his brother's direction.

The entire complex, and Bo's complete mastery of it, left Jerry awe-struck.

"I always knew you'd do something big, Bo," he said, letting the wind ruffle through his hair and clear his mind.

"Like I say, Jerry, it wasn't me. God did it. When I came out here two years ago at Dr. Naylor's insistence, this was someone's run-down dude ranch that had gone into foreclosure. Dr. Naylor helped me set up the Sky Ranch Foundation to get contributions from local businesses and from Christian organizations and benefactors throughout the country. We ran a few ads in magazines and newsletters and got listed on the World Wide Web. We're also listed on a nationwide help line that refers families to 'last-resort' centers like this. Now people everywhere know about us; it's very gratifying. The Lord has been good."

Jerry winced inwardly and tried to fight down the column of petty jealousy that rose up in him. How handily Bo had outstripped his struggling sibling! As if reading his thoughts, Bo responded perceptively.

"Jerry, I know this must be hard for you, after what's happened in the past few days," he said, as understanding crept into his eyes. "If the roles were reversed, I'm sure I'd feel a little competitive, too. I hope you'll look on Sky Ranch not as some great empire of mine but as a place that belongs to all of us. Try to see it as a place where you can get your bearings and move on to a successful life. Please be open to what God can do here, brother."

Jerry gave a slight smile of assent which he hoped would pacify Bo, but that smile soon faded into regret. Jerry knew that he must travel many miles before "success" was a word that could be linked with his name any time soon.

Jerry quietly began adapting to the pace and learning Sky Ranch's rhythm. The boys with whom he shared the barracks were testy at first with the new boarder. One morning he emerged from the shower to find his toiletry kit "relocated" onto the window ledge, as a practical joke.

Another time, he awoke to find his face decorated with his own shaving cream—the handiwork of some prankster.

Bo spoke sternly to the barracks' "R.A.," or resident assistant—an older youth who had reached level 6 and was close to release from Sky Ranch—about maintaining stronger discipline. The boy who pulled the shaving cream stunt was identified and given extra chores as consequences.

Gradually things settled down, and the "A" barracks boys actually seemed glad to have an adult in their midst. Several began to confide in Jerry, who reminded them of Bo, and Bo had their respect. Even though trust was a big factor at Sky Ranch, Jerry seemed to make the transition more easily than some newcomer staffers because the director already had established himself as someone who cared for them, and Jerry was the director's brother.

Bo sent Jerry to town to solicit among local businesses for the needed sports equipment for the new athletic program he was to head. Jerry began to follow the ranch's regimen for daily quiet times. Between 9:30 and 9:40 every evening, the time that the ranch set aside for the boys' daily devotions, Jerry closeted himself into his tiny quarters and opened the aging Bible like the ones provided every resident.

As usual, Jerry was easily distracted. He found himself wishing he could obtain some inspiration from the pages of the Good Book, but nothing resonated with him. He felt he was reading words intended for someone else, not for him.

When it came time to write on the sheets that Bo handed out for the boys to use to respond to their Scripture meditations, Jerry struggled to find anything to write in the blanks under the heading, "What God said to me in this passage" and "What I said back to God." He could have written something in Swahili more easily.

As for Bo's demand that contact must be made with Pop and Valley Lodge, Bo seemed to have forgotten about it, or so Jerry thought. Bo hadn't mentioned this commitment he extracted from Jerry on their drive to Sky Ranch. Jerry hoped Bo had let it slip his mind. The semi-denial he had crept into about his life felt comfortable to him. He would prefer to keep from stirring the waters.

On Friday evening, just before Jerry's one-week anniversary of his Sky Ranch arrival, Bo broke the spell.

"Jerry, it's time to call Pop. You've been here a week, and we have a job to do," he said.

Jerry breathed out a long sigh and said nothing, but his heart hammered in his chest so loudly he was afraid it echoed all over the campus.

"I'd like to think you're ready to make the call yourself," Bo continued. "Pop is owed some explanation. I'm sure he'd rather hear it from you than from me. I'd prefer to be out of the middle on this if I could."

Jerry sprang alive, stomping the floor with certainty. "I can't do it; not now, it's too soon!" he said, his face burning hot with conviction. "You said you would. Don't back out on me now."

"I said I *could,*" Bo responded, his voice steady despite Jerry's outburst. "But direct communication is always best. You'll have to someday, Jerry. That's part of your healing. I had hoped that a week might have given you some space to do it now, that's all."

Jerry's fingernails cut into his palms. He was stunned into speechlessness, but he opened his mouth and tried to reply. "What would I say to Pop?" he asked, a small sob choking him as he spat out the words. "That I'm sorry? That I know I ruined his and Carol's dreams? That I've had to come away to make some sense of my life and figure out why I shoot myself in the foot constantly?"

Bo put a comforting arm on his shoulders. "That would do for starters," he replied soothingly, his blue eyes unwavering.

Jerry took a few steps backward, causing Bo's arm to drop to his side. He turned away with his hands on his hips and considered Bo's words.

Then, with a determination he didn't know he had, he faced Bo again. "I want to wait until I can confront Pop, cleansed and whole," Jerry pleaded, holding his head in stubborn defiance. "I want to be confident. I want to be able to look him straight in the eye and speak with understanding. I'm not at that point yet, and I don't know when I will be. When that day comes, I'll know it. Until then, please be my intermediary. You'll know what to say, Bo. You'll know what to say."

Bo's long silence sent a jet of worry coursing through Jerry. He expected Bo to respond with undisguised anger. He swallowed the emotion that rose in his throat and waited for Bo to storm out or threaten to evict him from Sky Ranch.

Bo's only reply was a resigned, "Very well, then. I'll call tomorrow first thing. I'll give you a report afterwards." Then he left, quietly closing Jerry's door behind him.

The next morning, Jerry busied himself by yanking up fistfuls of weeds that had cropped up around the would-be softball diamond. As he savagely grabbed at them, Jerry tried to find some outlet for the anxiety that burned within him as he waited for Bo to appear on the horizon with the dreaded news. By noon the sun was high and penetrating, and he put down his hoe for lunch.

Stopping by his room on the way to the dining hall, Jerry found a note on his bureau that said, "Please see me," in Bo's handwriting. He could feel the hairs on his neck bristle as he read the message. He found Bo waiting in his tiny office that was a converted back porch on the ranch house. Jerry cast him a worried glance that Bo immediately addressed.

"You have nothing to fear, Jerry," Bo began. "Pop's not pressing charges or anything. You're not in any kind of legal trouble. We can all be thankful for that."

"However . . ." Jerry inserted irritably, waiting for the inevitable shoe to drop.

"However," Bo echoed, "as you can imagine, things haven't been pleasant at Valley Lodge." He related the story as spilled out by a broken Pop: During the first, answerless days, Jerry was the subject of a massive police search initially, but officers soon dismissed Jerry's disappearance as a case of engagement cold-feet.

When Bo identified himself only as a relative who had Jerry in safe-keeping, Pop responded angrily, demanding to know Jerry's location. Despite Pop's description of the untold heartache Jerry left behind for Carol and others, Bo firmly insisted that Jerry was better off at present with limited contact so he could work on his emotional and spiritual issues.

Bo arranged with Pop for Jerry's belongings to be mailed to a post-office box in Oakley, Kansas, about thirty miles to the southeast, and offered to repay the lodge for any monetary loss from Jerry's abrupt departure. The only family address that Pop's files at the lodge contained was their mother's on the East Coast. Pop would not have known about a brother in Kansas; therefore, his exact whereabouts was still concealed.

"In the end, he wasn't happy, but he acquiesced," Bo related. "I reiterated for him what you told me last night: that you would face him in person when the time was right."

Jerry blinked back tears and groped for control. He thought of his own answerless days as life loomed ahead as a series of question marks.

As Bo had related the story, Jerry grieved afresh for Carol—knock-dead, gorgeous Carol, her eyes perpetually swollen now from hours of empty tears. He grieved afresh for Pop, already withered from illness, now stooped under the weight of an even more baffling desertion than the worker strike had been. He grieved for his puzzled co-workers as Pop related to them the contents of Bo's call.

Even more than for these, Jerry grieved for himself and realized that he must pull the window shade down on all these people and events and focus only on his needs for a while, if he were to ever have a hope of a future. As he brought his eyes back to Bo's, Jerry blew out a defeated sigh and merely muttered in a hoarse, distant voice, "Thanks." Without anything further, he slammed out of Bo's office.

With all the energy he could muster, he headed back to the softball diamond. The weed patch was still in need of his attention.

FOURTEEN

Treasures from the Deep

❀

"Now swing wide, like this. Keep your eye on the ball."
Jerry reached around Chris, who at fourteen had never
been shown the finer points of softball, and demonstrated
the correct way to hold a bat.

"You can't teach me nuthin'," Chris replied to Jerry's
efforts. The ebony-skinned youth clunked the bat to the
ground loudly. A trail of curses followed him as he ran
off toward his barracks.

"No profanity, Chris. That's back to level 2 for you,"
Jerry shouted as the boy disappeared.

Although Jerry knew few of the boys' individual stories and what had brought them to Sky Ranch, Chris' was
one that Bo had shared. The youth was caught shoplifting
school supplies from a discount store and distributing the
items to poor kids in the housing project where he lived.
When police arrested him for theft, an astute judge picked

up on the boy's need for a parental figure. He referred Chris to Sky Ranch instead of issuing the usual punishment.

Bo had asked Jerry to take particular note of Chris and to try to spend special time with him. But the teen-ager's self-confidence was so low that the slightest mess-up made Chris surly. Jerry had patiently worked with him on learning softball skills, but Chris feared failure so badly that he wasn't making much effort.

Jerry had been at Sky Ranch for nearly a month, and he could easily say his work—or his *attempted* work—with the boys was the most difficult job of his life. Although a few had started to show some spunk at softball practice, most were still in a testing mode. They looked for ways to play pranks behind Jerry's back and interrupt him when he was teaching them.

The few boys who really seemed serious about learning how to play were those who had reached level 6 and were slated to return home soon. At this particular moment, it looked unlikely that Sky Ranch would have a softball team by late spring, as Bo had hoped.

What am I doing in a place like this? Jerry found himself asking no less than a dozen times a day. At Valley Lodge he had rubbed shoulders with people who really desired to perfect their skills. Here, at Sky Ranch, he was throwing his pearls before swine. *These kids should be grateful that they have my expertise around, but they could care less,* he grumbled to himself after Chris' disappearance.

That afternoon, he spilled some of this frustration to Dr. Naylor, with whom he was consulting regularly now, as Bo specified.

"What bothers you about them?" Dr. Naylor asked, whirling around briskly in his chair in a manner that nettled Jerry. He turned his back so that all Jerry could see of the counselor was the top of his balding head with its kinky, nickel-colored hair and his feet propped on the window ledge as he reclined behind his desk.

"They're acting out," Jerry complained. "They're taking their frustrations out on me. It's like an outcry for attention. They feel like they're not worthy enough to get someone interested in what's really wrong with them, so they'll get attention any way they can."

"Hmm," Dr. Naylor replied. He let a huge silence fall between them until Jerry wondered if the therapist had dozed off to sleep in his chair. His squat body was now so slumped down in his seat, Jerry could see nothing emerging over the leather headrest. Then, the doctor continued, "Tell me, have you ever felt like that before?"

Jerry smarted at the question. *How dare this guy?* Jerry thought. So far, Jerry had been vastly disappointed in this counseling experience. He looked forward to these enforced sessions about as much as eating paper. *How in the world could Bo say he personally owed everything to this bizarre shrink?*

Jerry had presumed that Dr. Naylor would empathize with him and tell him he was right for leaving behind all the pressure at Valley Lodge. He had expected the counselor to decry Pop's tactics and to declare Jerry an innocent victim.

Instead, the counselor, whose beady eyes were so stern that they could freeze hot butter, seemed to be trying to get Jerry to claim responsibility for his failings.

Any time Jerry started a sentence with, "But Pop . . .," Dr. Naylor repeated the same line: "You're not here to fix Pop. The only person you can fix is yourself. That doesn't excuse Pop for his mistakes. But the only person you'll have to answer for before God someday is yourself. Let's work on the one that you have 'fixing rights' to, OK?"

Today's counseling session, in the wake of Chris' rude behavior and the repeated disrespect on the part of all the boys, had the same theme.

"Let me just ask you, Jerry," Dr. Naylor interrogated. He pulled his half glasses far down on the bridge of his nose and shifted his eyes over the tops of them—another of his frustrating quirks. "What do you wish Chris would have done in this situation you just described? What would have helped you know how to meet his needs?"

Jerry didn't have to think for long on how to answer that one. "Instead of misbehaving, I wish he could tell me that he's not resisting because of me personally, but that he feels afraid he'll fail, and that's what keeps him from trying and causes him to shoot himself in the foot.

"Now, because he used profanity in front of me, he'll have to go back to sleeping on the floor of the barracks, just when he had achieved bunk status. Those are the rules around here. That's what Bo told me to do. Chris messed up just when he was on the brink of achieving."

"My friend, I'm asking you to listen to your very words," the counselor replied. He leaned so far across the desk toward him that Jerry could see his reflection in the doctor's mini-glasses. "It might help you understand these guys if you think about times when you've done the same thing. How easy was it for you to speak up for your needs? Did you ever tell Pop how pressured you were feeling, or how you felt when he tried to matchmake for you? Don't I recall you doing something to shoot yourself in the foot on the biggest night of your life?"

Jerry felt like slamming his fist on the doctor's desk and kicking his chair into the window. "Just exactly how was I supposed to tell Pop anything?" Jerry tiraded. "Pop had had a heart attack—and a relapse. Then the walkout happened. He was at the breaking point already. Surely you don't mean I was supposed to tell him off and run the risk of killing him."

Dr. Naylor let Jerry's words echo throughout Bo's small office that he borrowed for the counseling sessions when he visited Sky Ranch. "I didn't say anything about telling him off. Here, I want you to look at something," he finally advised. He picked up a sheet of paper and placed it in Jerry's hands.

Jerry scanned the paper absently and saw several long columns of words. They were adjectives that fell under a dozen or so overall headings. Jerry reviewed it momentarily, then look up at Dr. Naylor blankly.

"So?" he asked dully. "What's this supposed to mean?"

"Look at these words," the doctor instructed. "They're in categories of feelings, like angry feelings, sad feelings, and so on. Pick a couple. Tell me how you felt, for example, when Pop tried to rush things with you and Carol—

when he took steps that you wanted to initiate on your own."

Jerry bristled, clenching his fists so tightly that his knuckles went white. "I didn't come here for a grammar lesson. You have no right to waste my time," he yelled angrily. How long would it be until this interminable counseling session ended, anyway?

"You're proving my point right now, Jerry," Dr. Naylor replied. A knowing smile crossed his face. "The only way you know how to deal with frustration is either hold it all in and say nothing—or to tell someone off, to be confrontive, like you just did. Now, I'm serious. Which of these words would apply to how you felt then?"

Jerry had a befuddled expression as he looked at the paper. "I don't know what you . . ."

"Tell me, Jerry. Have you ever used words like this in your conversation? When you were growing up, did you ever say to your parents, 'I feel hurt because someone hit me at school today'? Did you ever say, 'I feel embarrassed because I made a bad grade on a test'?"

Jerry stared a hole through a tape dispenser on the desk, as though the object might yield the answer to Dr. Naylor's question. Finally he blared, defensively, "Of course not. That would have upset things. We had to keep things calm and quiet for Dad. He was sick. We couldn't rock the boat."

"He wasn't sick," the counselor fired back quickly. "He was drunk, right? That's what you've told me about your home life. The goal was, keep things calm around Dad and maybe he won't go into a rage . . . or won't be frustrated to the point of getting drunk again." Dr. Naylor's eyes suddenly lost their stern look and became deeply earnest as he asked the questions. Jerry sensed that the doctor wasn't trying to be mean, but his probing into these sensitive areas was about as comfortable as a paper cut.

"You're prying . . ." Jerry began, his hostility starting to spew.

"Jerry, how do you feel right now that I've asked you these questions?" the counselor asked quietly, not responding to Jerry's rancor.

"I want to get out of here. I don't want to be a part of this anymore," Jerry said caustically. He started to turn around in his chair and charge toward the door.

"The truth is, you feel shame, don't you?" Dr. Naylor gently pressed. "You feel shame about your dad's condition. You feel shame when I remind you what you told me about his drunkenness. You feel afraid when I suggest ways that you might have spoken up for your needs when you were growing up."

A small sob escaped Jerry's lips. Lowering his chin to his chest and letting a tear escape his eyelid, he nodded slightly, as he stared at his knees.

Dr. Naylor no longer whirled in his chair but faced him squarely, his eyes full of understanding. He went on to explain: What Jerry described was typical in families where a parental addiction, such as alcohol, governed those families' activities. In contrast to healthy families, in which various family members get their chance to be "needy"—that is, have a chance to air their feelings without fear of reprisal—everyone has to tiptoe around the addict, just as Jerry described. Children in those families won't get their needs met because all the attention is focused on the one needy family member. Usually feelings are suppressed—or only certain feelings are allowed. So it wouldn't be uncommon at all for someone like Jerry to be handed a "feelings chart" like the one Dr. Naylor showed him and to respond to it like it was written in a foreign language.

"In families with unhealthy patterns, words like this are like Greek," the doctor continued. "I gather you really aren't accustomed to speaking up for your needs, and when you do, it's usually in some stormy outburst that leaves you feeling guilty later."

Jerry nodded in quiet assent, his eyes still on the floor. This time, he offered no objection to Dr. Naylor's latest summary and studied it thoughtfully.

"See, you're an important person, Jerry," Dr. Naylor continued, as he evaluated Jerry's thoughtful gaze. "God created you as someone special, and God doesn't make junk. The Bible tells you that you're to love your neighbor as yourself. A lot of people get confused with that. They focus merely on the 'love thy neighbor' part and forget that it says you're to love yourself, as well. When you value yourself, you speak up for your needs."

"So?" Jerry asked with a shrug, wondering what those statements had to do with his dilemma.

"So, why don't you answer the question I asked you originally?" the therapist continued. "How did you feel when Pop tried to matchmake for you?"

Jerry looked bewildered. Dr. Naylor pointed to the list, and he surveyed it. "I guess I felt intruded upon," he finally answered. "I wish I could have proceeded at my own pace."

"Good, very good," Dr. Naylor nodded in assent. "See—you said it. You described your feelings, you did it courteously without raising your voice, and the world didn't cave in on you, did it? Now go one step further. You've told me that you often wished Carol had picked up on some of the distress signals you were sending off. How did you feel when she didn't?"

At first Jerry frowned, then remembered that the list might help him out. "I felt . . . I felt abandoned," he said, scanning the columns of words again for one that might fit. "I felt lonely. I felt I was suffering, and no one cared enough to ask me what was wrong. I felt like they were trying to accomplish their own agenda and were paying no attention to mine."

"And you deserve better. Right?" the doctor pushed.

"If you say so," Jerry said, acquiescing.

"OK, I do say so. You're a person of worth. God created you to be worthy, and you deserve better," Dr. Naylor pronounced. "When you start seeing yourself this way, you'll be able to demonstrate for others how you want to be treated. In the meantime, I suggest that you take this chart home, study it, and use it with your boys. See if you can get them to verbalize what's *really* going on with them when they refuse to listen to you. See if you can teach them a way of getting their needs met besides temper tantrums and rudeness—or simply sulking away. I promise you—there is a middle ground."

Jerry knew it would take longer than just a few days to digest all that had happened during that momentous visit. He still didn't know why Dr. Naylor had to dredge up old wounds from his childhood. He thought it was better to bury the past and move on.

He did have to admit there was something cleansing about finally being able to put a label on his feelings toward Pop and Carol. He *was* angry at them, for the reasons he had stated. Something about just admitting it during that counseling visit enabled him to view the world through slightly different glasses that afternoon.

Jerry soon had his first opportunity to use the feelings chart with Chris. Jerry saw the boy in the dining hall and asked him to come out to the ball diamond to hit a few.

When Chris balked and began darting out the door, Jerry tugged on his arm, beckoning him back. "Chris, tell me something. When I ask you to let me teach you, and you refuse, what's happening with you? How do you feel?" Jerry asked. He still formed the word "feel" a little gingerly, since it was new to his repertoire.

The boy merely stared, blinking amber-colored eyes at him at first. Then Chris replied, "Oh, you sound like Dr. Naylor and Bo. They're always asking me questions like that. I hate it when they do."

"OK, so you hate it, but what's the answer?" Jerry pressed. "When I show you how to hit the ball and ask you to do it, do you feel embarrassed, angry, humiliated, sad, afraid? Or something else?"

"That one—that last one. I feel afraid," Chris finally sputtered out.

"Afraid? Of me? Are you afraid I'll do something to hurt you?" Jerry questioned him.

"No. Afraid I won't do good; afraid that you won't like me if I do bad," Chris spat back. "My daddy stopped liking me when I messed up. He ran away. I thought you might, too." Suddenly uncomfortable, he pulled against Jerry's arm that had been resting on his shoulder and tried to spring free. "I gotta go now."

"You can go, Chris, but I want to thank you for being honest with me," Jerry said. He hesitated, as memories of

Valley Lodge and his own overwhelming fear of failure stampeded through him so powerfully he could hardly get the words out, "I've felt that way myself before. I've been afraid I'd disappoint someone. I understand."

By that time, Chris had slammed the dining room door and was gone. But in their brief interchange, Jerry thought maybe he now held the key to working with Chris—and perhaps the others, too.

If he could somehow convince the youth that he would accept them no matter what, if he could encourage them to express their feelings instead of turning to harmful behaviors, he might get beyond the bluster and actually do some real coaching.

Suddenly, things beyond simply how to teach softball to belligerent teen-agers came into focus as well. His dad's critical nature, his intense fear of failure—all these things had kept him in his comfort zone over the years. They kept him in "safe" jobs—from any kind of risk-taking. They had kept him at the comfortable ski apparel shop in Boulder long after he should have moved on. At Valley Lodge, when he started to panic that he could never learn new skills, his fears and memories had sent him back to the ski slopes as a security blanket any time he started to feel threatened. His liaison with Pop had been too close a reminder that the bugbear of disapproval could be just around the corner —even though, in truth, Pop had never expressed disapproval of him a day in his life.

Jerry felt an unexpected eagerness to go to his next session with Dr. Naylor. Instead of viewing it as a time-waster, Jerry saw the direction the counselor was headed with him and what he was trying to accomplish.

Certainly, uncovering past, painful memories was unpleasant. But maybe, just maybe there were more links than Jerry was willing to admit between his painful childhood and his current dilemma.

Just as Bo had assured him, probing in those deep, long-untouched places of his heart did seem to unlock buried treasure—treasure that just might help him make the mid-course correction in his life that he needed.

FIFTEEN

In the Father's House

Dr. Naylor's treasure hunt into the depths of Jerry's life became more bold in subsequent weeks. Jerry sent off signals that his crust of defenses was starting to crumble and that he was actually willing to do some productive work in the counselor's office.

Their sessions seemed to go in all directions. Sometimes they investigated why Jerry reverted to the con-artist role when things got tough. Jerry had learned that tactic in order to survive in his family of origin—not exactly lying, but not exactly telling the truth, either. Such duplicity kept him from being the brunt of his father's anger if he thought his behavior would let his father down.

They also delved into Jerry's tendency to bolt—why running away seemed to be his first line of defense, just like he had tried to do in Dr. Naylor's office when things got uncomfortable—and of course, had ultimately done at Valley Lodge. Jerry had seen this in the Sky Ranch youth, like Chris, as well.

"Your family pattern was to ignore your feelings instead of facing them," the counselor explained. "It's always easier to fly the coop than deal with what's really going on."

That tendency also caused him to shut down his grief over Natalie prematurely—to escape from Boulder rather than looking his loss squarely in the face and processing it over time, Dr. Naylor added. Unprocessed grief was what caused Jerry's sudden preoccupation with Natalie even after he fell in love with Carol, he told his client.

"Bolting, and shutting down emotions, may seem simpler, but it never settles things, really," the counselor advised him.

How well Jerry knew that one by now. Here he was several hundred miles away from Valley Lodge, but the hurt and pain accompanied him every minute of the day.

It was probably those aspects of the visits with Dr. Naylor—the occasions when he could just let the pain flow uninhibited—that were the most healing. Many times, the therapist merely listened to Jerry talk and then followed with the same type of affirming statement Bo made that day in the truck, "I'm sure that really hurt a lot" or "I'd feel awful, too, if that had happened to me."

Suddenly all those old childhood memories—Dad's drunken rages, Dad's long absences, hurtful criticisms, constant disapproval—could be reflected on and cried over, without Jerry fearing that Dr. Naylor would flinch. One day, after he poured out the sordid details of growing up in a home with liquor bottles hidden under the sofa, he looked up to see the counselor just sitting there, nodding and blinking at him with sympathetic eyes.

"You mean you still want to see me? You still like me after knowing all this stuff?" Jerry finally begged.

"I care about you, Jerry," was all the counselor replied. "I'll be here for you no matter what." When Jerry truly was trying to face issues, Dr. Naylor showed his approval by making eye contact with him again and stopping that preposterous whirling around in his chair.

On another occasion, they examined why Jerry had thought at Valley Lodge that he must assume more and more tasks without alerting Pop that he was overworked and why he thought he must perform all duties himself. Dr. Naylor helped Jerry see that his shame-based identity, which made him feel that something was intrinsically wrong at his very core, gave him a "works mentality."

"It seems that you're thinking, 'If I just do enough, it will make me acceptable'," the doctor explained. "At Valley Lodge, you were still playing those old tapes in your head."

Jerry nodded that such a supposition might be possible. Dr. Naylor reminded him, "You know, Jerry, what the Bible says about works, don't you? It says in Ephesians 2:8-9 that by grace you have been saved through faith in Christ and not by works, so that no one can boast. It's the Bible's way of saying that nothing that we do can make us seem any better in God's eyes. He created us. He sent Jesus Christ to die for us. He loves us without condition. We can't perform our way into heaven."

Jerry could swallow almost everything but that. When Dr. Naylor began quoting Scripture to him, it automatically gnawed a hole in his stomach—a reaction that he knew the counselor detected. Jerry hoped the doctor would never confront him about it, since it was so inexplicable to him, as well.

One day, however, Dr. Naylor handed him a series of charts. "I want you to fill out these today," he told Jerry. One chart was entitled "I see my father as . . ." and contained a series of boxes with various characteristics—everything from "loving," "gentle," "trustworthy," "forgiving," to "stern," "violent," "critical," "undependable." Jerry was to check these, where applicable.

"That's easy," Jerry remarked, making his checkmarks quickly. Any unflattering category that was listed netted Jerry's marks for his dad. "I've told you this already," he said to Dr. Naylor petulantly. "What difference does this chart make?"

"Because I want you to do this second one as well," Dr. Naylor told him. He handed Jerry a similar chart. It had the same categories, only the heading read, "I see God as . . ."

Jerry's brows met in a frown. "I don't get it. Why . . . ." he began.

"Just answer as best you can," said Dr. Naylor patiently.

Jerry studied the chart. Certainly he didn't see God as available or dependable. Nor did he see God as loving. God was the source of all that had gone wrong in his life. *Gentle?* Nope. *Trustworthy?* No again. If he told the truth, he'd have to say that God to him was harsh, critical, undependable . . . the same things he said about his father.

"Do you get the picture?" the counselor asked, moving to Jerry's side of the desk so he could survey Jerry's work. "Our concept of our Heavenly Father is largely related to how we look at our earthly parents—in your case, particularly the male one."

"But these things are true," Jerry protested. "God's never done a thing for me." He looked to see if Dr. Naylor was shocked at his bold statement.

"Let's see if they are," Dr. Naylor replied calmly, opening the Bible on the desk. "Here's what the Bible says about God." He read two verses: Psalm 103:8, "The Lord is compassionate and gracious, slow to anger, abounding in love," and Psalm 46:1, "God is our refuge and strength, an ever-present help in troubles."

"I don't care what the Bible says. I only know what I know in my heart," Jerry said.

"Exactly my point, Jerry," the counselor continued gently. "They say the longest distance in the world is the one between the head and the heart. The reason you don't know this in your heart, Jerry, is because your dad was your earthly representation of the Heavenly Father. That's the only role model you had to draw from. It may surprise you to know this happens all the time with the people I counsel. Until they get their heart knowledge equal to their head knowledge of God, they have a permanent barrier to things of the Spirit."

Jerry started to argue again but stopped. He *did* have a barrier to God. How many times had he filled out his quiet time sheets, or attempted to, since he came to Sky Ranch, only to realize that God hadn't said a word to him.

He truly had sought to read the Scriptures and understand how they applied to him today. At Valley Lodge he had wanted to experience the same kind of personal, everyday faith that Pop and Carol exemplified. At Sky Ranch he saw daily how Bo and Sally lived out the teachings of Christ in the self-sacrificing way they took care of the difficult youth. He always wondered why, when Pop began speaking of faith matters, the picture of his father somehow mysteriously always entered his mind. Was this why Jerry and God always seemed to be in some arm-wrestling match? He looked past Dr. Naylor and let the thoughts bounce around through his mind for a few minutes, wordlessly.

The counselor went on. "Jerry, the God of the Bible *is* trustworthy. He *can* be depended upon. He *is* loving. He gave you the ultimate gift. He sent His Son to die for you. God knew all along that there would be a Jerry Rutgers and that he would sin and that he would need forgiveness. He wants you to have abundant life, but He knew that your sin would keep you from it. He gave up His only Son for your very soul. Because of that, nothing in the world you could ever do can make Him stop loving you. His love is irrevocable. He's the Father you can depend on—the Father who won't fail you."

"But Natalie . . . but my rotten childhood," Jerry protested.

"I have a feeling God's heart broke when Natalie died," Dr. Naylor said compassionately. "He doesn't want bad things to happen to the ones He created. But we're not robots. The plane she was riding on crashed into a mountain. The laws of gravity are no respecter of persons. Your dad was a sinner who needed the Lord. He had the choice to accept Him or reject Him. By his choice, your dad hurt many people, including you. God wanted him to choose otherwise. 2 Peter 3:9 says God doesn't want any of His children to perish in sin.

"But in all those things, Jerry, though God didn't cause them, he worked for your good in spite of them. He helped you survive those rotten days and gave you skills to pull yourself up by your bootstraps. Even when you weren't grieving properly, He helped you through your loss of Natalie and sent you friends to comfort you—and ultimately a new job and another woman to bring love into your life. Now, He's brought you here, to be around loving family, to heal. That was God who did that, Jerry. That wasn't just some coincidence. Through it all, He's been your friend."

Jerry batted away tears. "You say you've seen others like me—who have this same dad/God struggle?" he questioned in a broken voice.

"Yep, in fact, someone very close to you. I heard these same arguments out of your own brother once, years ago," Dr. Naylor said, smiling a little in remembrance.

"Oh, don't worry," the therapist quickly added, making the covert overt. "I'm not betraying a client privilege. Bo gave me his full permission to use his story any time I thought it might help people."

Bo. Suddenly Jerry yearned to see his brother. Bo hadn't pried about his visits with Dr. Naylor. Bo never let on if he knew what Jerry and the counselor talked about during their two months of work.

With these new facts in his head, Jerry wanted to hear from Bo first-hand. Bo seemed to have it so together spiritually. It helped to know that he had once struggled in this very arena as well. Jerry said a quick good-bye to Dr. Naylor, who didn't seem shocked at all at his request, and headed for the ranch house.

Jerry found Bo seated at the kitchen table, buried under a pile of income tax papers that were spread out on the table's red-and-white-checked cloth. Bo seemed a bit surprised to see his brother at the door, his face bearing an anxious expression, but he quickly motioned Jerry in.

"Well, look who's here," he called out cordially, pulling up a chair.

Jerry seated himself and quickly described to Bo the flow of the evening's dialogue with the therapist. "I just had to hear you say it, Bo," he begged. "Did you hate God too at one time because of Dad? What got you to the point where God could really be someone important to you instead of someone you were always fighting?"

Although immersed in business matters, Bo saw the opportunity he had been waiting on for weeks had finally fallen in his lap.

"I don't guess I ever really told you much about what led me to this point in my life," Bo interposed. "I fell madly in love with Sally, except there was this big difference in us. She was a dedicated Christian, and by that time, I hated everything that Christians stood for. She laid the law down: she wouldn't even date me until I started going to church, and she refused to get serious about me until I knew the Lord. So I did it—I told her that I asked Christ into my life, just like she wanted me to. Now, I realize I was just going through the motions. I was mainly doing it for Sally.

"Then, a week before our wedding, I went off the deep end. I wasn't yet at peace with myself, so I began drinking heavily—just like I did before Sally and I met. I got arrested for drunken driving. The judge saw I didn't have a record and agreed to suspend my sentence if I'd see a counselor. That's when I first met Dr. Naylor.

"For weeks Sally put the wedding on hold while I straightened up the mess I'd made of my life. Only when I began to understand the harmful family patterns and the hold the past had on me could I truly understand why Christ died for me. See, even though my past had primed me toward acting a certain way, I couldn't blame everything on Daddy. I made a conscious choice about whether to sin. I realized that I was a sinner—that I needed God horribly. Only when I understood that God wasn't Daddy did I see the kind of relationship I'd been missing that was mine for the taking. That's when I confessed Jesus in my heart, not just in my head."

Jerry looked at his brother squarely. Now he knew what Bo meant on their way to Sky Ranch when he said an emotional collapse ultimately led him to a life of peace.

"Why didn't you tell me all this that day in the truck—when I unloaded all the bad things that happened to me at Valley Lodge?" Jerry pelleted him.

"I'm not sure it would have served a purpose, Jerry. You had to realize these things on your own, in your own time. It would have seemed just like one more sermon to you then. But I want you to know—I *do* understand," Bo said, laying a sympathetic hand on his shoulder.

Jerry laughed a little. "You're right, it probably would have. Sermons right then, I didn't need."

Bo gave Jerry a long, studied look. Because Jerry's gaze was downward, he didn't see Bo close his eyes momentarily, his lips moving slightly in prayer. Then, with eyes open and shoulders squared, Bo sensed the time was opportune. He took the crucial plunge.

"But, Jerry, it's not a sermon now, is it? I detect that somehow you've made the connection, just like I did a few years back. You see that God has been pursuing you in a love relationship with Him. You see that He's vastly different from the earthly dad we both knew. You know that God's been waiting for you all this time, don't you?"

Jerry's eyes misted at Bo's words. "He's had to put up with a lot out of me while He waited," Jerry replied.

Bo breathed out a satisfied sigh and pressed further. "He puts up with a lot from all of us. But that's because, as it says in 1 John 2:1, He has Jesus at his right hand acting as our advocate. Jesus is there telling Him, 'It's OK, Father. I've wiped the slate clean for this one.' Because of that, when we confess, God remembers our sins no more."

He continued. "Jerry, Jesus is waiting to enter your heart just like He did mine. I had denied Him for so long, because I couldn't imagine He wanted me—flawed as I was. But John 3:16 says 'whoever believes on Him.' It didn't say 'Everybody but Bo has everlasting life'. It doesn't say 'Everybody but Jerry.' The word is 'whoever.' Would you like to take that step of faith to trust Him tonight? If you would, I'll help you."

Jerry knew what Bo meant. Sunday after Sunday, he had seen the boys from Sky Ranch respond during chapel services and pray at the altar to receive Christ. He had heard the minister explain to them how to invite Christ to be Savior: then repent, then confess, and then receive Christ as the way to salvation. He had heard the words, and he had seen the joyful looks in their eyes. But he had never fully realized until tonight that a loving God who wasn't like Daddy was actually wanting him—yes, him—Jerry!—to respond, too.

As Jerry's eyes searched Bo's genuine ones that looked like they could see clear to the depths of his soul, Bo continued speaking. He said, "Jerry, I'll just say a prayer like you've heard me say with the boys several times. After I've said it, if this is the desire of your heart, just repeat after me. The prayer goes: 'Father, I know I am a sinner, and I ask You to forgive me. I know You died on the cross to save me and to give me eternal life. Jesus, I ask You this very night to come into my heart and make You my Savior and Lord from this moment on. Amen.'"

Bo slid out of his kitchen chair and knelt on the floor by the table. He gestured for Jerry to do likewise. For a moment there was silence, and then Jerry was by his side—kneeling, with his hands folded on the seat of the chair, his head bowed, his chin on his chest.

"Great, Jerry," Bo whispered, his voice strained with emotion at this highly significant moment. He laid his arm around Jerry's shoulder, and the two of them prayed the prayer together—Jerry's voice tearful but strong as they made it to the last "Amen."

Bo's eyes opened first and met Jerry's moisture-filled ones as he lifted his head. "Jerry, my brother, and now my brother in Christ," Bo pronounced, his heart bursting at the significance of the event. Jerry buried his head on his brother's shoulder and sobbed. For several moments, they remained kneeling by the table, the chair supporting their arms as they leaned on it, their two blond heads pressed together.

Finally, Bo got them both seated back in the chairs again. He reached for some paper towels to serve as tissues.

"Look what I interrupted," Jerry commented, his eyes scanning the mounds of paperwork that Bo had been involved in. Then he checked himself. "But then, according to Dr. Naylor, I'm not supposed to apologize. If you hadn't wanted my company, you would have told me. "

Bo blew his nose loudly on the paper towel and nodded as he blotted his eyes. Finally, beaming at Jerry, he replied, "This is the best interruption I've ever had in my life—the night of my brother's salvation!"

"You did it, Bo," Jerry assured him. "You brought me here. You made me see Dr. Naylor, you lived a Christlike life in front of me. You helped me see the light."

"No, you did it," Bo said in rebuttal. "It's a step that a person must take for himself. No one can do it for you. I just provided the environment where God could work."

Almost in unison, the brothers seemed to have the same thought. "It's really Sally who is at the heart of this," Jerry declared, good-naturedly. "When she laid down the law to you and refused to marry you as a heathen, look what she started!"

"Let's call her," Bo offered. Soon Sally, wearing a pink terry robe and a pink headband over her profusion of blonde curls, appeared in the doorway—blinking from sleep but jubilant at the news. Her own tears of joy were soon mixed with those of the brothers as the three of them exulted over what had happened in the ranch-house kitchen that night.

When Jerry's head at last hit his mildew-smelling pillow, it was not as a child of God who had everything in life settled. Jerry knew that his journey toward wholeness had just begun—that many more treasures from the deep would need to be extracted in this expedition into his soul that was occurring at Sky Ranch.

But as his head hit his pillow, it was as a child of God who for the first time in his life knew Father as one who could be trusted, who cared, and who loved him unconditionally.

With those thoughts dancing around through his head, he fell into one of the most blissful slumbers he could ever remember.

SIXTEEN

The Long Journey Back

❀

Once Jerry discovered the source of his spiritual rebellion and became a new creature in Christ, he was like a veritable sponge. As though making up for lost time, he began soaking up knowledge about the Christian life so avidly that he could hardly pump those around him fast enough for information.

He found himself returning to his room each night far earlier than usual, so he could begin the quiet time process he once disdained. Poring over his assigned Scripture passages for that evening, he actually looked forward to answering the questions on his quiet time sheets that Bo distributed to all the ranch residents each day.

Now that God was becoming both the Father of his heart and his head, he was eager to fill in the daily exercise, "What God said to me" and "What I said back to God." It was like discovering gold to realize that the words of the Bible were guideposts for living as though they had been addressed to him personally. Even better, he could respond back to them.

Of all the passages that he read—and even began memorizing, as Bo encouraged the teen residents to do—two stood out as the most comforting of all. They were the Scriptures that Dr. Naylor gave him during the next counseling session after Jerry trusted Christ as he knelt on Bo's kitchen floor. When he told Dr. Naylor about the step of faith he took following their last, dramatic visit, the counselor wrote down for him two verses: Romans 8:1, "Therefore, there is now no condemnation for those in Christ Jesus," and Psalm 25:3, "No one whose hope is in you will ever be put to shame."

"I hope you'll be able to see yourself in that light now," Dr. Naylor offered. "It doesn't mean that you won't continue to have slumps or low self-worth attacks. But you can remember that Christ died to wipe out condemnation for you. If your hope is in Him, nothing can truly put you to shame again. He—and not anything you've done—is the source of your identity."

"It's all starting to fit like never before," Jerry told him, his eyes containing a spark that he hardly recognized when he looked at himself in the mirror. On some mornings, when the freshness of his new life dawned on him, Jerry had the same exhilarating feeling he had experienced at the top of the ski run as he pushed off to soar down the slopes. For the first time in his life, his heart was actually learning to soar free of all the things that had shackled him—both spiritually and emotionally.

Bo arranged for Jerry to be baptized at the church in Colby that opened its baptistry to Sky Ranch residents whenever any of the boys began their Christian journey. On a Sunday night in early April, the minister took Jerry through the baptismal waters—as a symbol of his death to an old life and his birth into a new one. A delegation of about twenty staff and residents from Sky Ranch, including Dr. Naylor, sat in the congregation in support of him.

Afterwards, Sally fixed a giant, celebratory meal and invited in all the residents. Bo asked Jerry to give his testimony to the group. After all enjoyed heaping portions of dessert, Jerry stood to speak briefly.

Still a little awkward as he verbalized about his new faith, Jerry told the boys, "I'm glad it's never too late for Jesus to accept me as I am. But I wish I had become a Christian long ago—when I was your age. I could have been in step with God all these years. Knowing Christ is changing my life day by day. Don't put it off. Then you won't have to regret all the time you wasted."

Jerry surveyed the unlikely but devoted new "family" gathered around him. Suddenly, he was hit with the surprising urge for Pop and Carol, wherever they were, to know about this amazing thing that had happened in his life. Of late, Jerry tried not to let himself think about the two of them very much, other than when he had to in the therapist's office. Allowing his thoughts to roam back to Valley Lodge days was unnecessary pain. Sky Ranch was his world now, and he was determined to move ahead with his life.

The fact that he had now trusted Christ—the One that was the centerpoint of their very existence—made Jerry feel a strange kind of kinship with Pop and Carol that transcended the pain of past history. *What would they think of Jerry Rutgers, the consummate con-artist, master of verbal legerdemain, standing up in front of a group of people and confessing his sins?* he wondered.

Then he caught the improbability of this proposal. *Like Pop and Carol would even talk to me—like they'd even believe me . . . or care,* he thought sadly. Jerry knew that Pop would most certainly slam the telephone down on him the minute he heard Jerry's voice. As for Carol, well—even thinking about what he might ever say again to the fiancee he spurned was beyond his total comprehension.

However, Pop and Carol had actually started to become more and more the focus of his time with Dr. Naylor in the wake of his new religious ardor. Christ's forgiveness of him was intrinsically real to Jerry now, as he gleaned from Scriptures the fact that his sins were truly as far as the East is from the West. It was incredible to him that the Bible promised that nothing he'd ever done— not the sexual indiscretions, not the duplicity, not even the unthinkable desertion of Valley Lodge—was remembered even for a second by Creator God.

As he studied his Bible daily, he read about when Jesus forgave those who crucified him—not just people who had failed to meet His needs, but the very people who took His life. He read in Ephesians 4:32 where Paul said, "Be kind and compassionate to one another, forgiving each other, just as in Christ God forgave you."

Soon Jerry realized that the "forgiving each other" part was a mandate for him. He knew, for starters, he must forgive Pop and Carol for their actions at Valley Lodge that he continued to hold against them.

"But how do I do it?" he asked Dr. Naylor one afternoon when the subject came up in yet another session. Jerry understood that forgiveness didn't mean condoning, it didn't mean the other person was right, and it didn't mean continuing to make yourself a doormat to someone.

"Does it happen only when the pain stops?" Jerry queried. "If so, I may be waiting forever. The pain of Valley Lodge may not ever go away, or at least not any time soon."

At that question, Dr. Naylor reached into his pocket and removed his billfold. Jerry watched curiously as he unfolded a small slip of paper stuffed among a handful of credit cards. The paper was a sheet torn from a desk calendar. It bore the date April 21, 1993.

"On this date I heard a preacher say that forgiveness is a conscious decision—an act of the will," the counselor explained. "He said it involves simply resolving, with God's help, that you forgive a person his trespasses. I went back to my desk, ripped out this calendar page, wrote the words 'forgive, forgive, forgive' on it, and stuffed it in my wallet. It helps me remember that this was the day I resolved to no longer let a particular act I was brooding over have any further hold on my life."

"Will I never think or talk about it again?" Jerry queried.

"Certainly not," Dr. Naylor explained. "You'll continue to study what happened there and how it applies to you. You'll continue to look at what it all means. But it does cause you to quit keeping emotional bank accounts—with a sort of 'you-owe-me-one' mentality. It keeps you from being chained to the past and allows you to live in the present and even look to the future."

"I guess it also means trying to walk in their moccasins and understand that they had their reasons," Jerry said, his head lowered.

"Seeing it their way does help," the doctor replied. "Carol was so eager to find love with someone she could relate to that she was willing to put on blinders. Pop was so grateful to find someone reliable to run his business that he did likewise. You're the last person they wanted to hurt. But excusing is not forgiving. Even if there were no excuses, forgiveness is still, ultimately, the only answer."

"I can forgive them even if I don't tell them I do, right?" he asked, almost frantically.

He knew that Bo once cautioned him that he would need to confront Pop directly someday—a thought he dreaded. But Bo had taken care of things with his phone call early on. Weeks ago, Pop had sent a package with all of Jerry's belongings to the anonymous post-office box, as specified. After that initial contact, Pop had made no other attempts to reach him. That told Jerry that he was a closed case where Pop was concerned.

Dr. Naylor reassured him, "In forgiveness, the only person you have to talk to is God. Just tell God the desires of your heart." Jerry nodded, compliantly, and sucked in a sigh. "You don't have to rush forgiveness, Jerry," Dr. Naylor advised gently. "God will tell you when it's time."

One day not long afterward, when Jerry woke up and started to say his morning prayers, he realized that the resentment was suddenly gone. By talking about his hurt and pain, working through it, and consciously setting it aside, forgiveness had become a reality. Suddenly he felt his heart soar free again—like a skier taking off from the top of the most complicated run. He had taken the next step of his long journey back to emotional healing.

As Jerry began to use some of the insights he was gaining into his own behavior, he was amazed at how much more easily life went for him in general. Softball practices with the boys were far less of a struggle now—in fact, they were starting to pay off.

After the conversation in which Chris told Jerry he feared failure, Jerry changed his tactics. Instead of pushing Chris to perform, Jerry set small, incremental goals with the boy. He used a positive reinforcement system that merited Chris some special favor if he merely showed he was even trying to learn a skill. If Chris would put on a catcher's glove for just ten minutes and make an effort to receive some throws that Jerry sent his way, Jerry allowed Chris to help him carry the equipment back to the storage area after practice. If Chris seemed frustrated, Jerry tried to get him to identify why—whether he was embarrassed, defeated, or some other emotion that the two of them could uncover. The main tool with Chris was demonstrating consistency—that Jerry cared about him no matter whether he ever scored the winning hit. As Chris kept practicing, he naturally added abilities. So did the other boys. Jerry studied each case and tried to get behind the acting out to get some real work done.

By mid-May, softball fever reigned at Sky Ranch, as Jerry demonstrated some of the hard-charging work ethic he employed in his previous occupations. Jerry divided the groups into two teams that squared off against each other in the afternoon practices. After the boys showed proficiency, Jerry arranged with the YMCA in Colby for a "Y" team to travel out to Valley Ranch to take on the "Rancheros" in a game one afternoon a week.

Then, a church youth softball league included Sky Ranch in its schedule and brought its team regularly to the Sky Ranch diamond for games. Jerry saw the boys' self-confidence increase as they began to envision themselves as capable in some new area.

Jerry's own self-confidence burgeoned as well. As the Ranchero "boys of spring" became the "boys of summer," Jerry took great personal pride in what he saw develop with these random misfits.

Before Dr. Naylor could even ask him the standard "How do you feel?" question that began each of their sessions, Jerry was ready with the word "valuable" on his tongue.

"It makes me feel like I still have something to give to society after believing I was the world's worst goof-off," he explained to Dr. Naylor. "It shows me that I can take on new things, too, and do well at them. I never coached team sports before. I stepped outside my comfort zone, and it's working. We may not win every game. These guys are learning, and so am I. But it does show me that I can stretch and grow, without everything collapsing on me."

This fit right in with the area where Dr. Naylor was taking him next in his rehabilitation—helping Jerry learn self-care in a holistic way. The more Jerry coached, the more out of physical shape he realized he was—a far cry from his days at the ski shop when he worked out daily on a mountain bike and lifted weights. Walks around the diamond winded Jerry in a way that astonished him. Dr. Naylor urged Jerry to develop a fitness routine to rebuild his body. With Bo's permission, Jerry went into town several times a week to work out on the Y's exercise equipment, and he got up 30 minutes early each day to run.

Mustering enough courage to ask his brother for time off was initially a challenge, but Dr. Naylor coached Jerry into taking this step.

"If you ask not, you have not, Jerry," Dr. Naylor reminded him. "Don't expect someone to read your mind. Jesus wasn't the meek and mild Savior that we sometimes depict Him to be. How would He have developed his itinerant ministry without asking friends for food and lodging? How would He have obtained the donkey to ride into Jerusalem on Palm Sunday if he hadn't said, 'the Master has need'?"

The area of biblical acumen was where Jerry stretched himself even more as fall advanced. Bo asked Jerry to lead some of the older teens in a Bible study on Sunday mornings—again, using skills that Jerry didn't realize he had and boosting his self-confidence even further. Rico, the demanding youth who had been so attached to Bo, widened his affections to include Jerry—much to Bo's delight. One morning after the Bible lesson, Jerry helped lead Rico to Christ. Jerry's excitement knew no bounds, as he realized the thrill of sharing that same life-changing message as Bo had done with him earlier.

"I can't imagine that God can use me in that way," Jerry exulted to Dr. Naylor. "The most lost, the most rebellious child—now being able to point others to Christ." Jerry couldn't believe that miles from the slopes, without the crutch of skiing that had been his confidence blanket for so long, he was able to stand on his own two feet in new and promising ways.

Fall brought football—and soccer, both areas that Bo had on his wish list for Sky Ranch youth to learn. Building on the summer's momentum, Jerry taught the Rancheros these two sports. His soccer team won a "Best Effort" award that the Colby Chamber of Commerce devised just for them and received a special trophy at Sky Ranch just before Thanksgiving.

As he accepted the award, Jerry found himself remembering the long-ago night that Carol described her joy in coaching college soccer at Wooster. It launched him into a surprising reverie about Carol. Was she back at college these days? Had her team won regionals this year like they had in the past? Such a tide of unexpected nostalgia suddenly blindsided Jerry that he lay awake for several hours trying to decide from whence it sprang.

As the fall wore on and the winter set in, Jerry's heart turned back to Valley Lodge more and more often, no matter how he tried to fight the memories down. Sky Ranch and his new world there were so much a part of him now, he was shocked that he continued to feel a tug about the place that hadn't been a part of his universe for almost a year.

Suddenly the memories of Pop, once full of bitterness, were strangely warm again. The twinkly-eyed man who wandered into the ski shop and charmed Jerry away from Boulder took the place in his mind of the meddler and intruder. Pop's consistent words of affirmation that once boosted Jerry replaced in his memory the occasional words that led to regret.

Then one morning, as he did his workout in the frosty air and looked up at the gray, churning clouds that likely would bring the first snowfall of the season to Sky Ranch, Jerry realized what had brought on these sudden stirrings of his heart. His thoughts abruptly roamed to the bountiful snow that was already painting the mountains white and energizing the valley in a spot many miles to the west.

"I've put my house in order in every way," he told Dr. Naylor that afternoon. "I feel better. I look better. I'm part of Christ's family. But I still have a job to do, don't I? I can never have real peace until I face the ones I've hurt and try to make amends."

Dr. Naylor nodded, as though nothing about this development caught him off guard. "It's called closure, Jerry," he explained. "You can forgive. But that's really only part of the battle. The Bible tells us to become reconciled to people that we have injured, as well."

"I couldn't have done it earlier," Jerry expanded. "I had to start feeling good about myself. I had to feel confident. I feel like I have something to offer now—that I'm not the mush pot I was then."

"That confidence will shine through," the counselor assured him. "Whatever happens now, you can know that you're OK."

Together, they strategized the best plan as Jerry developed his approach. Within days it would be December— the busiest month of the year at Valley Lodge, with visitors pouring in to romp in the fluff of the luxuriant white playground. Planning a visit back there now to see Pop might be foolhardy, with tensions already high and people's nerves frayed. Waiting until January—a full year away from Jerry's departure—might make more sense and might find Pop in a more malleable mood, since the anniversary date would weigh on his mind.

As Jerry considered that timing plan, he realized that he needed to strike while the iron was hot—to go now, while he was motivated, while God seemed to be giving him that forward push—while he was ebullient and sure. The weight of the January anniversary event could drag

179

him down. It could be too heavy, too sad—too much of an added burden to the important work he had set out to do. Acting now was the only way that made sense, he rationalized.

Alternately, with his confident moments, Jerry was hit with the foolishness of what he proposed. "There's been no contact with these folks in eleven months," he told himself. "I don't know what I'll find at Valley Lodge. Pop could have retired by now. He could be living somewhere far away. The place could have changed hands."

As he soul-searched, he realized that a still-insecure corner of him wanted to beg Bo for help again—to place the initial call, to pave the way. *How can I make such a move, having absolutely no idea what lies ahead of me?* he asked himself miserably.

"I understand, Jerry," Dr. Naylor comforted him as he discussed his concerns. "You're afraid. You're embarrassed. You feel helpless when you realize the odds. But also realize that Satan can plant that negative self-talk into your head. He wants you to believe that the deck is stacked against you. He doesn't want you to act Christlike and make things right. Listen to what God—not the enemy—is telling you to do. God won't steer you wrong. He'll give you the courage to take the steps that are necessary."

He wrote out on a sheet of paper the words to Philippians 4:13, "I can do everything through him who gives me strength."

"God gives you a 'can-do' mentality, even when you think the battle is uphill," the counselor assured him.

During the next few days, Jerry and Dr. Naylor rehearsed every eventuality. "You're asking forgiveness, not asking him take you back," the counselor reminded him. "You may do the right thing and still not get the response you desire. The fear of another's response can't keep you from your errand."

They role-played possible scenarios between Jerry and Pop. They prayed together, and Jerry prayed some more. Bo and Sally joined them in prayer time. Finally one morning, Jerry decided to take the plunge.

No amount of rehearsing could have fortified Jerry for what he discovered, however, when he finally made the call to Valley Lodge.

He asked the switchboard operator to put him through to Pop. The female voice that came on the line was one he strained to recognize.

"Mr. Hartley is . . . is not available," came the strangely muffled tone. "Who's calling, please?"

Jerry heaved in a breath and launched out nervously. "This is Jerry Rutgers," he said, his heart clattering so violently he was sure it reverberated all the way through the receiver.

"Jerry—oh my gosh! This is Shannon," he heard the woman say, and he knew then why the voice rang a bell, except Shannon's characteristic, excitable chirp was gone, replaced by a sad monotone. "Jerry—you're not really calling for Pop, are you? But then, of course, you wouldn't know."

"Wouldn't know what, Shannon?" Jerry demanded, as he felt the blood drain from his face. "Where's Pop?"

Her voice quaked in reply. "Pop's in ICU at the hospital in Gunnison. He's real bad. In fact, we've been waiting for them to call any minute with—with the worst," she blurted out hoarsely, her voice failing.

Jerry caught his breath in a sob. "No, no, no! It can't be!" he groaned into the phone, his hand covering his mouth in terror. "Tell me it's not true."

Shannon continued, stammering, "He's been sick for months. He never did get his strength back after . . ." She trailed off, and Jerry completed the sentence for her in his head—*after I deserted them.* "I stayed on to help—to do whatever I could. Carol left, but the college gave me another sabbatical. I wanted to do anything possible for Pop. He would rally—he always did seem to have nine lives. You know how tough it always was to get him down, even when he seemed on his last leg."

Jerry knew. He had seen it happen many times.

"This last heart attack. It was the biggie," she moaned. "There's nothing they can do. They didn't even try to operate. They've just kept him comfortable. He took a turn for the worst last night. They told us this morning he only had a few hours, at most."

Jerry stomped his feet with fury, as though that very act could halt time in its flight. His trembling hands clutched the receiver in desperation.

"Shannon, I've got to talk to him. I've got to get there—to see him. I'll leave at once. Tell him, Shannon. Tell him to hang on, OK? Pop can't die yet. I haven't told him what I have to say."

He dug his nails into his palms, waiting for Shannon to turn judgmental. He knew that this soulmate of Carol's easily could lecture, blame, and demand to know why he hadn't come earlier, or why he thought he had the right to come at all.

Somehow, by God's grace, Shannon was matter-of-fact. "Jerry, it's no use," was all she replied, weakly. "Wherever you are, just stay there. It's too late now. He's really bad off, I promise you. You can't make it in time. He's in a coma. You'll rush around to get here, and he'll never know."

Jerry was practically yelling now. "He will too know!" he insisted angrily. "I'll make him know. You'll see."

Shannon sighed helplessly. "OK, Jerry. Have it your way. Just remember, though—you'll probably be coming to a funeral."

SEVENTEEN

Character Reference

❧

The raw, antiseptic hospital smells that bespoke of suffering and death irritated Jerry's nostrils as he bounded from the elevator. He followed signs to the double doors labeled "Intensive Care Unit."

"Visiting hours are over, sir." A nurse stationed nearby intercepted him crisply, as he attempted to push his way past the entrance. "You'll have to wait until morning. Are you family?"

Jerry paced in front of her, exasperated. He had spent a long, tedious day traveling from Sky Ranch, and now it was late evening. Dropping everything after the alarming phone conversation with Shannon, he persuaded Bo to drive him to Denver—retracing their steps from almost a year ago when Jerry first pled for help. From Denver he had caught a commuter flight, which Bo and Sally had generously funded. At last he was in Gunnison, where Pop was hospitalized.

As he whirled around to survey the nearby waiting room, he saw no one he recognized—a fact that seemed to confirm his worst fears.

"I'm here for Mr. Hartley," Jerry told the nurse, his breath coming in short gasps after he raced through the lobby. "Is he . . . ?"

She scowled. "Someone will need to talk to you," she answered gravely, starting to vanish through the doors.

Jerry put a cautionary hand on her arm and whispered, frantically, "Look, ma'am, if he's still alive, I've got to see him. NOW. It won't keep until morning. What I have to tell him won't wait."

"Sir, we must follow policy," the nurse began. "Now let me get . . ."

Jerry caught sight of a familiar form. From a waiting-room sofa, where he must have been sleeping, stumbled Doug—Doug, the chef, whose party Jerry deserted so many months ago.

At the gut-wrenching sight of Doug, who must now despise him bitterly, Jerry felt his insides crater. "Doug . . .," he began. He extended a tentative hand in greeting yet tried to brace himself for the worst.

At first, Doug stiffened. His arm hung rigidly at his side as he shifted his considerable bulk away from Jerry.

This will be harder than I expected, Jerry thought, cringing. Remembering "I can do everything through him who gives me strength," the verse from Philippians 4:13 that Dr. Naylor had written out for him, Jerry straightened his shoulders determinedly.

Thankfully, however, Doug turned back in his direction and at last stuck out his hand in return. With that welcome gesture, Jerry's restraint quickly gave way to anxiety about Pop. Jerry grasped Doug's entire arm and jiggled it wildly.

"I've gotta see Pop, Doug," he begged, his voice breaking. "I've traveled all day, since Shannon told me. Please, Doug, is he . . . ?"

"Barely alive," filled in the chef, his face drawn from the strain of vigil. "All day long, they've expected him to go. Several of us are taking shifts. Shannon was with him earlier, and now I'm staying here while she's gone back to the lodge to sleep."

Although Jerry knew his efforts were close to futile in the face of such conditions, he remained insistent.

"Doug, please understand," he implored. "I need to talk to Pop. I've got something to tell him—he can't die without hearing it." Doug averted his eyes from him momentarily. Jerry knew Doug probably fought the urge to remind him that he missed his chance long ago. He stepped in front of Doug to restore eye-contact.

"Doug, this is critical to me," Jerry begged. "Please tell the nurse it's OK to let me back there."

The nurse intervened. "I'm sure, sir, that you don't want to take responsibility for upsetting Mr. Hartley, in his state," she adjured him.

Jerry knew he had no choice. He went for broke, his muscles hardening. "Ma'am, it already *is* my responsibility that he's in this bed in the first place," he pleaded. "His body is broken because of everything I've done to him. That's why I've got to ask his forgiveness—before he leaves us. He's got to hear this before he dies. Do you understand?"

The nurse looked over his shoulder searchingly at Doug, who was familiar to the hospital staff by now. Jerry couldn't see Doug's face, but he was certain that the chef signaled his assent, because the next thing he knew, the nurse reluctantly parted the heavy double doors just wide enough for him to slip through. With that, Jerry blitzed down the hall to Pop.

The sound of Pop's labored breathing echoed through the corridor even before Jerry stepped inside the station where a nurse hovered over his lifeless frame. Oxygen canula covered the lower part of Pop's unshaven head, now prickly as a pine cone from days of stubble, and Jerry could see two slits of eyes shut tightly. The once-wild hair lay fanned out and impotent on his pillow. The familiar, mirthful face was sunken, and a cadaverous white.

At last standing over Pop in the utter stillness of the moment, Jerry frantically gulped down sobs that threatened to choke him. A welter of pent-up feelings assaulted him, and Jerry thought for a moment that his heart would literally tear apart from grief right there on the spot. He squeezed his eyes tightly and prayed the most desperate prayer of his life—for calmness, for strength—that he could pull the crumbling pieces of himself back together.

When he regained composure, however, Jerry thought he detected the faintest movement of Pop's hand. Touching it with his own trembling one, Jerry bent over the comatose form on the bed.

"Pop, it's Jerry. Wake up. I need to talk to you," he said, his voice raspy but firm as he put his lips near Pop's ear.

To Jerry's shock, the two slits of eyes fluttered open. Jerry maneuvered his face so it was directly within Pop's line of vision.

"Hi, Pop," he continued, tentatively, as he faced him. "I'm so glad to see you. I've come a long way to find you, so I'm glad you opened your eyes. Don't close them, now. Look at me." And Pop did. Jerry thought he saw the two slits grow a slight bit wider, as they strained to focus on the features in front of him.

"Pop, I need you to wake up more now, so I can talk to you," Jerry coaxed urgently. As Pop seemed to recognize Jerry, his face began to contract in what seemed like a sob, and a racking sound escaped from his throat. The nurse who hovered at the bedpost grabbed Pop's arm worriedly and took his blood pressure. Finding no change, she stepped aside again.

As the racking sound subsided, Jerry made another attempt.

"Pop, something very exciting has happened to me," he continued, his voice a bit more steady. "I've become a Christian. I asked Jesus into my heart—for real!" The beady eyes continued fixed on Jerry, and he now saw an almost quizzical look cross them.

"That's right, Pop. You and I are brothers in Christ now. Thank you for all the things you did to teach me about Him," Jerry managed. Emotions threatened to overwhelm him again, as memories of his duplicity reverberated throughout his heart. For a moment, Jerry again thought he would snap completely. A tear pushed through the corners of his eyelids. Although Jerry tried to check it, it fell unheeded until it splashed onto the white bedsheet near Pop's arm.

The ICU nurse who stood nearby seemed unmoved throughout Jerry's monologue, as she kept a sharp eye on her patient. Portly and officious, she possessed all the charm of a hand grenade. She watched Jerry warily while he pled with Pop.

Jerry sensed from her impatient look that his time was fleeting. He regained control of himself and focused on the reason he'd come. Sucking in all the air he could possibly pack into his lungs and forcing his shoulders up to their maximum height, Jerry leaned over Pop a final time.

"Pop, I know I've hurt you badly. I sinned against you, and I'm sorry. Please forgive me, Pop." More tears followed the first one, and Jerry didn't even try to stop them this time. Jerry searched Pop's eyes for the merest sign of recognition that anything got through. The eyes were still opened and focused on him but remained blank, expressionless. *Did Pop hear me?* Jerry thought, panicking. *He's got to hear me. It can't be too late. I've got to know that he hears my heart.*

"Do you hear me, Pop?" Jerry cajoled him. "You heard me say I'm sorry, didn't you?" His voice broke on the last sentence. The nurse gestured for him to move away. The minutes were slipping, slipping . . .

He made his last appeal. "Pop, I'm going to hold your hand," he said. He grasped the bony appendage that felt more like a bundle of sticks than part of a human form. "Pop, if you'll forgive me, will you just give my hand a little squeeze?"

Seconds passed, and nothing happened. Pop's tired eyelids began sinking down, starting to form horizontal slits again. The nurse tugged at Jerry's shoulder and gestured demandingly for him to move toward the door.

In the final moment, Jerry made one last entreaty. "If you forgive me, squeeze, Pop. Squeeze!" he boomed. He moved his lips near Pop's ear again and continued to hold on as the nurse pulled at him sternly.

Then, in the last instant, it happened. Jerry felt pressure on his fingers—ever so slight, but unmistakable! "That's right, Pop! Keep squeezing!" Jerry yelled, his face swathed in tears of relief and joy. And glory to God, he felt Pop press—stronger now, and beyond a doubt! It was the sign he sought.

"Oh, thank you, Pop. Thank you, for forgiving me," Jerry cried out. "Thank you," he repeated joyfully as he turned to the nurse, whom he felt like hugging despite the fact that she ushered him by his shirt sleeve toward the door. With a face that was tear-streaked but radiant, Jerry moved toward the lobby, where he would offer to relieve Doug as loved ones continued the death vigil.

But Pop didn't die—not that night, nor the next day either. With typical Poplike indomitability that Jerry and all of them had seen before, he rallied radically. Three days after Jerry arrived, he was transferred from ICU to a private room.

"Must not have used up all his nine lives yet," Shannon quipped, after Pop was moved off the critical list. "The Lord must still have a purpose for him."

Jerry thought he knew part of that purpose. As the doctors gradually removed what tubes and monitors they could and Pop woke up a bit more every day, Jerry was able to talk with him at a deeper level than he had in the ICU that night.

Although Pop spent most of his days moving in and out of sleep, Jerry managed to catch him in enough wakefulness to describe his life since Valley Lodge. He talked about teaching the troubled youth, working alongside Bo and Sally, leading his Sunday School class, and consulting with Dr. Naylor to understand why he messed up.

"So many times I thought about you, Pop," he confessed to the aging patient. "I know you wondered why I dropped out of sight. I wanted to call—to let you know what was happening in my life. I had to wait until I was sure my head was on straight. You wouldn't have wanted to see me in those early days. I was lost in every way a person can be. When I found Jesus, my life started to change."

Then, when strength finally began returning to his voice, and after he shed some of the tubes that earlier blocked his throat, Pop was able to communicate a little, as well. Somewhat sadly, but openly, he gave Jerry a glimpse of what life was like at Valley Lodge in the wake of his departure. Shannon and several others who did double-duty managed to hold things together until Pop could hire a new part-time assistant—a former P.R. man for the Crested Butte/Mt. Crested Butte Chamber of Commerce—who was working out well.

Jerry cratered inwardly as he thought about someone occupying the coveted role that he threw over, but he tried to respond in gratitude in the wake of Pop's revelation.

"I'd like all their names, so I can write every one of them a thank-you," Jerry offered.

Matter-of-factly, Pop also outlined what became of Cindy. As soon as possible, Pop shifted her to another hotel, with all expenses paid, plus covered her plane ticket home. He wanted to free her from the gossip of the Valley Lodge crew as well as act in good faith before she pressed charges.

"As far as I know, she went back to where she was from, in Oklahoma," Pop said in a whisper. Jerry knew that in the whole scheme of things, he owed Cindy a heartfelt apology, too, although he couldn't quite imagine exactly when or how. Even though Cindy had been a willing partner to his lust, he had sinned against her and God by making the first, improper move. His senseless behavior had impacted so many people, it was hard to even keep track of those he'd wronged.

For an endless time, Pop was silent—the heaving of his chest the only sound in the room. Jerry figured another day would pass without their discussing Carol. Pop had barely mentioned her, and Jerry thought Pop had drifted off to sleep once again without the subject being broached. He breathed a thankful sigh. Talking about Carol would be, for him, still too painful to be borne.

Just as Jerry was about to slip from the room so Pop could rest, the elderly man blurted out, "Carol's back teaching again, you know."

Jerry halted and edged back into the room, taking his seat so Pop could finish. "She left about a week later, after the police called off their search," Pop croaked hoarsely. "Too hard for her to stick around here. I'm sure you understand."

Jerry stared at his hands folded somberly in his lap and nodded. He understood too well. What else would there have been for Carol to do except return to her old way of life and try to pull the curtain down on Valley Lodge? His heart felt like a lead weight was suddenly attached to it. Part of Jerry wanted to throw himself on Pop's bed and sob in his arms.

Remembering his promise to Dr. Naylor to keep positive, Jerry straightened his shoulders again. *"I can do everything through him,"* he told himself, recalling the encouraging verse. Besides, it was time to go. Pop's energy was spent, and Jerry had an appointment to keep. Since it was Jerry's last night in town, Doug and Shannon had offered to drive him up to Valley Lodge before his flight out tomorrow morning.

"Well, tell everyone I'll be back soon," Pop whispered as Jerry told of his plans. "The doctors say I've gotta retire now—that I can't take any more chances. But I'll be back."

Jerry had no doubt that Pop would keep his word. Some things never changed, and the irrepressible Pop was one of them.

Jerry braced himself for the sensation of a million knife-points jabbing into his heart the moment the Valley Lodge's stone exterior came into view, with the familiar, sumptuous hills as a background. He expected to feel like an alien on foreign soil when he spotted the registration desk and realized that someone else now had more rights to stand behind it than he. He dreaded the moment when he saw all those once-dear faces—Henny, Jessie, Max, the other staff members he had disappointed. He imagined himself being struck dumb in the process.

But as Doug stopped the car under the overhang and Jerry heard the recorded greeting, "Welcome to Valley Lodge—the happiest little hotel in the Rockies," a great peace fell over him that settled his fears. He realized that at that very moment, Bo and Sally and Dr. Naylor were all back at Sky Ranch praying for him. Jerry had phoned them last night, telling them he expected to arrive at the lodge about three in the afternoon. He asked them to intercede for him while he made this critical foray.

In truth, it was as though guardian angels rested on his shoulders, literally picking him up and lifting him from place to difficult place. Jerry kept the visit low-key and simple. At the hospital while tending to Pop, Jerry had already had a long and honest conversation with Doug and Shannon, in which he explained himself as best he could and apologized to them personally. They seemed to bend over backwards to ease the awkward nature of his return visit. He suspected they even deliberately guided him away from personnel who might be critical and directed him toward those who would affirm.

Even his brief conversation with David Pollard, the new lodge assistant, was far less agonizing than Jerry feared, even though the man clearly knew the worst.

"I learned a lot from being in this job, and I hope that you will, too," he told the individual who probably would succeed Pop. Life, indeed, had gone on without him at Valley Lodge. He would try to hold his head high as a forgiven child of God and act as one with a clean slate.

Thankfully, his visit didn't take him past the room of his wrong choices, although he tried to mentally arm himself for that, as well. As he sat on the sofa in the Great Hall and sipped hot chocolate with the others, Jerry reminded himself that Valley Lodge had been necessary for him to learn the things God intended to teach him. Dr. Naylor had told him the biblical story in Genesis 32 of Jacob's wrestling match with God at Peniel and Jacob's warning to the wrestler, "I will not let you go unless you bless me." If Valley Lodge had been Jerry's Peniel, then he would be eternally grateful for it. Jerry's exit from Valley Lodge had been an entrance to his new life in Christ.

What he was unprepared for, however, as he inched his way gingerly throughout his former workplace, was how literally every corner was permeated with another presence—that of Carol. Everywhere he stepped—the laundry room, the gift shop, the Ripping Rock, the staff dining hall—Jerry fully expected Carol to walk in any minute, so overpowering were the memories of their weeks together there.

As the moonlight fell on the snow-dusted hill behind the lodge where they had skied at night, Jerry experienced a haunting tug for Carol that he hadn't known since his first days at Sky Ranch. From the long-closed-off portions of his heart sprang a yearning that he had thought was dormant, as Jerry moved once again through the places where he and Carol had talked, and sighed, and loved.

Then, and only then, did he realize how far down into his memory he had pushed her and how much he had denied the impact of their love. These strange, new emotions that coursed through him alarmed him, as emptiness clutched him afresh.

Jerry was relieved when Shannon, whose once-ditzy demeanor had melded into maturity now, excused herself to answer email and Jerry no longer had to make polite conversation. Jerry then made his way to his guest room and tried to deal with the strength of these renewed memories.

In his solitude, perhaps he could better process the kind of pain that came with having lost someone he had loved so completely.

Pop was sitting up in bed, counseling one of the nurses, when Jerry arrived at the hospital the next morning to say his good-byes. Pop was engrossed in the thing he enjoyed most—helping people. Jerry held back for a minute before going in. He wondered if Pop might be too preoccupied for any parting words.

But as he glimpsed Jerry in the doorway, Pop waved him in and turned his attention to him immediately and obsessively.

"Son, come over here," he attempted to bark. His voice was still not at full strength but had far more punch than on the first days of his visit. When Jerry was finally at his bedside, Pop grasped his shirt and pulled Jerry to him intently.

"Son, before you go, I've gotta ask you. Will you forgive an old codger for pressuring you?" he begged. "You've had courage to come here, and you've been thoughtful to apologize. But I did some things wrong, too—some things that probably hurt you. Oh—they were all done in love. Goodness knows, I only wanted for you the best. But I rushed things. I put too much on you. My heart has broken over it a million times since . . ." His voice trailed off in a cough, so forceful that the nurse, who had stepped out, came running to check him.

Jerry was incredulous. So Pop knew and had regretted matters, as well. Jerry never expected this serendipity. He came to the hospital on a singular mission—to hear Pop say, "I forgive." God had been working in Pop's heart too, bringing conviction, without Jerry even having to say a word. He grew warm all over at the thought of it. Suddenly his love for this man who once had mentored him was sweet and overwhelming.

"It's OK, Pop," Jerry managed to blurt out, making no effort to suppress the tears that literally spurted from his eyes at Pop's remarks. "I accept your apology." Then he straightened, since he didn't wish to depart on a tearful note. "Hasn't God been good to let us spend some time together once again?"

Jerry thought the intensity in Pop's eyes would dissipate after his confession, but he saw that a determined flame still burned brightly in them, and that there was more.

"Son," he called again. Jerry realized how comforting it was to once more hear that familiar, endearing term of long ago. "I hope you'll go see Carol. Promise you'll think about it. It'll be a good thing to do."

His request caught Jerry so off-guard that he had no time to conjure up anything but a transparent answer.

"It would be too hard, Pop," Jerry confided, with a vulnerability totally unlike his false bravado of former days. "I don't see how . . ."

Pop interrupted him. "You're right, son. It will be hard—harder than you even know. I understand Carol has someone new in her life, and I think it may be pretty serious."

Jerry startled like he had been shot from a cannon. He digested the words, as if they described a total stranger instead of the woman whose face and form and scent he now saw had pervaded his every thought for the past year, even when he tried to repress it.

Carol has someone new. Jerry repeated the words in his mind, his fingers forming a fist at the mental image of Carol with another person. *But why shouldn't she? Who am I to Carol any more?* Her last, wretched sight of him was unthinkably awful. A whole year had passed with no communication. Carol had no idea that his Christian walk was now all that she could have ever wanted for him. And even if she knew, would she really care? Why should she not seek a future elsewhere? He should rejoice that she was on the road to freedom from the horrible scars he inflicted.

If I should be happy, why do I feel like my heart has just crashed into pieces on the floor? Jerry asked himself, as Pop's words stabbed at his insides. He pushed several breaths out as he tried to comprehend it all.

Pop didn't rush Jerry, giving him plenty of room to process this latest announcement. But in a few moments he spoke again.

"Son, 'forgive me' is the sweetest phrase on earth, and if you and Carol can exchange those words, it will enable you both to go in peace," Pop said.

Silence settled on the hospital room. Pop's morning had been tiring. He turned his head to the side in a sleeping pose.

As Jerry patted his hand and turned to go, Pop whispered a parting offer.

"Son, if you ever decide to see her, let me know. I'll write you a letter—a character reference. I can tell her we've talked. It might . . . help."

Jerry managed to make his way through the hospital lobby, thinking it odd that a man whose heart had just disintegrated back there as he learned the dreadful news about Carol could still be walking and breathing and ultimately, boarding a cab for the airport.

The buoyancy, the pride, the cleansing of the past five days in Colorado seemed insignificant beside the crushing picture of Carol that Pop had just painted.

Then, Jerry remembered his Scripture promise—"I can do . . " He *had* done it. He had scaled the Great Wall. He had apologized to Pop on his deathbed, only to see Pop rally, by God's grace. He had confronted Valley Lodge and stared into the lion's mouth to come out the victor.

If God had brought him thus far in his recovery—surmounting more obstacles than he could ever enumerate—then Jerry knew he must trust Him to take him one step further.

EIGHTEEN

Five Minutes Early

❖

The fingers on the door handle trembled slightly and then clutched the knob for support.

There was no room for nervousness now, Jerry knew. The fact that he had managed to avoid speaking into the monitor downstairs as he entered the apartment complex had been a miracle of the highest order. He had leaped over that hurdle and hadn't had to blow his cover by identifying himself.

Still, thousands of other obstacles lay ahead. Jerry knew he must be in total control and thoroughly clear-headed, for the next few seconds held the key to the rest of his life.

He exhaled a final prayer as he watched the apartment door in front of him swing wide open.

Jerry's first sight of Carol in more than a year was that of a face creased in a playful grin. Carol was clearly expecting someone—a very *lucky* someone, Jerry concluded, as he regarded the ravishing form in front of him.

She was wearing a black velvet cocktail dress, with a scooped-out design that enhanced her creamy neck and shoulders and a form-fitting bodice that clung to every curve. Carol had been so eager to greet her companion for the evening and so confident of his identity, she had merely pushed the security button, giving her caller access to her stairway without his even having to announce himself. Jerry knew she fully anticipated seeing this expected individual—very likely, Kevin, the new suitor Pop had told him about—on the other side of the door.

The eyes that Carol met were not Kevin's. As she swung the door wide exultantly to greet her date, Carol stared into a face that she had spent the entire past year trying to forget.

Jerry somehow managed to get her name out without his voice quivering.

"Carol," he called, and steadied himself with a deep breath before he proceeded. The laugh lines on her face instantly drained into horror. She went white—as white as the pearl drop earrings that dangled alluringly next to her skin.

Clutching her chest, Carol grabbed the door frame for support. Jerry used every ounce of restraint he could muster to keep from pulling her to him protectively. He stood quietly in wait for these first waves of shock to pass over.

Jerry could almost feel the shape of her in his arms as she stood so close—too close. Her scent so familiar and heightened by her heady perfume that invaded his senses became dizzying. The splendor of her in stunning black velvet was almost irresistible. His hands ached to encircle her shapely waist—to merge past into present in one intoxicating embrace. As he watched her full, russet-colored lips tremble from the shock, he could almost taste their warmth, their sweetness, their passion.

But once Jerry had become determined that he indeed must make the visit to Carol that he and Pop discussed several weeks ago, Dr. Naylor had counseled Jerry that he must not touch her, must do nothing physical that would be off-putting in any way.

So Jerry waited, drank in the long-awaited sight of her, bit his lip, and prayed.

The next few broken seconds were the most difficult of Jerry's life. Carol lifted her eyes as though trying to focus. For a few minutes that seemed like eternity, she surveyed Jerry frantically, as though to convince herself that what she saw was not a ghost. After all these months, to finally be standing so close to the face Jerry had wept over and prayed that God would enable him to see just one more time—his heart flipped with fear that he would lose any strength he still harbored. Tears spurted to the corners of his eyes, threatening to spill.

However, Jerry knew he absolutely must NOT cry at this moment, so he frantically blinked the moisture away. Looking sure, confident, and in control was vital to what he sought to accomplish in this brief window of time while Carol adjusted to the shock.

The last time Carol had seen him, he was wild, irrational, and hopeless. The Jerry he was determined Carol would view this time must be assured, deliberate, and above all things—believable.

As the shock ebbed, Carol spewed the anger he anticipated. Shoving her hands out in front of her as though to push Jerry away, she blared, "No! No! You will NOT do this to me. You will NOT intrude into my life again. You will NOT mess me up. I don't know where you came from, but you can NOT be here. GO BACK!" Each NOT was punctuated by a fierce shove of the arms, as though she could by sheer force banish from reality this reprehensible thing that was happening at that very moment.

Jerry waited for the wave to subside before he spoke. Despite her verbal protests, he saw that the door to her apartment was still open. She had not shut him out immediately. It was a tentative, but first, victory. Her shouts echoed in the stairwell, but he still had an entree, albeit weak. He made his next approach.

"Carol, I have no desire to intrude into your life," he ventured, as his gaze locked with hers. "I don't intend to—using your words—mess you up. I don't want anything except for a few minutes of your time. I'm here because I need to do this in order to recover. Many things in my life contributed to the hurt that I caused you and others at Valley Lodge. I'm working through those, but I need to talk with you and ask your forgiveness so I can heal completely. I hear anger in what you say, and you have every right to be angry at me. I know I hurt you deeply. But I have asked God to forgive me for those times, and I'm here to ask you, as well. Will you please let me visit with you? Just a few moments is all I ask."

As Jerry spoke, his voice still steady only by the grace of God, Carol turned her back to him but stepped away from the door, leaving an opening wide enough for him to enter. Seizing the moment, Jerry made a quick, bold approach that landed him quietly within the doorway.

A second, tentative victory. Undoubtedly aware of his location, Carol wheeled back around again.

"Then why didn't you do this months ago, when it might have mattered?" she yelled, fairly hissing the words as they emerged through hot tears that now started to flow. "You left me dangling. I didn't know if you were dead or alive. I didn't know why you disgraced me, slinking away and never contacting me—as though nothing had ever happened between us. You cared nothing about my hopes and dreams that were dashed. Now, it doesn't matter any more. I've started a new life. Then, you come back unannounced—for *your* healing, you say. And you have the nerve to drag God into it!"

The bitterness she spat out with her last sentence especially troubled Jerry, based on something Pop revealed when Jerry called back to tell him he'd decided to make the Ohio trip. Pop disclosed that Carol's own faith had waned in the wake of her struggle. That made Jerry all the more remorseful and determined to make things right.

Inwardly Jerry winced at Carol's tirade he knew he deserved, but he still held up under her onslaught. Again, his words were deliberate, measured, in contrast to her own fiery ones.

"You have every right to be angry. The things you're accusing me of are true. I did desert you, but not because

I didn't care, Carol. But again, I'm not here to ask anything from you except a few minutes of your time. Then I'll go out of your life forever, if that's what you wish. Will you please grant me just that one request?"

His last sentence was punctuated by the rasp of the buzzer—the call that Carol had thought she was answering seconds earlier.

"Carol, it's Kevin," came a lilting voice at the other end of the monitor. "Got detained by a traffic pile-up, so I'm running late. Let me come up, and I'll whisk you away to the Terrace."

Carol's dress, her grin of anticipation when she answered the door, and the miraculous luck that enabled Jerry to pass through the security system without giving himself away—the reasons for these were now confirmed. It also confirmed what Pop had warned him about. Someone named Kevin *was* in the picture and was, at that moment, occupying Carol's time.

Jerry's heart sank, its beat hammering in his ears as the next few seconds passed. Carol's eyes darted between Jerry and the open door.

Jerry remained wordless but was certain his eyes pled volumes. "Lord God," he prayed silently, desperately. "Give her the courage to stay and not go."

The buzzer rasped again. "Carol, are you there? Where are you, baby? You gonna make me wait again?" the syrupy voice pressed.

"Can't you see?" Carol finally asked Jerry, her face awash in tears that soaked straight to Jerry's heart. "I'm going out for the evening. I can't talk to you. This is all behind me. Why do you have to show up now?"

She swept shaky hands across the front of her dress. "Can't you see?" she blared again, her sobs coming even more violently as she gestured to the black dress. "This is the first time in a year I've bought anything new—the first time I've really started to think of myself as attractive again. You made me feel ugly by what you did. Now the world looks brighter. Someone else cares about me now. Then you have the nerve to show up. Can't you see?"

Jerry could see—too well. The sting of her insults was overpowering.

He also could see the moment he'd waited for slipping through his fingers, if he didn't act quickly. He pulled out every stop and pled with all that was in him.

"Tell him you're sick," he begged. "Tell him anything. I need to see you, Carol. I've come a long way. Believe me, you won't be sorry."

Slamming his eyes shut tightly, he prayed frantically—so frantically he barely heard the swish of fabric as Carol dashed down the stairs to her awaiting caller.

When he finally looked up, Carol stood with her back to the door, which she had closed quietly, and leaned against it, the very life drained from her. No Kevin was with her, and the plaintive buzzer was at last at rest. Sobs quaked her body as she pressed against the door for support. Wispy tendrils fell from the French twist that had caught up her dark hair, and she shoved them out of her eyes as she wiped her tears.

Her red eyes were bleary, her cheeks puffy, and her nose runny. To Jerry she had never looked more irresistible.

Despite the disturbing scene, Jerry was quietly triumphant. In spite of her anger, Carol HAD stayed. Tears of relief choked Jerry's throat, but he again swallowed them back. He braced for what he sensed would be Carol's next onslaught. He didn't have long to wait.

"Now you've meddled in my last bit of happiness," Carol finally assailed him, sobs still convulsing her. "Why couldn't you just leave me alone? He'll probably never come back again. He'll never understand—never."

"Carol, please come sit down. Come over to the sofa," Jerry beckoned. Backing over to a mauve print sofa in the center of the room, Jerry seated himself and motioned her over, ironically becoming the host to Carol in her own apartment. Almost blinded by her own tears, she fairly stumbled to the couch.

Seeing her makeup stream down her face in muddy puddles, Jerry offered Carol a couple of cocktail napkins he found laid out on the coffee table—cocktail napkins obviously intended for entertaining Kevin. She sat there, crying into her napkin, the bottled-up pain of many months pouring forth in these silent minutes. Those quivering shoulders he once knew every curve of were so close, so close . . .

"Dear God, help me," Jerry prayed silently once again as he deliberately held back from the embrace his arms ached to give.

Finally, the storm subsided, and from swollen eyelids Carol blinked, "Just what do you want? Now that you've REALLY ruined my life, what do you want from me?"

Jerry cleared his throat, hoping to steady his voice that was heavy with emotion.

"First, I just want to say thank you, Carol," Jerry began. "I know I barged in on you. I know you had other plans. I know you could have sent me away. From the bottom of my heart, I'm so grateful to you. I know your friend will understand when you explain to him."

"I *lied* to him!" Carol shrieked. "I made up an excuse. I told him I had a headache. He'll have no respect for me when he finds out I wasn't sick. Do you know what this looks like?"

"I know it puts you in an awkward position, Carol, and I appreciate it, more than you'll ever know. "

"You could have called; you could have given some notice," she assaulted, her lips tight with rancor.

"You're right, I could have, and I prayed that God would show me the way. In my heart, this was the only recourse that gave me peace—to take a gamble that you would be here and that we could talk."

"You PRAYED!" Carol yelled, mockingly, with a caustic tone that pierced Jerry to the core. "What's all this God-talk from you suddenly? I can't remember your being this interested in God when I tried to get you to be. Why is God all of a sudden so much a part of your vocabulary?"

For the first time, Carol's words evoked a slight smile from Jerry, as Carol broached the subject of his conversion.

"I'm sure you do wonder about what you just asked. Probably from your perspective, it does seem puzzling," he responded. "But God is exactly why I'm here. I'm not the same person I was, Carol. God is an important part of my life now. I wish He had been all along. That's part of what I'm asking you to forgive me for—for playing like I was a committed Christian, when my heart wasn't in it.

"God has changed me," Jerry went on. "I gave my life to Him totally and completely about nine months ago. It's because of Him that I realize that I am a sinner saved by grace. He's shown me all I've done to hurt Him and others. I'm here to try to wipe the slate clean."

Carol drew back in haughty laughter. "You expect me to believe that?" she belittled. "You expect me to trust this, after all that's happened? How can I be sure this isn't some act as well?"

"I don't expect that you on your own power can, but I believe that God living in you can give you the ability to trust me if you allow Him to," Jerry responded. "And I also have this as a testimony to what I'm saying."

From inside his pocket Jerry pulled out his trump card—an envelope bearing a Valley Lodge imprint. With trembling hands, he handed it to Carol.

There, in Pop's familiar handwriting, was the character reference that Pop promised Jerry he would deliver.

As Carol pored over it, she read these words:

"My dear Carol: I'm writing to commend to you Jerry, our brother in Christ. I know his visit to you is a shock, as his was to me a few weeks ago. But God has been doing a great work in his life, and his coming to you at this time is a part of his healing.

"He told me of the great hurt and confusion that was going on in him, undetected, when you and I knew him at Valley Lodge. It doesn't excuse what he did, but it does explain it. It also makes me aware that I contributed to it by acting on my own agenda instead of failing to notice his pain. I have confessed to him how wrong I was.

"Carol, I pray that, as a fellow Christian, you'll hear him out. He asks nothing of us except understanding and forgiveness. I pray that however painful for you it might be to open old wounds, you'll allow Jerry to put closure on this time in his life. Please remember my great love for you. I'll pray for you as you read this letter and as you decide how God would have you respond.

Love to you always, Pop."

Tears sprang afresh as Carol read these lines from her friend. "How was he?" Carol asked, a sob choking in her throat. "Shannon called me when it happened."

The man they both adored had just been fighting for his life. Something about that fact still linked Carol and Jerry in a solemn bond, even though their relationship was through. Jerry knew that Shannon had kept her posted on all the developments—on everything but Jerry's visit, which Jerry had asked Shannon not to report until he could see Carol face-to-face.

Jerry lowered his eyes as he answered her, his emotions reeling. "Alive, at least. Oh, he's weak, tired, discouraged about being ordered to retire, as you might expect. But he knows God spared him for a purpose—maybe even so he could see the prodigal son return."

He stared at the crease in his trouser legs as he anticipated Carol's accusation.

"I know, I know," he admitted sadly. "His second attack happened because of what I put him through. I'll spend the rest of my life trying to make it up to him. But God has been gracious. He let Pop live long enough for me to ask for and receive his forgiveness."

Fresh pain stabbed Carol as she thought of Jerry, the self-described prodigal, returning to Valley Lodge, where she had left in such embarrassment. He could almost see new waves of anger rippling through her as she heard Jerry describe Pop's pardon. He knew she wondered how in the world she could be expected to respond in like fashion. After all, she had been his fiancee—the one who found him with another woman.

As though reading her thoughts, Jerry began chronicling what life had been like for him since the night both their worlds tumbled to the ground and Jerry vanished into the blackness. He told of his rescue by Bo and the intervening months at Sky Ranch—submitting himself to the ministrations of Bo and Sally like any other boarder whose life was a mess. He described the hours of counseling with Dr. Naylor, who helped him as he helped the youthful Sky Ranch residents gain understanding of their behavior.

He enumerated insights—why ungrieved losses from Natalie's death, unresolved past pain from his childhood, fear of failure from rushing too quickly into a management role for which he felt ill-trained, and inability to speak up for his needs made him a prime candidate for crashing and burning as he had on the night of the disaster.

He assured Carol that his sexual liaison in no way reflected on her personally but symbolized pain he could not express. He told Carol that since his visit to Pop, he had even written Cindy, difficult though it was to do so. He asked her forgiveness for innocently dragging her into his web of destruction.

He told Carol about the times he had wanted to call her, write her, come to her, yet knowing that he would be offering only an empty shell of a man to her until his healing was complete.

Then, with the tears that he had held back all evening finally unable to be stemmed, Jerry described how in the midst of understanding himself, he saw for the first time how God loved him, a sinner, and how nothing he did could separate him from God's love. He told how Bo and Sally witnessed to him, lived godly lives in front of him, and eventually led him to Christ. He described Bo's own struggle against the concept of God as a loving father and how he had to come to understand their own earthly father before he could learn that God could be trusted and believed.

"Only through the dark night of my soul did I truly understand what salvation meant," he shared with her.

He asked Carol to forgive him for the times he misled her into thinking his faith was genuine. "But what you see before you is a changed life," he told her.

For probably half an hour, Carol listened to Jerry's monologue in stunned silence, her eyes cold and distant as he spoke. But his last statement pricked the boil that he sensed was festering, and she lashed out.

"Well, what you see before you is a *wrecked* life," she fired back, her eyes glowing with anger.

In an emotional purging that Dr. Naylor had warned him to expect, Carol reiterated for Jerry the basic outline that Pop shared about her pilgrimage in the past year. Back in Ohio after her dreams crashed around her, she even contemplated ending her life.

Teaching her students no longer had meaning, and all the old activities—including church, which she didn't mention but which Pop had confirmed—seemed empty.

Only when she went to a teachers' convention two months ago and met Kevin, who sat across from her at one of the dinner meetings, did the winds of change begin to blow into her life and new shoots of hope spring from the dead winter of her soul.

"I learned that he taught math at a college in Akron," she confided, sharing details that Jerry cringed at but knew he must absorb as part of Carol's catharsis. "From then on, he sat by me at every convocation. With him around, the long treatises on educational theory were less deadly dull."

Once back home, Kevin called regularly, making the hundred-mile trip over several weekends. They had been to the theatre, to movies, to dinner.

"He couldn't believe I'd never been to the Terrace—a night club right here in town. So that's where he was taking me tonight. I'm usually late—he's usually having to cool his heels on the sofa and wait for me. I thought he'd be surprised tonight when I was ready five minutes early. It had been sort of a joke between us, but I was planning to show him this time and be ready when he buzzed. I showed him, alright, didn't I? It wasn't even him at the door." She collapsed into another storm of bitter weeping—ducking her head into her hands to absorb the force of her sobs.

When her sobs eventually subsided into a few sniffs, she continued, looking up at him with searching eyes.

"You really expect me to believe this . . . this story you've regurgitated? I'm not like the saintly Pop; he always wants to think the best of people. But how can you have had such an about-face? All this talk about prayer—how often I begged you to have an in-depth conversation about spiritual matters, only to give me some shallow answer. And now my own prayer life . . ."

Jerry was sure he correctly read her thoughts. Now, ironically, when Jerry was claiming that faith had made him whole, Carol found herself the one estranged from God because of life's circumstances. Jerry couldn't help notice that she mentioned nothing about Kevin's Christian walk as being a factor in their courtship. Surely she hadn't lowered her standards in her desperation.

Jerry sat quietly and let Carol process what she had just heard. Dr. Naylor had cautioned him that this would take days, even weeks for her to absorb.

Don't press for an answer right away, Dr. Naylor told him. *Give her time. Realize this is a big shock. You do the right thing regardless of how she responds.*

All these words of advice rang in his ears just at the moment Jerry realized he was most vulnerable.

All that was in him wanted to pull Carol to him, declare his love once again, and cover her face and lips with kisses. The hair that she at first had worn in the upswept do had come down from its pins while Carol's body quaked from sobs, and now it fell tantalizingly loose around her shoulders. He saw that her spectacular, chestnut mane still had unimaginable hold over him, the way it always had. He wanted to bury his face in it and breathe in its sweet, exotic smell.

But Dr. Naylor warned him that to bombard her hastily with physical affection might put any chance of reconciliation in jeopardy. If he ever hoped to be convincing, Jerry must take a disciplined path. His resolve must be immutable, come what may.

Jerry sensed it was time to bring closure—that Carol had reached her saturation point.

"Look, Carrie . . . ," he began. He caught himself in a quiet gasp.

By accident, Jerry had slipped and called Carol the name of affection that he used for her at Valley Lodge. He sucked in a breath, as he again fought back tears. The slip of familiarity obviously did not escape Carol, and she glanced away.

Jerry recovered quickly. "We've talked enough for the evening," he told her. "You need some time to process all I've said. I know this has been exhausting for you, and you need to get your rest. We'll have other chances to talk, if you desire to."

He would stay through the weekend at a motel on the south side of town, about a thirty-minute drive from her apartment, he explained.

Then he essentially left the ball in Carol's court.

"I'll be there through Sunday noon," he added. "My plane leaves at two o'clock. If you'd like to talk again, I have the phone number. I realize I've caught you off-guard. Maybe after you've had time to rest and think about things, you'd like for us to get together again. I'll come over, we can go out to dinner, go for a walk—anything that would make you comfortable. Or, you may decide that you have nothing further to say to me. If you decide that, I'll accept it—I won't like it, but I'll accept it. Of course, I'd like to leave here having heard you say that you forgive me. I've come a long way to hear those words. But I won't beg you. I can only do what is right for me, and that's to come forward to ask your pardon. The rest is up to you. If you want for us to visit again, just give me a call."

"Haven't I made it clear to you?" Carol implored him, furiously. "I'm involved in a relationship with someone. I don't have room for anyone else in my life."

Her tongue-slicing words stopped Jerry's heart, but he did his best to keep his feelings from view.

"I'm not asking you to do that," he replied, as longing burst through him afresh. "Certainly, if I had my druthers, you wouldn't be, but I have no claim on you now. That's the consequence of my leaving, my being gone for so long. I can't fight that. All I'm asking is that you find it in your heart to forgive me, and that you'll tell me so. As I said, I'll be in town for the weekend in case you want to talk further—after you've rested, after my being here doesn't seem like such a shock."

"Two nights in a hotel, plus your air fare and expenses," Carol protested, her face incredulous. "You don't have this kind of money. You said yourself your work at this place only pays for your room and board. How can you finance a trip like this? And *why* would you?"

"Some people who care about me and my being whole again have made this possible, and I'm very grateful," Jerry answered. It didn't seem necessary at this point to disclose that Bo and Sally were paying his way because they believed in him and knew he must take this step to heal.

Jerry stood to go, and Carol tensed. Jerry could tell she must fear he would try to kiss her good-bye or to smooth everything over with physical affection, as was his custom. She shrank away, hesitantly, and he knew she probably caught the look of pain that rippled across his features as he felt her rejection.

Vanquishing all urges to pull Carol to him in a final go-for-broke embrace, Jerry made no move toward her. He would not try to palliate things in this fashion. He passed to her the telephone number of the motel and walked to the door.

As he started to slip from the apartment, he realized that unless she called again, this might be his last time to ever be in her presence—to ever look on the face that had haunted his days and nights for the past year now, even though he had tried to push it away. A colossal sense of his own loss overwhelmed him, and he felt momentarily paralyzed with sadness.

Half-crazy with love for her, Jerry acknowledged anew that his own foolhardy actions had created the situation that he now faced. By his own hand he was cut off from Carol. He had dug his own grave. He *should* go dig his own grave. He should walk out the door, step into the traffic, and let someone put an end to him.

It's what I deserve, he thought.

Then he caught himself. "This is Satan trying to trip me up, pure and simple," he thought. He willed away the urge to shout it aloud so he could fight down the warfare he knew had seized him. "I won't let Satan triumph over me again."

Dr. Naylor had read to him a passage from Job 23 that said, "When He has tested me, I will come forth as gold." If Jerry accomplished nothing else during this time with Carol, he wanted to come forth as gold—as a struggling child that God could be proud of.

He knew he must leave immediately before he said, thought, or did something that he would regret.

Jerry stuck his head back in the door for one last, languishing glimpse of her, pale and shaken as her fingers gripped the cushions of the sofa where he left her.

"Good-bye, Carol," he called, his eyes riveted to hers for one final second as she stared in stone-cold silence.

Then he was gone.

N I N E T E E N

A Door Left Open

❀

Once in the privacy of his rental car parked outside Carol's apartment building, Jerry bent over the steering wheel and wept out all his bottled-up tears.

Not even Dr. Naylor's meticulous coaching could have prepared Jerry for the anguish of facing Carol again—and for the realization that getting her back was about as likely as a July snow.

A spate of "if-only"s strangled him as they poured forth. If only he had arrived earlier . . . Kevin had been in the picture for only two months. If only Jerry hadn't been so confoundedly cautious, he might have made his appeal before another man began vying for Carol's heart. If only he hadn't tried to convince himself that he was over her . . . After seeing Carol tonight—more to-die-for gorgeous than he had remembered, even when she sparred with him—he couldn't imagine how he ever believed that his love for her had halted.

Yet two months—even two days earlier—and he would have never been the same person he was tonight.

Jerry knew he had had to wait until he could face her as a recovering, fully accepted child of God. It was not something he could have rushed, even if he'd wanted to.

Even with that, Jerry sadly acknowledged that the whole, confident person that he presented to Carol wasn't enough to reclaim her love that he once recklessly tossed over.

Back at the motel—the cheapest he could find in Wooster—Jerry collapsed on the bed, face-down and fully clothed. He passed a sleepless night this way, inhaling the stale smoke fumes from the worn bedspread as he mulled over the visit. The next several hours were an agonizing post-mortem, as he took each scene at Carol's apartment and slid it under the lens of his mental microscope.

Gaining admittance to see Carol had been nothing but God's own handiwork. So was her excuse to Kevin in that desperate moment which meant success or failure to Jerry's mission.

But the words that his ears most ached to hear—"I forgive"—had not been forthcoming, and might not ever be.

Carol clearly had made her decision to move on. As he replayed every minute of their conversation, Jerry saw no evidence that Carol would meet him on his terms. Her glassy, embittered stare was permanently etched on his memory. There was no hint of the sweet, malleable Carol with the sincere, dark-pool eyes that had warmed his days and nights during the months at Valley Lodge. The scars of life—scars that Jerry knew he had inflicted—had left her raw. Nothing about his visit penetrated that sheet-metal exterior. Nothing about his life change made any difference to her at all.

Pop's reference letter *had* been helpful. At least it had kept her from throwing him out initially. But was it enough to convince her that Jerry wasn't the charlatan she had believed him to be for the past year?

Kevin obviously was very much a part of her life now. He seemed like all she could ever want or need—this slick-talking playboy who took her to glitzy places. The Carol that Jerry once knew would have never gone to a nightclub. Jerry sickened to think what other principles she might have violated. Had Carol decided she had paid too great a price at Valley Lodge for abstinence? Was she in spiritual rebellion partly because she now believed that good guys finish last?

If I could just assure her that God's way was the right way, Jerry said to himself. Tears gathered in his throat once again. He wished he could show her what Dr. Naylor helped him see—that the hurts inflicted on her at Valley Lodge sprang from human choices, not from God's design. If he could only remind her that God's principles are the sure ones, even when people fail.

As much as it chafed him, Jerry had to acknowledge that Carol did seem content in this new relationship with Kevin. In truth, how could Jerry expect her to turn her back on the beguiling Kevin? To Carol, Kevin must look like a prince. He was devoted to her, compared to one who had disgraced her. Just what was it that made Jerry think she would give him the time of day?

Maybe his restraint back there at her apartment was the wrong tactic after all, Jerry debated. Maybe he should have seized her in his arms and overwhelmed her with passion. Always before, his kisses and caresses had worked like magic on her. Maybe if he had tried that tactic again, he could have maneuvered her his way. Then she could decide for herself whether he or Kevin were the better lover.

Truth was, Jerry knew he had so much more to offer her now—not only the qualities about him that she once found attractive, but all the things she had hoped he would be—that she had thought he was, until his deception became apparent. Now, they would have much more in common than just their devotion to skiing. The fundamental things would be right this time. God would be their common denominator. *With that combination, I could overthrow Kevin hands down,* Jerry fumed.

Then, he realized how Satan was working overtime on his thought life. He knew that if Carol came back to him, it wouldn't be because he had overpowered her physically—or because he spouted "God talk," as she put it. He

213

reminded himself that he came to Ohio only to ask for Carol's forgiveness. He would be whole regardless of whether she agreed to see him for even one more minute.

All he could hope was that his confidence in himself and in who he was in Christ had shone through. He hadn't groveled. He hadn't begged. He had only pled for a hearing. He had relied on rational instead of emotional appeals, even in his contrition. For that he was proud, and he knew Dr. Naylor would be as well—even if it made no difference to Carol at all.

Right now Jerry's thoughts weren't coming too clearly because of his exhaustion. Jerry knew that the more spent and fatigued he was, the more vulnerable he was to saying something he regretted, where God and Dr. Naylor *wouldn't* be proud. He wanted to come away with a clean conscience—to think again that he had come forth as gold. Feeling a fresh wave of tiredness from this blitzkrieg of emotions, Jerry decided he would try to take a nap.

Since this classless motel lacked alarm clocks, Jerry called the front desk to wake him at three. After his sleepless night and agonizing morning, it was getting close to noon on Saturday, and no call from Carol seemed to be forthcoming. At three he'd get up and try to decide whether he should merely give up on Carol and catch an early plane out, or stick it out until Sunday in the final death-watch of their relationship.

He drifted off to sleep, shoring himself up for the inevitable and thinking about what he would report to Bo and Sally and Dr. Naylor. He studied how he could possibly put this onerous visit behind him and get on to other things, although for the life of him, he didn't know what those other things would be.

Jerry sensed he had barely dozed a little when an annoying, clanging noise jarred him from deep slumber. Time to wake up already? He was still *so* tired.

He picked up the phone, barked "Thank you" to the desk clerk for the call, and started to slam the phone down and grab a few minutes' more shut-eye.

Then, though the fog of sleep, he heard a voice, just seconds before the receiver hit its cradle. Carol's voice. It had been Carol. Carol! "Carol," his lips finally shaped the word. "Is that you?"

Carol responded fast and all at once, spitting her words out quickly to be done with them.

"I see nothing at all to be gained by seeing you again," she said colorlessly. "It prolongs the inevitable. You spoke your piece last night. You've done what you came to do. I think you should just go back to Kansas and put the whole thing behind you. That's what I have done—put it in the past."

So this was the bad news he expected. Jerry braced for the worst, his chest aching so profoundly it felt like he had broken a rib. He assessed her voice: it sounded weary, even faint. *She's probably trying to sound pathetic so she can put a guilt trip on me for disturbing her yesterday,* he reckoned. She was making special effort to be guarded as she delivered this statement that would pull the curtain down on all his hopes.

Then she went on.

"I see no point in our continuing to talk. But I'll do it for Pop's sake, because he asked me to treat you decently. Whatever you want to do, I'll be here this afternoon."

Jerry fairly leaped through the phone, his heart doing so many flips, he thought it would catapult out of his chest cavity. He realized he must stay steady, so he calmed quickly.

"OK, Carol, that will be fine," he said, trying to copy her impersonal tone. He mustn't let her detect his exuberance. "When can you be ready?"

Thinking with lightning speed, Jerry suggested a winter picnic. The weather was unseasonably warm for Ohio in January. Perhaps on some neutral turf, they could have a civil talk. Last night he had spotted a place on the way to her apartment—just in case he needed it.

"I saw a little park as I was driving to see you. Lots of pansies and a little lake and some picnic tables. I can stop by a sub shop and get some sandwiches."

Carol consented to the arrangement, and he agreed to pick her up in an hour. With the phone back on its hook,

Jerry whooped out a "ya-hoo" that could be heard all over the motel.

As he leaped into the shower and dressed, Jerry tried to avoid being too hopeful. Nothing in her insipid voice offered a shred of encouragement. She was doing this only out of loyalty to Pop, she had stated. Carol clearly had written Jerry off as some kind of wacko nut that she had met in the intoxicating atmosphere of the ski lodge but was over now. She obviously had constructed many props and support systems to confirm this belief, and she wasn't about to let Jerry shoot them down as he tried to move the past into the present.

He wondered whether she had yet explained to Kevin her sudden "headache" of last night. Did Kevin know by now that Carol actually stood him up—for her old fiance? Was Kevin likely to knock on his motel room door any minute to blow Jerry's brains out with a shotgun? Jerry felt like one of Bo's Charolais steers that had wandered into another rancher's territory—territory another man fiercely possessed.

Yet, the faintest glimmer of hope glinted. Carol *did* have an alternative. Whether she had acted out of loyalty to Pop, or for whatever reason she mustered up, she *had* called. There now would be yet another time for the two of them to be together—for better or for worse.

Jerry praised the Lord for another victory. Carol had left the door open once again.

TWENTY

A Rush of Compassion

❀

A light wind whipped up a few frothy waves on the lake as Jerry and Carol munched their turkey subs.

The late-afternoon, winter picnic in the scenic spot that Jerry had located was proving to be a good idea, he assessed, as they downed their lunch and watched the petals of some pansies quiver in the breeze.

We might be just any ordinary couple who found a creative way to escape the winter blahs, Jerry thought. He brushed a stray leaf off their gold plastic tablecloth that came from Carol's kitchen.

Carol and he both had managed to show up for the picnic in some comfy-looking jeans, and their casual attire set a laid-back atmosphere for the meal. The unseasonable January temperature was warm enough for Jerry to roll up the sleeves of his dark blue denim shirt, exposing lower arms that remained tanned from his summer of softball. The wheat-colored cardigan Carol wore over an ivory pullover softened lines of her face that had been taut during last night's interchange.

Jerry opened a bag and offered Carol some grapes he had dashed into the grocery to buy for their meal. *We're lunching so casually that no one would ever believe that some critical issues are hanging in the balance here,* Jerry thought.

Those critical issues hadn't entered the conversation yet, and Jerry hoped he could keep them at bay a little longer. He tried to steer their dialogue to pleasant matters as they dined.

He coaxed Carol to speak about her work and the things that she was involved in on campus. Now that he was in her habitat, he at last could picture her working here, living here, going about the day-to-dayness of her life—the way he'd envisioned during all those times he had tried to push her out of his mind.

All he had known of her previously, at Valley Lodge, was in connection with her passion for skiing.

Now, here in Ohio, it was as though Jerry couldn't soak up enough of Carol's turf. He wanted to see it all for himself—her grocery store, her post-office, her shopping mall, the place where she stood in line to renew her driver's license.

That way, if today were all he had of Carol, he would have memories to keep him going for a little while, at least.

In turn, Jerry told her about coaching the Rancheros and how he had brought the softball team to life. He talked about starting soccer and football at Sky Ranch and about life as a boarder with Bo and Sally. He thought he even saw a hint of a feeble smile on her face when he described waking up to the shaving cream shower the week he arrived.

But the fragile filament that held them above last night's heaviness quickly broke when Jerry innocently asked Carol about her teaching load this year.

"It's been horrible. I've had to take on a lot of Shannon's responsibilities as well as mine," she snapped stiffly, as the previous bitterness crept into her voice. "I coach both the girls' softball and soccer teams, now that she's not here, and it's a real killer."

Both Carol's and Jerry's eyes shifted downward with those remarks, and the unspoken fell between them like a lead curtain.

Jerry knew he was the reason that Carol carried such a maddening schedule. Had he not acted irresponsibly, he and Carol would be at Valley Lodge right now—married and managing for Pop. Carol might be teaching a classroom of kiddies somewhere, the way she had wanted to. Shannon would be back at Wooster, with roles completely reversed, as they should have been.

From that downturn in spirits, Jerry could never get things on the upswing again. He tried to interject open-ended questions. How did Carol outfox students who had an "attitude" like he found in Chris? How would she deal with pranksters like the ones who gave him the shaving-cream bath?

"Sometimes I wonder what these clever ones will make of themselves someday," Jerry commented. He hoped that might spark Carol to tell a classroom anecdote or two.

Carol's eyes repeatedly darted away from his during the conversation. She poked at the crust on her sandwich, further avoiding eye contact and sidestepping any hint of intimacy. When she looked up, her eyes skittered over the lake and the nearby parking lot to avert Jerry's gaze.

In every way, Carol continued to signal that she was only passing time with him out of an obligation to Pop. That gritty, determined streak that Jerry had once found so appealing about her was now working against him. She wasn't about to make him believe she found this pleasurable at all.

As they began packing away their picnic items, Jerry took a gamble to shift gears. He asked Carol if she would give him a tour of the College of Wooster.

"I've pictured it so many times," he confided. "I'd like to drive through the campus, if you don't care."

Carol at first glowered at him. Then she sighed with resignation, as though deciding no harm could come from a quick driving tour. They motored around the school that Jerry had tried for months to envision.

As they approached the athletic complex where Carol had her office, Jerry gathered his courage and took an additional plunge. Could they merely step inside?

Carol tensed, nervously adjusting the woven leather headband that held her hair back. Jerry knew why Carol hesitated, since a scenario of having to introduce him to colleagues might prove awkward. Some of them, no doubt, knew about Jerry and his antics—that he was the reason she returned so abruptly from her sabbatical. Some probably knew about Kevin entering her life, as well.

He saw Carol scan the parking lot for familiar cars. On a late Saturday afternoon, the place was fairly deserted. Anyone who might have been putting in weekend hours probably had shoved off by now.

Finally Carol relented again, with a disinterested toss of her shoulders. Leaving the car behind and threading their way down the sidewalk into the building, Carol led Jerry past the classrooms to a small academic office. A brown metal name plate on the door read "Ms. McKechnie."

Once inside the office, with the door closed behind them, Jerry became absorbed in her teams' trophies. At his insistence, Carol described for Jerry several photos of her with some of her winning squads.

In one, a group of triumphant softball girls toted Carol off the field after some victory last year. Jerry's eyes fixed on Carol as she was pictured there—her brown locks tucked into a softball cap, her face widened in a smile that covered up her heartbreak.

Jerry became so preoccupied that he only heard the last few clops of footsteps that had begun at the far end of the hallway. Despite the deserted look of the academic building, Jerry and Carol had not been alone on their Saturday foray.

Presently, a sharp rap came at the door. As Jerry opened it, a stockily built, older woman, with a referee whistle hanging around her neck, peered in to see who was making noises in Carol's office.

The woman glanced at Jerry, thrust out a hand, and introduced herself. "I'm Dr. Northcutt," she boomed gregariously, her bowl-cut hair tossing as she spoke. "Are you checking out our department today?"

Jerry recognized the name. At Valley Lodge, Carol had mentioned Dr. Northcutt on numerous occasions—the department chair whose approval she had needed to extend her sabbatical.

Jerry's eyes connected with Carol's for some sign as to how he should respond, but Carol's face merely registered the same shock that he felt inside. Without a cue from Carol, Jerry knew he had no choice but to let the chips fall.

"Yes, Carol's giving me a tour," he announced in a friendly voice, as he shook their guest's extended hand. "I'm Jerry Rutgers visiting here from Kansas. This is a nice facility you have here, Dr. Northcutt."

At the mention of his name, Dr. Northcutt's smiling eyes changed to horror and then darted back and forth from Carol to Jerry to Carol again, knowingly and in rapid succession. The look stealing over her face couldn't have been more pockmarked with disgust if he had said he were Adolf Hitler.

This woman was obviously fully aware of Carol's story and his role in it. She brusquely drew up her shoulders and faced Jerry squarely, her once-kind eyes shooting needles of disdain.

"Mr. Rutgers, I'm sorry I can't say it's a pleasure," she said curtly, icicles falling from each syllable as she pinched them out. "Good day, now," she huffed, and was gone.

Jerry's eyes followed Dr. Northcutt down the hall. He observed her bent-kneed, stoop-shouldered gait that looked as if she had carried a few too many barbells in her time. This supervisor of Carol's must consider him to be pond scum. Jerry was sure that this embarrassing scene with her boss would exhaust whatever shred of goodwill Carol had left. She would be furious at him for insisting they come inside.

He dispatched a quick prayer for wisdom and restraint. *God, only your approval of me matters,* he reminded himself quickly. *Please help me stand firm.* He turned his eyes back to look at Carol and braced for her negative reaction as well.

Oddly, though, as he lifted heavy eyelids toward Carol's blanched face, he saw her push her hands out in front of her as if to object.

"I'm sorry, Jerry," she murmured, and then almost instantly looked shocked that these sympathetic words had tumbled out from within her. "She shouldn't have treated you so rudely."

Jerry spoke up quickly, trying to dismiss the subject. "Clearly, I'm a household word at Wooster," he replied. He managed a weak smile and shrugged a little. He mustn't let his shoulders wilt; he must look self-assured even if his gut-level reaction was to crumble.

Carol seemed determined to explain.

"Dr. Northcutt is a confidante—one of only a few," she protested, her voice suddenly lacking its familiar sarcasm. "She's protective of me. I thought everyone was gone from here. I wouldn't have put you through . . ."

"Look, Carrie," Jerry quickly interjected, using the nickname because the sudden intimate turn seemed to merit it. "I'm glad you had friends during a rough time. You needed them. I can't blame Dr. Northcutt for wanting to choke me. She has no way of knowing how my life has changed. She doesn't know that I'm a sinner saved by grace. Maybe I'll get the chance to tell her sometime. Now, please. This isn't going to ruin *my* day, and I hope not yours, either. Let's go back to the car. We can drive some more. Why don't you show me the nursing home where you teach aerobics?"

As matter-of-factly as he had entered the office, he exited it, holding the door for Carol. She quietly followed him toward the parking lot. Along the way, and for the first several minutes they were settled in Jerry's rental car, silence reigned, and Jerry couldn't read Carol's thoughts for a second.

She mostly looked down, but occasionally Jerry saw her lashes lift as she studied him while he steered the car through the maze of campus roadways. As they pulled back onto the thoroughfare, Carol suddenly turned in her seat, her back toward the passenger door so she could face him. A touch of wonder in her wide eyes replaced the glassed-over look, and she raked her gaze over him while he drove.

"You're right," she finally pronounced, speaking in a decisive voice, as though rendering some verdict she had been contemplating. "You *have* changed. The Jerry I knew back at Valley Lodge would have let something like that devastate him. You're confident now. It's the way you were on the ski slopes, but not any other time. I saw it last night, and it baffled me. But now you've confirmed it. You've learned to have grace under fire. It's amazing."

Jerry blinked in disbelief. Although Carol's blunt words smarted a little, he was astounded at what he heard. For a brief moment Carol was letting down the impenetrable front she had so rigidly maintained.

Thank you, Lord, Jerry prayed silently, fervently. *Keep working, Lord. Keep her open, please.*

"Yes, by God's grace, I have," Jerry finally responded, forcing the words past the lump in his throat that threatened to choke him. "Thank you for acknowledging it, Carol. I've learned that God's approval is the only one that really matters. I just wish it had been a way of life for me earlier. It could have helped us both."

Silence flooded in again momentarily, and Jerry wondered where this development would lead. Was something about his appeal actually soaking though to Carol? Was God truly stirring her spirit in a way Jerry thought not possible?

Delight suddenly sluiced through Jerry, as he pondered the possibilities. Could it be that more of his conversation registered with her last night than he realized? Could her intrigue with his confidence—and not just loyalty to Pop—have been one reason she consented to today's visit? The plaintive sound in her voice on the phone this afternoon—he thought it had been a guilt trip on her part. Was it possible that she had endured some sleepless hours as well—pondering the matter she was baffled about?

And what had it meant back there at the college, when Carol had that strange rush of compassion after the rebuff from Dr. Northcutt? Had the snub truly caught Carol off-guard so she didn't have time to put her usual barriers in place? The spontaneous response contained a hint of her loving, sincere nature that initially attracted him to her during Valley Lodge days.

Just as quickly as his optimism surfaced, Carol dashed his hopes.

"But Jerry, you've been in a cocoon," she assaulted him, as though she couldn't give him the joy of toying with those delicious prospects. "Everything you've described about that place where you live—it's not the real world. You've got family to pick you up when you fall. You've got a counselor to coach you through things. You've got your room and board. No wonder you get along so well—look at all these anchors. Life is cushy. If you get back into a pressure-cooker situation, you'll crumble in a minute. You'll flash it again. You'll just go on hurting people, yourself included."

Carol's words unsettled Jerry in more ways than one. He knew that Carol, in part, spoke the truth. Jerry had been so caught up in seeking forgiveness and trying to get that difficult step mastered, he hadn't thought too much about the future. He knew many decisions about life after Sky Ranch would have to be made after these fundamental matters of his recovery were out of the way.

"I know it probably looks that way to you, Carol," he finally ventured, his voice unwavering with conviction. "You're right. Sky Ranch has been a special setting. It's the only kind of setting that could have worked to help me begin recovery. I'm grateful for the props I've had. God sent them to me just at the right time. I hate to think the mess my life would have been without them."

"But," Jerry continued solemnly, "I'm trying to build in some healthy patterns that will continue wherever I go or live in the future. My daily quiet times and my physical fitness plan are two of them. Dr. Naylor has told me to always stay connected to a Christian counselor—where I can check in if I feel old habits starting to creep up."

Carol shifted her body away from Jerry and turned her eyes out the car window. She looked unmoved by his testimony. Jerry determined to make one more stab at explanation.

"Again, Carol, I know I can't do any of this on my own power. In fact, that's what you told me the first time I met you, when I asked you why you were so eager to help at Valley Lodge. You said if it were up to your nature, you might not, but that it was Christ living in you that made it possible. That's how I feel now."

He saw Carol wince a little at the reference, a wince that made him uncomfortable. If Pop was right, Carol was feeling very alienated from these concepts right now, since her spiritual life was sagging. Jerry hoped that maybe this might gently remind her that Christ's power was still operative in her life, as well.

The remainder of their drive was mostly silent, except when Carol indifferently pointed out the nursing home that Jerry had asked to see. Now that Carol had dumped her venom on him, she seemed eager to return to her apartment. Although they had not discussed a deadline, it was approaching six o'clock, and she began looking at her watch nervously. She had mentioned no evening plans, but Jerry presumed she must have some sort of session arranged with Kevin to smooth over hurt feelings from last night. Jerry would have certainly lingered if invited to, but no invitation seemed forthcoming. He didn't want to push his good fortune after this emotion-laden day.

As they approached her apartment, Carol began fidgeting for her purse—gathering up her keys as though preparing to make a quick exit.

However, as Jerry opened the passenger door and Carol stepped from Jerry's car, Carol caught her heel on the curb, and Jerry spontaneously grasped her elbow to break her fall. It was his first time to touch her even slightly during the entire weekend. An electric shiver rippled through his entire body at the familiar curve of her arm. He weakened and almost broke his resolve. How easy it would be to gently pull her to him in this moment before they proceeded on toward her apartment.

At the last second, he resisted, but Jerry felt the heat rise inside him all the way to the apartment door. Carol bounded a few steps in front of him—probably to make sure he didn't grab her arm again. He observed how the legs of her jeans clung to her calves and thought again about how trim and cute she looked. How he wished that accidental touch had never happened—it would make saying good-bye torture him all the more.

As he watched her insert her key in the lock, his heart flamed up like a furnace. Tomorrow he must leave without any indication of what the future held for their relationship. With the flickering gas lamp outside her apartment outlining the fullness of her lips, the softness of her eyes, he found himself fighting tears again as he thought about this visit ending.

Little had been left unsaid—little, that is, except Carol's forgiveness, which Jerry realized he now likely would return to Kansas without.

Suddenly, Jerry felt new courage blast through him. *This doesn't have to be good-bye,* he thought, determinedly. *I won't let it be.*

Something had led Carol to feel sympathy for him in front of the brusque Dr. Northcutt. Something had led Carol to admit to a change in him, even if she followed with a diatribe. That something was God's activity, he acknowledged. Right now, Jerry was going to gamble that God would continue to deal with her intractability and lead her one step further.

"My plane leaves at two tomorrow," he called out as she breezed across the threshold, with her back to him. "I'd like to drop by on the way to the airport. I'm sorry if it cuts in on your church time."

As expected, he saw her duck her head at the last part of the statement. Her body language confirmed what he suspected—church attendance hadn't been part of her life, of late.

"If you think you must, alright," Carol finally consented wearily, as she turned to face him but strategically leaned on an antique hall tree as a physical barrier. "For Pop."

"Yes," Jerry parroted. "For Pop."

Then, to his surprise, she added, "You'll need lunch, I suppose. You bought mine today; I'll return the favor. I'll fix some sandwiches."

Jerry's heart bounded so at that suggestion, he was momentarily dumfounded. Then, regaining control, he tried to respond matter-of-factly.

"That's nice of you, Carol," he commented mildly, his voice tinged with more relief than he intended. Their eyes locked for one brief moment before she caught herself and looked away.

With the pressure off slightly, then, since there now *would* be a tomorrow, Jerry said his farewell, again without so much as a handshake.

Back at the hotel, he collapsed into a desperate sleep, exhausted from the day's string of events. Jerry dreamed of tomorrow and today's piercing words, "I'm sorry, Jerry. She shouldn't have treated you rudely," that continued to mystify and, oddly, to hearten him.

Even in his dreams, Jerry was sure he was entreating God for wisdom as he prepared to tell Carol good-bye, perhaps forever.

TWENTY ONE

Three Healing Words

❀

Jerry found Carol in a refreshingly expansive mood when he arrived at her apartment for their early lunch on Sunday.

When she opened the door, her brown eyes looked straight into his blue ones, more directly than usual.

"Hi," she said, simply, and rather pleasantly. It was her first civil greeting of the weekend.

"Hi," he responded back, in a quiet, husky voice, masking his surprise.

His eyes immediately zoomed in on the attractive table she had set for their meal. A spongeware vase held two fresh red rosebuds and some baby's breath. It sat in the middle of a white cloth draping an antique oak pedestal table.

Waiting for him on the table, set with spongeware dinner plates that matched the vase, were some tempting meatball sandwiches, a veggie tray with dip, and brownies for dessert. Carol clearly had taken some effort to prepare.

Jerry's eyes quickly roamed around her apartment inquisitively. On Friday night, his survival mode left little time for him to note his surroundings. Today, with things more relaxed, he could scope out added details of Carol's environment.

The mauve-print sofa on which they had conversed sat in the middle of a braided rug, with an antique rocker and an oak trunk Carol used as a coffee table as the room's other furnishings.

Several items of needlework—probably stitched by Carol's mother—were framed as accessories in the room. A large quilt with lively colors matching the rug and sofa was the focal point of one wall.

The homespun touches and the warm, vibrant colors were so like the Carol he remembered—so fitting for a place she would call home. Jerry was glad he hadn't found her living in one of those ultra-sleek, chrome-appointed, antiseptic-white numbers, although it would have been more in keeping with her cool overtones since he arrived. He hoped the cozy decor of her apartment proved that the old nature still thrived somewhere beneath Carol's crust of hurt.

"I thought I remembered that you liked mint tea," Carol stated cheerily, as she set two tall goblets on the table.

"This spread sure beats that dried-up airplane food that I would have had for lunch otherwise," Jerry replied appreciatively, nodding toward the meal laid out in front of them.

At his request, Carol directed Jerry to the hallway bath, so he could wash up before dining.

As he headed back to join her, Jerry caught a glimpse of Carol's bedroom off the hallway. Not surprisingly, it was warmly appointed like the living room. Her antique oak bed with a carved headboard was covered with a handmade quilt. Snapshots in a potpourri of interesting frames lined her bureau.

Two pieces of fitness equipment—her stationary bike and a stair-climber—flanked the windows. *So that's how she stays reed-thin,* Jerry assessed. He filed that detail away with all the other delectable Carol-trivia that he had collected this weekend in Wooster.

Then he spotted it—the telltale item in one corner of her room that created a maelstrom in his heart.

At the end of her dresser was an enormous bouquet of red roses—two dozen of them, at least—spilling over the top of a tall, crystal vase. They were undoubtedly the source of the two she had plucked out for the table arrangement. Jerry noted ruefully that they were fresh, tight buds—too new to have arrived much before last evening. That would explain the pervading scent of roses that greeted him in the apartment today. Unless he was mistaken, it was a scent that hadn't been present yesterday or the day before.

Kevin must have come to call, Jerry conjectured. As he suspected, Carol's new suitor had likely paid her a visit last night after Jerry's afternoon with her. He must have toted the roses to ameliorate Carol's "headache" after the broken date.

Now Carol could entertain Jerry with a clear conscience, knowing she could be hospitable to him today and still keep her relationship with Kevin safe.

A lump lodged in his throat, and he wondered how he could possibly force down a bite of the lunch Carol had prepared. His steps slowed in the hallway, and he took his time rejoining her at the meal.

With this new knowledge lumbering around in his head, Jerry's mind played all kinds of tricks on him as he eyed Carol studiously from his hallway vantage point.

Her hair was pulled back in a youthful French braid, and her makeup was perfect. Her full, outlined red lips matched the red, ribbed sweater that she wore over navy pants. Could it be that she was headed for a date this afternoon with Kevin, after Jerry was out of the picture?

With these prospects, Jerry found himself about as steady as a loose board as he seated himself at the ladder-back chair at the table. His hand shook as he took hold of the veggie tray Carol passed him.

But once they began to dine, he found his spirits lifted by Carol's chatty banter.

For the first time since he arrived, she actually initiated a conversation, asking him, "So, what's on tap for you when you get back to Sky Ranch?"

Jerry described his schedule for the near future. The boys were working on a talent show that they would present in about six weeks. It would be a commencement for some who would go home permanently at the end of their level 6 stage at Sky Ranch. Parents who could do so would attend. It was always a highlight of the ranch activities.

Beyond that, Jerry planned to take several of the residents on a four-day trip to Topeka to be part of a student panel on alternative schools like Sky Ranch. While there, they would hear a contemporary Christian group in concert and see some tourist attractions.

"For several of them, it's their first time off campus in a year," Jerry explained. Pride in his young charges was unmistakable in his voice.

Then, when it was Carol's turn to talk, she volunteered without prompting what life would be like at school for her in the days ahead: softball schedules to coordinate, practices to coach, and a conference in Akron where she would present a paper.

When lunch was finished, Carol went to the kitchen and brought out a piece of plastic wrap and a brown paper sack. In it she encased several brownies that remained uneaten. She gave them to Jerry for a snack on his airplane flight home.

"When everyone else on the plane gets their peanuts, you'll have these," she suggested.

Oddly, Jerry found himself thankful for the roses and for Kevin's visit. In a bittersweet reflection, Jerry mulled, *If this is what it takes to see the brighter side of Carol again, I won't complain.*

Then, because of Carol's almost playful mood that had underscored their visit today, Jerry took a gamble. Looking at the to-go package of brownies he turned around in his hand, Jerry quipped, "It's amazing, isn't it? To think I once proposed to you without ever even tasting your cooking."

He waited for Carol to turn dour at the mention of their painful past relationship, but to his relief, she maintained the lighthearted spirit of things.

"So you did," she reflected, squelching a hint of a slow grin that started to creep over her face. "Well, now that you *have* sampled it, just think what you missed out on."

This time, it was Jerry who turned somber, as his thoughts went beyond Carol's culinary skills.

"I do—every day," he murmured remorsefully. Such a burst of sadness suddenly seized his heart that he instinctively put his hand to his chest. It was the closest he had come all weekend to revealing to Carol the depth of his love for her still. Dr. Naylor had coached him that this was not yet the appropriate time to lay himself bare in that arena, lest Carol perceive it as manipulation, so he had tried to avoid anything that might seem like pressure for a commitment.

For a minute these words that pulled back the curtain on his soul hung heavy in the air. Because he saw there was no way to withdraw them, he simply let them hang there, swagged with the intensity of the moment, and let them find their home in Carol's heart, for better or for worse.

After Carol sat there, looking frozen at him and making no response for what seemed like centuries, Jerry suddenly remembered his watch. He knew it was time for his parting remarks, which he had carefully rehearsed with Dr. Naylor.

He thanked Carol for making time for his unexpected visit. "You've been a real trooper," he said, trying to smile, and failing miserably.

He then handed Carol a slip of paper containing his mailing address and phone number at Sky Ranch. Just as he directed her on Friday night, Jerry advised her that the ball would be in her court with regard to their further communication. He offered to phone her, write her, come back to Wooster to visit her again, or even send her a plane ticket to visit him at Sky Ranch, if she desired. He again saw no point in telling her that all this had already been arranged with Bo and Sally, in their great-hearted desire to help make him whole.

"Maybe it would help if you came to this place that has meant so much to me. You could meet some of the people who helped me," he offered. "Maybe you could piece together the past twelve months more easily if you visualized how I've lived."

At this invitation she visibly shrank a little—why, he wasn't exactly sure. She merely thanked him courteously and, not surprisingly, made no commitment. Jerry looked at his watch, saw that their visit was approaching an end, and rose to take his leave.

Suddenly Carol stopped him.

Lifting her eyes, which had been focused on a fold in her napkin, she said, "Jerry, you said you came here seeking only one thing from me, and I haven't given it to you. I've been so numb and then in such denial, I hadn't thought much about forgiveness. When you mentioned it to me this weekend, I remembered that it's part of the process. That's what Pop told me—way back there, at first—that I would have to do it eventually—but I had forgotten. I've heard your apology and I forgive you."

Jerry was incredulous. Those three healing words that he thought he would go away still craving—they had just tumbled from Carol's lips! Maybe her blithe spirits today weren't totally due to preoccupation with Kevin. Maybe the Holy Spirit had truly done a work in her heart. Maybe she felt released from the tentacles of unforgiveness, the way Jerry remembered feeling a few months back.

With all that was in him, Jerry wanted to grab Carol and hug her and express his boundless joy.

He resisted by merely saying, "Thank you, oh, thank you. That really means a lot." Tears stung the corners of his eyes, but he fought them back. His confidence and uncharacteristic strength of character seemed to have caught Carol's attention this weekend, so he must remain confident still. He smiled at her and turned toward the door.

Carol called him back. "Jerry, just tell me this. Do I have something to apologize for, too? Pop said he did. In his letter, he said he recognized that he played a role in what happened to you. Please tell me. What should I have seen? What should I have done? What could have made a difference?"

Jerry couldn't believe what he just heard. So Carol *had* been listening to him. He chose his words carefully as he answered.

"This is no time for recriminations, Carrie. The past is past. I'm not here placing any blame, except on myself."

"Please tell me," she begged. "I have to know. For months I searched my soul, asking myself what I had done. The things you've said about yourself—Jerry, was I blind not to see them? Did you drop hints that I missed? What did I not pick up on?"

Jerry looked at his watch and swallowed hard. Here at the eleventh hour, with an airplane schedule to meet, Carol had suddenly come alive—with questions that even Dr. Naylor didn't provide him a script to answer. His emotions felt like they'd been caught in the blades of an electric mixer. He prayed frenziedly, quickly. How in the few remaining seconds could he bridge the gap and take leave of her in a way that would honor Christ?

Jerry sat back down at the table beside her and looked at her squarely. "I put other gods before me, Carol. Instead of making serving God my priority, I made pleasing others my god. I took on too much. I refused to take care of the body God gave me. I refused to speak up for my needs and refused to give God first place in my life. If I had served Him as I should have, I would have taken time to grieve properly. I would have stopped before I rushed us both into a commitment, and I would have learned to cope better under stress. I didn't know what I was doing was wrong—but that doesn't make me less responsible for my mistakes."

"Then that doesn't make me less responsible, either," Carol replied. "I'm sorry I didn't know how to help you."

"I forgave you long ago," Jerry said, and Pop's words suddenly rang in his ear, as the fulfillment of a prophecy. Pop had told him, "'Forgive me' is the sweetest phrase on earth, and if you and Carol can exchange those words, it

234

will enable you both to go in peace." The words were now out on the table.

"We can't look back except to learn," Jerry tried to add, consolingly. "But I hope in the future that if anyone sees me abusing myself or others in that way, they'll hold a mirror up to me, in love—and if I don't pay attention, then bop me in the head."

He tried to laugh a little at his last statement, but the laughter didn't come quickly enough to cover up the sob that shoved its way through his throat.

It was suddenly too much. Jerry lowered his head. A tear slid down each cheek. His time had gone, and no more minutes were left. The tears had fallen, and he made no effort to apologize or check them.

Now, he must go. He took one last, long, loving look at Carol, with the stranglehold she had on his hurting heart threatening to overpower him, and drank in her face in case he saw it no more. He knew she need have no worry this time about whether he would smother her with physical affection. He was moving so rapidly to make his plane connection that Carol, still seated in the ladder-back chair, could rest assured that she was safe.

Jerry backed toward the door and called out, straining to keep his voice from breaking, "If you ever want to talk some more, you know where to call."

Then he was down the steps—headed toward a waiting plane, rushed, sad, with a myriad of feelings that would take weeks to sort out.

But thanks to Carol's three healing words, he felt free, at last.

TWENTY TWO

Hope's Smallest Ray

❁

Sky Ranch had never looked so beckoning as it did when Jerry finally pulled in about seven o'clock on Sunday night after his grueling trip to Ohio and Carol.

Bo had been there when his plane arrived in Goodland, the closest airport to Sky Ranch. Their hour-long trip by car to the rural area beyond Colby had been one continuous monologue, as Jerry poured out his experiences.

Later that evening, they settled in around the kitchen table, with welcoming hot tea and cookies served them on the red-and-white checked cloth. Sally wanted to hear everything first-hand, as well, so Jerry repeated his story—gladly, as part of his catharsis.

Carol had been right. Sky Ranch might have been a protective bubble for him, sheltering him temporarily from the world's hard knocks, but right now, it was the bubble he needed. The support he felt from this devoted couple was all that carried him along as he tried to make sense of what had transpired in his time away.

Then, on Monday, Dr. Naylor made a rare, special trip to Sky Ranch in the afternoon, so he could help Jerry process this critical visit.

All three of them—his counselor, as well as his brother and sister-in-law—affirmed Jerry for his courage. They commended him for how well he conducted himself amid Carol's initial hostility.

Dr. Naylor praised Jerry for remaining secure in himself throughout the rebuffs and for constantly reminding himself of God's approval.

He applauded him for refusing to beg or grovel, even when everything in his nature pulled him to do otherwise.

"It sounds as if you kept your focus on your own sense of self, and you kept your eye on the goal of forgiveness," Dr. Naylor told him.

After a few days, Jerry telephoned Pop to give him a report, since Pop's letter had played such a crucial role in how Carol received him.

He confirmed for Pop the two disturbing matters about which he had warned Jerry: the appearance of Kevin as a new date, and Carol's declining spiritual condition.

"I know you wished it otherwise, son," Pop said in a weak but consoling voice. "We must never stop praying that Carol will find the joy of her salvation."

Most rewarding to Pop was the fact that both Jerry and Carol had asked for and obtained forgiveness.

"I hope that in the long run, this fact alone will bring you great peace," Pop told him warmly.

Jerry did feel at peace. He felt that before God, he had done all he could do to make things right with Carol. He believed that from God's perspective, the slate was wiped clean.

He went about his duties at Sky Ranch with a lighter heart. Returning to the routine, he threw himself into the details of the upcoming Talent Night, which thoroughly occupied the boys these days.

As days dragged by and no communication of any kind arrived from Carol, Jerry felt sure that her rejection of him was a reality. After all, nothing in her demeanor when he left her apartment that Sunday indicated anything but a permanent good-bye. *She's got Kevin now—she made it clear I'm history*, Jerry kept reminding himself again and again, any time thoughts of Carol surfaced.

Bo and Sally and Dr. Naylor combined forces to give Jerry a new focus. Bo began helping Jerry work in the very area Carol targeted—goals for his life and for his coping beyond Sky Ranch.

"It's not that I wouldn't like to have you here forever," Bo explained to him one night after dinner. "But you're too qualified to remain here for long. I know that coaching athletics for troubled youth isn't the terminal job for you. Besides, I'm sure you'd eventually like to earn a salary."

"And you'd probably be happy to be minus one boarder," Jerry teased back.

Actually, his conversation with Carol about his future had started his wheels spinning already, even before he and Bo talked. It *was* time that he moved on, or at least used his work at Sky Ranch to augment employment outside.

He began to think he might like to attend graduate school for a master's degree in social work. He would be better trained to work with alternative youth, as he had at Sky Ranch.

He had thought about combining a part-time job with graduate school. He started writing for graduate school catalogs.

But employment and higher education weren't the only areas where Jerry had been doing some pondering. Especially during the time in Ohio when he was waiting for Carol's forgiveness, Jerry's thoughts had turned more and more to the breached relationship with his father.

It was actually Jerry who brought up the subject first in Dr. Naylor's office one afternoon.

"You've been very patient with me and haven't pressed," he told the counselor. "I know you've been wondering when I was really going to try to make things right with him."

Dr. Naylor gave him an all-knowing nod.

"These relationships with Carol and with Pop are all-important to you, but they're actually peripheral in the whole scope of things," he responded. "The primal relationship, in the long run, is the one with your parents. It's the rudder that steers the boat. You've learned some important skills as you've sought forgiveness and sought to maintain some kind of equilibrium with Carol and Pop, but the most important restoration goes far deeper than these."

Jerry acted as though he understood.

"Those days in Ohio, when I was waiting to hear from Carol—when it seemed I might have to live the rest of my life without ever hearing her pardon me—that's when it hit me—how truly sweet it is to extend forgiveness, how sweet it is to know that the person you had wronged has released you," Jerry said. "That's when I knew—I had to do that for my father. Even if he never knew it, I wanted to be able to free him in my heart. I've now forgiven him, fully and completely. I release all that from any hold it might have over me."

Jerry was amazed that he could remain dry-eyed, without feeling torn limb from limb emotionally. He had shed many tears over this matter long ago, including that weekend in the motel room in Wooster. His tears of relief and longing over Carol had been co-mingled with his tears of joy at forgiving his father as well.

Then he looked at Dr. Naylor questioningly.

"Did it take me too long? Am I overly slow, or something? Were you about to give up on me, wondering when I'd reach this stage?"

The counselor looked not the least bit surprised or disturbed or frustrated.

"No," he shook his head kindly. "What you did was perfectly logical. You understood the hold your past had on you; you gained insights from it; you identified the source. You were able to see the unhealthy patterns that sprang from these harmful relationships in your early life.

"But forgiving those that hurt you to the core, like early adult role models—it takes a long time, sometimes years. If I had tried to rush you, it would have only thwarted the process. I knew you'd hit upon it eventually, and it would unfold just as naturally as it has this morning."

"Wow," was all Jerry could say, as the counselor's words dawned on him. He had released his father—years and years of anger and bitterness were suddenly erased.

As Dr. Naylor waited silently, Jerry's thoughts then moved to a new level.

"I know Bo goes down there—goes to see him. Sometimes Bo invites him here," he mulled, thinking out loud as he explored the prospects. "They get along, tolerably I guess. He says our dad has changed a lot, that he doesn't drink anymore. It's been hard for me to imagine him any other way."

"When you think about it, it might be hard for him to imagine you as the mature adult that you are, too—one who doesn't get ruffled by people's criticism as you used to," Dr. Naylor ventured.

Jerry cogitated over that one for a while. The confidence in the face of rebuff that he had exhibited at Carol's—could he do that with his dad, as well? Could he unlearn a lifetime of old ways of relating?

The therapist interrupted his thoughts. "You told me your dad bought a small business and moved down to western Kansas a few years ago after his last layoff," he stated. "Why do you think he chose this part of the country to live?"

Jerry shrugged. "I've tried not to give it much thought," he said. "Maybe he was trying to get away from the place where he had his problems. Maybe he was a bolter, like me. Maybe I come by it honestly."

"Hmm," Dr. Naylor mulled. "That could be part of it. Sometimes, though, people hold out hope that being close in proximity will make up for being close emotionally. You and Bo both were in the West. Does he feel better being nearby? Was this one feeble attempt to show love for you, even when he really doesn't know how?"

"I don't know," Jerry frowned, as fear gnawed at him. "I'll have to think about that one a while. I don't know if I could ever visit him. It's been easier for Bo to go down there. He just doesn't have the baggage that I have with Dad. Even if I decided it was the right thing to do, I just don't know if I can trust myself to hold up."

"Then you just think about it," Dr. Naylor counseled. "I believe that seeing him again *is* something you'll want to do someday. When God gives you the nudge, you'll know it. Just remember, when you decide you're ready, I'll be here to help."

Soon it was time to take the boys to Topeka for their presentation. The trip represented a first for Sky Ranch: Bo had always held tight reins on the residents' comings and goings, since some were lawbreakers and some were there against their will. It was what the state—and the parents who called on Sky Ranch for help—expected of him. Only on rare, and closely guarded, occasions had Bo allowed a few of the level-6 boys to go into town, escorted. These safety measures had paid off. In his two years of operating the ranch, Bo had experienced no runaways and had foiled the occasional attempt or threat.

But the invitation for Jerry to take the boys to speak at the state-sponsored program on alternative schooling was such a grand affirmation for the Sky Ranch program that Bo was willing to take the gamble. It came at an especially crucial moment for Jerry, who had worked tirelessly with the four boys selected to get them ready for the event.

One afternoon before they departed, Bo sent Jerry with the four panelists to town to buy the boys sports jackets for the event.

"While you're shopping, find something for yourself," Bo directed. "No sense in these guys out-dressing you." He shoved $500 in crisp $100 bills into Jerry's hand. "This is just for you. Spend all of it," Bo instructed.

Jerry was speechless with gratitude. Bo and Sally had spent more on him than he could ever repay—especially during his weekend in Ohio. Now, they wanted to replenish his closet, as well.

Jerry knew his wardrobe sadly did need a boost. In the year he'd lived at Sky Ranch, he only bought a pair of athletic shoes and some white crew socks. If he were about to start interviewing soon for jobs or grad school, he would need more than his array of blue jeans, sweats, and sneakers. While the boys purchased new threads, Jerry found a sports coat, two pairs of slacks, two shirts, and a tie with an equestrian motif.

The clothes were confidence-builders in themselves, Jerry decided as he surveyed himself in the fitting room mirror. Over the years, people had often told him he was a handsome man. In high school, he had been voted best-looking, and in college, girls told him he was hunky. Jerry never could see it, really. In fact, he always had qualms about his appearance—qualms that he now understood were related to his self-concept. This time, as he assessed himself, it was as though Jerry saw himself through new eyes.

Interesting that how the inside always colored the way I looked at myself on the outside, Jerry realized. *Now I'm actually starting to like what I see—inside and out.*

The trip to Topeka came off successfully, with Jerry decidedly in charge of the boys, all level 6-ers, and with few significant behavior challenges. The boys were so proud of themselves for remembering their lines and for sounding competent when talking about Sky Ranch that they fairly danced out of the conference center.

That night, they were invited to a reception where the governor attended. Jerry arranged for photos as each of them shook the governor's hand. Well-groomed and not the least bit ill-at-ease in their new jackets and ties, they acted polished as any prep school youth might, Jerry thought.

The Christian concert afterwards was a special perk. The entire trip was an experience that none of them would ever forget, Jerry included, and that would shape their lives and their self-images forever.

If only I could tell Carol about this, he said to himself almost instinctively, and then of course thought better of it.

Bo and Sally and the rest of the staff were eager for a full report when Jerry and the boys got back. Jerry pushed a videotape of the program into Bo's VCR so all could see the performance first-hand.

Bo gushed with praise. "This is every bit your handi-work," he beamed at his brother. "I could have never done this without you, Jerry. Having you here has been such a blessing to me."

Jerry did feel great personal pride—the boys had come through, and he had squeaked by without a behav-ior incident. He accepted Bo's kudos with a smile wide as Kansas.

But as soon as he could politely slip away from the viewing, he darted to his mailbox to look for letters or messages. Nothing.

"Sorry, Jer," Bo yelled out to him, sensing his angst about Carol's continued silence. "We've all been on the lookout for you. Wish we could make it happen, like magic."

Jerry tried to keep from crumpling in front of every-one who had been so affirming. "I wish so, too," he said, struggling to hide the fact that his heart was shattering into a million pieces.

After taking polite leave of the well-wishing group, it was a race for Jerry to see whether he could get back to his room and kick the door closed behind him before the tears that he held back started to gush.

Jerry had left word for Bo to call him in Topeka the moment something surfaced, and no calls had ever come. Still, he had hoped beyond hope to find some shred of evidence of Carol by the time he arrived home.

Sorrowfully, he hung in his closet the new clothes he had bought for the trip—clothes, he now realized, he had picked out partly with Carol in mind. Any scintilla of hope had evaporated—Carol would never see them.

"Carrie. Carrie. Will I ever get over you?" Jerry sobbed plaintively, as he slammed his closet door too loudly.

Then, as Jerry's eyes roamed around his room, trying to make sense of his world, they halted on a folded piece of paper that stuck out from the edge of his desk pad.

He pulled out the item and saw it was actually the edge of an envelope. A yellow note attached to it read:

"Jerry—This was stuck in my box by mistake. Jason." The note covered up his address on the envelope—in Carol's handwriting!

It was a letter from Carol—a letter that, according to the postmark, arrived while he was away. Hadn't Bo known? Jerry resisted his first urge to rip into it. He ran outside his room where the boys were gathering.

He spotted Jason's towhead. "Hey, Jace!" Jerry called out to him, trying to keep from sounding anxious.

"Jerry! Welcome back, buddy," Jason hollered, scrunching Jerry's shoulder in a firm grip. Jason was a level 5, and one of his favorites.

"Thanks. Say, about this envelope on my desk—I just now found it."

"Yeah, it was weird. My mom forgot to seal her letter. When I turned it over, yours was tucked under the flap—like the two had gotten stuck together. I brought it to you as soon as I found it. Was that OK?" Jason wanted to be a level 6 badly and began looking at Jerry a little sheepishly. He feared Jerry had discovered some infraction that would keep him from his goal.

"Fine, just fine," Jerry answered, as the picture of this mystifying event came into focus. "Just curious, though—did you happen to tell Bo?"

Jason looked horrified. "Gosh, no. I didn't think to. I mean, should I have?" Jason was visibly edgy now, his defenses rising. Jerry saw he had to act quickly to keep the boy from panicking. He knew that Bo and Sally didn't always sort the mail personally—and if Carol's envelope was actually hiding under the other, it could have slipped past discerning eyes.

He slung an arm around Jason's frame. "Not at all, buddy. You did just great. I just appreciate your getting it to me. Thanks. Now get on to your quiet time."

"I got Hilda to put it in your room," Jason called as an afterthought, halfway down the hallway. Hilda was the woman who swept out the "A" Barracks. Jason wanted to make sure he covered every base in his explanation.

"Thanks again. You did absolutely right," Jerry said, determined to reassure the boy.

Now, with this mystery settled, he fairly sailed back to his room—slamming the door quickly again this time, but for a far different reason than he had a moment ago.

Carol *had* written him—a letter that eluded even Bo's most watchful eye. Instead of ripping into it, as he had almost done earlier, Jerry merely tossed it on his bedspread and stared at it for a moment. It had been almost three weeks since his visit to see Carol in Ohio. Was this letter her final good-bye?

His arms suddenly froze at his side. He tiptoed around the letter for a few seconds, as though it were a bomb getting ready to detonate.

Finally, though, he breathed a prayer, stuck one of his keys in a corner of the envelope flap to make a rough tear, and pulled out the single sheet of paper, written on by hand. Brief. Too brief. His heart sank even further. *It doesn't take many lines to give a brush-off,* Jerry thought, his hands trembling as he held the flimsy page.

As he finally allowed his eyes to make out the words, he saw this:

"Dear Jerry:

It's taken me a while to think of what to write. When you were here, I was in such shock, I'm not even sure what I said to you. I know I was probably not the best host. I have more questions— some things I'd like to understand better, now that the dust has settled. You said you'd be willing to make another trip. I'd like you to come to Wooster again. I promise to be more cordial and show you a better time.

Please let me know if you can do this. Our campus drama group performs *Steel Magnolias* in two weekends, on the 27th. Some of my students are starring. Could you visit then? Just let me know.

Sincerely, Carol"

This time, the phrase "for Pop" was nowhere in sight. Jerry tore through the barracks like a wild man and raced outside, charging to the pay phone by the dining hall. Before picking up the receiver, he looked around. Dr. Naylor wouldn't be back until Tuesday. Bo and Sally had turned in for the evening—the light in their bedroom was already out. No time to consult—should he wait until tomorrow to call, after his heart stopped slamming through the wall of his chest?

Then he remembered. The letter was postmarked almost a week ago and had lain on his desk for his return. Carol had waited several days already for an answer. He would give himself five more minutes to pray about this to avoid answering in haste.

At the end of three, he realized he was chanting the same prayer over and over—"God, help me." With his heart drumming furiously, he gave up and dialed the number.

It was 11 o'clock in Wooster, but Carol's voice gave the impression she was wide awake.

"No, just grading quizzes," she answered, when Jerry asked if he'd disturbed her sleep.

Jerry explained about his trip to Topeka and how he'd just now found the mail. He waited for her reply, hoping the invitation stood.

Her response still seemed eager. "Well, what about it? Can you come?" she asked pleasantly.

Jerry knew he hadn't checked with Bo, but he also knew Bo. His brother had demonstrated he would do everything in his power to help him put his life back together.

He took the plunge and committed.

"I'll be there," he promised, saying words that half an hour ago seemed hopelessly impossible.

Then he took another plunge, a more critical one, but on a score he had to settle.

"Look, Carol, if we're going to do this, I have to know about Kevin," he ventured, swallowing hard.

"Kevin? What about Kevin?" she asked, her tone suddenly more cautious.

"Well—where things stand with him. I mean, last time I was there, you made up excuses. You acted under subterfuge. It was a cloud over things. What about this time?"

Long silence followed. Jerry sensed he had tread into dangerous waters. His eyes felt hot, and his stomach knotted.

"It's not a problem, Jerry," Carol finally snapped out, her voice now as clipped as a crew cut.

"What do you mean, it's not a problem?" Had she and Kevin called it quits? Was Kevin acquiescing to his visit so Carol could get this former fiance out of her system?

More tremulous silence.

"He'll be away that weekend," she eventually said, her voice growing icier.

So Carol was playing her cards close to her vest on the matter of Kevin. Perhaps she was hedging her bets—clinging to the boyfriend she had while allowing herself to feel curious about the love from her past. Had she picked out the weekend of the 27th deliberately because she knew Kevin would be away?

Just as Jerry started to flare, he gave himself a refresher course in history. Could he really blame Carol? After all, Jerry was still in the trust-rebuilding mode with her. Carol had every right to keep her guard up. He would try to look on this opportunity as a gift of grace, to do simply what Carol asked—to return to Ohio, to fellowship in a more relaxed setting, and to share more about how the Lord had been at work in his life.

No promises, no commitments, no declarations of love. Just one more chance that God had allowed. He declined to press further, realizing that to do so would put things at risk.

"Good. Glad to hear it. See you on the 27th," he said, parting on a cordial note. He promised to call her back with travel information And so the conversation ended.

Back in his room that night, Jerry propped Carol's letter in a prominent place on his desk where his eyes could fix on it any time he walked in the room, whenever he wakened, while he was changing clothes, before he began his quiet time.

It was only a piece of paper, but for Jerry, it represented the first, small ray of hope that he had dared allow himself to feel.

TWENTY THREE

Lingering Questions

❄

This time, Carol met Jerry at the airport when his flight landed in Wooster. As soon as he stepped into the waiting area, he saw her leaning against a pillar, watching for him in another direction.

Jerry hurriedly scanned her face to see what he could read. Although somewhat somber, she looked relaxed, unstressed—far different from last time.

Then he noticed something else different about her. Her hair was cut several inches shorter—chin-length, with one side pulled back provocatively behind her ear. Although Jerry had considered her long, delectable mane worn down as she had at Valley Lodge to be her true beauty, the shorter cut looked stunning on her. It gave her a slightly more mature appearance—older and wiser, Jerry thought a little wistfully—and seemed appropriate, under the circumstances.

When she finally glanced in his direction, her eyes widened in recognition, and she stepped toward him.

Jerry kept his canvas duffel in one hand and a magazine in another so his arms would be visibly occupied. He didn't want Carol to worry that he'd try to hug her in greeting.

"Carol," he called out brightly, as strode up to her side. "You look terrific." Then he added, "Your hair looks great."

"Thanks," she responded simply, without elaboration. Carol clearly warmed to Jerry's spontaneous compliment, and a pleasant smile spread across her face. "I'm parked right out front. I'll pull my car around to the luggage area and meet you there."

Carol was sparing no detail to be sure she was more hospitable this time. As they drove from the airport to his motel, she outlined for him the itinerary she had planned for them.

They would dine that evening, a Friday, at a downtown restaurant she had picked out. During the day tomorrow, Carol wanted to take him on a more thorough tour than last time. Tomorrow night was the campus play she mentioned, with her students performing.

Then Carol took a deep breath and broached a more difficult subject hurriedly, as if to get it behind her.

"After what happened last time, I'm sure you'd wonder," she said. "Most of the people we might run into this weekend have no idea that you and I had a connection once. The only person even clued in is my friend Cathy. She knows everything that goes on in my life. I'm lucky to have her since Shannon's away. She's completely understanding and will be friendly to a fault, I'm sure. And Dr. Northcutt—well, we've had a good talk since you were here before. I doubt we see her, but if we do, she'll be cordial."

Jerry tried to squelch a bemused smile. He'd hardly given a thought to the issues that Carol nervously mentioned—the accidental stumbling onto people who knew her story—but he loved the way it seemed to matter to her. A self-conscious, almost shy look had crept across her face as she struggled to get the words out just then.

Then it was Jerry's turn to clear his throat and make the covert overt. "Well, sounds like we're defining house rules for the weekend, so I'll mention one, too," he said, as Carol's eyes narrowed in curiosity. "Carol, I really want us to feel comfortable around each other. I don't want you to worry that you have to be on guard. I know you remember me as a guy who likes to get amorous. I still do—after all, I'm only human."

He smiled a little in remembrance, and her eyes grew wider, as she pondered what he might say next.

"But you have my promise," Jerry continued. "While I'm here—in fact, any time we might be together in the future—while we're trying to sort things out, please know you have my assurance. I'll be the picture of discretion. I won't touch you. I promise. We probably got into that too early at Valley Lodge. What's done is done. This time, I want to do things right."

By that point, Carol's eyes were wide as plates—looking thoroughly incredulous at the pledge he just made. For minutes, she sat motionless as a tree stump—saying nothing, gaping, as though she had heard him wrong.

Finally, she stammered, "That's . . . that's very . . . thoughtful of you." He wasn't sure she totally believed him, considering his past history, but he hoped that his restraint on his last visit had made a deposit in the bank account of trust he was building with her.

As they stopped by her apartment briefly, he thankfully saw no hint of his competitor, as he had before. No scent of roses wafted through the door this time. No framed portraits of Kevin could be spotted, nor anything else to indicate Carol had a special beau, but that didn't mean that Kevin wasn't a regular presence here.

Jerry cracked his knuckles sharply, as though he could wipe the dreaded thought away by doing so. *I'll make myself sick if I dwell on it,* he decided as he drove Carol's car to his motel to get ready for the evening. *Carol says Kevin's not a problem this weekend. I've got to stop letting him preoccupy me, or else I'll tear down everything I'm building.*

They dined at The Embassy Room, a upper-story restaurant where the city lights against a dark sky were an enchanting backdrop. Carol had pulled out all the stops to make it a cordial evening—reserving a table with the best view and pre-ordering a special meal that was feast for a king.

Carol was equally a feast for the eyes in her deep hunter green crepe pants suit. The flattering new hairstyle showed off some pearl and jeweled ear clips that sparkled like the panorama behind her.

Jerry wondered if it recalled for her, as it did him, memories of the first romantic meal they shared together—at The Wild Goose—on the night in Crested Butte that they first began to fall in love. How much water had fallen under the bridge since then—how many regrets!

He stopped himself and remembered his old pledge about self-flagellation. *I'd never be the person I am if those times hadn't happened,* he remembered. *God used all those to grow me, and I wouldn't be sitting here now, with Christ in my heart, without them.*

As their meal was served, Jerry proudly told Carol about his trip with the boys to Topeka and their reception with the governor. He talked about applying to graduate school so he could get advanced training in working with difficult youth. He shared other ideas he was considering for future employment.

Then, he boldly brought up the matter that Carol had mentioned as a reason for inviting him.

"You said you had some questions—some things you want to clarify," he said, inwardly sweating bullets but trying to appear eager. "That's what I'm here for."

Without hesitation, Carol's queries came pouring out. They were obviously pent-up from many weeks of digesting their last talk.

One of them he anticipated—a question Dr. Naylor warned him was typical for friends and family of persons in recovery.

"You said everything that happened at Valley Lodge stemmed from unresolved hurts from your childhood," Carol stated. "But why couldn't you just forget the past? Sure, your father hurt you once. Why couldn't you just say, 'That was then. This is now'? Why'd you have to let it spill over to so many areas of your life?"

Jerry knew gaining understanding would not be easy for someone who had not walked his same pathway, but he did his best to explain.

"It was complicated because I had so many bad habits to unlearn," Jerry began. "From my dad I got the message that I was no good, that I didn't measure up, and that I had to achieve in order to please. Once I got around Pop, all those messages got transferred, because he was in the father role. I became terrified of disappointing him, just like I had my father. Growing up, no feelings were allowed, so I kept everything suppressed. Until I met Dr. Naylor, I didn't even know I had a right to hurt about what happened when I was young. It would have been hard to put behind me something that I didn't even know I had a right to feel."

Carol looked puzzled. "No right to hurt—about a father who criticized you and tried to run your business?"

Jerry knew this concept would be especially difficult for her, because of the loving relationship with her own father.

"When your father is an alcoholic, you learn to suppress feelings. In my family, his feelings were the only ones that mattered. If I came home from school sad because I made a bad grade, I couldn't cry on someone's shoulder. If I did anything to upset my dad, it might cause him to drink even more. I didn't have any other frame of reference. I thought it was normal—that expressing any kind of feelings was wrong."

"You couldn't tell your parents if you had a bad day at school?" Carol inquired. Her mystified but earnest expression said she was genuinely trying to tune in.

"Or that I needed new jeans. Or that I wanted to have a birthday party. Basically everyone's needs were secondary to Dad's," Jerry answered.

"You didn't have birthday parties?" Carol probed. As an only child of loving, doting parents, Jerry imagined she never missed a year.

"Or be allowed to invite friends over. If someone ever came to visit, there'd be the risk that the person would

252

find a liquor bottle under the sofa cushion. So we just kept that our family secret."

"What a bummer," Carol said, her voice now empathetic and sweet as in former times, and he could tell from her face that she meant it.

"It was, but I didn't know it. I just knew that resentment kept building. Pop caught the brunt of it, because he took on the father role. The more he pushed me to do, the closer to the brink I came, except, of course, I didn't know how to speak up, so I just let it keep happening."

"Pop never said a harsh word to you."

"Right—that's what makes it doubly bizarre," Jerry agreed. "It wasn't what he said or didn't say. It was what I perceived—because of the way I was programmed. I was so afraid of failure that I put everything on myself. I perceived Pop was waiting for me to goof up so he could rail at me, the way my dad had."

"But you did a good job—everyone said so," Carol protested, defending him.

"You're trying to make it logical, Carrie," Jerry explained. "This isn't head knowledge, remember. It's heart knowledge. I'd had the failure message all my life. I believed I wasn't capable of much."

"Did you think you were a good skier?" she asked, still searching to get a grasp on things.

"People told me I was—I got awards," Jerry answered her. "I felt better skiing than I did at most things. It came naturally to me. That's why I gravitated to it. But no, at that time, it was hard for me to point to anything I really felt successful at."

Carol dug a little deeper. "Why was I such a threat to you? I wasn't critical of you."

"You seemed so perfect. There was no way I could measure up. I felt I didn't deserve you. Once we were engaged, I was sure I'd be a failure at marriage. It would just be one more thing I couldn't succeed at."

"But your first fiancee—why didn't you bolt on her as well?"

"Who knows what I might have done in the long run? But in your case, you pointed out my spiritual inadequacies. I courted you under a terrible facade. The prospect of having to blow my cover—and run the risk of failing at love—was too much for me."

Carol looked away—out the window into the dark, starlight night. The city lights in the distance reflected in the lonely gaze of her eyes, and the heaviness of the conversation re-creased her face in stress lines he knew he probably had put there originally.

Last time, Carol had acknowledged she had played a role in his downfall and asked for his forgiveness. But Dr. Naylor had warned him that she likely would still be on an emotional seesaw—with alternate periods of insight and confusion—before she reached a final equilibrium.

Carol was silent for so long, Jerry thought for a minute the dialogue might be over. But once she had gone this far, Carol came back for the most difficult, most necessary question of all.

"But why sex? Why was that your way out? Why, of all the rotten ways you could have responded, did you have to pick this way to humiliate me? Couldn't you have just broken our engagement? I would have been hurt, sure, but not disgraced—not the object of gossip . . . of all those stares." Carol's voice trailed off. The old humiliation surfaced again, as hot tears sprang from her eyes before she had time to stop them.

It was a gut-wrenching moment—one that Jerry would have given the whole world to avoid. It was also a question he knew must be answered—and answered honestly—if he ever stood a chance with Carol again.

Shoulders up, he told himself. *You're a forgiven child of God. Just answer her truthfully, and remember, God cares. Carol's watching how you cope right now, and your only hope is in being strong.*

"It wasn't premeditated—this means of acting out. That doesn't mean I'm not responsible. I take full ownership of my actions. But by that point, I seized any cry for help that I could find. If an available woman hadn't been in that lobby, I might have embezzled. God forbid that it's possible, but who knows? I might have pulled a gun on someone—or even on myself. In my mind, I had no options. Going to the people involved and telling them how I felt—it would have never occurred to me."

She looked down, letting her tears splash with abandon on the tablecloth. Jerry could almost hear his heart ripping end from end. If he could just take her in his arms and make it right . . .

"Carrie, remember, it wasn't you I was spurning. It was my whole wretched life. You just had the misfortune to get mixed up with me. It was me I hated—and continued to until God came into my life and showed me how loved I was in His eyes, and that He forgave me."

For the next few minutes, Carol buried her face in her hands, and Jerry didn't know what to expect when she lifted it. He knew how foreign all this must seem to her, and he couldn't imagine that she'd ever really understand.

When she finally spoke, her words pierced straight through to Jerry's soul.

"All this time I've thought only of my pain and how I suffered," she told him, wiping her eyes with the heel of her palm. "But your pain was worse. I'm so sorry you had this kind of life—that would then ricochet and mess things up for everyone."

It was, undoubtedly, a half loaf—this back-handed affirmation—not precisely the kind of concluding line that Jerry would have written for Carol at this very moment. But some important ground had been covered in this conversation high above Wooster, in The Embassy Room. Jerry was glad they'd had this talk. God had clearly been active and had sustained him so far. He would try to wait for His activity during the rest of his visit.

If Jerry thought that Carol had reached the end of her lingering questions last night in the restaurant, he continued to be amazed. They had hardly begun their tour of the city on Saturday afternoon when Carol began pelleting him again.

If things were so bad with his father, why couldn't Jerry simply go to western Kansas and try to make up with him? Why couldn't he just tell his dad how he felt—go tell him off and get this thing settled once and for all?

"Why don't you just go with Bo to see him, like you say he wants you to? Why continue this breach?" she besieged him.

Jerry assured Carol that he'd struggled with these questions many times himself. He explained to Carol that people with painful childhoods are continually seeking their parents' blessing—just like the Jacob and Esau story in the Bible.

"I spent my whole life trying to please him, and getting nowhere," he testified. "Now I see that there was nothing I could do that would ever get the approval I needed from my father. He didn't have it in him to give."

"Don't you think he was proud of you—somewhere, deep down?" Carol inquired.

"Whether he was or not, he didn't know how to express it. It was his nature to be critical. I feared rejection so much, the last thing I wanted to do was to go visit him and have more heaped on me."

By this point, they were driving aimlessly. Carol was forgetting to give Jerry directions, and he had simply pointed the car one way and followed his nose. He knew that traveling this road emotionally was far more important than any city tour.

"Now that I've forgiven him, I've released this hold he had on me, and I do hope to visit him someday—no, not to tell him off. That would accomplish nothing. If I sensed he was open to talk about the past, and sensed God's leading, I might. But not to accuse—mainly to ask for and grant forgiveness."

"You came to see me, even though I was rude to you," Carol commented, with gentle understanding. Jerry couldn't believe his ears. He diverted his eyes from the road long enough to see if he could read genuineness in hers. He saw not only sincerity but tears as well, and he loved her for taking this small but significant step to relate.

"You're right. I did. God gave me the courage to take tough actions. I have to pray that He will again, when the time is right."

256

Then, just as quickly as she had been compassionate, Carol rose up again with pathos in her voice.

"Why did it take you so long—so painfully long?" she flung at him. "I'll never understand the year you waited—never!" It was another trace of unresolved bitterness that she needed ousted. Jerry saw that her jaw was set once again in that rigid, disbelieving way.

Will Satan forever have a toehold in this situation? he ranted to himself. *Will we never get to the bottom of Carol's hurt and anger?*

Instead of going ballistic, however, Jerry tried to listen reflectively. "I know that must have hurt you badly," he said. "I can't imagine how awful that felt."

It was his eyes that misted this time—so much that it got in the way of his driving, and he decided to pull off the road and into a parking lot. For what seemed like a long time, they just sat there—Jerry gripping the steering wheel and praying for the right response; Carol crying her needed tears to expunge the pain.

Finally, he said softly, "The process of recovery is long and tedious. You can't will any part, or rush it. It happens in God's good time. It took years for me to learn these hurtful patterns of relating. It takes a long time to unlearn them as well."

The silence dragged on so long that Jerry groped for what to do next. Was this the end of the dialogue? Had they hit the brick wall beyond which Carol no longer could go?

Finally, it seemed that God alone sent the answer.

"Look, Carrie, I asked you last time, and the offer still holds. Will you come to Sky Ranch? Maybe if you see the people and the place, you'd understand the process. Bo and Sally would welcome you. You could talk to Dr. Naylor. Maybe he could do a better job with these topics. And—" Jerry suddenly injected comic relief—"you could come see me! Best part!" He grinned at her almost flirtatiously as he said it.

Carol shook her head slightly. "I don't think . . . ," she trailed off. But somehow Carol wasn't convincing. He could tell she hadn't turned it down flat. He perceived, from the way she always flinched when he brought up the subject, that she held a trace of resentment toward Bo and Sally because they had access to him and she didn't during the year he dropped out of sight.

Surely that was highly fixable—only the coldest heart could dislike Bo and Sally after five minutes in their presence.

Carol at Sky Ranch! The mere thought of it sent him somersaulting. Although he'd dreamed about it, never in a million years could Jerry imagine she might actually be there—in the place that had been his lifeline. Heady images of Carol meeting Bo and Sally, Carol greeting the boys, Carol with him, flitted through his mind.

Jerry dismissed her protest. "Talent Night, that I told you about last time—it's in two weeks. You could come then." The salesman in him suddenly popped to the surface, but this time, for a use he thought God would honor. Jerry had to restrain his excitement—and himself—to keep from floating all the way back to Carol's apartment at the prospect.

She hadn't said yes. She had objected, meekly. But his heart continued doing flips. Back at his motel, he couldn't resist calling Bo with his mid-stream report. "Pray about Sky Ranch. Pray," he begged his brother.

Under that cover of prayer that he knew was emanating from points west, he moved into the evening.

The drama that the students put on had some light-hearted parts to it. It was good to sit and laugh with Carol again—as in former times. During several scenes, as the audience roared, Jerry and Carol snared each other's laughing eyes, and Carol made no effort to look away. After their heavy afternoon of conversation, it was a touch of normalcy they both needed.

Afterwards, Carol's students who were in the audience and cast—as well as her friend, Cathy—besieged her in the lobby. Her students yelled, "Hey, Miss McKechnie!"

and "Did you like it?" to their pretty instructor who looked as young as they.

Before they knew it, Carol and Jerry had formed a veritable receiving line, as the students filed past to greet her and to survey her eye-popping date.

Some were less than subtle as they gawked at Jerry, dapper in his navy blazer with the pin-striped shirt and tie that he once picked out with Carol in mind.

Two were especially unpretentious. "Wow, is he *cute!*" one girl proclaimed, linking her arm with this man she had hardly met. "Let's go, Jody," she called to her friend, motioning for Jody to grab Jerry's other arm. "Sir, we're taking you home with us," she teased, and they pretended to squire Jerry toward the doorway.

"GIRLS!" Carol shrieked, blushing hotly, yet pleased with the attention focused on her escort. If any of them had ever seen Carol with another man—Kevin—they thankfully kept quiet about it.

When the girls finally freed Jerry from their playful grip and returned him to Carol's side, he noticed that she took a few territorial steps backward and stood with her shoulders faintly brushing against his chest for the rest of the time they greeted people.

Jerry saw that standing closer than sardines in a can wasn't exactly covered under his "no-touch" clause. So he soaked up every second of the remaining few minutes, with Carol's body heat penetrating through his shirt front and her hair so near his face that he could smell the clean, herbal scent her shampoo had left.

When the lobby started to vacate, Jerry and Carol moved out into the crisp night air. His chest felt strangely cold since Carol had stepped away.

A front with snow flurries had blown in on this late February evening while they had been inside. A few flakes clung to their jackets as they made their way from the theater. It had become a cold, biting night.

A Valley Lodge-like night.

Though neither mentioned it, both clearly recognized the *deja vu.* They smiled in recollection in the dark, all the way back to the car.

259

"I think they love you," she said mischievously, able to laugh now at her students' outrageous behavior toward Jerry.

"I *know* they love you," he replied, with an affirming smile. "You're so good with them." He thought of the children from her Kiddie School that she had been good with, as well. He expected that she'd mention it, like she usually did, when she reminded him how unhappy she was—being here, and not there.

She surprised him. Staring down at red nails that peeked through her open-toed pumps, Carol said thoughtfully, "I'm actually glad I had this year with them. I never believed I'd say it. But it's true."

"What Satan meant for evil, God used for good," Jerry stated, thrilled at what she acknowledged. Carol, as usual, didn't reply to his spiritual reference, but she didn't contradict him, either.

It was time for another good-bye, and Carol pulled up in front of his motel. Because of their agreement, Carol didn't have to tense up any more at his leave-taking, although Jerry suspected he might even have kissed her without protest this evening, so high were her spirits after the play.

He did the right thing, of course, and desisted. But he did have one more thing to say.

"Last time you told me I had made you feel ugly. I understand why you'd say that. But I want you to know, Carol. You're a beautiful woman, inside and out. I hope you'll feel that way again someday."

"You made me feel that way tonight," she replied simply. Her eyes never even blinked, they were locked on his so tightly.

"Have beautiful dreams, then," he said, closing the door gently as he left.

It was their most peaceful parting yet—and oh, Jerry thought to himself, how they deserved it.

✿

On their way to the airport on Sunday, with Jerry driving, Carol shocked him.

Out of the blue, she announced, "I've thought about your invitation to Kansas. I'll come—in two weeks."

Jerry turned delighted eyes in her direction, but she stopped him from commenting.

"See, Jerry, it's not hard to believe you're better— more self-assured. I see it oozing through every pore of your body. But I still don't think it can hold. I believe you've gotten yourself into such a cushy set-up, you think the whole world looks like Sky Ranch."

Jerry was momentarily stung. Carol always seemed to throw in some zinger—to protect herself from further hurt. *Confound her!* Jerry thought in fury and frustration. *After all our progress.*

Then he realized—she *had* said yes. Never mind the escape clauses. Carol was coming to Sky Ranch.

Bo and Sally would lavish her with their special brand of welcome. Dr. Naylor would captivate her with his insights. The spiritual atmosphere would stir her soul.

Besides, Jerry had a surprise in his hip pocket—an idea that had germinated since their conversation yesterday—that would win her heart, for sure.

After one weekend at Sky Ranch, Carol McKechnie would once again be well on the way to being Carol Rutgers. He had never been more convinced.

TWENTY FOUR

Primary Sources

❁

Sky Ranch had never hummed with such hubbub as the kind that occurred for Talent Night weekend when Carol made her visit.

Sally had been cooking all week to prepare for the hoards of parents and benefactors that would descend on the ranch on Saturday for the talent show and dinner on the grounds.

Students had doubled up on chore time to ensure that horse stalls were clean, shrubbery was pruned, and fences were whitewashed. Barracks were spotless from stem to stern. Schoolwork was neatly displayed on desks, and students received etiquette instruction until they were ready to scream.

The community of Colby even got caught up in the act. Bo had invited the heads of key businesses—people who had donated money, time, or equipment to the ranch —to attend Talent Night. Several of them brought out pastries, coffee, soft drinks, ice, and folding tables and chairs for the occasion. The party goods store donated decorations for the fiesta-themed event. Sally was up to her armpits in details, coordinating it all.

When Jerry saw what a busy period it was, he offered to postpone Carol's visit until another time. Bo and Sally wouldn't hear of it.

"Let her see us at our best," Sally insisted.

Bo was preoccupied with a new problem—some behavior challenges from Rico, of late. Rico had transferred his obsessive attachment from Bo to Jerry. When Jerry had traveled to Topeka to the conference and to Ohio to see Carol, Rico had acted out uncharacteristically.

Then, as Talent Night approached, Rico seemed more angry than usual. Talent Night was one of the rare parental visits Bo permitted while the boys were rehabilitating, but Rico's mother had just lost her job and couldn't afford to attend. Bo and Jerry were spending extra time with Rico, who after nearly a year had almost achieved level 5, to try to get at the root of his problem.

Jerry again suggested that Carol's visit might add too much to the strain. Like Sally, Bo wouldn't hear of a cancellation.

"What's one more guest?" he shrugged. "Let's get her here now while the motivation's strong."

But the place *was* busy—so busy, in fact, that Jerry had to arrange for a Sky Ranch staffer who was coming back from Goodland to drop by the airport to pick up Carol when her plane got in. By Friday morning, Jerry was wrapped up in getting the boys' final talent acts ready. He was relieved when Chuck offered to make the pick-up, with Carol's full permission. Jerry knew he'd be more relaxed when she arrived if his duties were done beforehand.

So engrossed was Jerry in driving nails into the back fence to hold up a huge banner that he didn't even hear the crunch of the driveway gravel that signaled someone had arrived.

As he bent his plaid-shirted torso over a nail he had hammered in crooked, a soft voice called out, practically in his ear, "You look like someone who belongs on a ranch."

He glanced up to see what he first might have taken for a vision—like one that had appeared to him endless times in the past few weeks as he imagined this day. This vision was dressed in pale denim jeans, an ice-blue Western shirt with pearl beading, ostrich-skin boots, and a straw hat with a feather trim at the crown—and was standing right next to him.

This time he wasn't dreaming. Carol was there before him, at Sky Ranch, at last.

"So do . . . ," he said, slowly rising to his full height and never quite finishing his sentence as his eyes took in Carol's smashing attire.

Trying to pretend nonchalance at first, Carol made a perky, 360-degree turn in front of him to show off her outfit. A glorious, golden Kansas sun filled in the background behind her.

"Do I look like a ranch hand?" she teased, knowing full well that in her chic Western regalia, she looked anything but. She used the high heel on her right boot to pivot to display elaborate beadwork on the back of her shirt.

"Yeah, like one who's just arrived, before we put her to work," Jerry chuckled, entering into the playful repartee that continued to stall off official greetings.

"I borrowed it all from Cathy," Carol explained. "She used to live in Houston. They dressed to the nines for the rodeo there every year."

"It's perfect," Jerry murmured. Carol watched him continue to pull his gaze over her slowly, approvingly. If his arms and hands could not—would not embrace her, his eyes did what they could to make up for it.

"Welcome to Sky Ranch, Carol," his low-throated, husky voice said.

Their eyes stayed locked, each drinking in the sight of the other, without a muscle in their faces flickering, for timeless time. They might have remained that way forever if Jerry hadn't finally broken the spell with a logistical question.

"Did you stop at the ranch house as you came in?" he finally asked. "Hope you didn't think I was ignoring you. I didn't hear Chuck drive up. "

"No. Chuck showed me where you were, and I came out here first," she replied.

"I'll take you to meet Bo and Sally, then," he instructed. He picked up his hammer and directed Carol toward the family quarters. Her boots' staccato steps on the plank walkway seemed to dally a bit, the closer they got to the back door. Jerry wondered if she was dreading meeting his relatives.

He couldn't help believing that Bo's and Sally's charm would work its magic. He hoped Carol would turn loose of any lingering resentment she might have toward them for harboring him for so long.

Sally was standing at the sink, grating carrots, when they walked into the kitchen. When she spotted Jerry and Carol at the door, she ran toward them, strewing carrot peels in her wake.

She approached Carol with outstretched arms. "Carol," she trumpeted, racing toward her guest as though she were an old school chum. "May I give you a hug, hon? I've looked forward to meeting you for *such* a long time."

Carol at first stepped back a little hesitantly but then nodded her assent. She was clearly disarmed by the friendliness of this stranger. Sally swung her arms around Carol's neck—brandishing a half-grated carrot in one hand, peeler in another. When she drew back her face to look more closely at Carol—this one for whom she had uttered more prayers than Carol could ever imagine—Sally's eyes were tear-brimmed.

Partly to cut the critical emotional level, Carol looked around the kitchen at the flotilla of covered casserole dishes lined up on the counter.

"Looks like I've come at a really hectic time," she said, apologetically.

"That's not by accident," Sally quipped, recovering quickly and blotting her eyes with her knuckles. "I intend to put you to work."

As Sally announced her plan, Jerry remembered a similar take-charge spirit Carol exhibited on her first day at Valley Lodge long ago. He knew Carol would find Sally Rutgers to be a kindred spirit, if she would give her half a chance.

Then Bo, hearing the voices in the kitchen, burst through the door of his office and welcomed Carol equally warmly.

"Great to have you here," Bo boomed, approaching her with the same type of encompassing bear hug as Sally had. "May I give you one of our Sky Ranch embraces?"

This time, Carol managed a little smile, gradually giving into the overwhelming sincerity of this friendly couple who clearly wanted her to feel special. As Bo pulled away after hugging her, Carol saw that his cheeks were wet as well. Like Sally, he had stormed the gates of heaven more for Carol than she could ever think possible.

Bo wiped his eyes and blew his nose loudly on an oversized bandanna kerchief that hung from his pocket.

"Well, now that I have my tear ducts cleaned out, I guess it's time I told you, Carol," Bo said, leaning in toward her fraternally. "We invited you here to help us with Talent Night. You realize that, don't you? I have some information packets for you to stuff."

This time, Carol let out a vestige of a laugh and was able to respond light-heartedly.

"Uh, oh, this is sounding familiar," she quipped, rolling her eyes in amusement as she looked back and forth between Bo and Sally.

"I get her first," Sally declared, impaling Bo with her eyes. "She's a teacher, too. She can help me in my classroom." As an aside to Carol, she said, "I've been so busy cooking, my bulletin boards aren't nearly ready for tomorrow."

Jerry snickered at his brother's and sister-in-law's antics. "You're hardly here half an hour, and they're fighting over you," Jerry cut in, his eyes dancing mischievously at Carol.

Although he laughed, Jerry was catching on to a serious game plan here. The two of them had contrived a way for each to spend one-on-one time with Carol—becoming sort of primary sources for her to tap into about life at Sky Ranch and about Jerry's pilgrimage.

"Just give me a job to do," Carol offered gamely, entering into the spirit of the banter.

For the next several hours, Carol disappeared with Sally down to the academic building. Bo went back to his office, and Jerry continued rehearsing the boys for their performance.

Then, as if on cue, about mid-afternoon, Carol and Sally emerged from the schoolrooms, laughing and smiling, walking across the courtyard arm in arm to the ranch house. When Jerry stuck his head into the kitchen a few minutes later, he found Carol already in Bo's office, with packets stacked to her elbows. The two of them waved at Jerry but kept right on working.

What transpired during Bo's and Sally's times with Carol, Jerry had no way of knowing. He was clueless as to what to expect when he met up with Carol at five o'clock for evening vespers in the chapel. He could read nothing on her face, and she gave him no report.

He only knew that when they sat down for the service, Carol moved so close to him on the wooden pew that a hymnal page couldn't have wedged between them. *Maybe this means things didn't go too badly,* he sighed in relief.

Soon, everyone in the chapel was caught up in the spirit of the service. Bo recruited a half-dozen boys, including two who were about to return to their homes after Talent Night, to tell about receiving Christ at Sky Ranch.

To Jerry's delight, one of the testimonials was from Rico, who wasn't one of the graduates but who told his conversion story eloquently. Jerry sensed he was over his earlier disappointment after his mother declined to attend.

A few minutes before the service, he had greeted Carol politely when Jerry introduced them. "Hello, Meees Carol," he said, taking her fair-skinned hand into his pecan-colored one. He had worried that Carol's visit might disrupt Rico, since he prized Jerry's attention so fervently. But Rico's testimony told about how Jerry led him to the Lord, and the boy seemed tickled at the applause that followed.

Another speaker was one of Jerry's Sunday School pupils, who talked about how Jerry had encouraged him through Scripture memory. Jerry was especially glad Carol heard these remarks. Scripture memory was one area in which she had tried to influence Jerry at Valley Lodge, much to his resistance then.

Dinner afterwards in the ranch house kitchen was a hearty affair around the familiar red-and-white-checked cloth. While Sally served typical ranch-style fare of barbecue and potato salad, Bo guided Carol into talking about her work, her family, and whether she thought her softball team this year at Wooster would be a success.

Again, Jerry sensed that Carol was responding warmly to both him and his brother and sister-in-law as the evening wore on. One by one, Carol seemed to be losing a few more of her objections to him, putting her back just where he wanted her.

After supper, when the dishes were put away, Jerry took Carol on a walk down to the barn. It was a delicious April evening, and they took in great gulps of spring air as they strolled toward the paddock. They passed the stand of lilacs that were in full bloom beside the L-shaped front porch, and the iris that Sally had planted last summer were just starting to peek through. As they talked, Jerry at last began to get a picture from her of what had transpired in her meetings with Bo and Sally that afternoon.

"I wanted so much to hate them," she confessed, confirming Jerry's presumption. "I came with an attitude about Bo and Sally, because they kept you here all those months. I felt like they had stolen you from me with their possessiveness. I felt they were the gatekeepers to you, and no one else could participate.

"This afternoon when they asked me to help, I wanted to be nice, but I secretly dreaded it. I figured their whole approach would be to 'hype Jerry'—brainwashing me about you, about wonderful you are—how I should see things your way.

"In a roundabout way, I guess they did affirm you—or at least, help interpret your situation for me. But they were also interested in *me*—in how *I* felt. Sally told me about how crushed she was when Bo fell apart on her before their wedding. She said she struggled to understand his family issues—since her own dad wasn't that way. It made me feel I wasn't some kind of side-show freak because I can't always identify with your stories."

Jerry said nothing but exulted to himself, "Way to go, Sally!" It sounded as if Sally had said just the right thing to begin to break down the barriers.

Carol continued, "Then with Bo—being your brother, I expected the old blood-is-thicker-than-water routine. But he really cared about me, too. He said that all the time you were recovering, he prayed for me. Even early on, when he knew he couldn't tell me where you were, he prayed for me. He worried about how hurt I must be. He told me how he once struggled with the same issues you had and what a help Sally was to him during that time. It just helps to see that another couple has survived after going down the same road."

"Touche', Bo!" Jerry thought, rejoicing even further. He caught her reference to herself and Jerry as "another couple." It was a small matter of semantics, but it thrilled him that she might view the two of them—instead of her and Kevin—as a couple again, in her estimation. The Kevin matter—and the issue of where things stood between Carol and the new boyfriend—continued to concern Jerry, but Dr. Naylor had cautioned him about any further probing with Carol just now.

"If things stay on course, Kevin will peel off just as naturally as an old scab," Dr. Naylor had adjured Jerry. "Just let the chips continue to fall, and you won't have Kevin to worry about much longer." Jerry wanted to believe him, but it was still hard for thoughts of this suitor not to haunt him at every turn.

However, Jerry couldn't resist a little good-natured ribbing.

"So—you didn't want them to 'hype Jerry,' huh?," he asked, feigning hurt but with mirth in his voice. "I guess hearing about how wonderful Jerry was would have just undone you."

Carol got tickled at Jerry's teasing reference to her sarcasm. Her suppressed laugh came out as a little snort, which she tried to hide, unsuccessfully. The harder she tried to ignore it, the more it filtered through, and Jerry caught on in contagion. Soon they were both giggling like teen-agers at her comment and at Jerry's response to it.

"I guess that did come across as catty," she replied, suddenly humble, once the laughter subsided. "I'm sorry." Despite the darkness that hovered over the corral fence rail where they leaned, there was enough moonlight for them to see each other's eyes. Jerry could tell from hers that the apology was genuine.

"I think I see," Jerry finally responded, addressing Carol seriously this time. "You like it because they took your feelings into account."

"Yes, that's it," she nodded. She seemed appreciative that Jerry understood and wasn't mad at her. He decided that now was as good a time as any to lead into tomorrow's agenda.

"Good. I think you'll find that to be true of Dr. Naylor, too." She cocked an eyebrow at him, and Jerry pressed on.

"He wants to meet you. He'll be here tomorrow to consult with the parents. He's leaving for Korea right after he finishes, but he said he'd make time if we came by."

Carol didn't respond negatively to this suggestion and actually seemed relieved. Perhaps she felt that with this unbiased third party—another primary source—she'd be totally free to spill her guts. Still, she cast Jerry a suspicious eye.

"This is precisely what I'm talking about," she retorted finally.

"What do you mean?" Jerry asked.

Carol rushed in to complete her thought but then hesitated. "I don't want to sound disparaging, Jerry. Please don't misunderstand. Sky Ranch is a lovely place—Bo and Sally are terrific. The boys are great. I can see why you find it so meaningful. But . . ."

"But . . ." he parroted her, knowing what she'd say even before she mouthed the words. It was her usual hesitation—her iron-willed determination to keep his expectations low.

"But it's artificial," she went on. "You're protected from life's bumps. When they come along, you've got all these people to wrap their arms around you and love you through it. You have your own shrink. Your own church. Your own cheerleaders. If something like a worker strike at Valley Lodge happened, you'd be sunk, if you were away from these protective confines."

Jerry wanted to retaliate so badly, he literally had to put his hand to his mouth to seal his lips shut. They were back to the cat-and-mouse game Carol was playing with him, and had been for several weeks, in which she would seem to draw closer to him and then spit back with some dig. Carol had no idea how much stress he had confronted at Sky Ranch, and she had no idea what he was capable of now.

Instead of firing back, he thought about the direction he believed Dr. Naylor would take with her in their counseling session tomorrow. He replied simply, "I hope you'll tell Dr. Naylor about these concerns you keep having. I know he'll be a good listening ear." Then he walked her back to the ranch house, where she was to lodge in a spare bedroom Bo and Sally hoped to use for a nursery some day when they had children of their own.

Jerry knew that if Carol needed to feel like the Sky Ranch folks considered her feelings, then tomorrow should reassure her by the bucketloads.

By the end of the day tomorrow, after she spent time with Dr. Naylor and after Jerry involved her in the special surprise he had been planning for two weeks now, Carol would feel more taken into account than she had in many months.

After tomorrow—after she would be the center of attention more than she could possibly imagine, Jerry believed that Carol—and their relationship—would never be the same again.

TWENTY FIVE

Under the Microscope

❁

So many people made their way to the waiting area outside Dr. Naylor's office on Saturday morning, an observer might have thought he was giving away tickets to a cruise instead of dispensing counseling advice.

From early morning, when parents of residents began arriving at Sky Ranch for the weekend activities, people regularly filed into his office for their scheduled appointments.

Jerry kept waiting, a little nervously, for the traffic to subside so that he and Carol could have their turn with the counselor, but he tried not to be selfish about their needs. Jerry knew how critical Dr. Naylor's advice was to the loved ones who were about to get their boys back.

In the anxious meantime, Jerry brought Carol down to the barn to help him polish the rough edges off plans for the evening.

As Jerry suspected, Carol was a natural with the boys. Her teacher instincts and her take-charge demeanor that attracted him to her at Valley Lodge surfaced instantly. She attached herself to a group who fumbled over lines of a skit they were to perform. When Jerry was about to throw up his hands in exasperation, Carol pulled each of the five aside individually and drilled and drilled until they had it down cold.

"Looks like a few of the guys would like to run off with *you*, this time," Jerry joked with her later, recalling the night in Wooster when her students had squired him away by the elbows.

Several boys cornered Jerry outside the barn and teased him about Carol's sudden presence at the ranch. One was Rico, who seemed particularly curious.

"Is Meees Carol your lady?" he asked his mentor, his black, straight hair like dark threads of silk as the sunlight hit it.

"She's someone who's very special," Jerry answered Rico. He was glad the boy was responding to Carol positively and not jealously.

Just after lunch, the stream of hand-wringing parents that poured into Dr. Naylor's office slowed to a trickle, and Jerry and Carol stepped in behind his last appointment.

Soon the door opened, and Dr. Naylor's beady eyes appeared around the door frame as he mopped the sweat drops on his bald forehead.

"What a relief!" he exclaimed, seeing Jerry and Carol in the waiting area. "I've been reminding myself all morning, 'You've saved the best till last.'"

He looked down at Carol in his typical appraisal pose—over the tops of his half-glasses. "You must be Carol. Welcome, my dear," he said, almost paternally. The somewhat bemused look Carol shot the eccentric counselor told Jerry she would soon be at ease around him, too, just like she had Bo and Sally.

He showed them to seats in front of his desk. Jerry remembered the way Dr. Naylor had officiously wheeled around in his chair with his back toward him, during Jerry's early sessions when he was in sullen rebellion.

With Carol, however, Dr. Naylor most assuredly wouldn't use that tactic. If Jerry's guess was right, the counselor would commandeer her more like Bo and Sally had—from the start, as one who was in her corner.

Dr. Naylor said nothing at first, quietly waiting for the two of them to disclose the nature of their visit. He and Carol continued to study each other, taking each other's measure, while the silence held sway. Jerry got the signal and plunged.

"I've told Carol how much you helped me," he began, choosing his words delicately. "Since she's here for the weekend, I thought you might give her some insights, as well."

The counselor immediately turned to Carol for her version, an act that Jerry saw won her respect.

"How about you, Carol?" Dr. Naylor asked gently. "Is that how you see it?" As Jerry had presumed last night, Dr. Naylor was hinting from the outset that her viewpoint would matter, too, in this exchange, and that he did not view Jerry as her mouthpiece. Although Carol hadn't mentioned it, Jerry was sure she suspected Dr. Naylor of a bias, like she had with Bo and Sally initially. Dr. Naylor must have sensed this, too, and was laying down tracks that said he would be even-handed.

"I do have some questions that keep bothering me," Carol replied, looking a little sheepish around the counselor who no doubt knew their past history well. "I agreed to do this because I thought you could answer them."

Dr. Naylor put his pencil down from scratching out notes and smiled a little. "Perhaps we can answer them together," he commented. With that, he put both hands on the edge of his desk and pushed up from his chair into a standing position, indicating Jerry was to leave.

"Carol and I need to talk privately for a while," he instructed. "Come back in an hour; then I'll see you both together."

Jerry, expecting this, responded quickly. He was, in fact, glad Carol could have private time with Dr. Naylor to get to the heart of her concerns.

"Of course," he said, backing toward the door. "I'll be in the barn if anyone needs me."

For Jerry, the next hour inched by agonizingly. He tried to do some work on the sound system he had brought in for the evening, but his mind wandered badly. All his earlier confidence about how the session would go began to be replaced by a creeping panic. He trusted that Carol would respond well to Dr. Naylor as he put her under the microscope, but there were no guarantees. Despite his high hopes, Jerry worried that this visit with the therapist was a stupid miscalculation.

When the hour was up and he first laid eyes on Carol as he entered the counselor's office, Jerry's heart stopped. Her face seemed to confirm his worst fears. Carol's eyes were almost swollen shut from crying. Her red, sniffly nose and tear-mottled cheeks left her almost unrecognizable. Jerry felt his heart pounding a hole through his chest, and he gasped audibly.

Dr. Naylor caught the gasp and spoke to it directly.

"Sit down, Jerry," he insisted. "You looked a little taken aback when you came in just now. I could hear you draw in a breath. Can you tell me what that's about?"

Jerry gulped, mortified that Dr. Naylor had trapped him in his visceral response. What could he say tactfully that wouldn't humiliate Carol in her tears? He sat in silence for a minute. Dr. Naylor wouldn't let him off the hook.

"Come on, Jerry," he nudged. "What were you feeling just then when you came in the room and gaped at us?"

Finally, Jerry struggled to comment, swallowing back tension in his throat. "I was feeling fear," he told him, using the "feelings-chart" technique from his counseling experience.

"What did you fear?" the doctor prodded.

"I saw that Carol had been crying . . . ," he began, but Dr. Naylor interrupted.

"Address this to Carol, please, and not to me," Dr. Naylor coached.

He forced himself to meet Carol's gaze. "Carol," he began, trying to practice the way the counselor had taught him to speak directly, "I saw you had been crying, and I felt afraid that things had gone badly in your visit." He thought better of what he'd said and amended his comment. "I'm glad you got to cry if you needed to. But I also felt afraid that you were hurting again."

As he spoke, Carol lowered her eyes, a tear oozing from the corner of one. He felt an uncontrollable urge to touch her arm in comfort, but knew he should avoid anything that smacked of coercion.

"Good," Dr. Naylor affirmed loudly. "Thank you, Jerry, for that honest response and especially the way you directed that at Carol so well. Now Carol," he called, and at his beckoning, Carol raised puffy eyelids in his direction. "Carol, after hearing what Jerry said to you, I'd like you to please respond, in a sort of reality-check. Jerry described what he fears you're feeling right now. Can you please—to Jerry, not to me—say how you *actually* feel after our talk? Just state it the way Jerry did—"I feel . . . . ," and then complete the sentence.

Carol hesitated, having to get used to Dr. Naylor's methods, which were as new to her as they were commonplace to Jerry. After some silence, Dr. Naylor guided her again.

"I feel . . . ," he prompted her.

"I feel confused," she finally ventured. "This has all helped me, but it's so new." The counselor, noticing that she dispatched her comments to him mistakenly, said nothing but with the index fingers of both hands pointing in a sweeping motion, directed her eyes to Jerry's.

Catching herself, she started over. "I feel confused," she told Jerry, this time her brown eyes connecting with his blue ones. "I've never thought about some of these things before, and it'll take a while to digest."

"Can you identify with that feeling, Jerry—of trying to adjust to new concepts about yourself?" Dr. Naylor asked, again coaching him.

Jerry picked up on the hint and replied to Carol, "Yes, Carol, I felt that same way when I first began seeing Dr. Naylor," he said sympathetically. "It *was* confusing. I digested it for weeks."

"Good. Now, how else do you feel, Carol? Is there another 'feelings' word that applies?" the therapist prompted again.

First looking as though she were about to answer to Dr. Naylor, then correcting herself and turning back to Jerry, Carol continued, "I feel happy," she disclosed.

"Happy?" Jerry blurted out in surprise, a sudden warmth washing through him.

"Yes, happy," Carol repeated. A little laugh got caught in her throat, and she struggled to free it. "Guess it doesn't look like it, does it?" Momentarily self-conscious, her hands went absently to her face as she spoke. She and Jerry both laughed a little nervously at her weak stab at humor. Then she went on. .

"Yes, I feel happy, because I think I'm finally beginning to understand some of the things that have puzzled me, and to realize that I'm not helpless," she attempted to explain.

Dr. Naylor intervened. "Jerry, how do you feel when you hear Carol say she's happy?"

"Great!" Jerry answered, a wave of relief seeping through his voice and posture, as he stretched an arm over his chair back and assumed a more relaxed pose.

"So your first presumption—the fear that Carol was sad and distraught, was pretty far off course, wasn't it?"

"I guess it was," Jerry replied, taking a sideways glance at Carol to catch her expression.

"And the only way you found that out was to compare feelings, right?" he continued probing.

"Right as usual," Jerry replied, flashing his therapist an admiring look. They'd been down this road before, in past sessions. "I had to check it out."

Dr. Naylor scooted back in his chair, much like he might step back from a blackboard after delivering a lecture.

"Congratulations, friends. You just passed your first exam in Communications 101," he told Jerry and Carol excitedly. "In this little interchange, I hope you've caught something important. Privately you've both told me you want to work on your relationship—to be sure you have coping skills when things get rocky. What I've been trying to show you—and what you've just demonstrated very well—is that you have all the means you need to see you through the rough times. There's nothing magic about it. Jerry, you checked out your perception about Carol by asking her. She identified for you how she felt, and you compared that to a feeling of your own. Nobody accused, nobody pulled away. Carol, you explained the reason for your tears; Jerry, you expressed relief that it wasn't as you first supposed."

At his summation, Jerry and Carol exchanged glances, and Carol even managed to acknowledge, with her eyes fixed on Jerry this time, "He makes it look simple, doesn't he?"

Jerry nodded, and Dr. Naylor affirmed her statement. "It *is* simple, but it *does* take practice. It's so much easier for us to presume we know what someone is feeling than to go to the trouble to verify."

The two counselees nodded to each other in agreement. Both looked a little chagrined, as they realized how in the past they'd fallen into the trap Dr. Naylor described. The exercise the counselor just led them through had had its effect. It cut the tension in the office and fostered an atmosphere for him to plunge further in the process.

With Carol now dry-eyed and composed again, Dr. Naylor expanded on some other points of their conversation. When he asked her to share with Jerry—in the same face-to-face format—how she told the doctor she felt about visiting Sky Ranch, Carol replied, "Anxious."

"Can you tell Jerry what you're anxious about?" he encouraged.

Carol looked down hesitantly, knowing that to be totally honest would betray an intensity she had been on guard about revealing. Silence was heavy in the room at first and might have had its way forever, had Carol not raised her eyes to the therapist and observed him nod at her encouragingly. His nod gave her the requisite push.

"I told him I was anxious that if anything were to come of our relationship again—if we were to . . ." Carol struggled, as if the very words would re-invite hurt, "to get back together again, that I'd get all attached to you, only to see you fall apart again."

The transparency was too much for Carol, and she dipped her eyes so low that her chin touched her chest.

Jerry bent his head over to try to make contact with her eyes, to reassure her it was OK that she laid her deepest emotions bare for him to see, but they were squeezed tightly shut against her face.

Dr. Naylor cut in quickly, to keep the momentum up. "How do you feel about that, Jerry?" he probed.

Jerry choked out a sad laugh. "I feel happy to know I've been on your mind. That's something, anyway. I feel frustrated that I can't convince you I'd do better now."

"But does she have something on which to base her concern?" the counselor continued to dig.

"Yes," he replied to Dr. Naylor, and then caught himself as she had. "Yes, you do, Carrie. I've let you down in the past. Your feelings are valid." Jerry's heart lurched as he said the words, and as he looked at Carol, she opened her tight-shut eyes a smidgen.

"Good!" Dr. Naylor boomed exultantly, as though he'd just seen two children successfully play with a new toy. "Good feelings exchange. You're getting the hang of it. Now let's explore further."

He then asked Carol to reiterate for Jerry some other elements of their consultation—specifically, how Carol had responded when Jerry had shown weakness. Dr. Naylor had asked Carol to retrace her steps at the ski lodge—what she had done when Jerry seemed beleaguered—during the days when she first arrived and he was about to crater from exhaustion.

"I offered to help," Carol answered, repeating what she had already told Dr. Naylor. "I jumped in to fix things. I thought that if I just did enough, it would make things better at the lodge and it would lighten the load on you. I thought that was the right thing."

"OK, now, Jerry, can you tell Carol what you realize now would have helped you most at that time?" the counselor guided.

Jerry squirmed a little but finally came up with the words. "Carrie, it's not that I didn't appreciate you. You were sweet and generous. That's part of what drew me to you. I know you started out wanting to save the lodge and save your sabbatical. I know that being Christlike motivated you. I know you have a servant heart and that you cared about me being overloaded.

"But what Dr. Naylor has helped me see is that I was allowing you to enable me. I allowed you to be a crutch that kept me from taking stronger action to save the lodge. I let it keep me from learning to administer like I should have—to delegate, to recruit aggressively, to make proper contacts—the kinds of things that Pop eventually had to step in and bail me out on."

"I never really thought about it that way, until I talked to Dr. Naylor," she responded, as understanding crept into her eyes.

"So—how do you feel about it?" Jerry asked, tapping his fingers together. Carol rolled her eyes at Dr. Naylor, as she heard Jerry pick up on the counselor's favorite phrase.

"I feel . . . regretful," she admitted, growing more thoughtful. "I can see how I overdid."

"No worse than my tendency to keep my mouth shut," Jerry responded compassionately. "I should have been more assertive to take care of my own needs."

"Aha!" Dr. Naylor chimed in, pointing a finger in the air for emphasis. "Do you see what good work you just did? You've just demonstrated another vehicle you can use during the tough times. Carol, you've confessed to being a rescuer and fixer. Jerry, you've confessed to needing assertiveness. Knowing that you have these traits, and that you would fall into them if left to your own devices, is half the battle. Now that you know this about each other, and have demonstrated that you want to change, you can serve as traffic cops for each other when one of you starts to slip into bad habits."

Both Carol and Jerry blinked at him wordlessly, as his instruction soaked in. Capitalizing on their thoughtful poses, the counselor took a third, critical step.

"Now, Carol, about the third base we covered. If you are willing, please tell Jerry how you believe you responded to him in the days before he trusted Christ at Sky Ranch—those times when you tried to pin him down about his faith, and he waffled."

"I was in denial," she said quietly, through her pain, as she remembered. "I didn't want . . . didn't want to lose you," she stammered. "You seemed so perfect for me. I had just gotten over a hopeless relationship, and I wanted things to work. Some things I was willing to compromise in order to keep you. I just shrugged off our differences. Now I see I should have asked more questions."

"You held your shoulders back in that characteristic pose and just sucked it in," Jerry commented, hardly above a whisper.

"I just sucked it in," Carol agreed, echoing his words.

"And the end, what happened, Carol?" Dr. Naylor asked gently.

"I lost you anyway," she murmured, and tears suddenly poured out afresh. "I let you get away with murder, when all the time you were crying out for help."

Jerry was so overcome with the honesty of her revelation, he couldn't help himself. Never mind his no-touch rule. At that moment Carol needed to be comforted. He laid his hand, light as air, on her left arm just above the wrist, and she didn't draw back. Instead, the touch seemed to trigger a fresh burst of emotion. Her right hand—the one unoccupied at the moment—went to her face, and she cried into it for what seemed like untold minutes.

Finally, Jerry said, "And I allowed you to turn a blind eye. I didn't know how to say, 'Help me, Carrie. Help me get to the bottom of this.' I could do it now; I couldn't then." As broken as she was, with his own emotions whirling, Jerry buried his own face in his free hand, the two of them still lightly linked by his fingers on her arm, from which Carol still made no effort to withdraw.

Dr. Naylor, who clearly had been waiting to seize the right opening, took advantage of this break in the conversation to move right in.

"Precisely my point!" he boomed. He enthused so loudly that they both turned buried faces up and toward him with such a start that Jerry's hand fell free of Carol's arm. "See? You just described another resource you have. Jerry, you now know that Carol has a tendency to deny. Carol, you now know that Jerry tends to shout for help in nonverbal ways. Now you can watch out for each other and hold each other accountable. You can be on guard for issues before they snowball. Carol, you can be alert to his passive tendencies and call him on them. Jerry, you can watch for times she's letting you off the hook too easily. It's all unmasked now. It'll be harder to play games with each other now that your little secrets are out."

Quiet descended again after Dr. Naylor's outburst, and he again gestured for Jerry to speak to Carol, so he said, "How do you feel now, Carrie? Did Dr. Naylor answer your questions?"

"I feel more confused than I ever have in my life," she replied, dabbing at eyes. "But maybe it's a good kind of confused . . . I don't know."

"Do you still feel helpless?" he asked softly.

"Not as much," she replied, in such a light murmur it was almost inaudible.

But Dr. Naylor heard her, or at least read her lips. Arms waving like a fiery evangelist, he pronounced, "Good! Because what you've done this afternoon proves just how powerful you are."

He cleared his throat and then used an approach Jerry had never experienced in any of their counseling sessions. He stood up, walked around to their side of the desk, and leaned over a world globe that Bo used for tutoring history students.

"See, here's Sky Ranch," he said, pointing somewhere in the middle of North America on the globe. "But what I told you works here," and he pointed to indicate somewhere close to New York, "or here," and he moved his finger to the southernmost tip of South America, "or even here," and he whirled the globe around dramatically until it stopped and he plunked his finger down on China.

He looked straight at Carol.

"Carol, you told me that you fear Sky Ranch is a protective cocoon from life's hard knocks. As counselor here, I can assure you it's no Garden of Eden," and he rolled his eyes at Jerry, who nodded in agreement. "I know what you mean, however," he conceded. "To you, it looks pretty cushy."

"But I assure you," he went on, "I'm far from the only counselor in the world. You can find far better ones, I hope, when you need them. Besides counseling, you can use these problem solving-skills you've demonstrated; you can work on communication; you can find other support systems—in any spot on the globe."

He moved back to his chair and turned to Carol again.

"Let me ask both of you—Carol, you first. What do you do for self-care? Self-care is a very important resource in tough times, as well."

"Self-care?"

"Yes, the things you do to be nice to yourself—to relieve stress—to be good to the body God gave you."

"Well, I . . . I work out on my fitness equipment. I play tennis, when the weather lets me. I used to needlepoint some. Is that what you mean?"

"Umm, hmm," Dr. Naylor nodded. Then he looked at Jerry, awaiting his reply.

"That's been hard for me to re-learn here," Jerry replied. "But Dr. Naylor's right. I had to re-create a fitness program for Sky Ranch, after I saw I wasn't being a good steward of my body. So now I work out at the Y, I run, I have my quiet times." Jerry thought to himself how quiet times, which Carol didn't mention in her list, had once been among her stress-busters as well. They had talked about them a lot at Valley Lodge but little since. Jerry wished they had time to discuss spiritual matters in Dr. Naylor's presence just as they had these other relationship dynamics.

The issue of Carol and her current walk with Christ was one that Dr. Naylor seemed to be deliberately leaving up to Jerry to probe with her at a later moment.

The counselor began gathering up his papers, indicating the session was ended.

"Got a plane to catch," he announced. "Some folks in Korea seem to want to hear me speak. Well, this has been fun. Have I given you two some food for thought?" And he addressed this to them as nonchalantly as if they had been talking about the morning's editorial page.

"Lots," Jerry answered, far more accustomed than Carol to the wrung-out-like-a-dishrag sensation that always occurred after being with Dr. Naylor.

The counselor and Jerry both looked at Carol for her impression. She fidgeted a little but managed a slight smile.

"I'm sure I'll do a lot of thinking," she promised, shaking the therapist's outstretched hand and looking a little shell-shocked.

"Good. Well, Carol, it's been a pleasure. Enjoy your stay. Jerry, see you when I'm back in three weeks."

With that, the iconoclastic therapist was out the door in a heartbeat, leaving Jerry and Carol alone in the office, staring at each other awkwardly in the wake of the volatile discussion. Jerry sensed her discomfort after having every emotion dissected during the past two hours, and he pondered what to do next.

He looked around, distractedly.

"Well," he finally said, cutting the silence, "what would you like to do now, Carrie? The ice-cream social for the parents is starting about now. I could introduce you to some folks. Or, I don't have to be there, really. We could go somewhere and talk. Whatever you want to do."

Carol was in no frame of mind to socialize with a bunch of strangers.

"I just need some time to myself—to absorb all this," she answered him. Her eyes sank shut as she rested her head momentarily against the chair back. "Would you mind if I just went back to my room for a while?"

Thunder like a drumroll in the distance punctuated her sentence. Carol jerked to attention, and they both glanced outside at the thickening, slate-colored sky that threatened rain on the evening's plans.

"Sure—besides, I'd better go check on that sound system wiring before it pours," Jerry said, covering his concern at Carol's response. "Shall I walk you to your room?"

"No thanks, I'll just make my way," she replied. Carol clearly wanted to pull into her shell for a while and reflect, and he would let her.

It suddenly seemed there was nothing more to say or do. Jerry felt more useless than he could remember in a while, yet he tried to think about his long-ago promise to himself—he mustn't grovel. Before God, he had done his best; he had spoken his heart; he had provided a way for Carol to speak her mind before the best of professional help.

He must now trust that the Holy Spirit would do His work as Carol processed all that had happened this afternoon.

"OK, Carol," he said, trying to muster a confident air through this stilted good-bye. "See you tonight, then."

Carol got about halfway down the back steps when Jerry called back to her.

"Carol?"

"Yes?"

Jerry took a few tentative steps toward her. "I just wanted to say thank you . . . for this afternoon," he offered, uncertain why he felt so clumsy around her all of a sudden. "I know Dr. Naylor's methods can be perplexing sometimes, but you did great. Thanks for being willing to come here . . . and do this."

He saw the beginning trace of a smile on her face as she looked back in his direction, acknowledging his remarks, but then wordlessly turned back to go. This time he didn't stop her.

He felt himself wilting inside, not knowing how this discussion would settle with Carol. He longed to see her characteristic vibrancy surface again, but all he read in her face just now was bewilderment.

Yet, for the next few hours, he could hold in his heart the recollection of Carol's penetrating words . . . *I didn't want to lose you . . . I wanted things to work . . . You were crying out for help*—the treasures from the deep he'd longed for her to tap into. And he could draw on the memory of her arm trembling under his touch, at long last, even if for a few, brief moments.

He had had such high expectations for their time with Dr. Naylor, and now he wondered, with an aching heart, where all this would lead.

At least he still had tonight.

TWENTY SIX

Tested and Tried

❃

The last group of parents had just made their way to the barn from the picnic area, where Sally and her assistants had served up dinner, when rain began pattering on the barn's metal roof.

For the first few minutes, it all but drowned out the brassy sounds of the instrumentalists warming up for the performance. Outdoors, gusty winds flung into the air the paper goods that had been heaped into trash cans after the meal. Jittery boys who felt hyper already about their acts seemed to have even more anxious spring in their steps with the thunder grumbling nearby. The air had been sticky and tense all afternoon as rain had threatened since midday. Now, just at the pivotal moment, the weather took center stage.

Eventually, the churning chaos of the elements quieted into a more civilized, late-March shower, and Jerry stepped up to the platform to begin his role as emcee.

He paused for a second to locate Carol in the audience. Earlier in the afternoon, when he stood at the microphone for a sound check, he had mentally marked the spot in the bleachers where he had asked her to sit. Even if the spotlight blinded him this evening, he wanted to be able to turn by rote toward the area where she must be.

She had arrived at the barn just before the picnic, at the agreed-upon time to rehearse with the boys once more before their skit. With fresh makeup applied and with a nap having settled her thoughts, Carol seemed convivial enough as she helped the young actors in a final run-through of their lines. The stage work with the boys invigorated her, as instructing always seemed to. Jerry could tell as he watched her from a distance that her spirits were lifted by interacting with them.

At a couple of points she called out to Jerry, to check signals with him about where he wanted an actor to stand at various times in the script.

After dismissing the boys, she waggled her fingers at Jerry from across the room, and he sauntered over. "Looks good," he said with a relieved tone about the dress rehearsal. "Something you did obviously worked. They were pretty pathetic this morning."

"Glad I could have a part," she replied somewhat cheerfully, although he still detected in her eyes a trace of a puzzled look in the wake of talking to Dr. Naylor.

They meandered out the barn door and over to the picnic tables. From that point on, any hope of a private moment with Carol was lost, as they both got swept up in conversation with parents and other guests. Jerry found himself pulled aside to consult with mothers and dads and VIP's. Carol's pretty silver and turquoise pendant in the shape of a massive cross became a conversation topic for numerous visitors. She wore the necklace over a cream-colored knit shell tucked into her jeans, with a tan suede vest over everything.

"Borrowed from Cathy again?" Jerry queried her about her outfit when he was able to sidle up to Carol for a second.

"No. My dad brought them back to me from Santa Fe," she replied, flashing him a pleased smile. Jerry was especially encouraged that she wore the cross. It could help him segue into a discussion of her current relationship with Christ. He had decided they absolutely must talk about it tonight, when he had her all to himself again.

Before that could occur, there were many things to be accomplished—monumental things. As the crowd in the bleachers quieted, Jerry stepped to the microphone in the darkened barn and kicked off the show that the audience came to see—Sky Ranch's second annual Talent Night.

"Ladies and gentlemen, we're proud to present some of the greatest talent you'll ever see and hear this side of our stockade fence," Jerry announced into the mike as the spotlight hit him. A drum player rattled out an intro beat as a barbershop quartet, complete with straw hats and handlebar mustaches, took the stage and began the entertainment. They were followed by a magic act, a pantomime, and a harmonica solo.

The more the evening progressed, the more invigorated the audience became. Many of the parents were speechless that their sons were displaying some of the talents they witnessed on stage, after Jerry had worked with them. He hoped that the Talent Show would boost the self-concepts of many of the boys who felt they had nothing to offer.

Although most of the time Jerry had to remain "backstage," which was actually a couple of horse stalls converted into dressing rooms, occasionally he stuck his head out to try to detect how Carol was responding to the show.

Like the other guests, Carol appeared to be caught up in the entertainment. When a magician strolled into the audience and plucked gummy-worm candies from behind several parents' ears, Jerry watched Carol laugh heartily.

The skit she had helped with was an audience favorite. Several of the boys waved at her unpretentiously as they took their places to perform. The skit was a satire on campus life at Sky Ranch. The young dramatists portrayed a group of captive monkeys who lived in "Ape" Barracks and who were released to their homes when they reached Level "Tree." One actor, in a spoof on Jerry, portrayed a zookeeper who taught the monkeys how to play softball, using bananas for bats. When the players stepped up to "bat," they swatted large balls of aluminum foil into the audience.

"That's so the umpire can yell 'foil,'" one of the monkey/actors announced to the audience, which roared at the pun.

Jerry didn't remember that line being in the script. He wondered if Carol had made a sly addition as she drilled them. With questioning eyes, he looked across the barn at Carol. She flashed him a mischievous grin in reply and shrugged her shoulders as though admitting nothing.

When the laughter died down and the applause stopped, Jerry could see vestiges of that slightly perplexed demeanor from the afternoon still settle in on Carol. It seemed obvious to him that the conversation with Dr. Naylor still weighed on her significantly.

Bo had insisted that every Sky Ranch resident have at least a minor role in the talent show, so none would feel devalued because he didn't star in some area. So the next-to-the-last number was a "glee club" mostly formed by boys who had not yet participated in an act. The glee club sang the ranch's theme song, "The Sky's the Limit"—urging the residents to overcome barriers that would keep them from their dreams.

As the final bars echoed throughout the barn, Jerry felt his throat tighten, not just from emotion over saying good-bye to a group of boys who had become like family to him.

He knew that after this group left the stage, it was his turn to preside over the grand finale—tonight's crowning moment on which he had pinned such massively high hopes. As he stepped onto the platform and took the hand mike, the four boys from the barbershop quartet, this time minus their top hats and handlebars, filed in behind him.

"Friends, this concludes our talent show except for one last event," he began, his eyes scanning the crowd. "As you all know, this is a special evening because we're honoring ten residents who have achieved level 6 at Sky Ranch. They'll be graduating tonight and returning to their homes. As their names are called, you can read their personal vignettes that appear in your program."

Jerry read off the names of the ten and asked them to walk on stage toward Bo, who extended to each a certificate and a hug.

As the recognized youths returned to their seats, Jerry continued.

"I'm so glad I got to emcee this year in Talent Night," he told the audience. "The inaugural Talent Night occurred last year just after I arrived at Sky Ranch, so this has been my first year to really participate. You see, Sky Ranch has been a refuge for me as well. I came here at a time in my life when I was just about as lost and as hopeless as some of you felt when you entered these gates. In all my confusion, I left behind all that was dear to me in my search for some answers. I'm so thankful that the Lord Jesus Christ came into my life while I've been here, to show me that He is the one true Answer. When I have Him in my heart, all the other answers to life's dilemmas fall in place."

Jerry spoke with such an air of earnestness that it stilled every rustle in the house. With his eyes moistening, he added, "You're a special bunch of folks to me, and I love you more than I can say."

The audience responded with an enthusiastic ovation. Jerry gestured warmly first to the ten honorees and their families who were seated in a roped-off section of the bleachers, then to the remainder of the audience where the rest of the boys were scattered out. He then motioned for Bo and Sally, seated on the bottom row, to stand and take appropriate bows. The applause swelled for this couple who were seen as life-changers by a far greater number than Jerry alone.

Then, when the crowd in the barn quietened, Jerry moved up closer to the spotlights that blinded his eyes. He squinted a little and let a few seconds pass.

"Now, I'd also like to take a moment to introduce an honored guest. Some of you have met her already, but I didn't want to miss the opportunity to formally introduce her. The Lord brought Carol McKechnie into my life in a very special way, and I've been thrilled to be able to share Sky Ranch with her this weekend. It's a great pleasure to have you here tonight, Carol, at Sky Ranch—all the way to Kansas from Wooster, Ohio. Would you stand, please, and let everyone give you a big, Sky Ranch greeting?"

Jerry let his gaze fall tenderly on Carol, and she looked surprised and happy to be the momentary focus of attention. A few of the boys couldn't resist a few raucous wolf-whistles at the attractive guest. The ripple of laughter that ensued lent a down-home feeling to Jerry's remarks.

As the crowd hushed once again, Jerry stepped to the front of the platform and reached for a guitar that someone handed him. It was a guitar his grandmother bought him in college and paid for him to take lessons on one summer. He hadn't played it much until he came to Sky Ranch and found it among some things he transferred to Bo when he graduated.

The barbershop quartet moved directly behind him and straightened themselves. Jerry ducked his head under the thick guitar strap and adjusted it around his neck. Shifting the guitar until it finally felt comfortable, he took an audible deep breath that seemed to emerge all the way from his toenails.

He pushed a strand or two of hair out of his eyes and retrieved the hand mike he had momentarily deposited in its holder.

"The final number in our show tonight is one that I felt that Lord was leading me to compose—and to sing to you. When I was thinking about what I wanted to say to each of you as we close, these words of appreciation came to my mind."

He looked down, a little modestly, and continued. "You'll quickly figure out that I'm an amateur. I doubt if I get an invitation to record in Nashville on the basis of this song. But I think you'll see it's sincere. It expresses my love for those here tonight who are dear to me."

The barbershop quartet stepped to the mike at stage right, but they were silent initially. The first verse bore only the simple accompaniment of a few chords Jerry strummed out as he sang and looked toward the honorees:

Remembering you—and all our times together—
Thinking of days we've laughed and loved and
  grown.
Though we may part, our ties no one can sever.
With you in my heart, I'll never be alone.

The guests who lined the bleachers listened respect-fully. The song had been written in private, with only the barbershop members clued in at the very last minute when Jerry brought them in to rehearse. Jerry wondered what Bo and Sally were thinking at this moment. They had no idea he had planned this blockbuster conclusion to the show

He transitioned the melody up a half-step, and the quartet joined in as backup for the second verse. To the whole of the audience he sang:

Remember, please—in all of life's tomorrows,
God's in control; He sees the bigger plan.
Although the past might have its share of sorrows,
We can look back and see His faithful hand.

The quartet's harmony swelled in intensity, moving the song to its monumental conclusion. With the first few chords of the final verse, Jerry stepped from the platform and moved slowly and deliberately to the bleachers where Carol sat. He pinned his gaze on her eyes and sang the final, moving words directly to her, broadcasting his feel-ings for her as nearly two-hundred people looked on.

Remembering you—how God brought us together—
Even through trials, He's kept us safe and strong.
Our hearts soar free despite the stormy weather.
It's been His way to teach us all along.

Carol's lower lip dropped in surprise, and her eyes never left Jerry's as he performed. Her first look was almost a bemused one, as her face said, *I didn't know you could sing and play.* Then, as one line followed another, her eyes took on a dazzled quality, as she realized how tenderly Jerry was honoring her with this musical tribute. The glassed-over gaze of confusion that she wore earlier was suddenly replaced by a look of unadulterated joy.

The quartet's harmony and the increasingly powerful chords Jerry added for the finale lent richness to the climactic lines, as he sang to Carol one last time, on the refrain:

> My heart's been true.
> Always I'll be
> Remembering you.

Then, easing back onto the stage, he paid the boys a final, musical homage.

> To all of you,
> Always I'll be
> Remembering you.

When the song ended, Jerry held his arms out to them as if in a giant embrace. His eyes glistened, as did the eyes of several in the audience, and he felt that his heart was suddenly clutched in a mammoth grip.

The response from the bleachers was overwhelming. Numerous boys instantly jumped to their feet and cheered. With a wave of his arms, Jerry guided the spotlight first to the ten honorees, then to Bo and Sally, and then to Carol, whose face was so luminous that the spotlight was hardly necessary.

Jerry boomed, "Good night, everyone!" into the mike, but it was useless against the audience roar as the barn lights came up and the rain began assailing the roof again. Jerry felt victorious. The adrenaline rush carried him high as he was mobbed by admiring boys who wanted to throw hugs on him and grateful parents who wanted to shake his hand. The crowd pressed so immediately that his attempts to climb down from the stage were futile.

All these solicitous faces bobbing up around him, but only one was he interested in seeing at this very second. From the crowd his eyes instantly sought out Carol, who he found was moving toward him slowly and in the distance, held back by the mob. He suddenly had a dreadful urge to order everyone out—to inform them they were intruding on a private moment between him and the only one for whom his heart beat at that hour.

As he tried to carry on polite conversation with those around him, he glimpsed Carol as she moved closer. Her face was as one transformed, and he saw the unmistakable glimmer of love in her dilated eyes like he hadn't witnessed it since Valley Lodge. All these admiring remarks about his song—and only one appraisal did he really want to hear. Her compliment would crown the moment in this emotion-packed evening.

Hurry, Carol, hurry, his eyes urged in a way that shut out everyone else in the room.

Then, as Carol penetrated the inner tier of well-wishers that pressed against Jerry, he felt a firm tug at his shirt-sleeve. It was Happy, the ranch cook, who had darted in from the dining hall. He was rain-drenched and worried.

"Jerry, come quick!" Happy hissed frantically into his ear. "Rico's gone. He's run away."

"What?" Jerry gasped, clutching his chest.

"He wasn't in the glee club number. Didn't you notice?"

"No!" Jerry's face blanched. He whirled around, hoping he might spot Rico in the crowd to prove the man wrong.

"Two of the boys from the glee club ran out afterward to look for him. I was outside cleaning up and saw them looking scared. He's not in his barracks. He's not anywhere."

"Search the barracks again," Jerry demanded impassionedly. "Keep it quiet until I can meet you there. I'll find Bo."

At that very moment, Carol broke through the last layer of people. Her joyous look melted as she saw Jerry suddenly whiten when Happy grabbed him.

"Something's wrong," she declared intuitively, as she edged up to Jerry at last.

Jerry nodded, swallowing hard. "Rico's run off," he told her, hardly above a whisper so no one around them would hear. "Happy's been looking for him." Jerry vaulted himself on tiptoe above the heads of the audience to try to spot his brother. "I've gotta find Bo."

Carol's face mirrored the turmoil Jerry felt. Jerry started to dash off, then looked back at Carol, whose eyes had held the glow of love only seconds before. "Keep it under wraps for now, please, Carol," he directed breathlessly. "Meet me in a minute at the ranch house." He leaped from the crowd to the area off stage right where he had spotted Bo just minutes before.

He pulled Bo by the arm and dispatched the frightening news. The two of them blistered through the crowd determinedly and pushed out into the rain-soaked night.

Spurred by momentum, and buoyed in part by the confidence he felt over the successful talent show, Jerry didn't wait for his brother's direction but began giving instructions himself. "I'll meet Happy at the barracks. You go to the gate and see what the attendants know," he told Bo.

Happy's repeat search of the barracks confirmed his earlier report: no Rico. No note, no missing personal items that he could tell. Jerry felt a modicum of encouragement. "Maybe he's still on the premises, then," he almost cried with relief to Happy.

They dashed through the yard toward the ranch house and encountered Bo, who shot through their hopes. "One of the gate attendants is sure he slipped out when they were admitting some of the late-comers, about a half-hour ago," Bo yelled as the rain slid down his face in sheets. "The downpour made it tough to see, but they believe they saw a blur slip by. One of them ran to tell me but couldn't find me in the crowd."

Jerry knew the situation had turned serious. Rico was apparently Sky Ranch's first runaway, just at the moment parents swarmed everywhere, wanting urgently to trust the ranch with their own offspring.

Jerry looked at Bo's eyes as they slowly filled with dread. He thought about Carol, likely waiting at the ranch house, just seconds after what he had hoped was the tide-turning moment of their day. He again saw Carol's eyes as they had moved through the crowd, glowing with admiration for how successfully he had produced the talent show, especially the final act.

This would be the moment of truth for them. All of Carol's fears that Jerry would disintegrate under pressure could easily be realized if he didn't take control of himself quickly. Jerry knew he could rightfully pound himself with guilt right now, since he hadn't noticed Rico missing from the glee club number.

He couldn't succumb; he must prove to Carol—and to himself—that even when he was tested and tried, he could stay in control.

While Bo momentarily reeled from shock, Jerry knew he must take charge—and do it instantly.

"OK, Bo," Jerry directed, sucking in his breath so rapidly that it made a shrill whistle in the damp night air. "Here's what we'll do. I'll go look for Rico. Happy, you come with me. Bo, you go back to the barn, visit with the parents, and keep a straight face. Word may get out, so answer any questions as low-key as you can. We might have to announce something later, but let's hold our cards close at this point."

Bo nodded in agreement, so Jerry went on.

"Get someone you can trust to staff the phones. Not Sally—she needs to press the flesh with the parents, like you do. I'll take the cell phone with me. If I don't turn up something in, let's say, an hour, I'll call the sheriff's office."

"Right," Bo agreed, offering no resistance. His eyes grew wider and his face whiter as Jerry spoke.

Sensing his brother's angst, Jerry shook him by the shoulder. "Bo," he said, right in his face, almost yelling. "God's still in charge. He'll see us through this, remember?"

Bo moved his head in the affirmative, wordlessly, and Jerry realized that for the first time, roles had reversed. Jerry was actually in the position of comforting and shoring up his brother, after all these years.

Then, Jerry tacked on one last, heavy-hearted message. "Bo—about Carol. I don't know how long I'll be away. Take care of things with her, promise?" Jerry begged.

"Yes," Bo assured.

"Thanks. I'm off, then." He spun around in a 180-degree turn on the slippery grass and sprinted toward the ranch house.

Before locating Carol, Jerry dashed into Bo's bedroom and traded his soggy garments for a dry sweatshirt, jeans, and socks from Bo's bureau. Bo's room was closer than his own, and Jerry could replace the clothing items later. He grabbed the cell phone from its holder.

He knew where Bo's rain slicker hung, in the closet off the entry hall, so he yanked it from its hook. He slid into Bo's galoshes that he used in the horse stalls. Stuffing the cell phone into his pocket, he opened the door into the kitchen—just at the moment the back door slammed and Happy entered, rain gear in place. He had brought the Jeep around, and they hadn't a moment to waste.

Carol stood by the sink, looking out the window onto the drippy, dismal night. One glance at Jerry revealed that this was a man on a mission, his purpose resolute. It was clear that the search was still on.

"We're pretty sure Rico's left the ranch," Jerry stated gravely, answering her inquiring look. "Happy and I are going out in the Jeep."

Concern flooded her face, as the thunder created havoc outdoors.

"I'll go with you," she announced. "I can help."

"No, Carol, you mustn't," Jerry replied quickly, trying to sound self-assured. "Bo and Sally will be here. They need to keep up a confident face for parents. Let's contain the damage as much as we can until we know more."

"What can I do, then?" she entreated him.

"Pray, Carrie. Just pray," Jerry replied. He remembered another time, more than a year ago, when Pop threw him the same desperate admonition as he headed for bypass surgery. *Pray, Jerry. Just pray.*

The look that Carol shot him was not altogether different from the helpless one he gave Pop then. Jerry knew that praying seemed to be something that had not been part of Carol's activity in recent months.

Nevertheless, she managed a weak nod.

"Promise?" Jerry breathed insistently to her.

"Promise," she agreed.

"Good."

Carol surveyed the anxious Happy and looked at Jerry's attire that would keep him warm and dry for only so long on a inclement night like this one. She saw the lightning blasting and heard the thunder exploding so close, it could be in the next room.

As Jerry started to wheel out of the kitchen, he felt a hand on his arm. Carol clamped urgent fingers around the sleeve of his rain slicker, just below the elbow. Even through the thick material, the contact sent his heart ricocheting

"Be careful," she exhorted him, her face lifted upward to his so closely he could have kissed her without moving an inch.

In that moment when victory was within his grasp, all Jerry yearned to do was to spend the rest of the evening by Carol's side, as he'd planned originally. In the panic over Rico, he still hadn't had a chance to find out what Carol thought about his special song. There were still other, crucial matters they needed to discuss.

But an impatient Happy held the kitchen door open for him and waved him into the vehicle. Jerry ducked into the Jeep that Happy left with its engine spluttering in the rain.

Even for the love of Carol, the search for Rico couldn't wait.

TWENTY SEVEN

Standing in the Gap

❦

Jerry didn't come back to Sky Ranch that evening or the next morning, either. He and Happy and the ranch's Jeep sloshed all night over back roads that had been made into mud pies by the rain.

At times they pursued Rico separately, on foot, as they followed the creek that roped around the back of the ranch property line and beamed their flashlights into the underbrush. Late into the night, they dodged lightning bolts to knock at adjacent ranch houses, thinking that someone might have admitted Rico for shelter.

After the first forays around Sky Ranch failed to turn up the boy, Jerry alerted law-enforcement officials. They broadened the search and gave Rico's description to officers in several surrounding counties. Wet and weary, Jerry and Happy plowed on without food or rest, believing that they must find Rico before serious harm came to him.

Jerry had stayed in touch with Bo by cell phone, in case Rico returned on his own or tips came in to the ranch. Bo reported that thankfully, in most cases, parents left the ranch quickly after the program with no clue that Jerry and Happy were chasing a runaway. In the few cases where boys told their parents, Bo answered frankly but tried to assure them that the situation was in hand.

At bedtime, when word had begun to spread throughout the barracks, Bo called the boys together and informed them all at once about Rico. He led a prayer for Rico's safety and assured them that by morning he hoped to have more encouraging word.

"Sounds like you dealt with it well, Bo," Jerry commended, still taking the lead in all that was happening for Rico. The prayer meeting with the boys had been Jerry's suggestion, during one of the times he telephoned Bo late that evening.

Then he asked, in a jagged whisper, "How's Carol?"

"Concerned, of course," Bo replied. "She came with me and Sally to the prayer meeting. She's having a tough time with it, like all of us are. You and she sat with Rico at dinner, just before it happened. I guess that's the part that's most puzzling to her."

"I know," Jerry told him gloomily. "I keep going over it in my mind. He seemed OK. He didn't drop a clue. I keep asking myself—was he crying for help, the way I was at Valley Lodge? What did I fail to notice that would cause him to act this way?"

"We may never know until we find him," Bo commented. "We can only pray that's soon."

"Yes," Jerry replied. He hoped that the morning light might find him back at the ranch-house kitchen, with Rico safely in tow. He wanted to snare some brief time with Carol before she had to leave for Ohio.

But at 10 o'clock, only a few minutes before Carol needed to leave Sky Ranch to catch her noon flight, Jerry was nowhere near familiar territory. Sheriff's officials had received a tip that a youth matching Rico's description had darted into a farm outbuilding miles down the road. The retired man who owned the farm feared the boy would find the rifles he stored in the outbuilding and was afraid to approach him on his own. Jerry was alone now

301

since Happy had to return to the Sky Ranch to cook breakfast. The tip sent Jerry and a deputy racing to the man's farm to investigate.

With an aching chest that felt like one of the Jeep's tires had backed over it, Jerry regretfully called Sky Ranch and told Carol that he couldn't return to say good-bye. Bo had already assured him that Chuck could take her back to the airport.

"I have a bad track record for cutting out on you," he told Carol breathlessly. He cradled the cell phone between his ear and his shoulder as he ran toward the farmhouse. "Guess this doesn't help matters much."

Carol tried to sound upbeat, but this disappointment was the latest of events to assault her in the emotional see-saw she had been on since the visit began.

"I just keep thinking about Rico and how sweetly he shook my hand," she told Jerry, her voice quavering. "He's such a beautiful boy. Please keep working until you bring him home."

Jerry knew the Rico situation carried critically high stakes with Carol. No tender song, no magical evening, no insights from a therapist would weigh on her balance scale as much as how well he responded in this crisis. He couldn't believe Dr. Naylor was out of the country just when he needed his counsel most. Carol had wondered how Jerry would perform, away from some of his props, when difficulty hit. Jerry knew that the outcome of his search for Rico would impact not just Sky Ranch. It would be the real bottom-line if he wanted a future with Carol.

The tip that led Jerry and the deputy to the farmer's outbuilding proved to be a blind alley. Although all braced themselves for a shotgun blast when the deputy flung open the outbuilding door, the shed was empty. The farmer's guns were intact on the rack above the door. There was no indication that anyone had ever been inside, even though the owner held fast to his story that he had seen a youth hovering around that morning.

The false lead caused Jerry, much to his chagrin, to return to Sky Ranch about midday, empty-handed and stooped with fatigue. Jerry knew that he needed to dispatch a fresh team of searchers while he rested, ate, and regrouped.

Carol called Jerry as soon as she got back to Wooster that evening, to check on the status of things. By the time she called at six o'clock, Rico had been missing for almost 24 hours. A statewide police alert had been issued for him, and Jerry had worked with volunteers in Colby to organize citizen searches.

Some of the volunteers came on the premises at Sky Ranch to help staff the phone bank to receive tips as word spread, but the end result was the same. By Sunday, Rico was as lost as ever. Jerry tried to shore up Bo and Sally as they worked to keep Sky Ranch operational, but the strain in Bo's eyes was unmistakable. He had prided himself on the ranch's security record. Somehow, he had let one of his youth slip through his care.

Carol kept up her daily telephone calls to inquire. Jerry was touched by her concern but rarely had time to reply more than a few words, since he was usually dashing to pursue some lead.

On the third day, when the phone rang late one evening and Jerry answered it, he heard only a choking sound in the background.

"Hello?" he stormed, thinking it to be a prankster with a bogus tip.

"J-J-J-erry, it's Carol," he heard her finally manage.

"Carol, what's wrong?" he demanded, his voice instantly switching from irritation to concern.

"I n-n-need to talk to you," she sobbed, the tears in her voice unmistakable. "I know you n-n-need to go. Would you call me back sometime when you have a moment?"

Jerry felt a mixture of horror and curiosity. Carol never started conversations like this; that is, she certainly hadn't since Valley Lodge days.

"It's OK, Carol," he said, trying to soothe her. "We can talk now."

"You're busy," she interjected. "You might miss a call about Rico." Clearly she meant she needed to tie up the line more than just a few seconds.

"Tell you what," he replied. "I'll get Sally to staff this phone. I'll call you back on Bo's line." Jerry quickly made the transfer, and soon he was in Bo's office with the door closed, waiting for whatever Carol had to spill.

Spill, she did. She told him that she had taken his request to heart and had dutifully begun praying immediately for Rico; that he would be found, that he would be safe, and that Jerry would be protected as he searched.

"I prayed like that for a while, just like you asked me to do," she told him. "You probably figured out by now—I haven't done a lot of praying lately, not since . . . not since . . ."

Jerry finished the sentence for her. "Not since I left you at Valley Lodge."

"Not since then," she echoed sadly.

"I understand," Jerry replied, and he did. He'd rejected God, too, once, when things got rocky in his life. He couldn't blame Carol much at all.

"But then," she went on, "once I got on my knees and was standing in the gap for Rico, the floodgates opened. I began confessing to God all kinds of things. I knew He hadn't moved away from me; I'm the one that moved. I let go of Him, just when I needed Him most."

Jerry shot up, ramrod straight, disbelieving what he was hearing, as joy overtook him. The Holy Spirit had Carol in His grip and was bringing her to conviction.

"It took Rico's situation to get my attention, plus what Dr. Naylor told me. And the words to your song—Jerry, they were so beautiful. I didn't get a chance to tell you at first. All these times I've been on the phone with you, I just couldn't find a way to say it. It *was* God who brought us together, just like you sang. He *did* keep us safe and strong. His hand *did* sustain us during all those rough times. I've been blaming Him, when I should have thanked Him."

"Carol, I . . . I can't believe . . ." Now it was Jerry's voice that was choking, that couldn't complete a sentence.

"You knew all along, didn't you . . . that I had slipped away from Him?" she queried. "It was nice of you not to bug me about it."

304

Jerry sighed with relief, grateful for his restraint. "It's the Holy Spirit who convicts, not anything I might do," he answered her.

"But Jerry," she continued, "that's not all that happened to me. What Dr. Naylor said about my role in our relationship really has soaked in. I already told you I was sorry for my part, but Dr. Naylor helped me really understand about being a compulsive helper and fixer. I can't let you take the whole blame for what happened to us. I've confessed all that to God, as well. I want to make a clean start in my life."

Jerry said nothing in reply, because he couldn't. Carol's astounding confession, coupled with the stress of Rico's disappearance, clenched him at the core of his being. After a long silence, a few stifled sobs escaped him and drifted over the phone lines. At the sound of his own tears, Jerry panicked at first, fearing Carol would perceive he was falling apart. He thought he would suffocate from fear and embarrassment.

Carol's words of comfort were just the calming response he needed. "It's OK for you to cry," she reminded him gently, her voice caressing. "You probably haven't done this since Rico left, have you?"

Jerry choked out a few syllables. "I've tried to bear up, for Bo and Sally," he finally managed. "They're the ones looking to *me*, this time."

"You can tell me how much it hurts," she consoled him, and then added, with a slight touch of humor, "Remember what Dr. Naylor said. Use feelings words."

"I'd have to recite the whole chart," Jerry sniffed, his heart warming at Carol's compassion. "I feel scared, afraid, disappointed, humiliated, puzzled, enraged . . . because of what's happened to Rico."

Then he remembered her confession, and returned to it. "I feel joyful and gratified because of what you've told me. Thank God you've turned back to Him. For once, we're both in a good relationship with Him—at the same time."

He remembered to add, "I do accept your apology, Carrie. I already forgave you, long ago."

"Maybe it took Rico's leaving to knock sense into my head," she responded. "If he'd just come back now, before something bad happens to him."

The next few days did not bring Rico back, and Jerry's load increased. Calls from news media began pouring in, and Jerry had to answer all those questions—walking the fine line between soliciting help and sidestepping image problems for Sky Ranch. He printed multitudes of flyers and then mobilized volunteers to post them throughout the county. He dispatched Rev. Kinzer, the Sky Ranch chaplain, to organize prayer groups in area churches. He recruited one of Dr. Naylor's associates to visit the ranch and counsel with the boys who were distraught about Rico.

Amid the stress, however, Carol's repeated calls continued—each one more supportive and encouraging than the previous. She became his closest confidante—affirming him and helping him explore options. Most of all, Carol became someone with whom he could pour out his deepest frustrations and loss.

"Dr. Naylor really helped me identify secondary losses," she confided to him one evening, on the sixth night of Rico's disappearance. "He had me spell out for him all the losses I sustained the year you were away—not just the loss of a fiance, but others that I hadn't thought about—the loss of a dream and goal, the loss of image, the loss of a profession, even the loss of a hobby—skiing."

When Jerry gulped at what Carol had just shared, she quickly interjected, "I'm telling you this, Jerry, not as a guilt trip, but maybe so you could benefit, too. You've suffered a lot of losses in this thing with Rico—not just the loss of a resident. You lost your dream in the way the weekend ended so sadly. You lost the ranch's image, like Bo has. Just like Dr. Naylor said, it helps you understand why you feel so bad if you realize all the areas of your life that are impacted."

Carol was right. It did help. Just being able to verbalize it to someone who understood was half the battle. He marveled at how he and Carol, even in these few phone calls, were learning how to shore each other up through a crisis—in a really healthy way, this time, unlike the harmful patterns they adapted at Valley Lodge.

Their calls grew longer and longer. It seemed they never lacked for things to talk about, and they always seemed reluctant to part.

He talked about the search and where he was emotionally as well as logistically.

She talked about her current classroom challenges, and he listened and helped her reflect, as a diversion from his trauma.

She told him about a call she'd had from Pop and how he sent love to Jerry as he coordinated the search.

He told her about the substitute counselor, Guy Nelms, who was doing a fantastic job with the boys. He told about a postcard they'd received from Dr. Naylor, blissfully touring Korea without a shred of knowledge of what was going on at home.

She began to close their telephone visits by praying for him. Soon they were praying together—really sincere, meaningful, joint entreaties to God that were a far cry from the mockery of a prayer that night in the Valley Lodge kitchen.

He marveled at how in all their days of physical closeness at Valley Lodge, they had never communicated so effectively as they did, parted by 600 miles, in these recent phone calls. He felt his senses reach out to her powerfully across the several states that separated them.

By the eighth day, after Rico had been on the missing persons list for a week, law enforcement officials made less frequent calls to Sky Ranch, and the community interest began to quieten. Jerry, Bo, and Sally were sitting around the kitchen table with long faces, exchanging shocked, silent stares, when the phone rang. It was Carol.

"Jerry, can you go to Bo's office again?" she asked him urgently, meaning the call was private.

"What is it, Carol?" he questioned her, motioning for Sally that he needed her to take the phone.

"I need to tell you something," she insisted. It sounded like something needed to be stated quickly, before she had a mind change.

Jerry passed the receiver to Sally and called Carol back promptly on the non-emergency line.

"Is something wrong?" he asked, when they were connected again.

"No, something's right. Very right," she answered him, her words tumbling out more rapidly than usual. "I wanted you to know. It's all over with Kevin. I've told him I won't see him again."

Jerry was flicking away some pencil shavings from around the electric sharpener on Bo's desk when he heard the words, which Carol had uttered without either gladness or regret. He didn't respond right away but just let her statement seep down into his thoughts.

"What brought you to this decision?" he finally ventured, when he trusted his voice enough to reply.

"I realized that Kevin wasn't God's best for me," she told him. "I knew if Christ was going to really be Lord of my life again, I needed to set this relationship aside."

A long silence passed before either of them said anything else. The unspoken part of Carol's revelation almost deafened him. He was struck with awareness that something life-altering had just happened between them because of her comment. He realized his lashes had tears on them.

The silence went on so long that Carol finally called out, "Jerry?" thinking he might have stepped away from the phone.

"I'm here," he replied, releasing a pent-up breath. Then, he found the composure to admit, "I'm glad that's what you decided."

"Me, too."

"I'm glad you called to tell me."

"Yeah."

His mind began racing as he rejoiced inwardly, and he suddenly couldn't talk fast enough.

"Look, Carol, as soon as this thing settles with Rico—after he's back—you and I can plan something special. Maybe you can come back to Sky Ranch. We could have a big celebration welcoming Rico home. I won't have to dash off this time. Or, I can come to Ohio. We'll do whatever you want to do. One of these days we'll have more time, I promise."

"I know. Well, I've kept you long enough, I guess. You'd better go in and give Sally a break."

"Yes, I should."

"Well, good-bye then."

"Bye."

She could hear him hesitate, and she laughed a little. "You're not hanging up."

"I know—wait a minute, Carol, will you?"

"What?"

"About Kevin . . ."

"What about him?"

"You're sure?"

"Perfectly sure."

"OK, then, good ni . . ." Jerry stopped in mid-syllable as Bo slammed into the office forcefully. His brother didn't take time to excuse the interruption.

"Jerry, come quick. They think they've found Rico. They think he burned to death."

Jerry hung up instantly and followed his brother, who led him to an awaiting sheriff's car, but he did so like a robot. For the first few seconds, Jerry felt suspended somewhere just a few inches above awareness, a kind of odd disembodiment, even with all the frightening chaos that was transpiring around him.

At that moment, Carol's voice uttering the unforgettable words, "It's all over with Kevin," seconds earlier— was the only reality that he knew.

The blaring radio in the squad car brought him back to earth. Although incredulous at Carol's news, Jerry knew that how skillfully he saw this crisis through still would ultimately render the verdict in their relationship.

TWENTY EIGHT

A New Lease on Life

❀

The officer's monologue, yelled at them over the squawk of his radio, filled in the grim details about Rico as Jerry and Bo headed off to Colby on their miserable mission.

A fire that burned up a shed two counties over had claimed the life of a youth, most likely Hispanic and thought to be Rico's age. The fire was almost certainly self-imposed. The man who owned the shed had seen someone trespassing on his property just before the blaze began. The officer warned Jerry and Bo: be prepared for a grisly sight at the hospital.

"It isn't Rico," Jerry muttered adamantly, after hearing the report. "He's still alive. I just know it."

"But Jerry, it sounds like . . ." Bo cautioned.

"Rico wouldn't take his life," Jerry stated determinedly, his eyes intense.

"Jerry, please don't get your hopes up," Bo pled. "You heard the officer, didn't you?"

Jerry didn't reply, but within himself, he held firm. Jerry didn't know how he sensed it; he just couldn't believe that the effervescent, spirited Rico would deliberately self-destruct. Rico had come too far in his rehabilitation. He had merely become testy and reverted to some of his old attention-getting tactics, at a time when all eyes were focused on the other boys' talents.

"Only one of you has to go in," the medical examiner advised them after the trio arrived at the hospital.

Bo looked at Jerry consolingly. "I'll be the one, Jer, if it's too much for you," he offered.

"No. Count me in, too," Jerry swallowed stubbornly, digging his fingernails into this palms as he prepared himself. The official parted the doors, motioning, and they followed soberly.

A few singed, dark strands emerging from a sheet pulled up to the hairline was their first sight of the object they were required to view—a form that could hardly be called a body. Bo and Jerry both gasped as their eyes focused on charred bits of skin and muscle that still managed to cling to bone in spots. Jerry instantly was so nauseous he felt the room swaying. Bo gagged, partly from the hideous scene, partly from the odor in this holding chamber.

From hair, build, and height—the only real characteristics left to be identified on the incinerated corpse—there was no doubt, they could easily be Rico's distinguishing marks. Jerry looked away, shuddering, after his eyes could absorb no more of the maudlin picture.

Then he heard the medical examiner say, as he jiggled what was left of a jaw, "Poor little guy. Such bad teeth. Look at all these fillings."

Through the fog of nausea and stench and grief, something snapped inside Jerry. "Bad teeth?" he retorted. "Rico may have been poor, but he didn't have bad teeth. When the dentist came out for check-ups, Rico was one of the few with no cavities. Must have been some kind of hereditary thing. He bragged about it."

"Dentist?" the M.E. queried, his eyebrows arched. "You give these boys dental care?"

"Of course," Bo hissed defensively. "We have dental records on Rico. We'll match them up!"

"Take me back to Sky Ranch," Jerry demanded to the officer, his half-yell reverberating throughout the room. "This isn't Rico. I knew it wasn't Rico. I'll get those x-rays and prove it. Rico isn't dead!"

Flying back to the ranch and wildly tumbling through a file drawer, Jerry seized the vital records and sped with them back to Colby to prove his point. The official scanned them and acknowledged a case of mistaken identity.

"Rico is alive!" Jerry exulted with certainty. He embraced Bo and even the medical examiner in his gratitude.

"If only we could find him," Bo breathed wistfully.

For Jerry, the news was buoying. He found a boost of confidence in realizing his hunch was accurate all along. He went back to work with added vigor—attacking the boy-hunt with a new strain of resourcefulness.

First on his agenda, of course, was to call Carol. Because of the false alarm about Rico, Jerry hardly had a moment to process her announcement that Kevin was truly out of the picture, and most importantly, what it could mean for their relationship. Yet he knew that nothing for them could possibly be settled while the search for Rico went on.

Carol cried with relief when he told her about his producing the x-rays as the missing link.

"I'm so proud of you," she affirmed him, offering just the encouragement he needed. Then Carol added some news that warmed his heart: she had already started back to her church in Wooster, after her year's hiatus.

"I realize now much I've missed this part of my life," she confided to Jerry. "Just when I needed my church the most, I pulled away. It's great to have this support again. I've told them about Rico, and they're praying, too."

In his new toehold on the Rico search, Jerry prompted a fresh infusion of reward money to try to smoke out more tips. The citizens' watch in Colby organized a campaign for reward pledges from local businesses as well as in surrounding counties. Soon the reward pool was up to $5,000. Volunteers helped distribute press releases about

the reward money. Radio and TV stations in ten surrounding counties broadcast the message for a wider
appeal.

As Jerry hoped, the effort snagged a new batch of
clues—a large number of them totally bogus, of course,
but some worth checking out, too.

Jerry paid special attention to any tip that could per-
tain to Rico's food supply. Staving off hunger would be a
key priority with the boy after nine days away from Sky
Ranch.

Sure enough, the search soon hit paydirt. A rural
mom-and-pop grocery owner in far northwest Taylor
County reported that a youth matching Rico's description
sneaked out without paying for orange juice and two
packages of sweet rolls.

Jerry grimaced to think about Rico breaking the law,
even over a few pilfered items of breakfast food. He had
hoped that Rico could keep his nose clean while he was
away. Law infringements would complicate things for
Rico and for Sky Ranch when he did return.

However, Jerry knew that Rico's remaining alive at
this point was the key goal. Ancillary matters would have
to be reckoned with later, one step at a time. For now,
Rico needed finding.

The significant lead from the rural grocer helped law-
enforcement people isolate their search in a specific part
of Thomas County.

Within twenty-four hours, the crucial call came. Just
after dawn, a rancher led sheriff's officials to his barn,
where he was sure Rico was hiding. He had seen a dark-
haired youth filling a canteen with water from an outdoor
spigot in the paddock where the man kept his champion
stallions.

When the rancher yelled at him, the boy had run off
and darted up into the hayloft. He hurled empty cans at
the man when he tried to climb up after him.

For several nights previously, the man had thought
his horses seemed noisier than usual, but he had suspected small animals were agitating them. Now he was convinced the agitator was Rico.

To Jerry, it was at last a clue that was believable—something that the puckish, horse-lover Rico would be a party to. Jerry was off in a flash to the search scene.

Officers had asked Jerry to join them at the barn and to try to lure Rico down without incident. Although they could have used force to retrieve him, they wanted to avoid traumatizing the boy, if possible.

Jerry drove out into the county and found the property in question. The sheriff's cars that were on the scene looked strangely out of place in the tranquil, rural surroundings. He pulled onto a rutted driveway that led to a cluster of metal buildings, parked Bo's truck, and walked into the barn. The officers gestured toward a ladder propped up against a loft for hay.

Jerry shucked his jacket and vaulted up the ladder, but after only a few steps, he felt something clunk into his shoulder and saw a soda can hit the ground. Before he could look up, another object—this time a larger can, like it once held apple juice—struck him in the chest.

"Hey, man, what did you do that for?" Jerry yelled up to the loft. He heard no answer but saw two dark eyes peer inquisitively over the ledge. As Jerry inched a few steps further up, he got a better view of the assailant. It was Rico alright—his face looking a trace thinner than normal, his hair flattened from sleep—but alive, thankfully.

"Rico, it's me—Jerry. Wow, looks like you've got quite a nest made for yourself."

Jerry stretched on tiptoe to survey Rico's habitat. The youth's eyes were as wide and wild as a cornered animal now that he realized it was Jerry who made his way up to him.

As Jerry strained over the rim to look further, he saw Rico's canteen, his canvas backpack, some torn paper wrappers from junk food, and a one-quart orange juice carton—from the mom-and-pop grocery, most likely. Rico had mounded up a pile of hay which served as his bed. There was the arsenal of cans—his ammunition against intruders. His lower lip trembled as Jerry climbed higher. A look mixed with horror and relief crossed his face.

Finally the boy, who understood what Jerry's visit signified for him, yelled, "I'm not going back there." He meant to Sky Ranch.

Jerry ignored the remark and kept talking calmly.

"I've really missed you, Rico. Can you tell me how you're doing?"

His lower lip pooched out even further, defying Jerry to engage him in conversation. Jerry repeated the question.

"How are you, man? You must be hungry, huh?"

Jerry saw the brown head move in the faintest nod.

"I thought as much. Well, guess what? I happen to know that Sally has a big pot of chili on the stove, and some cornbread. I think we could take care of that hunger real quick."

"I already told you. I'm not going back."

Jerry scooted up to the top of the ladder enough so he could, by maneuvering carefully, now twist around and sit on the hayloft ledge, with his back to the rail. He was still a good twenty-five feet from Rico. He wanted to give the boy plenty of space so that Rico didn't feel surrounded. At least the ridiculous can-throwing had stopped.

"Rico, the guys are all worried about you. They miss you—we all do."

Rico heaved a sigh that could be heard clear out to the sheriff's cars.

"Nobody cares about me."

"Why, Rico, where did you ever get that idea?"

"That night at the fiesta. Everybody had somebody but me."

"I'm sure it may have looked that way. But if you're talking about your mom, lots of boys didn't have parents come. Besides, you had us. We sat by you at dinner."

The bottom lip went out again. "You had Meees Carol. That's all."

Jerry didn't get defensive with Rico's accusation but merely listened reflectively. "I hear you saying you felt left out of things," he summarized.

"Yeah."

"I'm very sorry if I caused you to feel left out."

Rico changed the subject completely. "Hey, Jerry, did you see the horses out there?"

"Yeah, I sure did. That why you came here?"

"The horses like me. I've been caring for them."

"You mean with Mr. Durwood, here?" Jerry asked, knowing the answer already. He gestured down to the hefty rancher with earnest eyes who helped hold the ladder.

"No, not exactly. At night, after the folks in the house were sleeping."

"I see," Jerry replied, confirming the owner's suspicions about the paddock noises. "Where'd you get your cans, here?" Scooting gradually on his haunches, he ooched a little closer to Rico in the hayloft as he gestured to Rico's pile.

"From the recycle bin up by the house. I thought maybe there was food in them."

"Then you used them to throw at people."

"Yeah, a few times. I didn't mean to hurt anybody. I just didn't want anyone bothering me."

"Not even people who might have given you food?"

"I got by."

"How?"

"My backpack. I filled it up with stuff from the fiesta—tacos and chips and cake squares, when nobody was looking. It lasted a long time."

"I see," Jerry replied, marveling at the youth's resourcefulness. "But Rico, that was ten days ago. Where else did you eat?"

Rico answered under his breath. "Got some things from a store."

"You have them still?"

"Nope. Gone."

Jerry had been right. Rico's hunger had been a crucial factor in tracking him down.

Rico changed subjects again. "Hey, Jerry, you think I could stay and help with the horses?"

"You really like them, don't you?" Jerry affirmed, as his mind raced.

"They're the most beautiful I've ever seen."

"Well, Rico, there's one little problem with that. You know, you've been trespassing on Mr. Durwood's property. You took items that didn't belong to you. You used his water to fill your canteen. You messed with his horses without permission. You tried to hurt him with a can. What do you think you need to do about that?"

Rico thought a minute.

"Maybe I could help take care of the horses."

"Maybe. But you know how we've talked about how important it is to make amends? You'd need to do more than work with horses to make up for the property violations."

Rico was quiet again, as he thought.

"What if you came back and did some other things to help—like clean stalls or whitewash fences or some other odd jobs he might have for you? I haven't asked Mr. Durwood about this," Jerry said, looking down at the ranch owner who held the ladder, "but I certainly could propose it to him." Jerry knew he had taken a gamble mentioning it. Thankfully Mr. Durwood was nodding his assent as Jerry spoke.

"I'd do anything to be around his horses."

"You'd work hard at some of the other things I mentioned?"

Rico nodded.

"OK, then, I'll talk to Mr. Durwood about it. Now Rico, here's what I want you to do. I want you to stuff everything—all your trash, your cans, your canteen—everything, into your backpack. You need to always clean up behind yourself, remember?"

Rico hesitated. "I gotta go back to a level 1, right?"

Jerry hesitated. At the moment, he wanted to sidestep answering what Rico's exact consequences would be for running away. Jerry didn't want to make false promises to Rico until he had a chance to talk to Bo.

"Rico, you've hurt a lot of people—not just here but also at Sky Ranch. Making amends to all of them will play a big role in what happens now. Also, I've talked to your mama. She says she wants to come see you real soon." Jerry knew that some major consultations must occur with

Bo and with Dr. Naylor about managing Rico's behavior in the future. He also knew that drawing Rico's mother into the picture and helping her learn better how to parent him—even funding her trip to Sky Ranch when she couldn't afford it—would be an important part of the process.

"I'll do anything to be with the horses," he replied assuredly.

Jerry appraised that Mr. Durwood could be an important new role model for Rico. The boy would need to develop some added ones, when the time came that Jerry wasn't always around.

"Come on, then," Jerry beckoned. "Come over to the ladder. I'll help you down."

Slowly, falteringly, Rico moved toward Jerry. When he got close enough, Jerry reached for Rico's backpack first and handed it down to an officer, who checked it for dangerous items.

Then, Jerry held out an arm to steady Rico, wobbly from hunger. His mind flashed back to another early morning, at a bus station, in another state, when Bo held out reassuring arms to a wobbly runaway.

Now Bo's gift kept on giving, as Jerry, safe and whole again from his long-ago flight, answered this distress call. He wondered if in God's providence, a restored Rico might reach out a hand to another recalcitrant someday, as well, and give him a new lease on life.

They got him down from the ladder, and as Jerry embraced Rico, the youth's haughty exterior melted. He wilted in Jerry's arms, sobbing from exhaustion and comforted at the familiar. His slight frame felt even slighter as Jerry held him, quaking like an aspen leaf.

Then, when Rico could manage it, Jerry turned him around to face his victim and benefactor, Mr. Durwood.

"Rico, this man would like to meet you," Jerry instructed. Rico stuck out a hand, much in need of a good washing.

"Hi," he said, sheepishly, his eyes lifting only to the man's belt buckle. "You sure have pretty horses."

"Rico . . ." Jerry chastened, and the boy seemed to follow Jerry's prodding.

"I'm s . . . sorry," Rico stammered, apologies not coming easily to this one despite his growth at Sky Ranch. Seeing Jerry's nod that urged him on to complete his statement, Rico followed with, "I'll come back to work for you as soon as I can."

They threw a blanket over Rico and herded him into the truck, but Rico didn't stay awake long enough to even wave good-bye as Mr. Durwood's prize horses whickered in the distance. Dozing, he didn't see the bevy of Sky Ranch residents that lined up inside the gate to greet him as he arrived. Catching up on sleep was the first order of business for this runaway. Greetings, consequences, and a new plan for his treatment would follow down the road.

When Carol made her regular morning call to Sky Ranch to check on Rico, Bo greeted her with the glad report: "They've just called from the sheriff's car. Jerry should be back here with Rico in about 30 minutes."

"Praise the Lord!" Carol yelled into the phone, her voice breaking with joyful tears.

Then Bo added something, believing enough barriers had crumbled that he could say this now without sounding like Jerry's press agent. "Jerry's been a rock through this, Carol," he told her. "Really. He's kept all our spirits up. He's managed this crisis very, very well."

Soon, after Rico was deposited in bed, Jerry followed up with a detailed call to Carol, giving her his account.

After soaking up the story and heaping on praise, Carol took a deep breath and conjectured to Jerry, "Wow, I bet all this experience with Rico really confirms it for you. I bet you see this as a sign that God for sure is leading you to work with teen-agers."

Jerry digested her comment and corrected her.

"No, quite the contrary," he said, setting the stage for a discussion that he knew would need to be on their agenda in the near future. "It's shown me something far different. I used to think I was incompetent in leadership roles. This has proved to me that I do have administrative skills— skills that I can use to run a business."

TWENTY NINE

Sweet Homecoming

❀

As though Pop had overheard these thoughts, he phoned Jerry two days later with news of his retirement date—May 1. Pop's doctors had finally lowered the boom on the stubborn lodge owner and ordered him away from management and off to a restful cabin near his niece in Durango. David Pollard, Pop's apprentice who had joined the lodge staff after Jerry's departure, had decided to return to P.R. work and was moving to New Mexico.

With this decided, Pop recognized that his original plan was God's way all along. He asked Jerry to pray about returning to Valley Lodge and becoming his successor—this time, for keeps.

Jerry and Pop talked regularly for the next three days after that. Carol had kept Pop posted on developments with Rico, so the older gentleman knew how unflappably Jerry supervised the search. Pop gave Jerry mini-briefings on the lodge's balance sheets, the esprit de corps among the staff these days, and the stable tourist season just past.

Jerry could launch out this time with things on a solid footing. Pop had already promised Shannon she could return to Wooster in the fall, but she had agreed to stay until Jerry could assume the mantle confidently.

As Jerry prayed, a profound peace settled on his heart, and he felt right about continuing these discussions. Bo long ago had released Jerry from any sense of obligation to continue on at Sky Ranch. Even though Bo grieved mightily as Jerry told him about Pop's proposal, he realized that the ranch for troubled boys was not his brother's ultimate destination.

Dr. Naylor was back from his trip and knew of all the happenings. He helped Jerry talk over the pros and cons of the job. Pop suggested that Jerry make a weekend visit to Valley Lodge soon to walk through the process, as a refresher, before he gave Pop his final word.

So that was why Jerry, at that moment, sat in the passenger cabin of a jet bound for Denver, with a connecting flight to Gunnison and on to Crested Butte.

By his side was Carol, whose hand he covered confidently with his own. As plans for this visit took shape, Jerry had broached the subject with her tentatively: would she accompany him to the place she left sadly and suddenly fifteen months before? Jerry knew how much it had helped him to go on his earlier, return journey, and he hoped it would be restorative to her as well. To his glad relief, she accepted. She had flown from Wooster, connecting with him at the Salinas airport, so they could board the plane to Denver together.

Unlike her restraint of past visits, Carol made no attempt to bury her excitement at seeing Jerry, nor did she mask her pride over his victory with Rico. Her vivid face glowed with adoration when Jerry spotted her moving toward him through the airport concourse. Her gaze told him she was focusing on him as through new eyes.

"Ready to go?" he inquired, as he reached down to tote her carry-on bag.

"Ready as I'll ever be," she sighed, partly to let out a nervous breath and partly because Jerry looked so incredibly hunky in his navy jacket and navy knit shirt.

When they were settled in their seats and Jerry moved his hand on top of hers, Carol laced her fingers into his eagerly. Other than his faint, comforting pat in the therapist's office at Sky Ranch, it was Jerry's first real touch of affection since before they parted long ago. Both were aware that their relationship had moved to a deeper level in recent days, since Carol officially ended things with Kevin. Jerry had promised to hold back from physical expression until he was sure they had dealt with the earlier barriers that separated them. Jerry knew that in both of their minds, those gears now had unalterably shifted.

He held Carol's hand for much of the flight. He relished in the warmth and sweetness of the simple act of his fingers fitting around hers once again as their hands rested against the leg of Carol's russet-colored silk pants suit. When the flight attendant served beverages, Jerry used his free hand to flip down both his and Carol's tray tables. He wanted nothing to cause Carol to have to disconnect this physical contact he had anticipated for so long.

It was thrilling to be able to gaze into each other's eyes for long periods of time now without fearing that they would give away their feelings, so they openly indulged in this luxury. They lowered their seat backs and turned toward each other so their faces were close on their seat cushions. Sometimes they murmured a few words to each other, but most of the time, they merely drank in each others' features, with a shared sense of wonder at what was happening between them again. They let their mutual glances speak volumes, and both seemed to recognize what direction things could be headed if this Valley Lodge trip was a success.

Jerry's only concern was how Carol would respond when the biting memories seized her. He remembered his own pain when he had initially laid eyes again on Valley Lodge, the place of their love and anguish. He wished he could spare her from these moments and worried it would set back their progress.

Sometime later, Jerry murmured to Carol, "How do you feel about going back?"

Carol smiled a little at his "feelings" question that had become such a standard, useful part of their conversations these days.

"I feel . . . excited, I guess. I can't wait to give Pop a hug and see Shannon and the others."

"And . . . ?" Jerry knew there was more.

"Oh, Jerry," she finally blurted, "surely you know how scary it is for me. I mean, just to realize what happened to us there . . . before."

"I know you're scared," he replied tenderly. "But Carrie, remember. I'm with you this time. I'm here to stay."

Another time, he whispered to her, "Tell me about your mother. Where does she stand on all of this?"

Carol smiled a little at the question he hadn't dared broach until now. "Mom is fine," she told him. "When things first happened, she reacted like you'd expect a mother to—protectively, but she's OK now. I've kept her posted, and she understands."

Jerry grew more insistent. "Carrie, please. It's important that I know. Do you think she'll forgive me, so I can talk to her again?"

Carol gave him a long, intuitive look. "She has already, long ago. Any time you want to talk with her, she'd be happy to. She's always been fond of you."

Her words provided him the assurance he craved, for the time in the future when he and Fayma would need to converse on some serious matters involving her daughter that they both loved.

They traveled by motorcoach from the airport to the lodge. Silence wove a web around them as their eyes drank in the familiar view of the mountains that had been their home months before. As their car drove into Crested Butte, nestled in the valley floor, it wound through the quaint streets of the venerable town. A few late-season tourists still clustered around the weathered, old storefronts on this spring day, but the customary mass of crowds had all gone home. It was now after Easter, traditionally spring's last hurrah in ski country.

As they pulled under the covered entry and heard the familiar shibboleth, "Welcome to Valley Lodge, the happiest little hotel in the Rockies," it was the moment of reality that Jerry had dreaded most for Carol. Jerry saw Carol's lower lip tremble and a single tear course from each eye. He rubbed the top of her hand consolingly.

"I'm here," he assured her quietly, and she nodded and sniffed.

Shannon was waiting just inside the lobby to seize both of them at the same time, with arms flung around both of their necks in a marathon squeeze. Momentarily, Jerry stepped away from her grip so she could cling exclusively to Carol, and the two friends rocked together like a pair of buoys in the water. Both women sobbed at this poignant meeting. Jerry stood a few steps behind, his own eyes moistening, as he remembered the long-ago day when he first welcomed them both over the registration desk.

Soon others joined the greeting party, as well—Doug, Henny, Max, Jessie, to name a few. Jerry had reunited with most everyone during his visit in December, so he moved back to let Carol be the focus of the attention—her first time to see these dear faces since her tortured good-bye. With each new embrace, Carol was a fresh font of tears. Jerry tried not to let her intense reaction discourage him. He believed that the more she plunged herself into this final stream of her grief, the more quickly she could begin looking to the future.

They both saved the biggest hugs for Pop, who hosted them in his residence quarters instead of over his desk. It was an encouraging sign that he was, indeed, emotionally disconnecting himself from the lodge helm. Jerry's last sight of him had been in December at the hospital, when he was wan and skeletal and just back from death's clutches. He was more prepared for Pop's spare appearance than was Carol, who had last seen Pop fifteen months ago before his second attack.

"It just can't be you, looking this way!" Carol moaned when she saw Pop's wasted frame and his tallow face.

"I'm gonna be just fine, now that the two of you are here," Pop assured. His eyes traveled immediately to Jerry and Carol's clasped hands as they arrayed themselves in front of him.

"Yes, and you'll be even finer after you get the retirement that's long overdue," Jerry reminded.

"Well, you can help speed that along, son," Pop retorted cheerfully, and they were back to their old badinage again, matching wits almost as if nothing had happened in the intervening months.

He sat them down and spent a long time briefing Jerry on the current state of lodge matters. He showed him a new P.R. campaign that David had kicked off and explained some major repairs on the heating system. He went over each department of the lodge operations. Pop addressed his business comments strictly to Jerry, as prospective manager-to-be.

Unlike his meddling of the past, this time Pop strategically made no reference to any dreams he might have for adding Carol to the picture. He seemed determined not to interpose himself wrongfully into a budding romance again.

After a bit, Pop pushed away from the breakfast table where they had been sitting huddled like coach and quarterbacks.

"Jerry, you and I can go over the finances later. I want to give you both a tour to show you some good things that are happening here," he directed. Moving with more struggle than they had ever seen him, Pop ushered them out the door and toward the stairs leading to the second-floor rooms.

Jerry's heart knocked like two billiard balls colliding. He knew exactly where the stairs headed that Pop pointed them toward. On his last visit Jerry had managed to avoid walking by the scene of his disgrace—the room where Carol had found him on the night of his frantic departure. But Pop was just now pointing them purposely in that direction.

I'm not ready, Jerry found himself panicking. *I need more time. I can't walk by there with Carol. I need to ease into this gently.* Carol kept her gaze fixed and avoided his eyes, but he felt the muscles in her arm grow rigid as their linked hands fell beside them on the way up the stairs.

She's dreading this, too, Jerry thought. *Why doesn't Pop realize how difficult this is? Why doesn't he stop before things get too awkward here?*

Pop kept talking, as though oblivious to Jerry's hesitation. "We had a good season, so we were able to make a few capital improvements," he burbled as he gestured to his right. "I've always felt we needed more storage at this end of the hallway. Guests wanted us to add a concession area. They complained it wasn't right to make them go up to third floor for ice and things."

As they passed the room that Jerry had dreaded seeing, he realized that it was no longer a guest accommodation at all. Pop had made it into a storage closet and carved out an adjacent niche in the hallway to install snack and ice machines. Nothing about the area bore the slightest hint of its previous use. Every trace of the former was gone!

Pop didn't break stride at the site. He didn't even look back at Jerry to see the baffled yet relieved look on his face. He just kept on prattling, "Look down here. I had them add this small closet for linens . . .," as he continued to point out touches of refurbishing. Although he assumed a casual air, it was Pop's way of signaling to them that the past had been dealt with at Valley Lodge—that he had done everything he could to eliminate ghosts that might threaten their future.

Jerry threw a glance over his shoulder at Carol, who was taking it all in quietly, the tension in her arm relaxing a little. Later, when they were alone, he would need to discuss all this with her, to see how she felt about what she was viewing. They weren't going to sweep anything under the rug this time—following Dr. Naylor's instructions, all emotions were going to be on the surface, even if the subject was difficult.

For now, his heart overflowed with gratitude to Pop. He felt that one huge question mark that stood in the way of his final decision about managing the lodge had just been lifted.

Another question mark got dealt with later that afternoon, when Carol and Shannon slid off somewhere for girltalk and Jerry went back to look at some documents spread out in Pop's kitchen. A knock came at the door, and when Pop answered, he ushered in Frank DeMoss, mayor of Crested Butte. Jerry had worked with Frank on some civic fundraisers during his Valley Lodge employment. Frank had been one of the last people he conversed with on the night of the engagement party, just before Jerry slipped out the door.

Frank stepped directly over to Jerry.

"Jerry, Pop gave me the good news—he thinks you're coming back to take his job," Frank told him, pumping his hand in a cordial shake. "Delighted to hear it. I can't think of anyone I'd rather work with. It was such a pleasure before."

Jerry was incredulous. "Frank, you came here just to tell me this?" he asked. "A busy man like you?"

"Well, I have to admit," the man said, lowering his eyes modestly. "The Rippling Rock's new menu had something to do with it. I wanted to grab an early dinner before council meeting tonight. But Pop told me you were here, and I couldn't pass up the opportunity to wish you well."

Jerry knew a politician like Frank DeMoss, who was up for re-election in November, never made a social call without mixed motives. Gaining the new Valley Lodge manager's support would strengthen his cause.

The deliberate effort Frank took to affirm Jerry still gladdened his heart, as did the affable hug the man gave him as he left to go.

"I've thought a lot about you, Jerry," he said in departing. "Glad to see you're doing fine. It'd be the city's gain to have you back here, for sure."

When Pop closed the door and commented on the mayor's courtesy, Jerry's brows knit soberly, and he turned to Pop with the matter that concerned him most. "Pop, I need to know the truth. Please be honest with me. Frank was kind, but what about the others? Are people in CB really going to trust me, after what happened? It's a small town. Most of the movers and shakers were here that night. They all know I ran off. Most people don't know I've changed—that I wouldn't do it again. What's it gonna be like, trying to do business with people who are suspicious?"

"Son, you heard the man, just like I did. The city will be the benefactor, with you in the business," Pop responded.

Jerry wouldn't be quieted that easily. It was an area he had to feel right about, before he could proceed with any future plans. "Seriously, Pop. How tough will it be—restoring trust? You've been around. You know what people think."

Pop got serious, too. "It's like any other area of human relations, son. Some people—most, I believe, will be cooperative. They're after the bottom line. If Valley Lodge keeps up its reputation and its profits, nobody cares who's in charge. When the dollar signs are good, folks will have short memories.

"I imagine there'll be some others where you'll, frankly, have to do some convincing. But, son, if you're consistent, if you prove yourself trustworthy, it'll work itself out in time."

Jerry pondered Pop's comments for a while. "I just don't want anyone to get hurt this time," he acknowledged wistfully. Jerry didn't identify the particular "anyone" who was chief object of his concern, and Pop tactfully didn't press him about anything to do with Carol this go-around. He had learned his lesson the hard way.

"Crested Butte has a big heart, and I think folks will stick by you—here and in town," Pop reassured. "And don't forget—I'll be praying."

Jerry reached over to hug the lovable bag of bones that was Pop these days. "I know you will. You're the one who taught me that prayer works."

"It has," his grizzled mentor reassured, patting his arm in a tender moment Jerry would remember forever. "It brought you back here."

❈

As dinner approached, Jerry reconnected with Carol. He gave her the option—a memory-lane meal in the Ripping Rock, overlooking the skating rink that was closed for the season, or a trip through the staff dining-room cafeteria line.

"Would you be too disappointed if I picked the cafeteria?" Carol asked him. "I'm really loving seeing everyone again."

Jerry believed Carol chose wisely. Fellowship with her peers was what Carol needed most right now to move her past these first few hours of re-entry and make her homecoming sweet.

"But you'll have to make it up to me," Jerry teased, as he affirmed her decision.

"How?"

Jerry nodded in the direction of the hill behind the lodge. "Go skiing with me, after dinner." As though cooperating just for them, tonight's moon was full, and there was plenty of light.

Carol instantly protested. "I couldn't! I haven't skied in fifteen months. I've forgotten how. I'll look like an idiot. I need to start back slowly."

"Then we'll look like idiots together. I'll be just as shaky as you will. Come on, is it a deal?"

"Guess you've hornswoggled me."

"Good. After dinner then." He gave her hand a squeeze, and his eyes held promise about a later time.

Dinner was a good time for both of them. All the lodge folks who hadn't had an opportunity to speak to them circled by their table. Even those who were a bit reserved in their greetings to Jerry were effusive with Carol, which Jerry understood and accepted. He knew that a few of them still hated his guts for what he did to Carol. Warming up to him would be a matter of time.

Frequently, between greetings, despite how much she was enjoying the fellowship of others, Carol's eyes met his across the table. To his delight, he sensed an urgency, a tacit message that said she hadn't forgotten him and wanted to spend time with him, exclusively. Her eyes said, "Later."

His eyes affirmed, "See you soon." After that exchange, it would be difficult for Jerry to take his gaze off her and to concentrate on what anyone else was saying.

Eventually, at the first moment Jerry found he could extract himself and Carol without seeming rude, he stood and told the others, "Well, good night, everyone. It's time I keep a date I made with a pretty lady."

Carol rose concurrently with him. She gave good-bye hugs to several on her side of the table and left without regret or delay. The evening had wiped out any reservations about what kind of reception she'd receive among Valley Lodge chronies. The light conversations had left her happy and upbeat.

When Jerry stood to leave, she quickly moved to his side, where he reached for her hand again, and they went out the door.

They had to scrounge ski equipment from available sources, since neither brought their own. Carol found most everything she needed in Shannon's supply; her parka was teal and black, with a teal headband. Jerry saw that Pop still had a closet behind the registration desk where he kept a stash of outdated ski wear that staff sometimes grabbed in an emergency. He raided the closet and fished out the necessary items. He cringed at the thought of using these antiquated skis, boots, and poles and not his own, which he had had custom-made for himself during the peak of his competition days. They were all stored away back at Sky Ranch now.

He surveyed himself in the full-length mirror that hung on the supply-room door and wondered whether Carol would remember him as looking thrown-together and seedy in the years to come as they would both reflect on this night in Crested Butte. The basic black, standard-issue ski bib and jacket certainly wouldn't put him on any magazine cover.

He tried to remember to keep things in perspective. His appearance and form would, in the long run, be far less important than other priorities he had for the evening.

They met outside in the night that was downright balmy at 40 degrees, compared to the single-digit temperatures they had skied in on previous days. At this point in April, only a handful of ski buffs kept showing up in Crested Butte for the late-season rates after the snowfall ceased, but there was still sufficient base to keep the trails working. Without its wintertime bite, the air felt fresh on their faces, and the night was clear and starry.

"Oh, I'm gonna be such a klutz!" moaned Carol, as her skis went up onto her shoulders for the uphill trek they had made many times before. "Are you sure you want to do this?"

"Absolutely sure," Jerry replied.

He had never been so sure of anything in his life.

His eyes danced as he looked down on Carol, standing before him now, outfitted in Shannon's borrowed teal attire, as the vibrant ski lover he remembered from their early courtship.

Motioning her onward, they headed toward the area the moon illuminated as it had in the days when they first began to fall in love.

Once again, they prepared to soar down the mountains on which dreams were made.

THIRTY

His Gift Again

❀

Despite Carol's misgivings, it was Jerry who proved to be the klutz on the slopes as they made their initial foray at night skiing. As they climbed to the top of the hill behind the lodge, Jerry reminded Carol that late spring snow can be gluey and wet and can throw skiers off balance sometimes. Just as they reached the summit, Jerry's feet went out from under him, and he skidded on his right thigh for some distance, kicking up powder as he slid. An embankment thirty feet away finally stopped his tumble.

At the sight of Jerry, championship skier, flailing clumsily, Carol tried to suppress a laugh but failed.

"How do you *feel*, Jerry?" she razzed him, with mock derision in her voice as she sped to him and bent over his sprawled-out frame. She extended her hand, and Jerry stomped the ground in an effort to right himself.

"Aw, come off of it," he retorted, trying to appear good-natured in his embarrassment. "I told you I'd be shaky, too, especially using this dime-store equipment." He shook the borrowed objects in disgust and glowered at Carol gently.

"I don't think it was the equipment, Jerry," she continued to goad.

Fully straightened now, with his boots re-clamped, Jerry attempted to ignore her teasing and moved away from the summit and onto the trail.

"I'll remember this abuse in a minute after *you* fall," he chided, rolling his eyes dramatically toward the chuckling Carol.

But Carol didn't fall, and he didn't either, after the first time. Energized by pursuing their common love of the slopes again, the two took off confidently, as though only yesterday were their last time to ski. The act of negotiating turns on the icy-covered hills returned to them naturally. They became Carol and Jerry, ski experts, again.

Though he stayed behind her, Jerry glimpsed the wide grin that Carol flashed him over her shoulder as she reached the midway point of her descent and was by then skiing assuredly. She was in her element now, and he was, too. The sport that had brought them together long ago was providing the same intoxicating joy as it had then.

"More!" Carol yelled headily, as she reached the base and began clambering her way up the hill again.

"Alright," Jerry agreed, following behind. As they climbed, he remembered how she had listed this hobby as one of her secondary losses as a result of his betrayal.

"So you've got it again," he commented, as they reached the top of the hill once more.

"Got what?"

"Your hobby. You hadn't lost it after all, like you told Dr. Naylor."

"Oh," she replied, remembering. She looked up at him, her eyes teasing, her face exultant. "Some things, and some people, have a way of . . . well, coming back."

"You're glad you're here, then?"

"Very," she answered happily.

Jerry's joy knew no bounds at her answer. It was the last boost he needed to clinch his impending plan.

The second time down was even more magnificent than the first. Although the trees around them hadn't felt fresh snowflakes for almost two weeks now, they still had a fairyland aura about them, as the moonlight white-washed them.

Jerry pushed off in front of Carol this time and aimed for speed. He flashed down like a meteor, his rapid turns washing waves of snow over him. By the time he reached the bottom of the hill, Carol was just coming into his field of vision some distance away. He hoped his jetting ahead hadn't bothered her, but he needed to buy a few seconds' time before she reached the bottom.

Finding himself an area at the base of the hill, Jerry began to go about his work. Jamming his pole into the latch, he released his right ski and pushed it and the pole aside. Bending down, his gloved hands scraped up a small mound of snow at the base of his right foot.

Carol zoomed in directly in front of him and eyed him curiously. "What are you doing? Don't you want to go again?" she queried, breathing rapidly and impatiently. While the thrill of the slopes had overtaken her and made her eager for more, he was here playing in the snow like a student in her old Kiddie School!

Jerry didn't answer her question but kept his eyes to the ground, as he continued to add to his snowmound. Soon he had it perfect—a giant white anthill pooching up between them. With eyes still glued to his feet, he eased his right knee down on top of the soft, packed pile of snow, using his left pole and his bent left ski-leg to balance him.

Once he was successfully in this position, he tossed his left pole aside as well, removed both gloves, and flung off his knit cap, fluffing up his hair that the cap had flattened.

Then slowly, as he settled himself into this position, he lifted his eyes toward Carol, who now stood over him, peering down. Her baffled look said she couldn't imagine why they weren't headed back up the hill, preparing for him to race her down again.

Below her, Jerry eased off first one of her gloves and then the other one, until he had both of her hands free and encased in his larger ones.

At that point Carol realized that the bending form she saw before her was, in fact, a suitor, on his knees.

Then came the words that accompanied the pose.

"Carol," he began, rubbing her hands in an effort to warm up all four of theirs, "last time I did this, I took the chicken's way out. I wrote it in frosting. That was artificial. This time, I don't want anything to rob me of the joy of saying the words."

He stopped, because he had to. Memories of that first proposal, offered so fearfully in the hotel kitchen when his emotions ran wild like rats in a maze, blindsided him, and he gulped back a fist-sized lump in his throat. It was an overwhelming reminder of how far God had brought them and healed them. His voice might have broken right then, stalling the whole process, had it not been for Carol's eyes, which took on the most incredible, urgent quality he had ever seen and commanded him to pick up his words and go on. So he plunged again.

"Carol, I love you. I want you to be my wife, my business companion, my prayer warrior, my lover, my fellow ski fanatic, my accountability partner, my friend. I want to be with you for the rest of my life. God gave us to each other once, and he's given us back to each other again. I think it's time we recognize that and get on with our life together. Carol, will you marry me?"

"Jerry . . . ," she breathed, her own voice faltering this time. "Jerry," she said again, repeating his name. It was all she could say, as though the meager human language contained no words sufficient to express what she felt. Now it was Jerry's turn to look up at her with urgent eyes, as the silence played havoc with his imagination.

"Carrie?" he finally implored, when he could stand her lack of an answer no longer.

Then the words billowed out, and he loved the look that overtook her face—full of delight mixed with disbelief at what had just transpired.

"Say it again, Jerry."

"I love you, Carrie. I want to marry you," he repeated, stunned at the sound of his own words—words that it seemed, at one point, would never be uttered again.

He turned his face into her palms and kissed them.

"I know! I know you do," she finally managed. "You've said it in so many ways in these past few months. You didn't even have to say it tonight, but I'm glad you did. I love you, too!" She bent down a little, trying to see his face that was buried in the cup of her hands. He was savoring the feel of her palms on his face, after long months of trying to remember what this touch had ever felt like.

He roused with a determination to complete the process. "Then, darling, tell me . . ." he began, but she finished his sentence for him.

"Oh yes, Jerry, yes! I want to marry you, too. You've convinced me in every way a man can convince a woman that you love me. I love you for all the things you've done and how determined you've been."

By this time he had pulled himself up to a standing position and stood flush in front of her. His foot with the ski still attached was planted between her two outfitted feet, and his foot wearing only the boot had to arch, a little awkwardly, on tiptoe to equalize his balance.

It didn't stop him from the embrace that his arms had waited until this moment to give. His arms encircled the waist of her parka, and she leaned against him with her hands pressed onto his chest, her forehead on his chin.

He pulled his head back so he could see her eyes, which brimmed with tears of love and wonder at what was occurring at the foot of the moonlit hill where they first courted long ago. Their mouths were close and almost touching. Jerry's gaze dropped to Carol's lips.

Still, he didn't kiss her. Instead, he pulled back and reached for her hand.

"Come on. Let's get our stuff and go inside. I have something for you."

"What now?" she begged, as he collected all the poles and skis and gloves that had been tossed to make way for his proposal.

"You'll see."

They wordlessly clomped their way back to the lodge. Once inside, Jerry dumped everything beside the back door, with a promise to gather it up later. In the rush of momentum, he didn't want to waste precious moments on being orderly.

At nine o'clock, the Great Hall normally would have still teemed with people in a lively *apres*-ski scene, but since this was off-season, only a few scattered guests sat around the big-screen TV. Jerry was grateful for the empty lobby, but peak-season crowds observing wouldn't have stopped him from the final act he had to take to complete his task.

Drawing Carol to the sofa in front of the fireplace, he finished the process that began many months earlier in the same, atmospheric spot—with a fire crackling in the background, just like then. He pulled Carol to him and covered the lips she willingly offered—the lips he had refused to claim until this very moment and they were pledged to each other again.

"It had to be here, in this place," he said against her skin, as his mouth pulled away from hers and trailed kisses down her chin, neck, and hairline.

"When you told me you would wait to kiss me, I didn't believe you," Carol confessed to him, ruefully. "I'm sorry I didn't, darling. You kept your word, just like you said."

"Only God could help me keep that promise," Jerry countered. "So many times I wanted to give in, but I had to honor my pledge. We had to get some other things right first."

"We did that, alright," Carol murmured into his lips. This time she initiated things, pulling his head toward hers and kissing him hungrily, holding nothing back.

When this second kiss subsided at last, Jerry pulled his arm from around behind her on the sofa and grasped both of her hands again.

"I'm sure you'll want to get married in Wooster, like before," he asserted. "Your mother had all those plans for the church there."

Carol looked at him, genuinely shocked. "Not at all. It hadn't even entered my mind."

"Where, then?" Jerry replied, stunned.

"The chapel at Sky Ranch, of course. I thought about it that day we went to vespers there. I knew it would be perfect for a wedding."

Jerry howled. "Don't give me that nonsense. You weren't thinking about a wedding on that day you were in the Sky Ranch chapel. You hadn't even broken things off with Kevin."

Carol grew dead serious and leveled her eyes straight at Jerry. "There's something you should know."

"Yes?"

"I never saw Kevin again after that first weekend you came to Wooster."

Jerry's jaw dropped to his knees.

"Why?"

The silence was so overpowering it even drowned out Pop's noisy little recording that infiltrated the lobby from outdoors.

"I think you know why, Jerry."

"Because he got mad at you?"

Carol laughed. "He got mad, for sure. But the truth was, I just didn't have the desire to be around him, after I saw you."

"But when you called me at Sky Ranch . . ."

"That was the day I had told him officially: we were through. But I hadn't gone out with him for all those weeks before. I couldn't. He wasn't you."

"Why did you not ever tell me?"

She shrugged. "I don't know. Frightened, I guess. Because my feelings were so all-consuming. Because I had been hurt before. Afraid to look too available to you, before I knew I could trust you again."

Jerry pondered this a while. Should he get mad at her because she bluffed him?

Then he realized Carol had been right in playing her cards close to her vest. For their relationship to be worth anything, trust had to be rebuilt, in both her mind and his. If he hadn't convinced both of them that he could function well in a crisis, they wouldn't be sitting at Valley Lodge this minute, with him feeling fully confident that he could take over from Pop. If Carol hadn't kept her guard up and had sped up their reunion too quickly, they might have taken the easy road back—coerced by physical passion that had tempted on every hand. Carol might not have resolved her faith issues, they might not have gained the insights from Dr. Naylor, and Jerry might have folded in his search for Rico without his desire for Carol to spur his momentum. Eventually, they would have run into the same barriers that tripped them up last time.

They had walked through the refiner's fire, and their love was stronger for it.

Jerry marveled at God's goodness to them. In His own plan, things had unfolded in just the way He intended.

That reminded Jerry of another unfinished part of this proposal.

"Something else I want to do right this time," he told her. "I want us to pray."

"Jerry!" she cried, astounded.

"I mean it. I flipped it off once, when it meant so much to you. I know that hurt you. I've berated myself for it ever since. How could I make light of something so serious?"

"Darling, you didn't know the Lord then. I've forgiven you."

"I want to start everything off properly now. This is just one more way."

Carol bowed her head but not before tears of amazement began to flood down her cheeks. Jerry slid both arms around her waist and pulled her to him so his shoulder could brace her forehead and absorb her tears while he prayed, his lips touching her ear.

"Dear God, Thank You for giving me Carol again and for keeping her for me all these many months until I could ask for her back. Help us learn from the pain of the past and not be bound by it. Thank you that we now can have a Christian marriage and that you can be the Lord of our home. Help us in the days ahead, to put you first in every decision that we make about our future together. In Christ's name, amen."

He opened his eyes and pulled back a few inches, so he could reach for her chin.

"Better this time?" he asked her, turning her face toward him.

All she could do was nod, because sobs of gladness shook her. He merely kissed her hair and let this new wave of emotion pass.

When she could finally get the words out, they were words Jerry would never forget.

"Now, we have it all. We have it all," she said. Jerry nodded in utmost agreement. He wondered if there had ever been another moment so triumphant in all the world.

At that very instant, Doug sauntered through the lobby, on a break from the kitchen. A glance at the sobbing Carol instinctively red-flagged him, and he stepped in their direction. Jerry intercepted him with a wave.

"Happy tears," he assured over the top of Carol's quivering head, and waved him on. But Doug's solicitousness attracted other attention. Jerry knew he and Carol had to act quickly before friends grew suspicious and drew their own conclusions.

He looked down at the weeping form in his arms. "Carrie, we need to go see Pop. We've got to tell him first, before anyone else finds out."

Pulling herself together, Carol nodded. It was only fair, after all, that their employer, friend, and second father should be the first to know. God had, indeed, spared Pop long enough to see one of the fondest dreams of his life come true.

THIRTY ONE

The Heart Soars Free

❀

June—the traditional month of brides—was the month that Carol and Jerry had chosen for their wedding when they were engaged the first time.

Fayma had planned that flowers would blanket every square inch of the sanctuary of Carol's church in Wooster, and nearly nine-hundred persons had been on the guest list. Carol had selected a chorus line of eight bridesmaids, and the church's entire choir had been recruited to sing.

But it was the month of July, sultry in the Kansas midsummer and stifling enough that Bo's horses dozed all day, that saw Carol and Jerry actually marry after their romance collapsed and bloomed the second time around.

By the time school was out for Carol, Pop had relocated to Durango, and Jerry settled in at Valley Lodge, two months had flown by before they could actually get down to business and say their "I do's."

This go-round, their guest list for the 1 o'clock nuptials was limited to the one-hundred fifty persons, maximum, that the Sky Ranch chapel could seat, and their lone decoration was the single altar candle that burned each Sunday in regular services there.

Carol and Jerry decided to take the money that they might have spent on an ostentatious ceremony and endow a Sky Ranch scholarship. They wanted needy families like Rico's to be able to visit their kids there in years to come. It seemed like the least the couple could do to help pay back Bo and Sally for their munificence. The energy and money these two had invested in their future had been staggering, and the new Mr. and Mrs. Rutgers would be eternally grateful.

As for attendants, Carol and Jerry trimmed the number back to three—three of the most significant people in their lives at that moment. Carol let Jerry do his own choosing this time, instead of goading him like before. However, to no one's surprise, Jerry again picked Pop as best man, along with Bo and Dr. Naylor. Standing up with Carol were Shannon, Sally, and Cathy, her Wooster friend. They wore dresses the color of the lilacs that bloomed around Sally's porch on Carol's first visit to the ranch.

The wedding music came from none other than the barbershop quartet that had been Jerry's backup during his Talent Night solo. Before he moved away, Jerry had continued rehearsing them until they sounded quite professional on the strains of "I'd Rather Have Jesus" and "O Love that Will Not Let Me Go," which they sang just before the vows.

Then they harmonized softly in the background as Jerry serenaded Carol again with "Remembering You," just before Rev. Kinzer, the ranch chaplain, pronounced Carol and Jerry husband and wife.

The popular favorite of all their wedding attendants was their ring bearer, Rico. Sharp in a flax-colored sports jacket, and strutting like one of Mr. Durwood's stallions, Rico drew admiring whispers from the crowd as he strode up the aisle carrying the wedding pillow. On top were tied two gold wedding bands that were Carol and Jerry's choice this time around.

At Carol's request, they decided to bypass the costly, bejeweled route that they had chosen before. To avoid embarrassing him, Carol never queried Jerry about her original ring that he had turned over to Bo for safekeeping long ago. He knew she thought the ring was sold to fund his living expenses during that time.

Although he offered to take her back to shop for a new diamond, Carol said no. By then, she had spotted a pair of handsome bands in a showroom that featured religious jewelry. The simple, wide bands were of hammered gold, with a raised cross in the center. Jerry thought they were perfect—a symbol of the new direction that their joint lives had taken.

Some people also might have expected for Carol to spare nothing on her own bridal finery, since she had ample time to shop for the gown of her dreams. However, Carol's protracted wait made her all the more sure that her dress would be understated yet significant, just like the ceremony.

Instead of trailing clouds of tulle that would overpower the tiny, rustic chapel, Carol radiantly swept down the aisle in an ivory faille, ankle-length dress of Fayma's design. Although it broke with traditional bridal regalia, it could hardly be called simple. Carol's clever mother had richly embroidered the bodice and applied yards of hand tatting passed down from her own mother. The handkerchief hem of Carol's skirt also came from her grandmother's handiwork—points of hand-made, ivory lace that brushed the tops of her satin pumps as she slowly walked toward her groom.

In place of a veil, she wore baby's breath sprigs tucked into her piled-high, dark hair. A small bouquet of gardenias completed her ensemble on her day of days.

Jerry's eyes were fastened on Carol from the moment she appeared in the chapel doorway on the arm of Pop, who did double-duty in his best-man role as he led her to the front of the church and toward her intended. Dashing in his wedding pin-stripes, Jerry could scarcely conceal the flush that slid up his sun-burnished cheeks when Pop gave him his bride's hand at long last.

343

The wedding audience was decidedly male and youthful, since Jerry insisted that all the Sky Ranch boys, down to the newest level 1's, be included as guests. Colby, Kansas, wasn't on the beaten path for folks in either Crested Butte or Wooster, so only a handful of their friends from those places got to travel there for the event. Besides, Jerry knew no wedding would have ever been rescheduled between him and Carol if it hadn't been for what happened on those Sky Ranch acres, so it seemed terribly fitting that the ranch boys comprise the majority of weddingoers. Most of them wore T-shirts and jeans—the best they had. The wedded couple couldn't have been happier to see them than if the boys had worn tuxes.

Those few of their closest associates who did manage to travel to the Rutgers-McKechnie nuptials seemed to enjoy themselves to the hilt.

At their rehearsal dinner, Jerry whispered to Carol, "Wouldn't you like to have been a fly on the wall this morning when Pop finally laid eyes on Bo and Sally? Can't you just imagine the mental images they'd had of each other all these months?"

"Or how about this afternoon when Dr. Naylor picked Dr. Northcutt and Cathy up at the airport?" Carol chimed in, laughing.

They had expected Carol's supervisor at the college to send her regrets to the invitation that Carol mailed her merely out of courtesy, but Dr. Northcutt surprised them by answering with a hearty "yes." Carol paired her up with Cathy, who was already traveling west from Wooster. It was the first time the professor and Jerry had spoken since that awkward meeting in Carol's office in which she snubbed him.

Jerry and the department chair greeted each other as if no brusque words had ever been uttered. He and Carol were awestruck by the massive silver tea set she gave them as a wedding gift. Jerry thought, in retrospect, how Dr. Northcutt had truly been one of God's instruments in the eventual healing of their relationship. Jerry could have lost hope during that first, risky visit to Wooster, if Dr.

Northcutt's snub hadn't brought Carol to his quick defense and given him cause to persist.

Another notable guest was in the crowd. Jerry's mother had come down from the East Coast, bringing a young step-brother Jerry had never met, a child acquired in her recent, third marriage. After Carol's significant coaxing, Jerry had invited her, as he did his father.

His dad's reply came back promptly in the form of a check mark by the "regrets" line on the wedding invitation reply card. No note was attached and no explanation was given, as though Jerry were some random acquaintance instead of his own firstborn. It was the only time during the entire wedding preliminaries when Jerry almost lost his cool.

"He's just the same scumbag he always was," Jerry blared to Carol over the phone line when the envelope arrived. "I don't care what Bo says about him; he hasn't changed a whit."

"Darling, I know that must hurt a lot," Carol consoled, remembering how Dr. Naylor had instructed her to reply to him. "I guess he feels uneasy after all this time has passed. Maybe he thinks it would be too awkward if your mother happens to be around. I still wish you could go to see him . . ."

Then she followed up by saying, "I feel a little scared right now, though, Jerry. You wouldn't let this ruin our wedding, would you?" Jerry realized immediately that she needed reassurance, which she had every right to expect, after what happened before.

"Absolutely not!" He replied with total sincerity, hoping his words were the balm she needed. "I just needed to vent my frustration, that's all. I don't need to let him have this much hold over me."

"Then, darling, feel free to vent with me any time," Carol answered him. "We want to do this right this time, in every way."

However, the arrival of his mother might have just been the wedding's real serendipity. Her name was Lydia Shaw now, and Jerry hadn't seen her since she was Lydia Tomlinson, in the first few months after Mr. Tomlinson left her for a secretary. He had hardly met Mr. Tomlinson before that marriage of two years ended, and he hadn't met Mr. Shaw at all. Jimmy, the nine-year-old she brought with her, was the oldest of three youngsters she inherited in her latest hook-up.

She wasn't a bad-looking woman, with stylish, auburn hair that clearly got a boost from a bottle and blazing blue eyes that repeated themselves in her two offspring. Her flashy earrings and trendy mini-skirts were obvious efforts to deduct years from her appearance. But Jerry saw that the seven years since she'd visited him last had left their thumbprint on this youthful mother he remembered, and her face looked every inch the 52-year-old she was. Now she had three schoolkids to rear, at the age most women began easing into grandmotherhood.

Most of his time with Dr. Naylor had been spent on father issues, but Jerry had realized in the counseling process that he still harbored some resentment toward Lydia also. Jerry saw that he felt anger toward her because she had never spoken up when his father intimidated him and didn't put a stop to the belittling.

After studying the matter, however, Jerry gained insights into his mother's behavior that gave him new compassion toward her. He realized that Lydia, herself, had been on a quest for love with his father that caused her to come up empty-handed. She had carried that quest into two other marriages and saw a second one disappoint her, just like the first. Dr. Naylor had helped him see that his mother was trying to fill her own love-cup. In her neediness, she hadn't seen Jerry's unmet needs.

This softened Jerry's anger toward her and helped forgiveness happen. For their Valley Lodge engagement party, Lydia had sent a terse decline. So when she responded with a "yes" for the wedding, Jerry was genuinely glad for both himself and Bo. Bo had seen her only a little more recently than Jerry had, although he had communicated with her fairly often in his own recovery.

"Don't expect her to be anything like Fayma," Jerry had cautioned Carol after he got his mother's RSVP. "I wish I had a better in-law family to offer you."

346

Jerry knew that he would have to interpret his family situation to Carol many more times in the course of their marriage, since it departed from hers so drastically. At least he had Bo and Sally. Their sure, consistent love had reached out to encompass Carol, too, as a counterbalance to some of his other bizarre relatives.

Because of his mother's presence, Jerry was especially glad for the Christian overtones that he and Carol had prescribed for their marriage ceremony. Besides the traditional vows that Rev. Kinzer read, Jerry and Carol recited personal vows of love and commitment to each other and then ended with their testimonies of how they came to know Jesus as Savior. They knew that Lydia and other nonbelievers would be in the audience and wanted to leave no doubt about the way to salvation. Although Lydia had taken him and Bo to church occasionally in their youth, Jerry had no evidence to indicate she had a personal relationship with Jesus. As happy as this day was for Jerry and Carol, it would be an even grander occasion if someone trusted Christ because of attending their wedding. Jerry hoped for future visits with his mother so he could share more with her about the Christian way.

The reception that followed was all down-home. Happy, the ranch cook, had fixed fried chicken and assorted side dishes. They were served in the dining hall that the boys had trimmed in a clever mishmash of wedding/Western decor.

Despite the Country flair that suffused the wedding, there was one nod to the heart of Colorado ski country that would be their new home. The groom's cake was in the shape of a ski slope—white icing over chocolate. Plastic figures of two skiers were positioned over a heart carved in the "snow" with chocolate icing. Inside the heart appeared the chocolaty words, "Jerry loves Carol."

After folks had eaten all they wanted of Happy's fare, the dining room tables were pushed back so guests could enjoy Country line dancing, with Bo coaching the Sky Ranch boys who might not know the steps. Music came from the instrumental group that Jerry originally brought together for Talent Night. The band director at the Colby high school was working with them now, two afternoons a week. Jerry also had found a replacement from town who would keep the Rancheros going in their summer and fall sports. He didn't want any of these programs to go to seed just because he had moved away, and Bo didn't either. Though Jerry's time at Sky Ranch was just over a year—about the same length of stay as some of the youth—his impact would be felt there for aeons to come. He wasn't sure that even Carol understood the full extent of how much he'd miss the place of his recovery.

Jerry sat beside Carol at her dressing table in their honeymoon suite, with Carol fishing out pins and bits of baby's breath from her wedding coiffure. Carol tried to brush her dark hair down so that it settled around her chin again but got interference from Jerry, who nuzzled her earlobe and neck, his heart clubbing with joy at having her to himself at last.

They had finally managed to get away from the jubilant crowd of well-wishers at their reception by 3:30. By late evening they were in Colorado Springs, where their room awaited them at The Broadmoor.

"You can't even set business aside for our honeymoon," Carol had ribbed Jerry after he chose this particular place for their wedding night. She knew Jerry picked this legendary, old luxury hotel in part so he could scope it out as a model for Valley Lodge operations.

Jerry had other reasons for making reservations here. Couples for decades had picked The Broadmoor, this dowager jewel of the Rockies, as the site for starting married life. It seemed appropriate that the new Mr. and Mrs. Rutgers celebrate their first night together in one of the treasure spots of the state where they met and would live as newlyweds.

In fact, their whole honeymoon was designed for total ensconcement in Carol's new habitat, before arriving in Crested Butte as the valley began its annual, magical transformation from summer to fall to winter. Before her stint at Valley Lodge, Carol had never been any further west than Indiana, and her work as a ski instructor left her no time to tour. Jerry wanted to acquaint her with the other attractions—Pike's Peak, within the mountains surrounding The Broadmoor; Estes Park; Royal Gorge; Black Canyon of the Gunnison; and the western towns of Silverton and Durango, near Pop's new home.

Pop wouldn't be there yet. He was filling in for Jerry while they honeymooned—the old, indomitable war horse headed back to Valley Lodge, running things again for a while.

"Don't get too used to it," Jerry insisted, as he recruited Pop. "No offense, but I want you to put this place behind you and stay gone."

"Nonsense," Pop scoffed. "You and Carol are going to need some breaks from time to time. I want you to call on me whenever you need to get away."

Right now they were on the most important get-away of all, and Jerry had saved some surprises until just this honeymoon moment.

"I have something special for you," he murmured into her ear, winding his arms around the waist of her white terry robe that matched his own.

"I can't imagine what," Carol said curiously. Last night they had exchanged wedding gifts to each other. Jerry's to her was a pair of emerald-cut diamond ear studs that she wore now after removing her wedding pearls. Hers to him was an elegant watch with a two-tone band that Carol thought looked executive for his new job.

Jerry pulled from his deep robe pocket a tiny red moire box that Carol immediately recognized—the box that had housed her engagement ring, long ago. She looked at Jerry quizzically, since they already had their wedding bands.

Slowly she raised the hinged lid. Lying on the black velvety insides of the box was a familiar sight—her old ring, set into a pendant. The gold heart surrounded by diamonds was now suspended on a dainty gold chain. Jerry helped her free the necklace from its holder and draped it around her neck, clasping it securely. Against her milky skin, it was stunning.

Carol's eyes grew moist but were still questioning.

"But I thought . . . ," she began.

"You thought it was hocked to help me survive," he finished.

Carol was silent. It was clear she hadn't wanted to say it, but Jerry guessed right. She had presumed the ring was long gone.

"I tried, but Bo wouldn't hear of it," Jerry explained. "He kept it for me all these months. Maybe he thought I might need it again. When we chose our bands, it didn't have its old use any more, but I wanted to preserve it, to give it to you in a new form. I hope you like it."

His bride was overwhelmed. She just kept staring at it in the mirror, remembering the night she once was to receive it, which contrasted sharply to this night in which she finally had.

Before she could speak, Jerry went on. He captured both of her hands in his, as the terry sleeves of their robes brushed up against each other.

"This heart means something, Carol," Jerry insisted, his eyes burning with intensity as he spoke. "It symbolizes the fact that my heart was always true to you, even during the times it seemed otherwise, even during the times I skipped out on you. I never stopped loving you. Nothing I ever did reflected my lack of love for you. You understand that?"

She nodded, searching his eyes, trying to probe the very depths of what he was saying with such obvious feeling.

"Also, it means that our hearts have been set free to soar, the way they were always meant to, before we got shackled by the pain of the past. All that's released. This necklace will remind us of that, every time you wear it, and every time I look at it."

Jerry stopped and awaited the verdict from Carol.

Finally, it came, after a few minutes of the tears he expected, and even welcomed, because they, as always, were part of her healing.

"It's spectacular," she finally managed. "I'm so glad you did it, just this way. I just . . ." Her voice broke, as she fingered the heart lovingly, "It's just that . . . that there were days when I never thought I'd see it again."

"There were days when I thought you wouldn't either. But here we are! We have each other, and you have your heart back. God's been good, Carrie. God's been good."

She nodded, dabbed at her eyes, and just kept touching the heart—patting it, holding her hand mirror up to it to get a closer view, adjusting to the sight and feel of it. He loved watching her do this, and he knew he had made the right choice.

Then he added, "There's more."

"More?"

"Yes, this surprise isn't something for you to open, but it's something you want—something you've been urging me to do for a while now."

Carol's eyes squinted in thought, then widened. "You don't mean—about your father?"

Jerry nodded, his lips curling up into a proud grin. "I talked to him yesterday. I actually did it! I asked him, could I come by and introduce him to my new bride?"

"When?" She looked incredulous, eager.

"As part of our wedding trip. I told him we'd swing by his house in western Kansas. We won't be that far away when we drop down to Pueblo."

She threw her arms around him in a congratulatory hug. "I'm so proud of you, darling. That took a lot of courage."

"I can't take all the credit," Jerry explained. "Bo set it up for me, after Dr. Naylor helped me work out what to say. Bo placed the call and talked to him for a while, like he's used to doing. Then he put me on the line. Guess that might have been the easy way out, but it helped to have Bo as a go-between."

"Did he say anything about missing the wedding?"

"No, he didn't acknowledge it."

"I'm sorry. I know that hurts. Did you call him a scumbag, like you did that day to me on the phone?"

"I didn't, even though I wanted to. But the funniest thing was—he sounded almost relieved to be talking to me. It was like—he wasn't ever going to break down the barrier himself and make the first move, but once I did, he seemed glad."

Carol tossed her head back and shook it in amazement. "Oh, I'm so pleased, Jerry. I've hoped for this so *long*, ever since I began trying to understand things."

Jerry's brow knit a little at Carol's remarks, and he reached out to her, clasping both arms protectively.

"Please don't get your hopes up, darling, because I'm not," he warned. "He may get cold feet. He may not be there when we go. Or, he may not be receptive. How he'll respond is anybody's guess."

She nodded reassuringly. "It's like Dr. Naylor told us. You do the right thing, whether the other person responds correctly or not. Jerry, I'm so happy. I know you'll do well."

Then she asked him, with a teasing twinkle in her eye, "How do you *feel* about it?"

He liked this girl.

"I feel . . . free, I guess," he answered her. "Free, even if we haven't been there yet. Just talking to him that once, just taking that first step, was another way of releasing the hold he has on my emotions. I feel like I'm . . . I'm . . ."

She made the analogy for him. "Like you're taking off from the top of the ski slope."

"That's it!" he exclaimed. Then, turning to kiss her eyebrow, her ear lobe, and her under lip—cherished places of his beloved that he now could claim for his own—he murmured to her huskily, "You completed my sentence."

"I complete *you*," she told him, assuredly, as her own lips started to explore.

They'd both known that fact about each other all along. Now, they had the rest of their lives to put it into practice.

APPENDIX A

Resources to Help People Who Hurt

*

Support-Group Resources

People who deal with painful issues as did the characters in *When the Heart Soars Free* often resist seeking help because they believe no one else has ever experienced life's hurts in the same way they have. Participating in a Christ-centered support group enables people who deal with hurtful issues in their lives to experience hope and healing by relating to others who are fellow travelers. The following are biblically based support-group materials designed to be used in a small-group setting.

- *First Place: A Christ-Centered Health Program* (Nashville: LifeWay, 1992). Individuals learn healthy ways of eating, exercising, and caring for their bodies through an internationally recognized, Christ-centered program of weight and lifestyle management.

- McGee, Robert S. *Search for Significance* LIFE Support Edition (Houston: Rapha, 1992). Helps persons who struggle with low self-worth understand that the source of their self-concept is their identity in Christ, not others' approval or their own shame from past events.

- Pillow, Larry O. *Family and Friends: Helping the Person You Care About in Recovery* (Nashville: LifeWay Press, 1995). How family and friends can understand changes in the lives of people who are making positive life alterations through Christian recovery.

- Sledge, Tim. *Making Peace with Your Past* (Nashville: LifeWay Press, 1992). Helps people understand how painful events and issues in their past color their relationships to others in the present.

- Sledge, Tim. *Moving Beyond Your Past* (Nashville: LifeWay Press, 1994). This sequel to *Making Peace with Your Past* helps individuals, with Christ's help, move beyond the hurts of the past and into joyful, productive day-to-day living.

- Springle, Pat. *Untangling Relationships* (Houston: Rapha, 1993). Helps people understand how relationships become unhealthy and learn to develop Christ-honoring relationships with friends, spouses, children, co-workers, and others in their lives.

- Springle, Pat, and Dale W. McCleskey. *Conquering Codependency: A Christ-Centered 12-Step Process* (Houston: Rapha, 1993). Helps people whose lives are devastated by codependency, the compulsion to rescue others and to control. Utilizes a Christ-centered approach to the 12 Steps of Alcoholics Anonymous.

- Wright, H. Norman, and Kay Moore. *Recovering from the Losses of Life* LIFE Support Edition (Nashville: LifeWay Press, 1995). Offers encouragement and practical guidance for anyone who has lost a loved one through death or who has experienced other profound losses such as loss of a job, a broken relationship, leaving home, loss of identity, or loss of a dream or goal.

Order the above resources by calling 1-800-747-0738.

APPENDIX B

How to Find
a Christian Counselor

Just as Dr. Naylor reminded Jerry and Carol in chapter Twenty Five, God has helpers all over the globe to serve as unbiased listeners and coaches for people who want to make sense out of critical issues in their lives. A counselor whose Christian faith is central to his or her practice can help the counselee integrate psychological principles with biblical truth and will aid the person in processing issues through a Christian frame of reference.

Many competent professional helpers—psychiatrists, psychologists, social workers, professional counselors, marriage and family therapists, and pastoral counselors—are Christian and operate their professional practices within the moral and ethical teaching of Scripture. Be aware that many excellent Christian professionals work for local public or private agencies which do not use the word *Christian* in their title. And, unfortunately, incompetent, untrained and/or unethical counselors whose agencies widely advertise their "Christianity" also exist.

To find the right resource:

1. Ask your pastor or other church-staff members to recommend Christian mental health professionals in your community. Obtain several names so you can gather information and make your own informed decision. Call these suggested resources and discuss your particular need, their backgrounds, their beliefs, and their approach to therapy.

2. If you know a Christian friend who sees a counselor, ask that person about the professional's style and whether the person has confidence in the counselor. Ask yourself, "Do I see evidence of positive life change as a result of the work on issues this friend is doing?" Some counselors may do more harm than good for a counselee.

3. The local or state office of your denomination may also be a good source for names. A denominational staff member who concentrates on family-life issues may keep a list of counseling resources. Sometimes a county-wide or state branch of your denomination may sponsor its own counseling center.

4. Avoid counselors who merely recite Scripture or who tend to preach rather than listen reflectively. A skilled Christian counselor will avoid dispensing advice but will allow the counselee to make his or her own decisions after helping the individual process all options.

5. The American Association of Christian Counselors at 1-800-520-2268 can provide names of resources in your community. Another resource is RAPHA, at 1-800-383-HOPE, which has a nationwide network of Christian counseling centers in numerous communities.

Abstinence Education

In *When the Heart Soars Free* Jerry expressed regret that he had not been acquainted earlier with high-principled role models who stuck by standards of sexual purity. Today young adults who choose to remain sexually pure until marriage have much company, thanks in part to the **True Love Waits Campaign**, an annual emphasis designed for use in churches of all denominations to challenge teen-agers and college students to practice abstinence. It includes Christian sex-education resources for children, youth, and married couples. The resources include *Boys and Girls—Alike and Different* (ages 4-7); *My Body and Me* (ages 8-9), *Sex! What's That?* (ages 10-13); *Sexuality: God's Gift* (ages 14-17), and *Celebrating Sex in Your Marriage* (married couples). Other books are *Until You Say I Do*, which helps students understand the meaning of commitment; *Holding Out for True Love*, which shows students why pre-marital abstinence makes good sense for them and their future; and *When True Love Doesn't Wait*, which serves as a counseling tool for adults to use with youth who are seeking forgiveness and counsel in the area of purity. Order by calling 800-458-2772.

APPENDIX C

The Answer
to All of Life's Problems

The characters in *When the Heart Soars Free* learned that the core source of answers to all of life's most perplexing problems is a personal relationship with Jesus Christ. How can you have that kind of relationship?

1. The Bible says that you are accountable for the sin in your life. "For all have sinned and fall short of the glory of God." Romans 3:23

2. A penalty exists for that sin. "For the wages of sin is death." Romans 6:23

3. You cannot earn, by good deeds, a way to wipe out that sin from your life. "For it is by grace you have been saved, through faith—and this is not from yourselves; it is the gift of God—not by works, so that no one can boast." (Ephesians 2:8-9)

4. God provided for your sin by sending His Son to die in your place. Instead of you, Jesus took the wages of sin on Himself by dying on the cross. Then God raised Him on the third day. "But God demonstrates his own love for us in this: While we were still sinners, Christ died for us." (Romans 5:8)

5. How do you claim this free gift of salvation that God has provided? "Everyone who calls on the name of the Lord will be saved." (Romans 10:13)

If this makes sense to you, then pray a prayer similar to the one Jerry prayed in Chapter Fifteen: *"Dear God, Thank You for going to the cross for me. I believe You did it because I am a sinner and You wanted to spend eternity with me. Thank You for forgiving me of my sins and giving me a new life. I desire to change my ways and seek a relationship with You. Amen."*

Now, find a pastor or Christian friend to tell about your decision.

To order other items from Hannibal Books, fill out this coupon.

Please send me:

When the Heart Soars Free by Kay Moore. A heart-touching love story with a healing, biblical message. Set in a picturesque mountain wonderland.

_____ Copies at $12.95 = _____

Gathering the Missing Pieces in an Adopted Life, by Kay Moore. Pulitzer Prize nominee seeks her birth-family roots; includes helps from more than sixty others impacted by adoption.

_____ Copies at $11.95 = _____

Where Is God When a Child Suffers? by Penny Giesbrecht. How two Christian parents cope with their child's pain in the light of God's love.

_____ Copies at $8.95 = _____

How to Make the Most of the Best of Your Life by Kathryn Grant. A treasure-house of inspiration and guidance for making the most of the "mature" years.

_____ Copies at $9.95 = _____

Please add $2.00 postage and handling for first book, plus .50 for each additional book.

Shipping & Handling _____

VA residents add sales tax _____

TOTAL ENCLOSED
(Check or money order)_____

Name _____

Address _____

City _____ State _____ Zip _____

MAIL TO HANNIBAL BOOKS, P.O. BOX 29621, Richmond, VA 23242. Satisfaction guaranteed. Call 1-800-747-0738 for free catalog, or order from www.hannibalbooks.com